Praise for *The Silent Companions*

'Not since *The Little Stranger* has a book so entranced and haunted me. Compelling, bewitching and beautifully written. Read it if you dare' Anna Mazzola, author of *The Unseeing*

'Menacing and unsettling' *Psychologies*

'Frighteningly atmospheric, genuinely haunting and psychologically astute, the horror of *The Silent Companions* lingers like truth in the darkest corners of the human mind' Helen Sedgwick, author of *The Comet Seekers*

'Creepy and page-turning' *The Times*

'Unnerving and compelling in equal measure ... An atmospheric gothic tale that chills the blood' Sophia Tobin, author of *The Silversmith's Wife*

'A classic, *Turn of the Screw*-esque, ghost story' *Radio Times*

'Compelling and claustrophobic. The pages all but turn by themselves' Essie Fox, author of *The Last Days of Leda Grey*

'Neatly crafted and compelling' *Times Literary Supplement*

'If *The Silent Companions* lands on your night table, don't plan on leaving your bed anytime soon. Immersive, meticulous, and reminiscent of the masters of gothic fiction – not only a compulsively readable ghost story, but a skilful, loving ode to the entire genre' Lyndsay Faye, author of *The Gods of Gotham*

A Note on the Author

LAURA PURCELL is a former bookseller. She lives in Colchester with her husband and guinea pigs. *The Silent Companions* was published to widespread critical acclaim and was a BBC Radio 2 Book Club choice. Her second novel for Bloomsbury, gothic chiller *The Corset*, will be published in Autumn 2018.

laurapurcell.com
@spookypurcell

THE
SILENT
COMPANIONS

LAURA PURCELL

RAVEN BOOKS
LONDON · OXFORD · NEW YORK · NEW DELHI · SYDNEY

RAVEN BOOKS
Bloomsbury Publishing Plc
50 Bedford Square, London, WC1B 3DP, UK

BLOOMSBURY, RAVEN BOOKS and the Raven Books logo are trademarks of
Bloomsbury Publishing Plc

First published in Great Britain 2017
This paperback edition first published in 2018

A catalogue record for this book is available from the British Library

ISBN: HB: 978-1-4088-8809-4; TPB: 978-1-4088-8810-0;
PB: 978-1-4088-8803-2; EBOOK: 978-1-4088-8811-7

8 10 9 7

Typeset by Integra Software Services Pvt. Ltd.
Printed and bound in Great Britain by CPI Group (UK) Ltd, Croydon CR0 4YY

To find out more about our authors and books visit www.bloomsbury.com
and sign up for our newsletters.

For Juliet

ST JOSEPH'S HOSPITAL

The new doctor took her by surprise. Not that there was anything unusual in his arrival – doctors came and went often enough. But this one was young. New to the profession, as well as the place. There was a brightness to him that made her eyes ache.

'This is her? Mrs Bainbridge?' The *Mrs* was a nice touch. She could not remember the last time she had been given a title. It played like a tune she could only just recall. He looked up from his notes, intent upon her. 'Mrs Bainbridge, my name is Dr Shepherd. I am here to help you. To make sure we are giving you the sufficient level of care.'

Care. She wanted to stand up from where she sat on the edge of the bed, take his arm and gently guide him to the door. This place was not for innocents. Next to the stocky, middle-aged hag of an attendant he looked so vibrant, so alive. The limewashed walls had not yet leeched the colour from his face or dulled the tone of his voice. In his eyes she saw the gleam of interest. This disturbed her more than the attendant's scowl.

'Mrs Bainbridge? Do you understand?'

'Told you.' The attendant sniffed. 'You'll get nothing from her.'

The doctor sighed. Tucking his papers under his arm, he came farther into her cell. 'That does happen. Often in cases of great distress. Sometimes the shock is so intense that it renders the patient unable to speak. It seems likely, does it not?'

They bubbled up, the words in her chest. Her ribs ached and her lips tingled with the force of them. But they were ghosts, echoes of things that had been. She would never experience them again.

He bent forward so that his head was level with hers. She was acutely aware of his eyes, wide and unblinking behind his spectacles. Palest rings of mint green.

'It can be cured. With time and patience. I have seen it done.'

The attendant sucked in a disapproving breath. 'Don't get close, doctor. She's a fierce one, all right. Spat in my face once.'

How steadily he watched her. He was close enough for her to smell him: carbolic soap, cloves. Memory flickered like a tinderbox. She refused to let the flint spark.

'You do not wish to recall what happened to you. But you *can* talk. The smoke inhalation was by no means bad enough to render you mute.'

'She won't talk, doctor. This one's no fool. Knows where they'll put her if she ain't in here.'

'But she can write?' He looked about the room. 'Why is there nothing here for her to write with? Have you not *tried* to communicate with her?'

'Wouldn't trust her with a pen.'

'A slate then, and chalk. You will find them in my room.' He fished in his pocket and thrust a key at the attendant. 'Fetch them. Now, if you please.'

With a frown, the attendant took the key and shuffled out the door.

They were alone. She felt his eyes upon her – not hard but uncomfortable, like the tickle of an insect crawling over her leg.

'Medicine is changing, Mrs Bainbridge. I am not a man who will give you electric shocks or plunge you into cold baths. I want to help.' He cocked his head. 'You must know that certain . . . accusations have been made against you. Some people suggest you should be moved to a more secure facility. Or that perhaps you do not belong in an asylum at all.'

Accusations. They never explained the basis of the charge, only called her a killer, and for a while she had lived up to the reputation: throwing cups; scratching the nurses. But now she had a room of her own and stronger medication, it was too much effort to act the part. She would rather sleep. Forget.

'I am here to decide your fate. But in order to help you, I need you to help *me*. I need you to tell me what happened.'

As if he could understand. She had seen things beyond the comprehension of his small, scientific brain. Things he would deny were possible until they stole up beside him and pressed their worn, splintered hands against his.

A dimple appeared in his left cheek as he smiled. 'I see what you are thinking. Every patient says the same, that I won't believe them. I confess, there are many delusions here, but few are without foundation. Some experience has formed them. Even if it sounds extraordinary, I should like to hear it – what you *think* happened. Sometimes, the brain cannot cope with the information it has to process.

It makes sense of trauma in odd ways. If I can hear what your mind tells you, I might be able to understand how it works.'

She smiled back. It was an unpleasant smile; the one that made the nurses edge away. He didn't flinch.

'And perhaps we can turn your predicament to our advantage. When a trauma has occurred, it often helps the victim to write it down. In a detached way. As if it happened to someone else.' The door whined; the attendant had returned with the chalk and slate in hand. Dr Shepherd took them and reached towards the bed, offering the items like an olive branch. 'So then, Mrs Bainbridge. Will you try for me? Write something.'

Tentatively, she reached out and picked up the chalk. It sat strangely in her hand. After all this time, she could not remember how to begin. She pressed the tip to the slate and drew a vertical line. It squeaked – an awful, high-pitched squeal that set her teeth on edge. She panicked, pushed too hard. The end of the chalk snapped off.

'I really do think a pencil would be easier for her. Look, she is not dangerous. She is simply trying to do as we ask.'

The attendant glared. 'On your head be it, doctor. I'll bring one later.'

She managed to scrape out some letters. They were faint, but she was afraid to use force again. Just visible on the slate was a shaky *Hello*.

Dr Shepherd rewarded her with another smile. 'That's it! Keep practising. Do you think you could build it up, Mrs Bainbridge, and do as I asked? Write down all you remember?'

As easy as that.

He was too young. Too fresh and full of hope to realise there would be times in his life he would want to erase – whole years of unbearable moments.

She had pushed them down so deep that she could only reach one or two. Enough to confirm she did not want the rest. Whenever she tried to think back, she saw *them*. Their awful faces barring the way to the past.

She used the cuff of her sleeve to wipe the slate clean and write again. *Why?*

He blinked behind his glasses. 'Well . . . Why do you think?'

Cure.

'That's right.' The dimple appeared again. 'Imagine if we could cure you? Set you free of this hospital?'

God love him. *No.*

'No? But . . . I do not understand.'

'Told you, doctor,' said the attendant in her harsh, magpie voice. 'She did it, all right.'

She tucked her legs up and lay flat on the bed. Her head throbbed. She raised her hands to her scalp and gripped, trying to hold things in place. Bristles prickled from her shaved head. Hair growing, months passing, locked away.

How long had it been? A year, she supposed. She could ask them, write the question on the slate, but she feared to learn the truth.

Surely it was time for her medicine, time to deaden the world?

'Mrs Bainbridge? Mrs Bainbridge, are you well?'

She kept her eyes shut. Enough, enough. Four words, and she had written too much.

'Perhaps I have pushed her too hard for today,' he said. But still he hovered, an unsettling presence by her bed.

This was all wrong. Her mind was thawing.

Finally, she heard him straighten up. Keys jangled, a door creaked open.

'Who next?'

The door closed and muffled their voices. Their words and steps petered away down the corridor.

She was alone, but the isolation did not comfort her as it used to. Noises that usually went unnoticed came painfully loud: the rattle of a lock, laughter far away.

Frantic, she buried her face beneath her pillow and tried to forget.

———

The truth. She could not stop thinking about it during the cold grey hours of silence.

They didn't get newspapers in the day room – at least, not when she had been allowed in there – but rumours had a way of seeping under doors and through cracks in the walls. Journalists' lies made it into the asylum long before she did. Ever since she awoke in this place, she had been given a new name: *murderess*.

Other patients, attendants, even the nurses when they thought no one could hear: they twisted their mouths and bared their teeth as they said it, ravenous. *Murderess*. As if they wanted to frighten her. *Her*.

It wasn't the injustice she loathed but the noise, its syllables hissing in her ears like – *No*.

She shifted in bed and hugged her goose-pimpled arms tight, trying to hold herself together. Until now she had been safe. Safe behind the walls, safe behind her silence, safe with the beautiful drugs that drowned out the past. But the new doctor . . . He was the clock signalling with a dread knell that her time was finished. *Perhaps you do not belong in an asylum at all.*

Panic spiralled in her chest.

Back again to the same three options. Say nothing and be presumed guilty. Destination: the gallows. Say nothing and, by some miracle, be acquitted. Destination: the cold, sharp world outside, no medicine to help her forget.

Only one choice remained – the truth. But what was that?

Gazing back to the past, the only faces she saw clearly were those of her parents. Around them, shadowy figures massed. Figures full of hate that had terrified her and twisted the course of her life.

But no one would believe that.

A full moon shone in silvery lines through the window at the top of the wall, touching her head. She lay there, watching it, when the thought came to her. In this place of misrule, everything was upside down. The truth was mad, beyond the realms of any healthy imagination. And that was why the truth was the only thing guaranteed to keep her under lock and key.

She slid from the bed onto the floor. It was cold and faintly sticky. No matter how many times they mopped it, the scent of piss hung in the air. She crouched down beside her bed, finally facing the bulky shadow across the room.

Dr Shepherd had ordered it put there: the first new item in an unchanging landscape. Just a desk. But it was another instrument to crack open the charnel house and exhume all she had buried.

With her pulse pounding in her neck, she crawled across the floor. Somehow she felt safer down low, crouched beneath it, looking up the notched legs. *Wood*. She shivered.

Surely there was no reason to be cautious, here. Surely they could not take any piece of wood and . . . It wasn't possible. But then none of it was possible. None of it made the least bit of sense. Yet it *had* happened.

Slowly, she stood and surveyed the surface of the desk. Dr Shepherd had left all the implements out for her: paper and a thick, blunt-ended pencil.

She pulled a page towards her. In the gloom she saw a void of white, waiting for her words. She swallowed the pain in her throat. How could she relive it? How could she bring herself to do it to them, all over again?

She peered into the blank page, trying to see, somewhere in its vast expanse of nothing, that other woman from long ago.

THE BRIDGE, 1865

I am not dead.

Elsie recited the words as her carriage sluiced through country roads, churning up clods of mud. The wheels made a wet, sucking noise. *I am not dead.* But it was hard to believe, looking through the rain-spattered window at the ghost of her reflection: pale skin; cadaverous cheeks; curls eclipsed by black gauze.

Outside the sky was iron grey, the monotony broken only by crows. Mile after mile and the scenery did not change. Stubble fields, skeletal trees. *They are burying me*, she realised. *They are burying me along with Rupert.*

It wasn't meant to be like this. They should have been back in London by now; the house thrown open, spilling over with wine and candles. This season vivid dyes were in fashion. The salons would be awash with azuline, mauve, magenta and Paris green. She should be there at the centre of it: invited to every diamond-spangled party; hanging on the arm of the host in his striped waistcoat; the first lady escorted into the dining room. The new bride always went first.

But not a widow. A widow shied from the light and entombed herself with grief. She became a mermaid drowning in black crêpe, like the Queen. Elsie sighed and stared into the hollow reflection of her eyes. She must be a terrible wife, for she did not long for seclusion. Sitting in silence musing on Rupert's virtues would not help her grief. Only distraction could do that. She wanted to attend the theatre, to ride up and down on the rattling omnibuses. She would rather be anywhere than alone in these bleak fields.

Well, not quite alone. Sarah sat hunched on the squabs opposite, poring over a battered leather volume. Her wide mouth moved as she read, whispering the words. Elsie despised her already. Those mud-brown, bovine eyes that held no spark of intelligence, the pinched cheekbones and the lanky hair that always dribbled out of her bonnet. She'd seen shop girls with more refinement.

'She'll be company for you,' Rupert had promised. 'Just watch her while I'm down at The Bridge. Show her a few sights. The poor girl doesn't get out much.'

He wasn't exaggerating. His cousin Sarah ate, breathed and blinked – occasionally she read. That was it. There was no initiative, no yearning to better her position. She'd been content in her little rut as companion to a crippled old lady until the crone died.

As a good cousin, Rupert had taken her in. But it was Elsie who was stuck with her now.

Yellow, fan-shaped leaves came swooping down from the chestnut trees and landed on the roof of the carriage. *Pat, pat.* Earth upon the coffin.

Only another hour or two, and the sun would start to set. 'How much longer?'

Sarah looked up from the page with glazed eyes. 'Hmm?'

'How long?'

'Until . . .?'

Dear God. 'Until we arrive.'

'I don't know. I have never been to The Bridge.'

'What? You haven't seen it either?' It was incomprehensible. For an ancient family, the Bainbridges didn't take much pride in their ancestral seat. Even Rupert, at the age of forty-five, had possessed no memory of the place. He only seemed to recollect he owned an estate when the lawyers were ratifying their marriage contract. 'I cannot believe it. Did you not visit even when you were little?'

'No. My parents often spoke of the gardens, but I never saw them. Rupert took no interest in the place until . . .'

'Until he met me,' Elsie finished.

She swallowed back the tears. They had been so close, hadn't they, to creating the perfect life together? Rupert had gone up to make the estate ready for spring and the heir who would arrive to inherit it. But now he'd left her, with no experience of running a country house, to cope with the family legacy and an impending child, alone. She envisaged herself nursing a baby in a mouldering parlour with tattered, pea-green upholstery and a clock on the mantel swathed in cobwebs.

The horses' hooves squelched outside. The windows began to mist. Elsie pulled down her sleeve and rubbed it against the glass. Dreary images lumbered past. Everything was overgrown and shabby. Remnants of a grey brick wall poked up from the grass like tombstones, while clover and bracken swarmed around. Nature was coming into its own, reclaiming the space with brambles and moss.

How could the road to Rupert's house *be* in such a state? He was a fastidious businessman, good with numbers, balanced in his books. So why would he let one of his possessions degenerate into this mess?

The carriage rattled and stopped abruptly. Peters cursed from up on the box.

Sarah closed her book and placed it aside. 'What's happening?'

'I think we're getting near.' Leaning forward, she peered as far into the distance as she could. A light mist snaked up from the river running alongside the track and shrouded the horizon.

Surely they were at Fayford by now? It seemed as if they had been jolting along for hours. Boarding the train at London in the smudged, whisky-coloured dawn felt like an occurrence of last week, not this morning.

Peters snapped his whip. The horses snorted and strained in their harness, but the carriage only swayed.

'What now?'

The whip cracked again. Hooves sloshed in the mud.

Knuckles rapped on the roof. 'Hello in there? You'll have to get out, ma'am.'

'Out?' she repeated. 'We cannot get out in this filth!'

Peters jumped off the box, landing with a splat. In a few wet steps he was at the door, swinging it open. Mist swept in and played around the threshold. 'No choice, I'm afraid, ma'am. The wheel's stuck fast. All we can do is yank at it and hope the horses do the rest. The less weight in the coach, the better.'

'Surely two ladies do not weigh so very much?'

'Enough to make a difference,' he said bluntly.

Elsie groaned. The fog pressed against her cheek, damp as a dog's breath, carrying the scent of water and a deep, earthy tang.

Sarah tucked her book away and picked up her skirts. She paused, petticoats lifted above her ankles. 'After you, Mrs Bainbridge.'

In other circumstances, Elsie would be pleased to have Sarah defer to her. But this time, she would rather not go first. The mist had already built with surprising speed. She could just make out the shape of Peters and his hand, reaching towards her. 'The steps?' she asked, without much hope.

'Can't get 'em down at this angle, ma'am. You'll have to jump. It's only a little way. I'll catch you.'

All her dignity had come to this. Heaving a sigh, she closed her eyes and sprang. Peters's hand touched her waist for an instant before he set her down in the mud.

'Now you, miss.'

Elsie stumbled away from the carriage, not wanting Sarah's big feet to land on her train. It was like walking on rice pudding. Her boots slipped and stuck at strange angles. She could not see where she placed them; the mist floated up to her knees, obscuring everything below. Perhaps that was as well – she did not want to see the hem of her new bombazine gown edged with filth.

More chestnut trees appeared in patches through the fog. She had never encountered anything like this; it was not yellow and sulphurous like a London Particular, it did not hang, but *moved*. As the clouds of silver and grey slid to the side, they revealed a cracked wall by the line of trees. Bricks had fallen from it, leaving gaping holes like missing teeth. About halfway up there was an empty, rotting window frame. She tried to see clearly, but the images dissolved as the fog glided back.

'Peters? What is this ghastly building?'

A cry ripped through the damp air. Elsie spun round, her heart pounding, but only white mist met her eyes.

'Easy now, miss.' Peters's voice. 'You're all right.'

She released her breath and watched it seep into the mist. 'What's going on? I cannot see you. Did Sarah fall?'

'No, no. I caught her in time.'

Probably the most excitement the girl had experienced all year. A jest was on the tip of her tongue, but then she heard another sound: lower, more insistent. A deep, stretched groan. The horses must have heard it too, for they jinked in their harness.

'Peters? What was that?'

The noise came again: bass and mournful. She didn't like it. She wasn't used to these country sounds and mists – nor did she wish to be. Lifting her train, she tottered back to the carriage. She moved too fast. Her foot slid, the ground slipped beneath her and her shoulder blades smacked against the mud.

Elsie lay on her back, stunned. Cool slime oozed into the gap between her collar and her bonnet.

'Mrs Bainbridge? Where are you?'

The blow had knocked the breath from her. She wasn't hurt – she had no concerns for the baby, but she could not find her voice. She stared up into the billowing white. Moisture soaked through her gown. Somewhere, in a distant part of her brain, she cried over the damage to her black bombazine.

'Mrs Bainbridge?'

That groan came once more, closer now. The mist moved like a restless spirit above her. She sensed a shape over her head, a presence. She croaked feebly.

'Mrs Bainbridge!'

Elsie cringed as she saw them, inches from her face: two soulless eyes. A wet nose. Black wings like a bat. It sniffed her, then it lowed. *Lowed.*

A cow. It was just a cow, tethered by a length of frayed rope. Her voice came flowing back on a tide of embarrassment. 'Shoo! Get away, I have no food for you.'

It did not move. She wondered if it could – it was not a healthy creature. A stringy neck supported its head and flies hovered over its jutting ribs. Poor brute.

'There you are!' Peters moved the cow out of the way with a few kicks. 'What happened, ma'am? Are you all right? Let me help you.'

It took four attempts before he managed to heave her up. Her dress left the bog with a sticky rip. Ruined.

Peters gave a crooked smile. 'Not to worry, ma'am. Don't look like a place you need to dress up, does it?'

She peered over his shoulder, where the last tendrils of mist were twisting away. Surely not. Surely the village floating into view could not be Fayford?

A row of tumbledown cottages squatted beneath the trees, each with a smashed window or battered door. Holes in the walls had been hastily patched over with mud and dung. Broken thatch made a pathetic attempt to stretch over the rooftops, but it was flecked with mould.

'No wonder we got stuck.' Peters gestured to the road flowing before the cottages. It was little more than a brown river. 'Welcome to Fayford, ma'am.'

'This cannot possibly be Fayford,' she told him.

Sarah's pale face appeared beside them. 'I think it is!' she breathed. 'Oh, heavens.'

Elsie could only gape. It was bad enough to be trapped in the country, but *here*? Marrying Rupert was meant to lift her above her station, provide her with well-fed cottagers and humble tenants.

'Stay there, ladies,' said Peters. 'I'm going to get this wheel out while the mist is clear.' He walked back carefully over the mud.

Sarah crept up next to Elsie. For once, Elsie was glad of her presence. 'I hoped for pleasant country walks, Mrs Bainbridge, but I fear we will have to stay indoors this winter.'

Indoors. The word was like a key turning in a lock. That old, trapped feeling from childhood. How could she take her mind off Rupert if she had to stay indoors?

There were books, she supposed. Card games. It would not take long for them to become tedious.

'Did Mrs Crabbly ever teach you how to play backgammon, Sarah?'

'Oh yes. And then of course …' She froze, eyes widening.

'Sarah? What is it?'

She twitched her head at the cottages. Elsie turned. Grubby faces hovered by the windows. Wretched people, worse than the cow.

'They must be my tenants.' She raised a hand, feeling she should signal to them, but her courage faltered.

'Should we—' Sarah squirmed. 'Should we try to talk to them?'

'No. Stay away.'

'But they look so miserable!'

They did. Elsie cudgelled her brains for ways to help. Visit them with a basket and read a Bible passage? That was what rich ladies did, wasn't it? Somehow she didn't think they would appreciate the effort.

A horse whinnied. She heard a curse and turned to see the carriage wheel burst from the quagmire with an almighty gurgle, spraying mud over Peters.

'Well,' he said, casting a wry glance at Elsie's gown. 'That makes two of us.'

The carriage rolled forward a few paces. Behind it, Elsie saw the battered ruins of a church. Its spire had disappeared, leaving only a jagged spike of wood. Yellow, sparse grass surrounded it, crammed close with headstones. Someone watched them from the lychgate.

Bubbles fizzed in Elsie's stomach. The baby. She put one hand on her muddy bodice and used the other to take Sarah's arm. 'Come on. Back in the carriage.'

'Oh, yes.' Sarah scrambled forward. 'Let us get to the house as soon as possible!'

Elsie could not share her enthusiasm. For if this rat's nest was the village, what on earth would they find at the house?

The river whispered to them; a rushing, disembodied sound. Moss-speckled stone formed a bridge across the water – it must be the very bridge from which the house took its name.

It was not like any of the bridges in London. Instead of modern architecture and engineering, Elsie saw crumbling arches teased by foam and spray. A pair of discoloured stone lions flanked the posts on either side of the water. It made her think of drawbridges, the Tower of London – Traitors' Gate.

But this river was not like the Thames; it was not grey or brown but clear. She squinted, her eyes catching a flick beneath the surface. Dark shapes, swirling. Fish?

When they reached the other side, an old gatehouse sprang up as if from nowhere. Peters slowed the carriage, but no one came out to greet them. Elsie put the window down, wincing at the sensation of her clammy sleeve moving against her arm. 'Carry on, Peters.'

'There!' cried Sarah. 'The house is there.'

The road sloped down across a range of hills, where the sun was beginning to set. At the very end, crouching in a horseshoe of red and orange trees, was The Bridge.

Elsie put up her veil. She saw a low-slung Jacobean building with three gables on the roof, a central lantern tower and redbrick chimneys looming behind. Ivy poured out of the eaves and engulfed the turrets at either end of the house. It looked dead.

Everything was dead. Parterres lay prostrate beneath the soulless gaze of the windows, the hedges brown and riddled with holes. Vines choked the flowerbeds. Even the lawns were yellow and sparse, as if a contagion spread slowly throughout the grounds. Only the thistle thrived, its purple spikes bristling from amidst the coloured gravel.

The carriage drew to a halt on a gravel sweep, opposite the fountain that formed the centrepiece of the decaying grounds. Once, when the stone was white and the sculpted figures of dogs on top were new, it must have been a handsome structure. No water sprang up from the jets. Cracks wiggled across the empty basin.

Sarah drew back. 'They're all out to see us,' she said. 'The entire staff!'

Elsie's stomach plunged. She had been too busy staring at the gardens. Now she observed three women dressed in black waiting outside the house. Two wore white caps and aprons while the third was bare-headed, showing a coil of iron hair. Beside her stood a stiff, formal-looking man.

Elsie looked down at her skirts. They were patched like a rusty iron gate. Mud made the bombazine heavy and caused it to cling around her knees. What would her new servants think if they saw her in such a state? She would be neater and cleaner in her factory clothes.

'A mistress must meet her household. But I had hoped not to do it caked in mud.'

Without warning, the carriage door swung open. She jumped. A young man stood before her, his slim figure clad in a black suit.

'Oh Jolyon, it's you. Thank goodness.'

'Elsie? What on earth happened?' His light brown hair was swept back from his face, as if to highlight the dismay written there.

'An accident. The carriage wheel got stuck and I fell—' She gestured to her skirt. 'I can't see the household like this. Send them back inside.'

He hesitated. His cheeks flushed beside his whiskers. 'But . . . It would look so strange. What am I supposed to say?'

'I don't know! Tell them anything!' She heard the brittle sound of her own voice and felt dangerously close to tears. 'Make up some excuse.'

'Very well.' Jolyon closed the door and stood back. She saw him turn, the breeze lifting a curl of hair at his collar.

'Mrs Bainbridge is . . . indisposed. She will have to go straight to her bed. Set a fire and send up some tea.'

Mumbles sounded outside, but then there was the welcome crunch of feet trudging back over gravel. Elsie breathed a sigh of relief. She did not have to face them – not yet.

Of all people, Elsie found servants the most judgemental: jealous of their master's station, since it was tied closely to their own. Rupert's London household had turned their noses up at her when she arrived from the match factory. Her confession that she hadn't kept domestic help since her mother died had sealed their contempt. Only respect for Rupert, and Rupert's warning glances, made them civil.

Sarah leant forward. 'What will you do? You'll need to get changed straight away, without being seen. And Rosie isn't here!'

No. Rosie was unwilling to leave her London life and wages to live in this backwater. Elsie could not blame her. And to be honest, she was secretly relieved. She'd never felt comfortable changing in front of her lady's maid, having strange hands against her skin. But she would need to hire another one soon, if just for appearances' sake. She did not want to get the reputation of being one of those eccentric widows populating the countryside.

'I daresay I'll manage without Rosie for now.'

Sarah's face brightened. 'I could help you with the buttons at the back. I'm good at buttons.'

Well, that made one thing.

Jolyon appeared back beside the door, opened it again and extended a hand. 'The staff are safely inside. Come on now, climb out.'

She struggled down the steps and landed awkwardly with a sprinkle of stones. Jolyon raised his eyebrows at her dress. 'Good heavens.'

She snatched her hand away.

While he helped Sarah down, she looked over the house. It revealed nothing. Curtains were drawn across the windows in an unrelenting screen of black. Ivy fluttered against the wall.

'Come. The trunks you sent ahead are in your room.'

They climbed a shallow flight of steps to the open door. Before they crossed the threshold, a musty tang reached out and forced its way up Elsie's nostrils. Someone had tried to cover it with a softer, powdery note. There were scents of a linen drawer: lavender and green herbs.

Jolyon walked briskly on, as he did in London, his footsteps tapping over a grey stone floor set with lozenges. Elsie and Sarah dawdled behind him, keen for a look at the house.

The door opened straight into the Great Hall, a cavern of antique splendour. Medieval details stood out: a suit of armour, shortswords displayed in fans on the wall and worm-eaten roof beams above.

'Did you know Charles I and his queen once stayed here?' asked Sarah. 'My mother told me. Imagine them, walking right across this floor!'

Elsie was more concerned with the fire blazing in a black iron grate. She hurried towards it and held her gloved hands out to the flames. She was used to coal; there was something unnerving about these crackling logs and the deep, sweet smell of their smoke. It reminded her of the deal they used in the match factory to make the splints. The way it split under the saw.

She looked away. Either side of the fireplace stood two heavy wooden doors, embossed with iron.

'Elsie.' Jolyon sounded impatient. 'There will be a fire in your room.'

'Yes, but I—' She turned, and the muscles in her face set like wax. Under the stairs. She had not noticed it before. A long, narrow box lay on a table in the centre of an oriental rug. 'Is that . . .?'

Jolyon hung his head. 'Yes. He was in the drawing room at first. But the housekeeper informs me it is easier to keep this room aired and fresh.'

Of course: the smell of herbs. Elsie reared back, feeling her insides curl. She wanted to remember Rupert smiling and dapper, as he had always been, not as a lifeless doll on display.

She cleared her throat. 'I see. And at least the neighbours will not have to traipse through the house when they come to pay their respects.' That dreadful listlessness which had possessed her when she first heard of Rupert's death started up, but she pushed it back down. She did not want to be swamped by grief or bitterness – she only yearned to pretend it had never, ever happened.

'There do not seem to be many neighbours.' Jolyon leant on the banister. 'Only the vicar has come so far.'

How terribly sad that was. In London, men would be honoured to see Rupert one last time. She regretted, once again, that they had not brought him back to town for a fine burial, but Jolyon had said it was impossible.

Sarah walked to the coffin and peered in. 'He looks peaceful. Dear man, he deserves to be.' She turned to Elsie and held out a hand. 'Come, Mrs Bainbridge, and look.'

'No.'

'It's all right. Come. It will do you good to see how serene he is. It will help with the grief.'

She severely doubted that. 'I don't want to.'

'Mrs Bainbridge—'

A log exploded in the grate. Elsie yelped and jumped forwards. A shower of sparks dusted her skirts and melted to ash before they reached the rug. 'Goodness.' She put a hand to her chest. 'These old fires. I could have been set alight.'

'Hardly.' Jolyon ran his fingers through his hair. 'We must get you upstairs before the servants come and – Elsie? Elsie, are you listening to me?'

The leap away from the fire had done it. She was close enough to see the peaks of Rupert's profile rising over white satin: the grey-blue tip of a nose; eyelashes; curls of salt-and-pepper hair. It was too late to look away. She inched forward, each footstep placed with the care she would use to approach a sleeping child. Gradually, the high wall of the coffin receded.

Breath left her in a rush. It was not Rupert. Not really. What lay before her was an imitation, as cold and featureless as a stone effigy. Its hair was perfectly greased in place, with no hint of the curl that always fell over Rupert's left eye. The broken veins that had adorned Rupert's cheek were a mere smudge of grey. Even his moustache looked false, standing out prominently from drying skin.

How that moustache had tickled. She felt it again at her cheek, under her nose. The way she had always laughed when he kissed her. Laughter was Rupert's gift. It felt wrong to stand around him solemn and silent. He would not have wanted that.

As her eyes travelled down to his chin and the dots of stubble that would now never grow, she noticed small, blue flecks on the skin. They reminded her of childhood and sewing needles, sucking hard on a finger.

Of course, they were splinters. But why would he have splinters on his face?

'Elsie.' Jolyon's voice was firm. 'We must go up. There will be time enough to say goodbye tomorrow.'

She nodded and rubbed her eyes. It was not hard to drag herself away. Whatever Sarah thought, staring into a coffin was nothing like bidding farewell to her husband. The time for that had passed with his last breath. All they had in the casket was a pale shadow of the man who had once been Rupert Bainbridge.

———

It took two flights of steps before they cleared the beams of the Great Hall and emerged onto a small landing. Only a few lamps were lit, flaring in patches and revealing red flock wallpaper.

'This way,' said Jolyon, turning left.

Puffs of dust rose beneath Elsie's feet as she followed, her damp skirts swishing against the carpet. The corridor conveyed an air of shabby grandeur. Tapestry sofas lurked against the walls with chipped marble busts dotted in between. They were horrible things, watching her with dead expressions, shadows creeping over their cheekbones and sinking into the sockets of their eyes. She didn't recognise any as famous writers or philosophers. Perhaps they were previous owners of The Bridge? She searched their impassive faces for a trace of Rupert but found none.

Jolyon took a turn to the right, then another quickly to the left. They came up against an arched door. 'This is the guest suite,' he explained. 'I thought you would be comfortable here, Miss Bainbridge.'

Sarah blinked. 'A suite, just for me?'

'Yes indeed.' He gave a tight smile. 'Your box is in there. I will sleep down the hall by the servants' stairs.' He gestured with a sweep of his arm. 'Mrs Bainbridge is in a mirror suite on the other wing.'

Elsie raised her eyebrows. A mirror suite. Was that the level to which she had sunk? 'How thrilling. We'll be just like twins.' She tried to keep the tartness from her voice but feared she did not succeed.

'I will just settle in,' Sarah said awkwardly. 'Then I will come and help you dress, Mrs Bainbridge.'

'Take all the time you need,' said Jolyon. 'I will show my sister to her room. Then we will enjoy a late dinner together.'

'Thank you.'

Grabbing Elsie's arm, he frogmarched her back the way they had come. 'You must not treat Sarah like a servant,' he grunted.

'Indeed I won't, for she does no work to earn her living. She is a spinster here on my charity, is she not?'

'She was the only family Bainbridge had.'

Elsie tossed her head. 'That is not true. *I* was Rupert's family. *I* was his next of kin.'

'Oh yes, you managed to convince him of that.'

'What on earth do you mean?'

Jolyon slowed to a halt. He peered over his shoulder, checking there were no servants loitering in the shadows. 'I am sorry. That was crass of me. It is not your fault. But I thought Bainbridge and I had agreed, before the marriage, exactly what would happen in this situation. It was a gentleman's agreement. But Bainbridge . . .'

Unease crept into her stomach. 'What are you saying?'

'He did not tell you? Bainbridge changed his will a month before he died. His solicitor read it to me.'

'What did it say?'

'He left it all to you. Everything. The house in London, The Bridge, his share in the match factory. No one else benefits in the least.'

Of course he did. A month ago – that was when she told him about the baby.

To think that after all she had been through, she had managed to marry a considerate man, a prudent man – and lost him. *Careless*, Ma would have said. *Just like you, Elisabeth*.

'Is it strange that he should change his will? I am his wife, I am carrying his child. Surely the arrangement is perfectly natural?'

'It would be. A year or two down the line and I would have no quarrel with it.' Shaking his head, he moved off down the corridor.

She tried to keep up, unable to concentrate on the path he took; the wine-red walls seemed to billow like cloth. 'I don't understand. Rupert has acted like an angel. This is the answer to my prayers.'

'No, it is not. Think, Elsie, think! How does it look? A man everyone thought was a confirmed bachelor marries a woman ten years his junior and invests in her brother's factory. He changes his will to make her the sole beneficiary. Then, a mere month later, he is dead. A man who appeared as strong as an ox is dead, and nobody knows how.'

Glacier crystals formed in her chest. 'Don't be ridiculous. No one would suggest—'

'Oh, they are suggesting it, I assure you. And whispering it. Think of the match factory. Think of my good name! I have to steer through this storm of gossip, alone.'

She stumbled. That was why Jolyon wanted her in the country, why he refused to move Rupert's body back to London for burial: scandal.

She remembered the last scandal. Police officers in their iron hats, taking down statements. The whispers that buzzed in her wake like a trail of flies and those hungry, pointed looks. Years of it. It would take years to fade away.

'Dear God, Jo. How long will the baby and I have to stay in this place?'

He flinched. For the first time, she noticed the pain shining in his eyes. 'Damn it, Elsie, what is wrong with you? I am telling you about a stain on our name, on the factory, and all you can think about is how long you will be away from London. Do you even miss Rupert?'

She missed him like air. 'You know I do.'

'Well, I must say you do a good job of hiding it. He was a good man, a great man. Without him we would have lost the factory.'

'I know.'

He stopped at the end of the corridor. 'This is your room. Perhaps once you are settled inside, you will have the decency to grieve.'

'I *am* grieving,' she snapped. 'I just do it in a different manner to you.' Pushing past him, she flung open the door and slammed it behind her.

She closed her eyes and leant back, both palms flat against the wood, before she exhaled and sank to the floor. Jolyon had always been so. She should not take his words to heart. Twelve years her junior, he had always been at leisure to feel, to cry. It was Elsie who endured. And hadn't that been the point? To keep little Jolyon in ignorance of what she suffered?

After a few minutes, she was mistress of herself. She rubbed her forehead and opened her eyes. A clean, bright room lay before her with windows on either side, one facing out to the semicircle of russet trees that embraced the house and the other angled across at the west wing, where Sarah was staying. Her trunks lay heaped in the corner. A fire sizzled in the grate and Elsie was relieved to see a washstand beside it. Strands of steam rose from the ewer. Hot water.

She heard Ma's voice, clear in her ear. *Silly girl, making such a fuss. Let's wash all those bad thoughts away.*

Climbing to her feet, she stripped off her gloves and went to splash her face. Her sore eyes instantly felt better and the towel she used to wipe her skin was wonderfully soft – whatever the flaws of the place, she could not fault the housekeeper.

A heavy four-poster bed carved in rosewood loomed against the far wall. Cream bedclothes embroidered with flowers were spread across it. Then came the dressing table, its three-piece mirror swathed in black fabric. She sighed. It was the first looking glass she had seen since leaving the station. Time to assess the damage done by her tumble in the mud.

Placing the towel back on its rail, she walked over and sat on the stool. She drew the black material aside. It was a foolish superstition: covering mirrors to stop the dead from becoming trapped. Nothing was held inside the glass except three blonde-haired, brown-eyed women, each one a sorry state. Her gauze veil fluttered at the nape of her neck like a netted crow. Windblown curls frizzed around her forehead and, despite her brief wash, a smear of mud remained on her right cheekbone. Elsie scrubbed until it melted away. Thank goodness she had refused to see the servants.

Slowly, she reached up her weary arms to remove her bonnet and cap, and begin the long task of unpinning her hair. Her fingers were not as nimble as they used to be – she had grown accustomed to having Rosie do it. But Rosie and all the comforts of that past life were miles away.

A pin snagged on a tangle and made her gasp. She dropped her hands, upset beyond reason at this small annoyance. *How did this happen?* she asked the dishevelled women before her. They had no answer.

The glass here was cold and harsh. It did not contain the smiling, pretty bride she had stared at such a short time ago. Unbidden, a scene rose up in her memory: Rupert, standing behind her that first night and brushing her hair. Pride in his face, flashes of the silver-backed brush. A feeling of safety and trust, so rare, as she considered his reversed image. She could have loved him.

The marriage was a business relationship, cement to secure Rupert's investment in the match factory, but that night she had truly looked at the man and realised she could grow to love him. In time. Alas, time was the one thing they did not have.

A tap at the door made her start.

'Buttons?' Sarah's voice.

'Yes. Come in, Sarah.'

Sarah had swapped her travelling dress for an evening gown that had seen better days. Black dye mottled it in uneven patches. She hardly looked presentable, but at least she'd plaited her mousy hair. 'Have you chosen a gown? I could ask one of the maids if there is a flatiron . . .'

'No. Please just dig out a nightgown.' If Jolyon wanted her to grieve, that's what she would do. She would act exactly as he had, after Ma. That would serve him. He would see how irritating and useless it was to have her whimpering upstairs.

Sarah's reflection twisted its hands in the mirror. 'But . . . dinner . . .'

'I'm not going down. I have no appetite.'

'But – but I *cannot* have dinner alone with Mr Livingstone! What would people say? We are barely acquainted!'

Irritated, Elsie rose to her feet and went to find a nightgown herself. Had Sarah *really* been a lady's companion? She should know better than to stand and argue with her mistress. 'Nonsense. You must have spoken to Jolyon at the wedding.'

'I was not at your wedding. Mrs Crabbly was taken ill. Do you not remember?'

'Oh.' Elsie took a moment to pull a nightgown from a trunk and arrange her face before she turned. 'Of course not. You will have to forgive me. That day . . .' She looked down at the white cotton in her hands. 'It all passed in such a happy blur.'

Honiton lace, orange blossom. She had never thought to be a bride. One put aside such fancies after the age of twenty-five. For Elsie, the prospect had seemed even less likely. She despaired of finding someone she could trust, but Rupert had been different. He carried something in the air around him, an aura innately good.

'I understand,' said Sarah. 'Now come here. Let us see about that dress.'

Elsie would rather have changed by herself, but there was no choice. She could hardly tell Rupert's cousin that she owned a buttonhook – only whores were meant to use them.

Sarah worked deftly, her fingers moving over Elsie's shoulders and down her waist like the lightest taps of rain. The gown fell whispering into her hands. 'Such fine material. I do hope the mud will wash out.'

'Perhaps you can take it downstairs for me. There must be a scullery maid who will put it in the copper without telling for a crown.'

Sarah nodded. She folded the gown and hugged it to her chest. 'And . . . the rest?' She shot a coy look at the cage of petticoats, spring steel and hoops holding Elsie in. 'You will be able to manage—?'

'Oh yes.' Self-conscious, she put her hands to the tapes securing her crinoline. 'I didn't always have a maid, you know.'

It was Sarah's silence and stillness that made Elsie's flesh creep. Her eyes fixed on Elsie's waist and expanded, darker and strangely glittering.

'Sarah?'

Sarah shook herself. 'Yes. Very well. I'll be on my way.'

Elsie looked down at her body, confused. What had made Sarah stare? With a painful jolt, she realised: her hands. She had taken her gloves off to wash her face and revealed her hands in all their chapped ugliness. Work-hardened hands, factory hands. Not a lady's hands.

But before Elsie could say anything in her defence, Sarah opened the door and walked out.

ST JOSEPH'S HOSPITAL

It appeared overnight. No sooner did she lift her head from the pillow and wipe her gritty eyes than she saw it. Alien. Wrong.

She stumbled out of bed, her feet slapping against the cold floor. It hung before her. She narrowed her eyes. It hurt to look, too bright, but she dare not remove her gaze. Yellow. Brown. Swirling lines and shapes.

It had arrived without her knowing. If she looked away, would it move again? Though it was mute it seemed to scream, to crash inside her head.

She could not go back to bed; she had to hold it at bay. Daylight trickled through the high windows, stark and limewashed like the walls. Its beams crept across the floor, then past her. At last the door clicked open.

'Mrs Bainbridge.'

It was Dr Shepherd.

Without turning, she raised a shaking hand and extended her index finger.

'Oh. You have seen the painting.' The air shifted as he arrived by her shoulder. 'I hope it is to your liking.'

The silence stretched.

'It brightens the place, does it not? I thought that, since you are not permitted to go in the day room and the exercise yard with the other patients, you might appreciate a bit of colour.' He transferred his weight to the other foot. 'This is the direction our hospital is taking. We will no longer subject our patients to bleak cells. This is a refuge for recuperation. There must be cheerful, stimulating things.'

She saw now what the artist had tried to capture: a nursery scene. A sunlit room with a mother cooing over a crib. Her dress was like a daffodil, her hair like spun gold. There were white roses in a vase, standing upon a table by the baby.

'Does it . . . Does it trouble you, Mrs Bainbridge?'

She nodded.

'And why is that?' His shoes creaked as he retrieved her slate. Although the pencil was better for writing her story, the chalk and slate made conversation easier. He placed them into her hands. 'Tell me.'

Again. He was chiselling away at her, piece by piece. That was his plan, she supposed. To strip out every inch of her; another confession, another memory until she was spent.

Already they came at night: dreams which were really flashes of the past. Landscapes of blood, wood and fire. She did not want them. How far back into the squalid past must she delve before he considered her unbalanced and left her alone?

'Do you not like the colour? Does it not cheer your spirit and remind you of better times?'

She shook her head. *Better times*. He assumed she had those, in her past.

'I am sorry to have caused you distress. Believe me, I meant only to bring pleasure.' He sighed. 'Will you sit down? I will arrange to have the painting removed once we are finished.'

With her gaze trained on the floor, she stumbled back to the bed and sat down, gripping the chalk and slate as tightly as if they were weapons. As if they could defend her.

'Do not take this little setback to heart,' he said. 'I am pleased with your progress. I read what you wrote. I see you have followed my advice and written as if the events happened to someone else.' She could not look up at him; she was intensely aware of the painting, hanging there. Its brushstrokes, its frame. He forced a chuckle. 'Memory is a tricky one. They're funny, aren't they, the details that you recall? That cow—!'

She picked up the chalk, still clumsy. *The cow is not funny.*

He bowed his head. 'I did not mean – forgive me. It was wrong of me to laugh.'

Yes.

But actually, she envied him that chuckle. Envied the fact he still *could* laugh.

Laughter, conversation, music – all these things felt like relics, activities her ancestors may have adopted, long ago, but carried no relevance for her.

She looked back at the desk.

'You stare so intently at the desk. What is it that upsets you?'

Her fingers trembled as she wrote. *Wood.*

'Wood. You dislike wood?'

The word conjured other sounds: the whoosh of a saw, a door slamming shut.

'Interesting. Most interesting. Of course, after the fire and your injury . . . Perhaps that is why?'

She blinked at him.

'Perhaps that is why you do not like wood. Because it reminds you of the fire. Because it burns.'

The fire?

He was too quick. He was living at a rate three times the speed of her drugged, undersea world. Was that why her arms appeared so scarred, why they never let her see a looking glass? Had she been in a fire?

'But of course, there could be other reasons. I have been perusing your file.' For the first time, she noticed the papers he carried beneath his arm. He spread them on the desk: her past laid out, exposed, like a body on the slab at a mortuary. 'You grew up, I see, in a match factory. First it was owned by your father, and upon his death it passed into trust until you and your brother came of age. I expect you saw a good deal of wood and fire in a match factory.'

That, too? Nothing was sacred – all must be dredged up.

Doubt bloomed in her chest and he must have sensed it, for he said, 'I trust you understand it is not idle curiosity that prompts my investigation. Nor is it merely a desire to cure you – although I hope I shall do that, too. I am charged by the hospital and the police to write a report.' He picked two papers up from the desk and came over to her. 'When you first arrived, there was no question of interrogating you. Your injuries were too great.' He showed her the first item: a newspaper clipping with an engraving. It gave a grainy impression of someone swamped in bandages, dark patches appearing where blood had seeped through the linen. 'But now you are physically, if not mentally, recovered, it has become a matter of some importance to establish the cause of the fire.'

He was not implying . . . That mummy in the engraving was not *her*? Panic seized her. The paper was dated over a year ago. All that time had passed, yet she remembered little more than a cow and the faces of painted wooden figures.

He sat beside her on the bed. She flinched away. The heat of his body, the smell of him – it was all too real.

'The remains of four bodies were found. Two of the deaths had been registered already. It is these other two we must account for.' He pushed his spectacles up his nose. 'There is likely to be an inquest. Given your current condition, I will probably be asked to speak on your behalf. So you see why I must push you for information. Find the truth. I want to help.'

He kept saying that. Repetition only made it sound false. Presumably, what he really wanted was to establish his career by solving her case.

But even if she did not trust him, he was right about one thing: there must be a statement. However painful, she had to press on and remember the rest, or she might end up dangling from the end of a noose.

The gallows shouldn't scare her. God knew there was little enough left to live for. But it was instinct, she supposed, burrowed deep within her, fighting like a feral animal. She did not want to die – only to sleep, safe, here. Cocooned by white walls and drugs.

Splinters of gold flickered before her eyes. His glasses; he was leaning close, peering into her face. 'You may not remember everything yet, but I am sure we can do it between us – wake the part of your mind that lies dormant.'

She shifted away from him, making the bed creak. Putting the chalk against the slate, she began to write awkwardly.

Squeak, squeak. That was her voice now, it seemed: a high, abrasive sound, devoid of words.

Where was the fire?

Dr Shepherd's eyebrows shot up. 'You do not recall the fire? Your injury?'

Vague images floated back. She remembered a thousand insects of pain gnawing at her back. An odd impression of nurses, medicinal scents. All of it was too far down – she had layers and layers to peel back before she could reach it clearly.

Placing one hand on her shoulder, Dr Shepherd took the slate from her fingers. She thought, for an instant, that he was going to hold her hand. But then she realised he was showing her: showing her the shining, marbled skin at her wrist. Gently, he folded back the coarse sleeve of her gown. Pink patches welled up around her elbow, misshapen, wrinkled like old fruit. Scars burnt so deep they would never be erased. Yes, she saw it now. They were burns. How had she not realised before?

'This,' he said, laying her hand back down, 'this photograph was taken a few weeks ago. Do you recall?'

She recalled the flash and the smoke, the way they had seemed to burst inside her head. But when he slid the photograph onto her lap, the face looking back was a stranger. It was a woman – at least, the striped gown and kerchief tied around the neck seemed to suggest it was a woman – but her hair was stubby, growing in tufts from a mottled scalp. Dark, bumpy skin stretched over her cheeks. One eye sagged at the lower lid.

She saw her own name written underneath.

Elisabeth Bainbridge. Detained on suspicion of arson.

THE BRIDGE, 1865

Elsie jerked upright at a knock on the door, bemused by her surroundings. The grey afternoon had deepened into the charcoal of an autumn evening. The fire burnt low in the grate. Only a single candle flickered on the dressing table, a winding sheet of hard wax down its side. Memory lurched back: she was stuck in the country – and Rupert was dead.

The knock came again. She reached for her lace gloves and pulled them on. 'Enter,' she croaked. Her mouth tasted stale. How long had she been asleep?

The door creaked open. Metal clattered against crockery and a short young woman, perhaps about eighteen years of age, edged across the threshold carrying a tray.

'Ma'am.' She placed the tray on the dressing table, fired up the gas lamp and lit it using the candle.

Elsie blinked. Surely it was a trick of her eyes – was this really her housemaid? She was filthy from the kitchen, soot streaking her coarse apron. Her face was not altogether plain; she had long lashes and thick, rosy lips that would have been pleasing were they not quirked in an impertin-ent expression. She wore no cap. Her dark hair was parted down the middle in a severe fashion, then looped behind her ears into a knot at the back of her head.

Did such a creature pass for a housemaid in this part of the country? If Elsie had known this, she would not have worried about her own appearance earlier.

'Ma'am,' the girl said again. Belatedly, she bobbed an awkward curtsy. The tray rattled. 'Mr Livingstone said you might be hungry.'

'Oh.' She could not say if that were true: the combination of smells arising from the tray left her ravenous and nauseated in equal measures. 'Yes. That was very kind of him. I will take the tray here.' She propped a bolster behind her back.

The girl came forward. She did not have the careful gait of the servants in London; her bold stride jogged the bowl and sent soup trickling over the rim. Depositing the tray on Elsie's legs with a thunk, she stepped back and bent her knees in another curtsy.

Elsie didn't know whether to be offended or amused. The girl was clearly a bumpkin. 'And you are . . .?'

'Mabel Cousins. The maid.' She had an odd voice; a blend between a cockney twang and a country drawl. 'Ma'am.'

It occurred to Elsie that perhaps Mabel was not usually permitted above stairs. They may have grown desperate for a pair of hands and sent anyone. From the way she eyed the pile of Elsie's clothes on the floor and the lace collar of her nightgown, you would think she had never seen anything so costly in her life. 'Are you the housemaid? The kitchen-maid?'

Mabel shrugged. 'Just the maid. Me and Helen. Tain't no others.'

'Well then, that makes you the maid-of-all-work.'

'If you say so. Ma'am.'

Elsie adjusted the tray on her lap. Steam rose from the surface of a yellow-brown soup flecked with herbs. Next to it sat a dish of broiled beef and a cream-coloured, lumpy substance that looked like chicken fricassee. She was hungry, but the idea of food turned her stomach. Grimacing, she picked up a spoon and plunged it into the soup.

She was surprised to see Mabel still standing there. What on earth was she waiting for? 'You may go, Mabel. I don't require anything else.'

'Oh.' At least she had the grace to blush. Wiping her hands on her apron, she gave another hopeless curtsy. 'Sorry. Ma'am. The Bridge ain't had no mistress for nigh on forty years. We ain't used to it.'

Elsie lowered her spoon and let the soup slide back into the bowl. 'Really? That long? How very strange. I wonder why?'

'There were a bunch of servants what died, I think. In the old days. Put the family off living here. I heard talk in the village – something about a skeleton they dug up in King George's time. A skeleton in the garden! Imagine that!'

Really, there was so much dead in that garden, it did not come as much of a surprise.

'Indeed! You grew up in the village of Fayford, I suppose?'

Mabel's crack of laughter made her jump. The maid threw back her head like a common woman at a music theatre.

This would not do – it would not do at all. 'Do I amuse you, Mabel?' she snapped.

'Lord bless you, ma'am.' Mabel wiped an eye with the edge of her apron. 'No one from the village works here.'

'And why might that be?'

'They're scared of the place. Gives 'em the morbs.'

Weight settled around her neck. Superstition? Premonition? Whatever it was, she did not want Mabel to see it. 'Well, that seems very foolish. It was only a skeleton. There is nothing to be afraid of, is there?' Mabel shrugged. 'That will be all, Mabel.'

'Very good, ma'am.' Without a curtsy she turned, extinguished the lamp and strode out of the door. She didn't bother to close it behind her.

'Mabel!' Elsie called. 'You turned off the light by mistake, I cannot see to . . .'

But she could already hear Mabel's flat feet thudding down the stairs.

———

Nobody came to close the door or remove the food. Despairing, Elsie placed her untouched dinner tray on the floor and dropped back against the pillows.

When she awoke, the room was as black as a weeping veil. The fire had expired, leaving the air chill. The taint of that damned soup still hung in the air, making her stomach writhe. How could the maid just leave it there to fester and grow foul? She would have to speak with the housekeeper in the morning.

It was then that she heard it: a low rasp, like a saw against wood. She went rigid.

Had she really heard that? The senses could play tricks in the dark. But then it came again. *Hiss.*

She did not want to deal with another problem tonight. Surely if she kept wrapped up with her eyes shut, the noise would go away? *Hiss, hiss.* A rhythmic, abrasive sound. *Hiss hiss, hiss hiss.* What *was* it?

She pulled the cover up over her ear until it muffled the noise. At last, it stopped. Her head drooped with the weight of exhaustion. It was probably some foolish nonsense; animals in the woods. She would not recognise their sounds – she had always slept in a town. It was silent now, and she could go back to sleep . . .

Hiss, hiss. She started up, every inch of her electrified. *Hiss.* Teeth against wood. Scraping.

Blindly, she groped under the pillow for her matchbox. It was not there. Of course it was not there, she hadn't unpacked yet. Her hand felt empty, vulnerable, without the box. She had to be careful, she mustn't spiral into panic.

Half falling from the bed, she fumbled in the dark for a gas lever, a tinderbox, anything. Her fingers only met hard pools of wax where the candle had melted. *Hiss, hiss.*

The darkness was absolute – her eyes refused to adjust. It wasn't like London; there were no streetlamps outside. She was forced to inch along, feeling her way forwards. The leg of the dressing table, a round, springy shape – a hoop of her crinoline. She manoeuvred around it, ears tensed for the sound. The very stillness felt heavy – charged, as if it were waiting.

She placed her hand down and felt it sink into something. She recoiled and cried out. There was a crash and liquid seeped through her nightgown. The odours of chicken and beef announced she had crawled straight into her dinner tray.

Hiss, hiss. Elsie flung herself away from the tray. Black, nothing but black before her eyes. How could she get out of this room?

Finally, she made out a shade of grey. She crawled towards it and felt a solid surface. The door. Struggling to her feet, she groped for the handle and pulled the door open.

It was brighter in the corridor. She took a few steps out, her feet sinking in the dusty carpet. Little clouds floated up as she moved.

There was nothing to suggest what had made the noise. Everything was still. Moonlight fell through the lantern tower in silver bars and the marble busts glowed.

Hiss, hiss. Elsie headed in the direction of the sound. She had to stop it – she would never sleep with that racket. *Hiss, hiss.* It came faster, frantic. Her feet matched its pace as they turned past the gallery, towards the stairs. She was certain: it was coming from above.

The steps led to a narrow landing with whitewashed walls. The top floor of the house, traditionally the domain of servants. She followed the sound down a corridor, past the lantern tower, until the beacon of moonlight faded to a muted glow. Soft flooring gave way to cold tiles underfoot. She shivered, wishing she had brought a wrap or a blanket with her. She felt small, exposed in cotton and lace.

She stopped to rest and get her bearings. Up ahead, a faint yellow circle stained the wall.

Hiss, hiss. The noise was close. She put one foot forward – and felt something brush her leg.

'Damn it!' she cried out. She reeled, nearly losing her balance. 'Damn, damn.'

Tiny clicks sounded on the tiles. She did not dare to look down and see what made them.

The rasping, sawing noise was everywhere around her, like the voice of God. And just below it, a steady beat. Footsteps.

A yellow orb floated into the darkness, drifting towards her.

Elsie braced herself, hardly knowing what she expected.

The orb was coming closer. The figure of a woman loomed up behind it, her shadow stretched along the tiles at her heels. She saw Elsie, gasped – and they were plunged into darkness once more.

Hiss, hiss. Again something sleek and warm swept against her calf. This time Elsie cried out.

'Mrs Bainbridge?' There was a sound like fabric ripping, then the flare of a match. A woman's face appeared in a flickering halo. She was well past middle-age with wrinkles puckering her skin. 'Bless me! Is that you, Mrs Bainbridge, up at this hour? You gave me a fright. I blew my candle right out.'

Elsie's lips flapped, trying to find purchase. 'I came . . . The sound . . .' As she spoke, it started up again, that terrible *hiss, hiss.*

The woman nodded. Her eyes were liquid and jaundiced in the candlelight, as if her irises were swimming in honey. 'I'll show you the problem, madam. Please follow me.'

She turned, taking the candle with her. The gloom was all the more fearsome after a moment of illumination. In her tired fancy Elsie imagined a second pair of footsteps, padding behind her.

'I am the housekeeper here, Mrs Bainbridge. My name is Edna Holt. I had hoped to meet you under more trad-itional circumstances, but it can't be helped.' Her voice was gentle and respectful, without the awful drawl of Mabel's speech. Elsie followed the sound of it, a rope tethering her to a world of reality and servants rather than the phantasmagoria that raged inside her imagination. 'I trust you are a little better now, madam? I heard you were unwell.'

'Yes. Yes, all I needed was sleep. But then—' The rasping noise cut her off. It hissed and scratched as Mrs Holt stopped at the end of the corridor beside a case of wooden stairs.

What could it be? The circular saw in the factory made a sound vaguely similar, but it was rapid, more staccato. This was drawn out. Like a slow, slow rip.

Something glided over her feet, tickling her legs as it passed. She gasped. A small, dark shape moved up the steps ahead. 'Mrs Holt! Do you not see it?' Two glowing slits of green materialised beside the door at the top of the stairs. Elsie's breath locked in her throat. 'God have mercy.'

'I know,' Mrs Holt said kindly. But she was not looking at Elsie – her eyes were fixed on the door. 'I know, Jasper. Come down.'

Shapes fell into place – Elsie saw a little black cat, loping back down the stairs to Mrs Holt's side. A *cat*. She had never felt so foolish.

'I think it must be rats, madam. Or possibly squirrels. Something with gnawing teeth. They drive poor Jasper here distracted.'

The cat paced a protective circle around them, muttering in the depths of his throat. His coat and tail swished against their skirts.

'Well,' Elsie said, regaining the use of her voice, 'we must get a man up there to look. A nest is soon cleared out.'

'Ah, madam, but that's the problem.' With her spare hand, Mrs Holt pulled a bunch of keys from her belt and held them up. 'The garret was closed up years ago, before my time here. None of these fit the lock.'

'You mean to tell me there is no way of gaining access?' The housekeeper shook her head. 'Then someone must take an axe to the door. I cannot allow these creatures to nest unmolested. Think what they might do to the fabric of the building! Why, the whole place could fall down around our ears.'

The candle danced beneath her breath. She could not make out Mrs Holt's expression. 'Don't upset yourself, madam. They can't have wreaked much havoc. I've only heard them the past few weeks. Only, really, since the master came down.'

They both grew still. Elsie was suddenly aware of the body, three floors below – maybe beneath the very spot where her feet arched away from the cold tiles. She hugged herself. 'And what did Mr Bainbridge say about the matter?'

'Much the same as you, madam. He was going to write to Torbury St Jude for a man . . . I don't know if he ever did.'

All the unsent letters, the unspoken words. It was as if Rupert had left the party in the middle of a dance. She ached with the need for him to come and make everything simple, to remove the burden from her shoulders.

'Well, Mrs Holt, I will check his library in the morning and see what I find. If I have no luck, I will write myself.'

The housekeeper paused. When her voice came it was infinitely softer; a verbal caress. 'Very good, madam. Now I had better be lighting you back to bed. Tomorrow will be a long and weary day, heaven knows.'

Elsie wondered for a moment what she meant. Then realisation burst upon her: they had only been waiting for her arrival. Tomorrow, they would bury Rupert.

Her knees sagged. Mrs Holt's spare hand came quickly under her elbow. 'Easy, madam.'

All at once she was aware of her nightgown, damp with soup and sauce against her legs, and the cat's little tongue licking it clean. Revolting.

She thought of the mess she had made in her bedroom, then the mess she had made with Jolyon. Her eyelids grew unbearably heavy. 'I think you are right, Mrs Holt. I had better get back to bed.'

———

The sky was a cold, hard blue, devoid of clouds. Brisk wind kept the trees constantly in motion. A confetti of green, yellow and brown leaves lay strewn over the paths, crunching as the carriage wheels ploughed through them. Elsie was astonished just how far into the distance she could see, even submerged beneath her weeping veil. There were no soot flecks in the air; no pall of coal smoke dimmed the light. It unnerved her.

'Yes, this is the right day for Rupert,' Sarah sighed. 'Busy and bright, just like him.' Her long, horsey face looked worse than yesterday, washed out and baggy-eyed after she had sat up all night with Rupert's body.

Elsie regretted not keeping watch herself. In the Great Hall, right at the bottom of the house, she would not have been troubled by the scratching noise; Sarah made no mention of having heard it. And Rupert deserved a last vigil. She had not intended to slight him, but with the baby in her belly, she had grown selfish for her own comfort. Sleep, fire and an easy chair had become the vital things in her life.

She leant her head against the window. The land looked better in sunshine. She made out larch and elm growing between the chestnut trees, and a squirrel loping across their path. It paused on its hind legs, watching the funeral procession pass, then shot up the nearest trunk.

The featherman went first, a tray of black plumes balanced upon his head. Next came the mute with his staff. His hat trailed a weeper below his waist.

'You have put on a good show for him.' Elsie reached out and squeezed Jolyon's hand, keen to remove the tension between them. 'I'm grateful.'

'It is no more than he deserved.'

Rupert's coffin gleamed from the hearse. Poor Rupert, trapped forever in this dismal place. Overlooked for eternity by that abysmal church with only half a steeple. When they married, Elsie had never doubted they would spend eternity buried side by side. She might have to review that plan.

As the carriages ground to a halt, she was relieved to see that none of the villagers had ventured to their windows, although it did surprise her. At home a funeral was a spectacle. Here it seemed like no remarkable occurrence.

Jolyon picked up his cane. 'It is time.' His black cloak swished as he climbed down the steps and offered his hand, first to Elsie and then to Sarah.

She felt fragile once she touched the ground; as light as one of the twigs blowing about the churchyard. She didn't know how to behave.

Ma had been hysterical when Pa died. Remembering her shuddering sobs, Elsie felt an instant failure as a wife. She could not cry. She spent her days holding the knowledge of Rupert's death at a distance, like a dagger against her throat, afraid to let it plunge in and bring with it understanding. Her only sensations were numbness and nausea.

Blasted Sarah started crying the moment she was installed on Jolyon's other arm. The sight of her tears filled Elsie with an anger she could not justify.

'Mr Livingstone. Mrs Bainbridge, Miss Bainbridge. My sincere condolences.'

Elsie curtsied before the vicar. Through the net of her weeping veil she made out a young man with dirty blond hair. He had a long nose and large chin that suggested good breeding, but his stole was grimy, off-white.

'I have only had the pleasure of meeting Mr Livingstone before. My name is Underwood. Richard Underwood.' A genteel voice, each letter enunciated. What was such a man doing with the dire living of Fayford? Surely his connections could do better for him? As he folded his hands over a prayer book and held it against his stomach, Elsie noticed holes in the sleeves of his cassock. 'Now I must ask you ladies, before we begin, if you are sure that you feel equal to the service? There is no shame in resting at home.'

Sarah unleashed a fresh burst of tears.

'There there, Miss Bainbridge,' said Jolyon. 'Are you – would you – it is as Mr Underwood says. Would you rather stay in the carriage?' He looked over at Elsie for help. She nearly smirked. He wanted a sister with keener sensibilities, did he?

Mr Underwood stepped in. 'My dear Miss Bainbridge, take comfort. Here is my arm.' He detached her from Jolyon with such delicacy that Elsie was convinced: he must be a gentleman. Slowly, he guided Sarah away. 'You may sit in the vicarage until you are restored. My maid will fetch you some tea. Salts? Do you have salts?'

Sarah made a gasping reply that Elsie did not catch.

'Very good. Look, just here.' His house was one of the unsavoury hovels encroaching on the burial ground – hardly a home befitting a vicar. She was almost worried about Sarah sitting in there for the length of the service; it looked as if you could catch typhoid from the place. 'Ethel, fetch the stool. You are to watch over this lady for me. Make her a sweet tea.'

A bony hag with missing teeth appeared in the doorway. 'But it's the last of—'

'I am aware of that, Ethel,' he said sharply. 'Now do as I ask.'

Grumbling, the woman ushered Sarah inside and closed the door.

Mr Underwood returned to them, seemingly unperturbed.

'That was very kind of you, sir. Thank you,' Jolyon said.

'No trouble at all. Mrs Bainbridge, are we quite safe with you?'

'I would answer for her nerves with my life,' Jolyon replied.

Underwood appraised her with interest. His eyes were wide but strangely hooded; they peered, rather than looked. 'Very good. Now, Mrs Bainbridge, I will go to the door of the church and meet the coffin. That will go in first, then the mourners will follow.'

She nodded. It was all she could do.

The pall-bearers heaved the coffin onto their shoulders and shuffled forwards. Wind crept beneath the black velvet pall, flapping it in time with their steps. The Bainbridge crest waved in flashes: blue, gold, blue, gold then an axe.

She tugged on Jolyon's arm. 'I need to sit down.'

Weather-beaten gravestones lined the path to the church door: their inscriptions crude. Three memorials in a row bore the name *John Smith* with dates barely two years apart. Then came another pair, beside a rosebush, both *Jane Price, 1859.*

Elsie kept her gaze lowered. She did not want to see the mourners climbing out of their carriages or meet their commiserating gaze. Just months ago she had walked in the other direction, decked in silk and myrtle with the peal of wedding bells behind her. She had looked down at her white dress and known that the spinster Miss Livingstone was gone forever. Here stood Mrs Bainbridge, a fresh creation, newborn.

Ashes to ashes, dust to dust. How quickly fortune turned. The woman who walked into church after this coffin – who was she now? Livingstone, Bainbridge? Maybe neither. Maybe she was not a person Elsie wanted to know.

––––––––

'It was a lovely service.' A fat gentleman took her hand and pressed it against his moustache. He reeked of tobacco.

'Yes. Just – lovely,' she said for the thousandth time. 'Thank you for coming. Please, won't you take a memorial card?' She slipped her glove out of his sweaty grasp and replaced it with a piece of black-edged card. Then she moved on to the next one.

They looked ridiculous: these men of the City with their fine hatbands, braying voices and cigars, huddled together in a dilapidated graveyard. *What* must they think of Rupert's family seat and his factory wife?

The sun had faded to a primrose disc yet still she paraded up and down the line of strangers, thanking them. Handing out Rupert's life, compressed to a bare set of facts on a monochrome card.

> *In affectionate remembrance of*
> *Rupert Jonathan Bainbridge*
> *Who departed this life 3 October 1865*
> *in the forty-fifth year of his age*
> *Interred in the family vault, All Souls Church, Fayford*
> *MEMENTO MORI*

Jolyon played his part, passing from group to group, accepting their condolences. It was *him* the guests had come to see – few of them knew her. Would they really notice if she slipped away? Perhaps she should go and find her old companion, the starved cow. At least that miserable creature had shown some interest in her.

She stood for a moment, gazing abstractedly through the net squares of her veil. Birds she did not even have a name for called in the trees beyond. Fat, inquisitive ones that looked like London pigeons except they were beige. Bold, black scavengers. Rooks? Jackdaws? Ravens? She had never really known the difference. One she did recognise – a magpie – rattled at her from the lychgate. The cobalt stripe on his tail pointed to the poorest of the gravestones: lopsided, devoured by lichen and thistle.

'You are wondering about the gravestones.' The voice made her start. She swivelled round to see Mr Underwood, standing unobtrusively by her side. His hands were tucked under his surplice; either he was cold or he was hiding the holes in his sleeves.

'Yes, I was. There seem to be an awful lot with the same names.'

He sighed. 'There are. And no matter what I say to my parishioners, there continue to be. The people . . . Well. I need not dress it up for you, Mrs Bainbridge. You see how the village is. The people do not have hope. They do not even hope that their babies will live, and so they reuse names. Over there,' he pulled out a hand and gestured to the Jane Prices she had seen earlier. 'Those two little girls were alive at the same time. The elder was ailing and the babe was born sickly. They died within a month of each other.'

'What a terrible thing. Those poor girls! But at least their folk remember them with a stone.'

'A slim comfort.'

'You think so? Have you ever been to London, Mr Underwood?'

His brow furrowed. 'On occasion. Before I took my orders.'

'Then you will have seen the burying grounds? Twenty-foot shafts, one coffin stacked atop another, all the way to the surface. Horrible places. I've heard of bodies being disturbed, even dismembered, to make way for fresh corpses. So I say it is a mercy to be laid in your own plot of land under a stone with a name, even if it is a borrowed one. There are far worse things a parent can do.'

He peered at her, reassessing her. 'To be sure.'

She judged it prudent to turn the topic. 'My maid told me that a skeleton was discovered on my own property, years ago. Would you happen to know if that is buried here also, Mr Underwood?'

'Which skeleton would that be?'

She blinked. 'I do not understand you.'

'There have been . . . a few,' he admitted. 'But it is a very old house, Mrs Bainbridge. There is no cause to be alarmed.'

Mabel's words made more sense now. It would be silly for maids to steer clear of the house over a single skeleton, but she could understand they might be put off by multiple discoveries. No one wanted to come across a pile of bones while performing their duties.

'I am not alarmed, only . . . surprised. My late husband did not know much about the history of the house.'

'It is a strange one. The estate was left empty during and after the Civil War. Then, with the Restoration, the family began to come back. Never for very long, though. The Bainbridge family had a nasty habit of losing their heirs, and the house often passed to second sons who never returned to claim it.'

'How very sad.'

'Business kept them away, I expect.' He folded his arms. 'There are many records in Torbury St Jude; I would be happy to fetch some if you have an interest?'

From the sound of it, the history would read like a bad penny dreadful. The last thing she wanted was a tale of death and skeletons. But Mr Underwood looked so earnest as he offered, she did not have the heart to rebuff him. 'You are most kind.'

They fell silent, watching the graves. No hothouse flowers adorned the ground. Instead, thistles prickled. Their purple blooms were fading, turning to clutches of wispy seed.

'Perhaps, Mrs Bainbridge, I will go and fetch your cousin for you,' he said at last. 'I trust she will be recovered.'

'Yes. I hope she will. Thank you.' She inclined her head as he strode away, his blond fringe bouncing around his temples.

The magpie had flown. She stared at the gate where it had sat, thinking of the little Jane Prices. Her veil fluttered in the breeze and made it look as if their graves were undulating. Waving to her.

———

Elsie awoke in a bad mood. For a second night, she had not slept well. The infuriating *hiss* had begun again, although it only lasted for an hour. After it stopped she had lain uneasy, teasing her mind for a way to help the village, and remembering poor Rupert in the chill crypt.

The bed was far too large without him. Although she was not the sort of wife that slept curled up around her husband, there was something reassuring about Rupert's presence beneath the sheets and the occasional creak he made as he turned. It was as though he was guarding her. Without him, the other side of the mattress yawned cold and sinister. So much space, so much opportunity for something else to slip in.

Without any assistance forthcoming from the maids, she dressed herself and managed to pin on her widow's cap before making her way downstairs.

Mr Underwood's words continued to trouble her. There must be something she could do for Fayford. She hadn't seen any of the children, but judging by the state of the cow they would be skin and bones. Who knew what domestic horror they faced? Yet if their parents were afraid of the Bainbridges and their skeleton house, she could hardly go barging in with her goodwill basket and a condescending smile. It would be better to—

Motes danced in the air before her, making her cough. She stopped and glanced down at the steps. Her black skirts had brushed up a cloud of the stuff: a powder, unlike ordinary dust. Denser. She bent down, pinching a speck between her thumb and index finger. The grains were beige and coarse.

She raised her fingers to her nose. Her nostrils flared with scents that took her back to the factory. Something sharp and clean: linseed. And beneath that a deeper, nutty aroma. She sneezed. Yes – it was sawdust.

Here?

Sawdust, phosphorous, the whirl of the cutting blade . . .

Hurriedly, she brushed it away and slapped out her skirts, not wanting a trace of the stuff upon her.

Perhaps it was the beams supporting the ceiling; they might be crumbling, like everything else at The Bridge. She would have to ask Mrs Holt later on.

As she stood, the stairwell wobbled – she was going to faint. Leaning against the banister, she tottered down the last steps. *Breathe, breathe.*

Sometimes it happened like that; the slightest thing would hurtle her back in time, resurrect memories and reduce her to the state of a frightened child.

With the blood roaring in her ears, she reached the Great Hall and sucked in a ragged breath. She was here now, safe.

The past had taken enough from her already – she would not let it have her adult years too.

She took the door to the left of the fireplace and entered the dining room. Jolyon and Sarah were already seated at a mahogany table, the dandelion-gold brocade on the wall throwing a sickly shade over their skin. They took their napkins off their laps and rose to their feet as she entered.

'There you are.' Jolyon dabbed his mouth. 'I am afraid we started without you. We were not sure if you would be down.'

The grandfather clock chimed.

'I must go on as usual, I suppose.' Her voice shook. She slumped into the chair Jolyon pulled out for her, just in time.

Servants lurked by the sideboard – the shabby maid Mabel and an older woman who must be Helen. She was a stout, jolly-looking thing, her face flushed in a permanent strawberry hue – no doubt the effect of standing over hot water for many years. Wisps of ginger hair escaped her cap at the temples. Elsie guessed her age at around forty.

Supervising both maids was a tall grey-haired man. He looked as if he had never smiled in his life.

Jolyon poured coffee while Helen served up buttered eggs on toast with herring, but the sawdust smell had turned Elsie's stomach. She took her fork and toyed with the wobbly pile of egg.

'Miss Bainbridge was just telling me about her time in the vicar's house.' Jolyon lifted the tails of his coat and sat back down beside her.

Sarah blushed up to the roots of her lanky hair. 'Wasn't it good of him, Mrs Bainbridge, to take me in like that? When he was so busy?'

'Yes.'

'He strikes me as a superior sort of man,' Jolyon observed. 'Not bred for the church, I think. At any rate, not a church in Fayford.'

'No, he wasn't,' Sarah gabbled, warming to her subject. 'He left a rich family and an inheritance to try and do some good. His father cut him off without a penny, but he had a little of his own money. He used it to get the living at Fayford. Did you ever hear of such a noble thing?'

Elsie placed a morsel of food in her mouth and chewed slowly. It was a mistake – the texture of the egg made her want to gag.

'Are you well, Mrs Bainbridge?'

'Yes, yes.' She touched a napkin to her mouth and discreetly spat out the egg. 'But what about you? Have you recovered from your faintness yesterday?'

'Yes, thank you. I am much stronger today.'

'I am glad to hear it. I expect you have had enough of funerals, after the death of Mrs Crabbly and your parents.'

'Yes.' Sarah took a shaky sip of her tea. 'Although I didn't attend Mrs Crabbly's burial. She was awfully old-fashioned like that. She would have turned in her grave to know there had been a woman present at her funeral. But my parents . . .' She stared into her tea.

'Rupert did not tell me much about your parents,' Elsie said gently.

'Well, I can scarcely tell you more. I expect Rupert was better acquainted with them than I ever was. They put me out to Mrs Crabbly when I was eight, to train as a companion. We were never wealthy, you see, on our side of the family. Something to do with an argument between my grandfather and his father. So we all worked. My parents did not have a great deal of time for me.' Sarah took another gulp of tea, as if to give her strength. 'And then they were gone. There was no money for a funeral. I couldn't have buried them if Rupert had not . . . He was always so good to me.' Her voice thickened. 'I wish . . .'

Embarrassed, Elsie picked up her fork and shredded her herring. She was beginning to regret treating the girl so flippantly. Sarah may be dull as ditchwater, but she had suffered. 'I am so sorry.'

Jolyon cleared his throat. 'We understand, Miss Bainbridge.' He did not meet Elsie's eye. 'We also lost our parents at a young age.'

Sarah shook her head, hair slipping from her chignon. 'It doesn't do to dwell upon it. But you can see why I was so grateful to Mr Underwood and his servant for looking after me. Did you know that Mr Underwood gave me the very last of his tea? I felt awful taking it. His cupboards were so sparse. Only a sliver of sugar, and absolutely no milk!'

'Milk!' Elsie speared a piece of herring triumphantly. 'Of course, that is the answer. That is how I can help the village! Jolyon, you must make enquiries. I am going to adopt the cow.'

Jolyon snorted into his coffee. The maids shifted by the sideboard. 'What cow?'

'The cow I saw on my way here. Poor old beast, it looked quite done in. The more I think on it, the more I believe she was asking me for help. If I buy the cow, I can bring her here to get nice and fat, and then she will produce milk. We can make cheese. And I can give the milk and the cheese to the villagers, for free.'

'You are a goose, Elsie.' He placed his cup down. 'Why not simply call on the villagers with a basket?'

'It will feel less condescending this way. Don't you think?'

Jolyon raised his hands. 'It does not matter what I say. You are sure to do just as you please. But you will have to get Mr Stilford here, or Mrs Holt, to make your enquiries. I am returning to London by this afternoon's train.'

'This afternoon!'

'I am afraid so. Speaking to the gentlemen at the funeral made me realise how pressing business matters are.'

'But . . .' How could he abandon her, leave her alone with Sarah? 'When will you be back?'

'Not for a good while, I should think.' His lips compressed; she sensed there were things he could not say in front of Sarah. 'I am sorry, Elsie. But I have to go back. For the factory.'

And how could she argue with that? She, who had given so much for that place?

'Of course. Of course, I understand.'

———

When Jolyon's carriage departed in a spray of gravel, Elsie was left despondent. The place felt even bigger, emptier without him. She wandered around her room and the summer parlour but found nothing to do.

Grey clouds bubbled up outside. Wind lashed at the trees. Even the light within the house was subdued and grainy. All she could hear was the tick of the clock, the groaning of the walls and a maid, brushing a hearth somewhere on the first floor.

She did not like being alone in this house: she felt it was watching her. Sensing her movements within its walls, as she felt the baby flutter inside her belly.

It was no good. She needed company, no matter how dire. After two hours of boredom she padded down the maroon corridor, past the ghastly marble busts, towards Sarah's room.

Knocking once, she entered to find Sarah curled up on her bed with a book and Mrs Holt's cat, Jasper. The room was remarkably like her own – only, as Jolyon had said, mirrored. The trees waving outside Sarah's windows were a treasury of gold and bronze; Elsie's side had the coppers, the burnt reds.

'Oh! Mrs Bainbridge. I did not expect you.' Sarah placed a mark in her book and rose, embarrassed, to her feet. Jasper merely watched her – he did not forfeit his spot on the bed. 'I'm sorry. Did you need me?'

'Yes. As a matter of fact, I am going to explore the house. I want you to join me.'

'Explore?' Sarah's brown eyes widened. 'Why, are we – I mean . . . I suppose Mrs Holt won't mind?'

'Mrs Holt? What has she to do with it? This is *my* house. I can do as I like.'

'Yes. I suppose you can.' For a moment, Sarah's wide mouth sagged. Perhaps it occurred to her, as it did to Elsie, that she had been pushed out of the inheritance. But then a happier thought seemed to inspire Sarah, for she smiled and said, 'This house has belonged to my family for a long time.

It is the only part of them I still have. A connection. I would like to explore ever so much.'

Elsie held out her gloved hand. 'Come along, then.'

Sarah hesitated. Elsie suddenly remembered exposing her coarse hands the night they had first arrived: palms the colour and texture of pork rind. She tried not to let the consciousness show on her face.

'What are you afraid of?'

With a quick release of breath, Sarah stepped forwards.

They started at the very bottom of the house. The Bridge was, in fact, much larger than they had imagined. It seemed to twist into itself. Leading off the Great Hall, across from the fireplace Elsie had warmed herself at that first night, they found a drawing room panelled with dark wood up to shoulder height. Blue-grey paper covered the rest of the walls; its shade reminded Elsie of dead cornflowers. It was a cold room, full of marble urns and tapestries.

'Why would you withdraw here?' she asked. 'I'd wager there are workhouses decorated with more warmth.'

The drawing room connected to a vast, powder-pink space filled with instruments. A mottled harp leant against the window, as if pining to get out. One of its strings had snapped. Elsie ran her eyes up the rose-coloured curtains that blocked out the daylight. The ceiling was scalloped, like the white icing around the top of a cake.

Sarah flew towards the grand piano, opened it and pressed a key. A plume of dust rose up with the note. 'I can play the piano,' she said. 'Just little pieces. Mrs Crabbly used to like them. I will play for you tonight.'

It was a testament to how dreary Elsie felt that she actually looked forward to it.

Next came a card room, decorated in green. A stuffed stag head loomed over them from the wall, his antlers casting shadows like the branches of a tree.

'How macabre.' Elsie wrinkled her nose.

'Do you really think so?' Sarah gazed up at the mounted head. The fur was dirty. Each light brown eyelash was carefully separated, revealing the ebony marbles encased within the sockets. 'There's beauty in it. Ordinarily this fellow would be rotting, but instead he is here, still majestic. Preserved forever.'

'Stuck in The Bridge for the rest of his days? I can't envy him that.'

The stag marked the end of the wing; there was no escape but back through the music room and drawing room. When they returned to the Great Hall, the red-haired maid emerged from the green baize door on the servants' side.

'Helen!' The maid pulled up sharp at the sound of Elsie's voice. 'It *is* Helen, isn't it?' She nodded dumbly and her legs bent in a curtsy far superior to Mabel's. 'Helen, now that the funeral is over, I want you to turn the pictures on the second storey. And anywhere else, for that matter. Miss Bainbridge and I want to look at the portraits. Can you do that for me?'

'Yes, ma'am.'

'Excellent.'

Curtsying again, Helen turned and went back through the baize door. They heard her feet through the walls, climbing the spiral staircase. Elsie and Sarah ascended the wider, carpeted steps reserved for the family.

'There was sawdust here earlier,' Elsie said, watching carefully. 'It seems to have gone.'

The first floor started off well, with a honey-coloured parlour adjoining a billiard room in the west wing. But as they made their way to the east wing, Elsie felt a nauseous chill take hold of her. Some sixth sense told her what they were about to see.

'Oh, look, Mrs Bainbridge! How darling!' Sarah dashed forward, leaving her leaning on the door jamb. 'Look at the little nursery!'

A child might have played there only yesterday. It was spotless. The flower-patterned paper showed no signs of age and the carpet, a bright chintz of red and yellow, had been beaten and washed. A rocking horse stood proud and gleaming in the centre of the room, little dapples of white across its rump. Sarah pushed it and giggled as it bumped on green castors.

Elsie looked around. The horse was not the only toy. Dolls were arranged round a miniature table set out for tea. On the floor beside them was a wooden Noah's ark, complete with animals. A high screen sat in front of the fire-place. Within range of the heat hung a cot trimmed with swathes of lemon fabric. It was joined by an iron bedstead covered in a patchwork quilt for an older child. Her throat closed up.

'There is a schoolroom beyond,' said Sarah.

'I think I have done enough exploring for the day.'

She drifted back to the gallery and looked down on the Great Hall. The grey and black flags danced before her eyes. Dear God, she couldn't do it. They might as well ask her to go to Oxford and sit an exam. She could not be an ordinary mother to an ordinary baby.

All those toys, the memorabilia of childhood. Perhaps it was different if you grew up happy, with memories of your father dandling you on his knee and your mother kissing your tears away. But for Elsie there was nothing but fear. Fear for the baby. Fear *of* the baby.

Jolyon had turned out all right, she reminded herself. But it was easier with Jolyon being a boy. What if Rupert's baby was born a girl? She could not love a daughter that looked like her. She could not bear to glance upon a mirror of her past without being sick.

'Mrs Bainbridge?' Sarah crept to her side. 'Are you unwell?'

'No. Just . . . weary.'

'Will we explore again tomorrow?'

'There is not much left to see. The library and the summer parlour are on the same floor as our bedrooms, we can go there any time. And then there is only . . .' Her brow grew tight with the memory of the garret. That night and the sound rasping just beyond the door, out of reach. What *had* it been?

She could not believe it was rats – not a noise like that. She wanted to know the truth. Raising a hand, she pulled a pin from underneath her cap. Two blonde curls tumbled down.

'Mrs Bainbridge?'

'How would you like to see me pick a lock?'

———

The passageway on the third floor appeared less eerie by daylight. It was a different corridor to the one she had cringed down. The Dutch tiles revealed their copper colour and clacked beneath her boots. She noticed clouds of damp and little cracks she had not seen on the walls before.

'I don't believe you, Mrs Bainbridge. You are poking fun at me. You cannot really pick a lock.'

Elsie grinned. 'You will see. I am a most resourceful woman.' She turned the hairpin between her gloved fingers. It had been a long time since she'd done this. There were no locked doors at the factory, these days.

A pattering sounded on the tiles behind. She looked round and saw Jasper, scampering to join them.

'Oh, bless him.' Sarah stopped to wait. When Jasper drew level with her he brushed against her leg, making her dress sigh.

'How fortunate you are, Sarah. You have a firm friend there.' It was strange, but she did not seem able to traverse this corridor without the cat. Was he guarding something? Or did his arrival mean Mrs Holt was nearby? It was one thing to let Sarah see her pick a lock; quite another to do it before the housekeeper. 'Come along then. Hurry. We must do this while the light is still good.'

She saw the door at the end of the corridor; three shallow steps rising to a barrier of chipped wood. It did not look sturdy. She did not see how it could contain a nest of squirrels or rats. Surely their rapacious little teeth would have gnawed through it by now?

She was just about to mount the steps when Jasper streaked past her, mewing. 'Foolish chap!' He stood before the door as he had done that night, green eyes shining, and miaowed. She turned to Sarah. 'Perhaps it is a good thing we have him with us. Mrs Holt thinks there may be some type of rodent living there.' Sarah shuddered. 'Don't be afraid. They cannot hurt you. And the cat will kill them.'

'I do not think I can watch that. I hate mice.'

'Very well. You stand back here, then, while I attend to the lock. Jasper and I will go through.' She paused. Hopefully she was not about to make one of the skeletal discoveries Mr Underwood had mentioned. 'I must confess, I am curious to see what manner of beast is in there. You would not believe the strange sound they made.'

'Oh! But I have heard it, at night. Is *this* where it comes from?' Sarah looked at the door with wide eyes. Something in her expression made Elsie's stomach clench. 'Could – could an animal *produce* that sound?'

Jasper mewed, and scratched at the door. It was a dull imitation of the *hiss* she heard at night. Thin white lines marked the wood where he had worried it over time. 'Jasper. Come away.'

He looked at her, his emerald eyes inscrutable, his paw suspended. Then he swatted the door again. It creaked ajar.

Sarah stepped back. 'Look! It's open.'

Elsie could not believe her luck. 'Mrs Holt must have written to Torbury St Jude for a locksmith. I didn't expect her to be so prompt.' She jammed the hairpin back under her cap. 'I'm going in to explore.'

No creatures skittered out from the opening – that was a good sign. Mounting the steps, she stood next to Jasper and peeked inside. The air was still and heavy. There were no rats, no squirrels, no skeletons; just trunks and old furniture. Dust coated every surface, thick as velvet. 'Sarah,' she called back. 'It's quite safe.' She coughed, then sneezed. 'Rather dusty, but safe.'

She pushed the door and watched it swing back on its hinges with a prolonged whine. She expected Jasper to dart in ahead of her, but instead he turned tail and fled back the way they had come. She laughed; coughed again. 'Cats. They are such perverse creatures, are they not?'

She took four steps into the room, her hem sweeping up a cloud of dust. The garret looked as if time had stood still for centuries. Cobwebs festooned the corners but no insects writhed within them; all were dead in cocoons or shrivelled and dry. By the far wall slumped a clock that no longer ticked. Its face was smashed and the hands hung at odd angles. Holland sheets covered square shapes that might be portraits.

She walked to a table beside the smeared window. It was heaped with yellow-paged books. Dust obscured the titles. With the tip of one finger she prodded through the pile. A few volumes lower down the stack still had clean covers. Treatises on gardening from two centuries back. Some leather-bound pads that looked like journals. *Culpeper's Complete Herbal* and a *Generall Historie of Plantes* by Gerard. 'Sarah, come in!' She tried not to inhale too much dust as she called. 'There are no mice. But there are books.'

Sarah's long face appeared, hovering beside the door. 'Books?'

'Yes, if you can still read them. Mouldy old things! I think some of these have been here since the Norman Conquest at least.'

Sarah padded to her side. 'Oh! My goodness.' Reverently, she picked up the volumes with the tips of her fingers. Tidemarks misted some of the pages; others were as yellow and thin as onion skin. 'Receipts. Ingredients. A list of farrier bills. Oh, look at this! Sixteen thirty-five! Can you believe it?' She blew to clear dust from the cover. '"The Diary of Anne Bainbridge". Two volumes of it. Why, she must be one of my ancestors!'

'Not a very interesting one, if her diaries have been rotting here for two hundred years,' Elsie observed. She put a foot out and tested the floorboard. It creaked, but held. 'I wonder what could be under these sheets?' She threw one back with a flourish. Dust exploded out. They both gagged for breath. When the air cleared, it revealed a rocking chair and a small case that looked like a physician's travelling store of medicine. Elsie pulled it open. Clear glass bottles with cork stoppers rattled inside. 'Must have been an apothecary in the family,' she said. 'The residue at the bottom looks like herbs.'

Sarah turned, clutching a book against her bosom. 'Let me see.' She took two steps towards Elsie – then shrieked.

Elsie dropped the bottle she was holding. It cracked open and released a mouldy, underground smell. 'What? What is it?'

'There's something there . . . Eyes.'

'Oh, don't be ridiculous . . .' Her voice subsided as she followed Sarah's gaze.

Sarah was right. Green-brown eyes lurked in the shadows at the back of the room. A white sheet concealed most of the face, but she could see the pupils, trained on her with an unnatural scrutiny.

'A painting. It is just a painting, Sarah. Look, it does not blink.'

Elsie dug through the clutter, pulling and pushing objects out of her way. Dust powdered her dress grey, trailing from the hem in ribbons. The painted eyes kindled as she grew closer, as if greeting an old friend.

Elsie seized the end of the sheet covering the portrait and dragged it away. The material snagged as it moved, finally coming loose with a ripping sound.

'Oh!' Sarah cried. 'It's . . . it's . . .'

It's me, Elsie thought with horror.

It was a girl, about nine or ten. A button nose and pursed lips. Eyes that simultaneously beckoned and dared you to come closer. She was staring into the face of the child she had been: the girl with her youth ripped out.

How? Her mind stuttered and stopped. The face before her eyes was her own, yet she felt no kinship with it. *Go away*, she wanted to scream. *Go away, I am afraid of you.*

'It is not a painting,' Sarah said. 'That is – it's painted, but it is not a canvas. It seems to be free-standing.' She put her book down, pushed forwards and poked her head around the back of the figure. 'Ah, no. It is flat. But it has a wooden prop, you see?'

Elsie's field of vision expanded. The face shrank into proportion and she saw the painted girl in full. Waist-height, like a real child, the figure represented was dressed in olive silk with a gold lace trim. A tissue apron drifted around her legs. She did not have blonde hair like Elsie; it was red-brown and piled up onto her head in a kind of pyramid, threaded with orange ribbon and beads. She held a basket of roses and herbs at her waist. The other hand was raised, pressing a white bloom against her heart. She was not of this century; perhaps not even of the last.

'Remarkable.' Sarah rested a hand on the outline of a shoulder. The colours had faded with age and there were little scuffs on the woodwork. 'It is as if someone has cut out the figure from a painting and mounted it on a plank of wood.'

'Does it . . . Does it not remind you of anyone?'

Sarah nibbled her lower lip. 'A little. Around the eyes. It must be one of the Bainbridge ancestors. We cannot be surprised if she looks a bit like Rupert.'

'Rupert?' she repeated incredulously. But then she saw it: just a whisper, creeping through the chipped paint. *She looks like me and Rupert.* Her heart seized. Was this what her baby would look like?

Sarah ran her hand along the wooden edge of the arm. 'She's beautiful. We must take her downstairs. Let's put her in the Great Hall. We might be able to lift her between us. If we – oh!' She sprang back. A shard of wood impaled her palm. 'Ouch.'

'Come here.' Carefully, Elsie held Sarah's fingers within her gloved ones. 'Grit your teeth. One, two – three!'

The splinter slid out. Beads of blood welled up from the puncture mark; Sarah raised it to her mouth and sucked.

'These antiques do fall apart,' Elsie said. 'Probably best to leave the thing where it is.'

'Oh no, Mrs Bainbridge, please! I would so love to have her in the house.'

Elsie shivered. 'Well, perhaps you should get a servant to move it for you,' she said reluctantly. 'Thicker skin.'

Behind them, the floorboards screeched. 'Dash it!'

Elsie spun around. Mabel the maid lay crumpled beside the door with her skirts spread about her.

'Heaven above, what are you doing, Mabel?'

'Tain't nothing *I've* done! Floorboard gave way and swallowed me foot!'

'Goodness me!' Sarah rushed forward, her own injury forgotten. 'Are you hurt? Can you feel the ankle?'

'Yes, I can darn well feel it! Hurts like hell.' Mabel bit down on a spurt of pain. 'Miss.'

Taking an arm each, Elsie and Sarah wedged their shoulders beneath Mabel's armpits and hauled her free. A smell emerged from the hole in the boards; something reeking of wet ashes and decomposition.

Seated on the floor, Mabel reached out to prod her ankle. 'Torn right through to my stocking. Lucky the whole bleedin' leg didn't come off.'

'We had better fetch Mrs Holt,' said Elsie. 'I am sure she will have a poultice to put on it. Whatever were you doing, Mabel, sneaking up behind us?'

Mabel lowered her chin onto her chest. She looked more truculent than ever. 'Didn't mean no harm. This door ain't been open since I come here. Wondered what was inside. Then I heard Miss Sarah cry out, like. Thought she needed help. Lot of thanks I gets for it,' she added sourly.

'I'm very grateful,' Sarah said. 'Come here, I'll wrap your skirt around the cut. Keep pushing on it until we can bind it with some bandages.' She moved tenderly, but Mabel still moaned. 'How strange that you should come in just then! Mrs Bainbridge and I were about to fetch you. We wanted your help moving our new discovery downstairs.'

'What discovery?' Sarah pointed to the wooden figure. Mabel looked up and recoiled. 'Bleedin' heck. What's that?'

'Mabel,' Elsie said, 'I appreciate you are injured but that is no excuse for your continued bad language. Please remember the company you are in.'

'Sorry, ma'am,' she mumbled, although she did not sound contrite. 'It's just – I never seen anything like that before. What is it, a picture?'

'No. We believe it is some kind of ornament for the floor. A standing figure. Not a statue or a painting but somewhere in between.'

'I don't like it.' Mabel's jaw set. 'Looks at me funny. Would give me the creeps, something like that.'

'Hogwash,' said Elsie. 'It is no different from the portraits that hang in the corridor.'

'It is,' Mabel insisted. 'It's nasty. Don't like it.'

Elsie's skin prickled. She found it uncanny herself, but she was not about to admit that to a servant. 'It is not necessary for you to like it. You are required only to move it for Miss Sarah and clean it.'

Mabel pouted. As if coming to her defence, a fresh pulse of blood pushed up through the gash on her ankle. 'Can't do no cleaning now, can I?'

Elsie sighed. 'I suppose I had better fetch Helen.'

———

Helen regarded the wooden figure, hands planted on her broad hips. Crinkles appeared beside her eyes as she squinted through the dust. 'Is this new, ma'am?'

'New?' Elsie echoed. 'No, I expect it is very old.'

'No, ma'am, I meant new to the house. I'm sure the master had something like it.'

A spasm in her shoulder muscles. To hear Rupert spoken of like that, as if he were still present, still in charge here. 'He never mentioned such an object to me. We didn't have one in London, and if he found one here . . . Well, I have not seen another around the house, have you?'

Helen shrugged and picked up the figure. 'Can't say I have, ma'am.'

'Then what makes you suppose Mr Bainbridge owned one?'

'He was a nice man, Mr Bainbridge,' Helen said as she manoeuvred the wooden figure past the hole in the floor and out through the garret door. 'No airs about him. He used to chat with me, when I was dusting in the library. One day he starts to tell me about figures from Amsterdam, just like this one. Said he was researching them from a book.'

Outside in the corridor, Elsie squashed her crinoline against the wall to make space. 'Indeed? I cannot think why that topic would interest him.'

'Me neither, ma'am. I didn't ask, because I just presumed he owned one.'

Rupert always possessed an active, enquiring mind. That was what led him to Livingstone's match factory. He loved the idea of progress and new inventions. She had not realised he was interested in the past, too.

Helen's words made her feel better about taking the strange wooden girl downstairs. It might be unsettling, but it was another link to Rupert. He might have warmed to the figure himself, if he had ever opened the garret.

'Did Mr Bainbridge say what these figures were, Helen?'

'Called them companions. Silent companions.'

Elsie's lips curled. She looked down the corridor to where Sarah supported a limping Mabel. 'Did you hear that, Sarah? Helen calls it a companion! Mrs Crabbly might have saved her money. Your species have been replaced by wooden statues.'

'Oh, how wicked you are!' Sarah laughed. 'I would dearly love to see a piece of wood plump cushions, read poetry, play the piano and make gruel. If it did, I'd get one myself.'

Helen pulled her sleeve down over her knuckles and tucked the companion under her arm. It lay horizontally, as if it had fallen into a swoon.

'This way,' said Elsie. 'Miss Sarah wants it in the Great Hall. Not too close to the fire, mind. She can greet our guests as they arrive.'

'Guests, ma'am?'

She grimaced. 'You are right. I don't suppose we will have any for a while.'

'Oh!' Sarah pulled up in the corridor ahead of them. 'Mrs Bainbridge, would you mind going back? I'm terribly sorry . . . I left one of the diaries behind. What with poor Mabel's accident, I forgot to pick up the second volume. I would so dearly love to read my ancestor's story.'

Elsie glanced over her shoulder. She did not want to be running up and down; she was already tired out by the day's exertion. 'Can it not wait until later? I—' She stopped, confused. The door to the garret was shut. She had not heard it close. 'Helen,' she scolded, 'I told you to leave the garret door open. God knows it needs a good airing.'

'I didn't close it, ma'am.'

'Didn't close it? What do you think that is, then?' She pointed back.

Helen puffed out her red cheeks. 'Sorry, ma'am. I don't remember doing it.'

Where did Mrs Holt find such servants? '*I* will go and open it,' she sighed, 'while I fetch Miss Sarah's book.'

'Thank you ever so much, I do appreciate it. If you could leave it in my room I would be most grateful,' Sarah called. 'It might have a record of the visit from Charles I! I will put Mabel to bed. And perhaps you might see if Mrs Holt—'

'Yes, yes, I will fetch her too.' She walked back with sharp, irritable steps, her crinoline bouncing behind her. What was the point of being mistress of the house if you had to do all the work yourself?

Remembering how Jasper had simply swatted the door open, she stretched out a hand as she approached the garret. Her palm struck the wood hard; her shoulder jolted back. She grunted and tried again, using a little more force. The door did not budge. 'What?' She reached for the doorknob; rattled it from side to side. It would not turn. 'Damnation.'

There must be something in the latch that stuck – that was why it had jammed before. They would need to get someone in to replace the mechanism, or perhaps fit a whole new door. Another job to be done.

Wearily, Elsie retraced her steps and began the long descent to the ground floor. Really, she was not feeling entirely well. It must be this house: the weight of it pressing on her. After she had spoken with Mrs Holt, she would have a lie-down.

She passed Helen in the Great Hall, adjusting the companion beside the window. 'Thought I'd set her here,' Helen grinned, 'so as she can see out.' She cocked her head. 'Looks a bit like you, she does, ma'am.'

In the stronger light the wooden girl's resemblance to Elsie *was* more pronounced. It made the skin on her scalp tingle.

'A little. Isn't that strange?' Taking one last look, she crossed over to the west wing and disappeared through the green baize door of the servants' quarters.

On this side of the wall, the air was thick with mingled smells of soap, ash and burnt fat. A warren of bare walls and stone wound deeper into the house, the path just visible through oily light.

Mrs Holt's room was marked *Housekeeper* with white letters. Elsie knocked on the door – the second time today that she had knocked for admittance to a room in her own house.

'Come in.'

She squeezed into a room with an atmosphere that reminded her of pea soup. A single lamp burnt upon the desk, throwing an anaemic glow over Mrs Holt's papers and drawers. The housekeeper turned in her plain wooden chair and, seeing her mistress, started to her feet. 'Why, Mrs Bainbridge! This is unexpected. Please come in.'

A little table was set for tea with blue and white cups. Elsie sat down in relief. She was too ashamed of her weariness to ask for a drink, but she wished Mrs Holt would offer one.

'I was going to come and see you,' Mrs Holt confessed as she tidied the papers on her desk. 'We've just had a delivery from Torbury St Jude and I wanted to consult you about the menus I've drawn up.'

'I am sure they will suit perfectly well. We will live very quietly, Miss Sarah and I, until Mr Livingstone returns.'

'I expect you will, madam. But that is no reason not to enjoy your food.'

'Very true. Actually, Mrs Holt, while I am down here . . . There is a matter I need to discuss with you.'

'Yes, madam?'

It was only Mrs Holt looking back at her with those bleared, yellow eyes, so why did it feel like a furious light trained upon her face? She swallowed, not knowing how to start. This was nothing to be ashamed of, she reminded

herself. This baby was conceived honestly, however misbegotten it might feel. 'We will soon be in need of . . . extra
staff. Yet Mabel has led me to believe that no person from
Fayford will consent to work at this house?'

'Ah.' The lines in Mrs Holt's face deepened. Elsie nodded
for her to sit. 'It's a very strange situation, madam. There's
been a long feud between the village and the family – dating
back, I think, all the way to the Civil War. They believe one
of our ladies was a witch, or some other silly thing.'

Elsie stared down at the tablecloth and its small wreaths
of embroidered flowers. When Mabel had said the villagers were afraid of the house, she had imagined ghosts and
goblins, not a witch. But everyone knew that in those days
women could be, and often were, accused of witchcraft
for all manner of things. 'Did you at least try to recruit in
Fayford, Mrs Holt?'

'Oh yes. But you see my case was not helped by the
Roberts family. One of them was a footman here around the
turn of the century, and he met with an unlucky accident.'

'What do you mean, *accident*?'

Mrs Holt pressed a hand to her chest and adjusted a
cameo brooch. 'No one is sure how it happened. The poor
soul fell all the way from the gallery into the Great Hall.
Broke his neck, of course. A great tragedy. But some of the
Roberts maintain, even now, that he was pushed.'

'By whom?'

'Well, that particular master lost his wife shortly after.
There's a story about the Roberts man being the wife's
admirer . . . You know how these things go.' Mrs Holt
waved her hand. The flesh upon it was like chicken skin. 'A
jealous husband, taking revenge.'

'Upon my word, the village seems full of stories, and all of them about us.'

Mrs Holt smiled. 'Country folk, madam. They must have something to keep the winter nights occupied. But have no fear. I am sure we will find some excellent workers elsewhere, for both your house and your garden.'

'Let us hope so.' Clearing her throat, she went on, 'You see, I have cause to be particular about my staff. There will soon be – I mean, come spring – I have reason to hope there may be . . .' Heat rushed to her face. There was no delicate way to say it.

'You don't mean . . . Bless me, Mrs Bainbridge, are you telling me that you have sprained your ankle?'

Sprained your ankle. She hadn't heard that expression in years – a common phrase, but it did the trick. 'Yes. The baby should arrive in May.' It was unsettling to see tears sparkle in the old lady's eyes. Embarrassed, she hurried on. 'I will need nursemaids, and also a new lady's maid for myself. I mean to go into Torbury St Jude and visit the Registry Office. Is that where you found Mabel and Helen?'

Mrs Holt opened her mouth. Closed it. 'I – I did not have a large salary to offer, madam. And given the deserted nature of the estate, without a resident family or opportunity for progression . . .' She twisted in her chair. 'I found it better to take girls from the workhouse, madam.'

'The workhouse,' she said flatly. Of course, that explained so much. 'I suppose they did not have any formal training?'

Mrs Holt blushed. 'Helen did.'

'And how exactly did Helen come to leave service?'

Again, Mrs Holt fiddled with her brooch. 'I have not enquired into it.'

'I must say, I am astonished you could think such women suitable for employment in my house! You knew nothing of their characters. How did you ascertain if they were honest? And how can I trust them near my child? Mabel is a terrible influence. She has left trays of food to grow foul in my room. The language she uses, her inability to even curtsy – I cannot risk my child copying such behaviour!'

'I can only apologise. I will speak to her, madam. They're not used to serving a mistress and perhaps I have been too soft on them, in the past.' She took a breath. 'But I've found their general cleaning and cooking quite satisfactory.'

'I wish that I could say the same. The amount of dust in the maroon corridor is phenomenal. I even found *sawdust*, of all things, upon the stairs – where could that have come from? Some of the carpets look as if they have never been beaten, which I cannot comprehend when the nursery is in such perfect order.'

Mrs Holt's head jerked up. 'The nursery?'

'Yes. That is one room I will thankfully have no need to prepare. It is practically ready for my child.'

Mrs Holt looked at her strangely. 'Perhaps there has been some confusion. The girls rarely go into the nursery.'

'You are mistaken, Mrs Holt. They have even been brushing the rocking horse and setting up dollies' tea parties.'

'Dear me.' Mrs Holt shook her head. 'I had no idea. Helen told me she was afraid of that room. Everything was covered up with dustsheets.'

'Not this morning. Come, I will show you.' She stood.

Mrs Holt rose too, grasping at the keys dangling from her waist. 'I hardly ever go there,' she confessed. 'The servants' stairs lead up to the landing just outside. If you do not mind?'

'Not at all. I am quite capable of going up servants' stairs.'

Elsie spoke bravely, but she had cause to regret it. There was no space for her crinoline; it jammed and stuck out behind her in a hefty tail which she lugged from step to step.

They emerged onto the landing she had crossed with Sarah earlier that day. She followed Mrs Holt to the door. Once again, that tense, unsettled feeling held her captive. *It is just a nursery*, she told herself. *There is no need to cry.*

Mrs Holt jangled the keys at her waist and slipped one into the lock. It clicked as the tumblers moved.

'But it was not locked when—' It could not be. It was simply not possible.

The airy, perfectly manicured room had perished. Tatty curtains covered the windows, admitting only sparks of light. The dolls were gone. The ark was gone. A few toy chests remained, but they were coated in the dust of countless years. Great white sheets, like those in the garret, formed lumpy shapes where the rocking horse and the cot had been. Rust spotted the firescreen and the iron bedstead.

Mrs Holt did not speak.

'I – it's not—' Words swarmed into her mouth, but she could not form any of them. How could it be? Striding over to the crib, she took hold of the sheet. 'Right here, there was the most beautiful . . .' She gasped. As the sheet slithered away, a musty smell of camphor welled up. The shape of the crib endured, but the delicate draperies were moth-eaten and stained.

'I didn't think the girls would trouble it much,' Mrs Holt said carefully. 'It's a sad place. Not opened except for a sweep every few months, since the little ones went.'

Elsie stared at her. The nursery had been glorious. She could not have imagined the things she had seen. Sarah was there too – she had pushed the horse.

'What – what did you say? The little ones?'

Metal keys clunked together as Mrs Holt shifted her stance. 'Yes, God bless them.'

'Whose little ones?'

'The – the master and mistress. That is, Master Rupert's parents. He was the third child – or so I was told.'

Elsie leant against the crib. It creaked. 'You knew Rupert's parents? Before they died?'

'I did, madam. I did.' All at once she looked older and profoundly sad. 'I worked for them in London. Just a lass I was, then. Saw Master Rupert delivered.' Her voice grew hoarse. 'He – he was the first of the babes to be born away from The Bridge. The others died, they said, before the move. That was the reason they relocated to London.' She looked away. 'You can imagine how it would be, living in a house where you have lost a child.'

'The other babies *died*?' Elsie looked down at the decaying crib and felt sick. She released the edge and it swayed, empty. God, what a heritage for her baby: a nervous mother and a nursery of death. 'Mrs Holt, I do not wish to upset you. But –' She took a hesitant step towards her. 'You were one of the last people to see my husband alive. No one has told me exactly how he died. He did not write that he was ill. Was he taken, suddenly?'

Mrs Holt withdrew a handkerchief and dabbed at her eyes. 'Ah, madam. It was a shock to us all. He seemed hale and hearty – perhaps a little preoccupied. I was under the impression he was not sleeping. But he did not seem like to die!'

'And then . . .?' She held her breath.

'Helen found him. Gave a shriek I won't ever forget. Chilled me to the very bone, it did.'

'But *how*? How did he die?'

'Peacefully madam, don't you fret. Peacefully. In his bed, tucked up warm.'

'Not *my* bed?'

'No, no. The bedroom just next door. The coroner thought it was his heart. They can give out suddenly, he said. Sometimes a person carries an unsound heart all their life and they never know until – well, *they* never know.'

So the heart that was so warm and kind had burnt itself out. She sighed. 'I hope there was not much pain. I saw splinters, near his neck. Do you have any idea how they got there?'

Mrs Holt narrowed her eyes. 'Splinters? I don't know, madam. Sometimes those embalmers do strange things. But as to how Helen found him, it didn't look like there was a struggle. A sudden seizure, maybe. His eyes were open.' A tear leaked out of her eye and made a tributary of one of her wrinkles. 'I saw his eyes open, madam, and I closed them for him. God forgive us, what a world this is.'

'A cruel world to the Bainbridges.' Elsie thought for a moment. 'But Mrs Holt, you said you were present when Rupert was born in London. How did you come to be here?'

She patted her eyes and folded the handkerchief, staring down at it. 'That was the master's doing.'

'Rupert's father?'

'Yes.' She hesitated – Elsie thought she was choosing her words with care. 'He was fond of me. I helped him with the missus. She was in a bad way, the poor love. Never really recovered from the birth. Just before we lost her, she had the strangest notions about this place. Used to rattle on about it with a kind of . . . wild sadness.'

'What do you mean by strange notions?'

Mrs Holt shook her head. 'I don't know. Couldn't make much sense of it. She used to talk about this nursery and the rocking horse a great deal. All gibberish. But after she went, thoughts of it troubled the master too. That's why he asked me to come. Said his wife would rest easier, knowing someone was keeping an eye on the house.' The trace of a smile played at the corners of her bracketed mouth. 'I didn't want to go. Didn't want to leave little Rupert just when he was learning to walk. But the master talked me round, in the end.'

'How?'

She laughed. 'Flattery. Flattery and bribery, what else? For a girl so young to be promoted to housekeeper – that's not an opportunity you turn down. Not if you want to keep your mother in her old age. He was a hard, strange man was Mr Bainbridge, but he said the most curious thing. It's stayed with me ever since. "That house needs someone young and pure," he told me. "Someone good. Without bitterness. You must be its angel, Edna." Silly, isn't it? But it touched me. I've always tried, since that day. Tried to be the angel he thought I was.'

Elsie chewed her lip again. The skin was hot and raw. 'No. It's not silly. But why did Rupert not come to live with you after his father died? It would have made sense for him to come here.'

'I would have liked that.' Mrs Holt looked fondly at the shape of the rocking horse in its shroud. 'But family on his mother's side took him in. Town people. Didn't have time for jaunts to the country.'

'But all that time! Weren't they ever curious to see the house?'

'Well, they were his mother's people. They knew about the other poor mites dying here, and how she jabbered on about the place. Didn't think she would forgive them if they brought her child back.'

It seemed absurd that no one had attempted to claim the house for all this time. No lurking, four-times-removed connection. 'It is astonishing how unlucky a family can be. Three children and nothing remains.'

Mrs Holt cleared her throat. 'Except . . .'

Except her own baby. She placed a hand on her stomach. The nausea returned.

'I have been very neglectful, Mrs Holt. All this talk of Rupert's family has made me forget my original errand. I came to tell you that Mabel has hurt her leg. She was following me in the garret.'

'The *garret*, madam?'

'Yes. There is another thing I have forgotten. I was supposed to thank you. It was so good of you to write after we spoke. But whoever you got in will have to come back, I'm afraid. The door is quite stuck again.'

Mrs Holt regarded her as if she had sprouted a second head. 'I don't understand . . .'

'The door,' Elsie repeated. 'The door to the garret. You had someone come from Torbury to open it and it has got stuck again. I need you to write them another letter.'

'But – but I can't. I think there must be some mistake—'

'For heaven's sake, why? Why cannot you fetch the person back in?'

Mrs Holt shrank away. 'Because, madam, I never wrote to Torbury St Jude.'

THE BRIDGE, 1635

A fortuitous day to start my new journal! Josiah is home early and he brings the best of news.

Jane was coaxing the short hair around my forehead into curls when I heard a beat upon the bridge.

'Stop,' I said. 'Listen. It is Josiah.'

'Nay, it can't be the master yet. He won't be back until next week.'

'It is,' I insisted. 'I am sure of it.'

She gave me the look that I have grown accustomed to. Her hand twitched by her side, as if she longed to make the old sign against witchcraft. But she did not say a word as I stood and hastened from my bedroom into the summer parlour. Outside, the mist was up. I strained my eyes at the window, certain I could hear it still: the thump of my husband's heart. Colour fluttered in the mass of cloud. I pressed my forehead to the glass, the better to see. Yes. A tiny rectangle rippling blue and yellow, darting in and out of the fog. Our banner.

The beating sound built and turned into the steady pound of hooves.

'I knew it!' I cried, running back to my room. 'The herald is below. Make ready.'

Jane leapt like a doe. 'Well, bless me.' She draped a lace collar around my shoulders and pulled on her linen oversleeves. 'I'd better go and warn them in the kitchens. Do you want me to finish your hair, mistress?'

'No, there is not time. Josiah wants to speak to me immediately.' Her gaze flinched away. 'That is, I expect he will. He often does.'

Although I do my best to hide it from her, Jane is afraid every time my gift manifests itself. I cannot deny that it is strange – I have always heard things, always sensed things. But when I read Josiah's thoughts it is no sorcery – unless love be a spell. I simply know him through and through.

I did not stay long after Jane had quit the room. Checking the set of my ribbons one last time, I hurried out through the corridor and down the stairs, taking them in pairs. As I passed the first floor I called out to tell Hetta that her father was home. I should have gone and fetched her in person, but I was selfish. I wanted Josiah all to myself.

I had the servants set a fire in the dining room. Light played upon the tapestries and picked out the golden threads. I thought Josiah would take some refreshment after his journey so I made sure there was spiced wine and a collection of small dishes to suit his fancy: bread, cheese, cold meats and a tray of pastries. It looked most appealing on our new mahogany table. But when my husband swept in, raindrops pebbled on his doublet and his wool cloak steaming, he paid no heed to the food. Marching straight to me, he put his hands either side of my waist and lifted me off my feet.

'Well met, my love!' He set me down and gave me a smacking kiss. 'Can you guess why I have returned?'

'It is good news from court, I wager. I never saw you smile so wide.'

His eyes glittered. 'With good reason, Anne. Can you really not guess?' I shook my head. 'He is coming. The King is coming.' I must have gone pale, for his laughter boomed. 'Not *now*, sweeting. You will have ample time to prepare. The King and the Queen will stop here for a night on their summer progress.'

For a moment I could only grasp his gloved hand. 'Blessed God. This is . . . remarkable. What an honour. It is all we have worked for. How, how did you accomplish it?'

Could it be the chrysanthemum petals I put in his wine for luck? The bay leaves under his pillow for intuition? For while Josiah tries to raise our family at court I am working too, busy in my stillroom. I, of all people, will never underestimate the strength of plants.

Laughing once more, he peeled off his gloves and sat down at the table. 'We accomplished it together, Anne. I told you this house was just the beginning.'

He *has* told me. Ever since we amassed the money to build a great country estate, Josiah has been insisting that The Bridge will be the making of us. I had no idea it would happen so soon.

He picked up a hunk of bread and bit into it. 'We have made our name now. This year they stay a night, but who can tell of next year? If I obtain a title . . . Perchance we will be invited to Christmas at court. Perchance the Queen will take a fancy to you and offer you a place in her household.'

In all my wildest visions, I never imagined this. 'As long as the King holds you in esteem, I have nothing else to wish for.'

'Do not rein in your dreams, Anne!' He grabbed a flagon of wine. 'There is no telling how far we can rise. We will get the boys down – show what fine, strapping lads we have. They would make the King fine Grooms of the Bedchamber or Gentleman Ushers, one day.'

'Is it likely he would consider them?'

'Who can say? There is no limit to the success a titled family can achieve. With my mother's connections and your skills, we will make a reputation for ourselves. Look at the Villiers!'

'No,' I said sharply. 'No, we will not be like the Villiers.' He paused in his meal, staring at me. I tried a smile, but it was too small. 'Remember what happened to the duke.'

He tossed his hunk of bread back on the plate. Crumbs snagged in his beard. 'Do not fret, Anne, I am not setting out to become the next Duke of Buckingham. I doubt there ever was a more conceited, feckless fool in England. All I mean to say is that he has set the bar. He was born a nobody, and by the time he met his end he was richer than the King himself.

Anything is possible. And it seems to me it is our duty to get what we can for our boys.'

'I will write to tell them at once. And they will require new clothes! Heaven only knows how much they have grown. We will need to measure them anew.'

Josiah chuckled.

'I could write a masque for them to perform before the Queen!' I have always yearned to experience the theatre and pageantry of a court masque. They say the Queen herself dances in them, spun in the most luxurious costumes.

'Aye, I can see our James striding on stage to recite a poem.'

'And Hetta – she will be the nymph who—'

Josiah cleared his throat. He took another quick swig of wine before he said, 'I have not decided how large a part I want Henrietta Maria to play in this visit.'

My stomach clenched, the way it always does when people mention my daughter. Josiah never calls her by her pet name, Hetta; it is always formal, always Henrietta Maria with him.

'Whatever do you mean? Surely she will be involved just as much as the boys?'

'While we are still feeling our way with the royal couple, setting everything out to impress . . . It would be best not to draw attention to her little – aberration.'

Nauseous guilt swept over me. I told myself not to snap, not to reply too quickly. But of course I did. 'There is nothing the matter with her!'

'You know that is not true.'

Panic caught at me like nettles; I was sure that somehow he would see through me. See through to the truth. 'I do not understand why it should affect her role in the visit. She is our daughter. She deserves every advantage for her future, as well as the boys.'

'I will think upon it.' Quick as a cloud shifts on a windy day, his mood changed. The shadow of desire darkened his eyes. 'Enough for now. Come, sit by me. Lord, Anne, I have missed you.'

At the very first chance that offered, I ran to see Lizzy. Once she was my nurse, and she has nursed all of my children. She has been there for every significant moment of my life. I wanted her to share in my joy at this, the pinnacle of our achievement. But she has only made me most unhappy.

I found Lizzy and Hetta poring over books in the schoolroom. *Schoolroom*, I call it – in truth it looked more like a fairy den than a seat of learning when I walked in. Potted plants covered every surface. Baskets spilled over with ivy and periwinkle, trailing their foliage over the bookshelves. Hetta's pet sparrow hopped in his cage and trilled a song. It is not a sober or reflective environment, but Hetta refuses to attend to her studies if there is no greenery around her.

Today she was reading *Culpeper's Complete Herbal*, her very favourite book. It cannot be a coincidence, her interest in the natural world? Not with those eyes:

mixed brown, green and yellow just like a tisane; or with that hair, blushing every shade of autumn.

Lizzy rose at once to greet me, but Hetta only offered that shy half-smile which never reaches her eyes. That is not her fault, of course – it is mine. An incorrect measurement, a stumbled word. She is not responsible for my blunders.

'Hetta, sweeting,' I said. 'Perhaps you could go and do some drawing? Mother needs to talk with Lizzy.'

Obediently, she trotted off to the window seat. Pulling out her paper and pencils she sat, staring at a blank page.

'She will draw flowers,' Lizzy guessed with a chuckle. 'Always flowers.' She sat down once more in her rocking chair, adjusting the black partlet around her shoulders. 'Look at her! Don't you see a little more of Mary in her face every day?'

That was what I wanted, for certain. But it feels strange to see my dead sister's features on this shy, silent girl. Mary was always full of life.

'It is a remarkable likeness, indeed.'

'But you wished to speak with me in confidence? What news?'

I finally let the smile break on my face. 'Oh Lizzy, I have *wonderful* news. I am the happiest woman alive.'

She grinned, as she always does when I am happy. 'What is it, child? It cannot be . . .' Her eyes darted to my stomach. 'No, not that. One miracle is enough.'

'No!' I patted the creases out of my bodice. 'Far better. Josiah is home. He has told me to make myself ready. The King and Queen are coming in summer! Coming here!'

The smile wilted on her lips. 'Here? The King and Queen?'

'Yes!' By the window, Hetta had begun to draw, her head tilted to the side. I dropped my voice. 'How now, Lizzy? Why do you look unhappy?'

She squeezed my hand; her bony old fingers pressed into mine. 'Oh, I am glad for *you*, dearheart. At least, I think . . .' She shook her grey head. 'May I tell you the truth?'

'Always.'

'I do not think they will be well received in the village.'

The village: I had not thought of that. The stuffed-up, precise men of Fayford with their chessboard clothing. I have not warmed towards them. When we purchased this land to build The Bridge, I called upon the workers with salves for their chapped hands. They shrank from me in abhorrence. They mistrust my skill with plants, look at me askance, and so I have kept away ever since. With a talent like mine, I must take caution. Spurious accusations could harm far more than my pride.

'The villagers may be impudent with the gentry, Lizzy, but surely for their King—?'

'Not them. They have no respect for the King. Haven't you wondered why they don't take to our family? The master serves a King who drained the fens, and they all expect he'll be after more ship money soon.'

'Fie! That tax does not apply to us. We are not a coastal district.'

'*Inland* ship money.' Lizzy hunched her shoulders unhappily. 'It's been proposed. Can you imagine? I dread to think of the scene in the village if that happens. They'll throw vegetables at His Majesty as he passes.'

'They would not dare! Stop it, Lizzy, you are getting me into a fright.'

'I only speak the truth.'

'Then I will have to find a way to bring the court here without them passing through Fayford. But really, I can't see why I should. It is the King's village. *His* country.' Hetta's pencil stopped. I took a breath and it started again. 'I do not foresee King Charles demanding more ship money, Lizzy. He cannot be too poor of pocket. Josiah was just telling me of the new ceiling to be painted at the Banqueting House and the Queen's building project at Greenwich.'

'Oh aye,' she said darkly. 'He will spend money on his trifles. That is what makes people so angry.'

I looked at her anew. 'You sound as if you agree with the Puritans of Fayford, Lizzy.'

'I cannot say I like the idea of those royals bursting in here. You know,' she whispered, 'that she's a Papist shrew.'

'Lizzy!' Hetta looked up. I bent my head and lowered my voice again. 'The Queen may be a Catholic, but she is no shrew. You should not say such things. Must I remind you that my daughter is named for Queen Henrietta Maria?'

'I don't like it,' Lizzy repeated. 'Her in your house, chanting her popish spells and nonsense. Especially with the child so susceptible.'

'Whatever do you mean? Hetta is not simple; only mute. She will not sell her soul to the Pope just because she sees a fine Catholic queen.'

'Even so. An innocent child, in the same house! And the King! Why, you know what people said about him and the Duke of Buckingham.'

'I do not see what gossip—'

'Who could stand it? A papist and a sodomite under the same roof as our precious girl.'

'Enough!' I stood so suddenly that my chair squealed. Hetta froze, the tip of her pencil quivering on the paper. 'Hold your tongue, Lizzy,' I hissed. 'I will not have it, not in my house. He is your King. You will speak of him with respect.'

Lizzy's face closed: 'Yes, mistress.'

I had done it again. I had treated her like a friend and then thrust her back down to the role of servant. I always do this, and I know she resents it. But what else could I say?

We are dependent on the King. Josiah has fine blood – his mother was a dowager countess before she married his untitled father – but only the King's bounty can establish the Bainbridge name. Only the King can give my husband the knighthood he so craves. I cannot, *cannot* have one of my household spreading vile treason. Only last year I heard of a man who had his ears cut off for criticising the royal family. Would Lizzy want me to sit back and let that happen to her?

THE BRIDGE, 1865

There were two.

Elsie stared from one to the other, searching for a clue in their inscrutable wooden faces. One smiling her knowing, little-girl smile; the second, the interloper, a boy dressed for work in the fields. He faced to the right, leaning against a shepherd's crook. Black hair straggled out from beneath his cap, framing a sombre, tawny face.

'Who are you?' she wondered aloud, as if he could answer.

There was something distasteful about the boy. He seemed untrustworthy, wayward.

'Where have you come from?'

Perhaps Helen had found him in the garret? But no – the garret was jammed shut. Wasn't it? Her mind wobbled. After the strange business with the nursery, she could not be quite sure about anything.

She blinked rapidly, hoping one flick of the eyelids would show the gypsy boy gone and only the little girl with the flowers standing beside her window. But it was no use: he stayed put.

Unsettled, she turned her back and walked towards the stairs. She would not mention this new companion to anyone yet – not until she was sure. She'd already made a fool of herself in front of Mrs Holt.

Perhaps it was grief making her see things? Grief worked strangely on the mind – people always said so. But after all she had endured, it did not seem likely that Rupert's death would be the weight to unbalance her.

Her skirts puffed as she mounted the stairs; she ignored them, ignored the patina of sawdust they swept up. She would not think of the past, only the task in hand: she would go to the library and write for a man to fix the garret.

The library was on the second floor, the first room off the corridor branching away from her suite to the back of the house. Elsie had not troubled herself to enter it before. To her mind, a library was the domain of men, saturated in tobacco and deep thought.

There was no quibble with this door; it opened smoothly, gliding over worn carpet without a catch. She put one foot over the threshold and shivered. It was like stepping through the doorway of a tomb. And just like a tomb the library was dark and stale, tainted with the smell of leaf mulch.

Striding across the carpet to a trio of windows, she pushed back the floor-length curtains, coughing as dust fell from the valances. Pearly light crept in. The trees outside looked more ragged than before; patches of their flaming foliage had been extinguished and dropped down to the gravel. The flowerbeds were full of thistles. Winter was coming on fast.

She turned back to face the door. Still ajar – that was a good sign. She was not going mad. As for her shivers, the cause of them was clear: an empty fireplace yawned to her right, breathing out gusts of cold air as the wind swept down the chimney.

Now the curtains were open, she saw the room was not as she had expected. *Library* was a pretentious name for what was merely a shallow chamber, curved at one end, with perhaps five or six bookcases set along the wall. A polished, heavily built desk stood in an alcove, facing the fire, with a green-shaded lamp hanging over the writing space.

She approached it and sat down. The chair felt heavenly, easing the nag in her back and limbs.

She looked at the desk. The inkwell lay open, the feathers of a quill poking from the top. *Rupert*. He would have sat here, the pen ready for his left hand. His legs had touched this squeaking, slippery leather chair, yet nothing of his warmth remained.

She missed him terribly. Missed him and hated him. How could he abandon her? He was meant to be her saviour, her reward, the rich man who swept into the factory and fell in love below his station. She could not face the days ahead without him. She could not raise a child and cope with all the memories that stirred. She *needed* him.

Tears blurred her eyes as she groped for one drawer after another, yanking them open. The runners groaned and the metal handles rattled. She had to keep busy, she had to write to someone about the hole in the garret floor. There was serious work to do before a baby could live in The Bridge.

Sheaves of paper fluttered out of the drawers. She would have to go through every one and find out how far Rupert's plans had progressed. The horrid nursery would be completely refurbished – that much she knew. She might even move it; she hated to think of her own baby in the room where Rupert's siblings had died. They had space enough for a day nursery and a night nursery, not to mention—

Her hands fell still.

Something winked at her from the depth of a drawer. She bent closer. There, again – tiny sparkles scattered across the green lining. She reached in and closed her fingers around a velvet pouch. It felt heavy. She drew it out and dropped it with a thud on the desk.

The pouch looked old but not shabby; adorned, rather than eaten by time. It was designed to tie shut with draw-strings, but a rolled-up scroll of paper held the mouth open. Elsie did not hesitate: she upended the pouch and spilled its contents onto the desk.

The dazzle made her pull back in her chair. A rainbow-coloured stream rippled into a coil. She put out a finger to touch it; felt the solidity of jewels through her gloves. 'It cannot be,' she gasped, picking it up. But it was: a necklace dripping with diamonds.

The gems caught the light from a hundred different angles, blazing like white fire. Brilliants iced the chain all the way to the centre, where marquise-cut stones formed a twinkling bow. From it hung three enormous pear drops, each looking more expensive than the house itself.

Mesmerised, she laid the necklace back down on the desk and stared at it. The chain looked ancient, but the diamonds were flawless. She could not see a single cloud; only that hot, white flare that melted to colour at the edges.

But the scroll. What was on the scroll? She plucked up the paper and smoothed it out.

My dearest wife,

Like a conjurer, I wave my wand and – behold! Look what arrived from the bank vault in Torbury St Jude!

I can imagine the look on your face as you open this parcel. You did not realise you were marrying into a family with heirlooms, did you? The Bainbridge diamonds have been handed down for generations. Legend has it they were pulled from the river on the squire's fishing line! My father locked them away when my mother died and I have not seen them since. How well they will look around your beautiful neck! I only wish I had fetched them in time for the wedding.

I find there is more work to do at The Bridge than we anticipated. Besides redecoration and gardening costs – which are substantial – I now fear we will need to hire a rat-catcher. Over the past few nights I have been kept awake by a terrible sound coming from the garret. The housekeeper does not have the key, and although I tried to force the lock, I only succeeded in hurting myself. After I write to you, I must send for a locksmith and find out what is in there. If the cat does not take the vermin down, I must employ another man.

Rest assured I will not permit you to set a foot inside the house until it is quite worthy of you and our dear little stranger. I miss you both and await your next letter with much impatience.

Yours forever,
Rupert

Her hands would not stop shaking. The paper jerked wildly. All at once it ripped, and she began to cry.

THE BRIDGE, 1635

I want nothing more than the promise of spring. It was sore weather all through Lent and then the church flooded at Easter. Josiah writes that the court have suspended their festivities until Whitsun. Verily, I cannot blame them. These have been more like drear November evenings than spring days. Heaven knows what I will do if things have not improved by August. If the King cannot hunt in the woods and the Queen cannot enjoy the pleasure grounds, it will be a disaster.

This afternoon I was able to get out into the formal gardens for the first time in weeks. The sun shone, but there was no piping skylark, no sticky buds upon the trees. My Hetta worked in her physic garden where she raises herbs. She looked charming in her straw hat, intent on her work, her little scissors cutting off the dead heads – *snip, snip* – and releasing their earthy scents. I watched her with pleasure. In the shade she looked like a lily; her pale skin and the gossamer veins beside her eyes. Such a fragile, delicate girl: my sister Mary wrought in porcelain.

I tried not to let the smell of the herbs stir my memory, but I could not control it. I closed my eyes and journeyed back to that night, that tisane brewed under a full moon. Back to my own murky face reflected in the bottom of a cup. The guilt lingers, like the scent of fallen apples rotting in an orchard. It may have been wrong of me to interfere in the natural order of things, but I cannot regret it – I cannot regret *her*.

Harris tended the knot garden on his knees, trimming the shrubbery with precision and raking the coloured gravel. The high winds had scattered it out of pattern, so I made him redesign the twists. I asked for new shapes in the hedges, or at least the parterre – angels and fleur-de-lis for a daughter of France – but he doubts he will be able to train them before August.

'Purchase full-grown shrubs then,' I said. 'And cut them.'

He seemed to think this was amusing. Nonetheless, he has promised to do his best in that quarter. As to my planting requirements, he is perfectly hopeless.

'Roses and lilies won't grow together,' he said, picking the dirt from beneath his crooked fingernails. 'They don't suit.'

'I know that. We do not need them growing *together*, but they must both be in the garden. A rose for the King of England, a lily for the Princess of France.'

'A lily I might manage. The bulbs like to be deep and cool and shady. Though give me much more of this wet weather and they'll speckle up.'

'What about our rosebushes?' I demanded. 'Do they not thrive this year?'

He spread his arms with an infuriating sigh, as if it were not his job to make these things work. 'Full sun, mistress. They need full sun and drained soil to flower. Find me some of that and I'll sort your roses.'

I was afraid of losing my temper, so I fisted my hands upon my hips and looked over to Hetta. She had stopped working and stood on the soil, staring out over the green hills as if waiting for something. Small white flowers wound their way over her shoes; unruly twigs seemed to reach out and embrace her.

'Hetta,' I called. 'Step back, sweeting, you will tear your gown.'

She obeyed but did not look at me. By her side I heard the little scissors going *snip, snip*. Cutting nothing. Cutting air.

'As for thistles,' said Harris, 'I can't let you do it. They're a weed, mistress. Take over the whole garden, give them half a chance.'

'The thistle is the symbol of Scotland. The Stuart kings' symbol.'

'It's a weed,' he repeated. 'Invasive. Devouring. It creeps.' I took a sudden chill. The weather was not so very clement, after all. 'If you must plant them somewhere, do it in little Miss's patch. Happen it'll wreak less harm there.'

I had to confess that he was right – about the damage, I mean. It may well be that *he* cannot control the spread of a weed but I know my Hetta can. I have not seen a single plant she cannot grow or tame, from the rock sampier and gooseberries thriving in the kitchen garden to the coltsfoot and feverfew she raises for our aches and pains. I taught her to plant, but she has surpassed me. She has far surpassed me at just eight years old.

Sometimes I think it is the tisane flowing through her veins, which causes her flowers to bloom. She has inherited more than just her looks from Mary, for it was my older sister who visited the wise-women in secret and instructed me in their ways.

'Hetta. Hetta, my sweet.' I picked up my skirts and threaded my way through the unpruned branches to her side. She did not turn her eyes towards me until I placed my hand on her shoulder. 'I have a favour to beg.' Ignoring the dirt, I squatted down to her level. 'Would you grow some thistle for me in your patch?'

She blinked. Her head tilted to the side as if she did not understand.

I hesitated. Josiah has not permitted me to speak of the royal visit before Hetta, but he underestimates her. As I often say, she is only mute, not some poor natural. She hears others talk. She must have a hint of what is going on.

'The reason I ask is that the King and Queen are coming to stay. The thistle is one of the King's symbols, do you understand?'

She nodded. The pink, misshapen stump of her tongue moved and a sound came from her throat; not like speech, more a bleat.

I felt hollow inside. Gazing upon that tongue is like looking upon a gown I have stained or a letter

I have blotted. Once again I heard Josiah's words: *her aberration*. Mary would never have made such a mistake.

Prodded by guilt, I said, 'Indeed, sweeting, it may be that you can help me prepare in more than one way. The dinner I serve the King must be very fine. I will need rosemary, sage and thyme for seasoning. Basil, and perhaps some parsley too. Onions, quinces, parsnip,' I counted them on my fingers. 'Do you think you could manage to grow all this?'

A smile dawned on her face and my heart lifted. With Hetta's smile, you do not need words: it captivates you with upturned lips and soft dimples. How can people whisper that it is a demon that holds her mute? How can they even think it?

'Good.' I touched her cheek. The smell of her, so sweet and floral, and the feel of her skin, silky as petals. 'Good girl. You write down what you need and Mr Harris will fetch it.'

At least now she will be involved in the glory of the day, no matter what Josiah commands.

His words haunt me: *her aberration*. As I stand in my stillroom, trying to grind out my remorse with pestle and mortar, I see it again: that tongue. Josiah's expression.

I think that he knows.

He has never feared my power before. He will take herbs and brews for luck without question. But when he looks at Hetta, it is as though he sees not a flower – only the mucky soil beneath. As if he sees my hands, thick and claggy with dirt.

THE BRIDGE, 1865

The day was bright and crisp as an apple as their carriage tumbled back from town, packed tight with packages. Chips of periwinkle sky showed through the bare tree branches.

'They are so beautiful. May I see them once more?' Sarah reached out with her bandaged hand. A hint of blood bloomed to the surface. Although she had cut herself on the companion a week ago and the wound was only small, it showed no signs of healing.

Elsie passed over the package. 'Take care, or we'll need to go back and have them cleaned all over again.'

'I will not get my bandage near the gems. See, I only need that hand to unwrap them.' Sarah smoothed out the material and sighed like a girl in love. 'I never knew we had diamonds in the family.'

After a clean and polish at the jeweller's in Torbury St Jude, the diamond necklace shone brighter than ever. The pear drops flashed cinnamon, then white, then blue, as light streaked through the carriage window.

Elsie turned her face away. Whenever she looked at the necklace she thought of Rupert's letter, his dear voice coming to her from beyond the grave. *Rest assured I will not permit you to set a foot inside the house until it is quite worthy of you.* If only he had known.

'Rupert wrote that they were locked in a bank vault until he arrived at The Bridge.'

'I do not wonder at it.' Sarah wet her lips. 'When I think of my ancestors wearing this necklace . . . Perhaps even Anne Bainbridge, whose diary I'm reading! These diamonds might have touched her skin, moved with her. It is almost too wonderful to comprehend.'

The ancestors again. Every time Sarah mentioned them, Elsie felt another stitch of guilt. The girl had lost her family and now here was her cousin's widow, snatching her inheritance away. If Elsie had found the diamonds by accident, *perhaps* she would have let Sarah take them. But Rupert's letter made it clear what he wanted. She could never give away his last gift to her.

'But Mrs Bainbridge, you will not be able to wear diamonds until your year of mourning is over! What a shame. I should so like to see them every day.'

'I am only grateful that you *can* see them. After that episode with Mrs Holt, I was beginning to fear I had run mad.'

'You are not going mad.' Sarah rewrapped the package. 'Did any of the shopkeepers treat you like a madwoman today?'

'Thankfully, no.' Elsie had to admit that the trip had brightened her spirits. Amidst the bustle of Torbury St Jude, the market stalls, knife-grinders and cabs hurrying to and from the station, it was difficult to think of sombre matters. She had visited a carpenter, a builder and a draper to discuss her plans for the house. Then, with Sarah's period of half-mourning fast approaching, they went to order new gowns for her in lavender and grey. Elsie would remain in black – but that did not stop her from commissioning some new dresses to fit her growing belly.

'I have spent my life with an elderly person,' Sarah went on. 'Believe me, I know the signs of a mind beginning to wander.'

'Do they include placing reckless orders for home improvements and spending a fortune on new dresses?'

'No, indeed! If you are going mad,' said Sarah, checking her injured hand, 'then so am I.'

Unable to stop herself, Elsie reached out and seized Sarah's wrist. 'You *did* see them? You saw the dolls and the animals in the nursery?'

'Yes. They were beautiful! There is no possible way that . . .' Trouble puckered her brow. 'I cannot understand. It all seems like some monstrous joke. But Mrs Holt is not the sort of woman to amuse herself in that way. Maybe there was a misunderstanding? She led you to some other room?'

'That's hardly likely. Why would there be two nurseries, one a hideous mirror of the other?'

'We have mirror suites,' Sarah pointed out. Absent-mindedly, she chewed on the lock of hair hanging down beside her mouth.

Fayford looked better in the sun. The mud road had dried to a rutted track. Some of the villagers had ventured outside their cottages. Elsie waved to them. They pulled their fore-locks in acknowledgement, but she noticed them hustle their scrawny children back inside, as if it were unlucky to have her eye fall upon them. With all their superstitions, they probably thought widows spread bad fortune.

'Sarah, what about the second companion? Did you see him also?'

'The gypsy boy. Yes, I told you.'

'You are sure?'

'Of course. There are two.'

But how?

They were on the bridge now, flanked by stone lions. Elsie gave an involuntary shudder as they crossed the water. 'I shall have to speak to Helen. But I presumed she would tell me if she'd found another one. I have never known such slipshod maids.'

The gatehouse flitted past them and they started to roll down the hills towards The Bridge. Above, the clouds swept along at speed, casting shadows over the turf. The gardeners she had hired were out. Some pruned bushes while others knelt in the parterres, uprooting dead flowers.

The horses drew to a halt before the house. Through the window, she saw the silhouettes of the companions waiting in the Great Hall. Two companions.

The butler who never smiled, Mr Stilford, opened the carriage door and let down the steps with an efficient *clunk, clunk*. As soon as they touched the gravel, he turned and spoke to Peters. 'You will find a new charge when you take the horses round, Mr Peters. It seems they have a companion.'

Carefully negotiating the passage of her crinoline, Elsie stumbled down beside him onto the gravel. 'A companion?'

'Your cow has arrived, madam.'

She had almost forgotten. Dancing back towards the carriage, she gave Sarah her hand and pulled her out. 'It's the cow, Sarah. My little adopted cow. We will have a merry afternoon settling her in.' She was glad not to be forced back into the house. 'Take the boxes inside, would you?' she asked Stilford. 'We are going to see her.'

With one hand grasping Sarah and the other clamping down her skirts, she made her way past the scattered dirt and tools left by the gardeners to the stable block behind the house. It was a horseshoe of decrepit brick buildings. Paint peeled in curls from the hunter-green doors. A clock was mounted on the roof, but its hands hung still at a quarter to ten. Even the weathervane beside it had rusted to a halt in the east.

The cow did not look out of place beside these derelict objects. She stood next to the man who held her rope, her large black head hanging in dejection.

'Oh!' Sarah's voice shot up a pitch. 'Mr Underwood has brought her.'

It was indeed Mr Underwood: Elsie did not recognise him at first. He was dressed differently: a tweed trouser and jacket combination, clearly second-hand, hung from his tall frame. A low-crowned, wide-brimmed hat squashed his fringe over his forehead.

'Mrs Bainbridge. Miss Bainbridge.' He shook their hands. 'A pleasure. I trust Miss Bainbridge is recovered from her faintness since we last met?'

Sarah's cheeks glowed. 'Oh yes. Much, much recovered.' When he smiled, she released an absurd little giggle.

So that's how it was.

'But it appears that you have hurt your hand?'

Sarah touched the bandage. 'Yes. Just a scratch. How kind, how very kind of you to notice!'

'I must thank you for escorting my ward to The Bridge,' Elsie cut in. 'Dear thing. She has not even raised her head to look at us.' The poor animal seemed to expect nothing more than future misery. 'We will feed her up and get her healthy in no time. And she will need a name.'

'Betsy,' Sarah suggested. 'Or Daisy.'

'For heaven's sake, have a little imagination. Something more poetic.'

'She does not look very poetic at present,' Underwood observed.

'On the contrary! She is a distressed soul coming out of purgatory into a perfect cow-heaven – if that is not a blasphemous thing to say, Mr Underwood.'

A smile tickled his lips. 'She is Dante's Beatrice, then?'

Elsie didn't know who that was, but she liked the sound of the name. 'Beatrice the cow.'

'Well, I hope her expectations will be as grand as her name.'

Peters came and took the rope from Underwood's hand. Softly clicking his tongue, he encouraged Beatrice to follow him to a stall. She shambled off, her overgrown hooves slipping on the cobbles.

'I was so pleased,' said Underwood, 'when Mrs Holt told me of your plan to take the cow. Usually the villagers are reluctant to deal with the big house. But with winter coming on, they finally saw the sense of it.'

'I should think so! I offered a pretty price for a bag of bones.' As soon as she said the words, she regretted them. She sounded just like her father.

'I know, Mrs Bainbridge. You were very good to suggest the trade, I am well aware of that. You must not take their little eccentricities amiss. Poor people can be very proud.'

Elsie thought of the match girls, of Pa's grasping fingers. 'Not in London,' she said.

———

Elsie took Mr Underwood to the first floor. She felt it would be beneficial to bring a vicar near the nursery. His presence might banish . . . whatever it was. Whatever was making her and Sarah see things that were not there.

With Mabel laid up, the house was increasingly worse for wear. Elsie found a peppering of woodchips on the landing and long, deep scratches in the floor, as though heavy objects had been dragged across it. Thankfully the parlour remained presentable, pleasantly warmed by the afternoon sun.

Elsie gestured to a sofa upholstered in pale daffodil silk and bid Underwood sit down. She rang a bell for tea, without holding much hope for its success.

'A delightful room, Mrs Bainbridge. I like the framed butterflies exceedingly. But who are our friends?'

She followed his gaze. 'Oh!'

Standing either side of the dwindling fire were the companions.

But weren't they just . . . Hadn't she seen them in the Great Hall?

The girl looked sweetly apologetic, pressing the white rose to her chest as if begging for indulgence. But not the boy; his baleful eyes met hers with a direct challenge.

Sarah moved to take a chair opposite Mr Underwood. 'We found them in the garret a few days ago. They are curious items, are they not? Our housemaid must have brought them upstairs.'

But why would Helen do that? Did she make the scratches on the floor as she pulled them along?

'It is very clever artistry,' Underwood replied. 'They look almost as if they would speak.'

Sarah giggled. Elsie tried to laugh, but it came out in a strained wheeze. 'I *do* find myself a little lonely, knocking around this old place. These figures are my guests until I am permitted to invite real ones. But if I ever tell you that they have started talking to me, Mr Underwood, I give you permission to send me to Bedlam.'

He smiled gently. 'I am sorry to learn you are lonely. We shall always be happy to see you at church. Come along on Sunday.'

Unexpectedly, her throat closed up with tears. She looked down at her hands. For the first time in her widowhood, she felt she might scream and howl like Ma. 'I shall. I daresay it looks odd that I have not come before, but I did not feel . . . I was not equal to it. But I have had some encouragement today. The villagers seemed almost friendly as we drove past.'

'But of course. It is all thanks to – erm – Beatrice. I told everyone about your plan to feed her up and pass on the milk. She has not been healthy enough to produce for many a year. Butter and milk will make a huge difference to the villagers' lives. Especially the children.'

'To be sure. I would do more if I could. I would employ the people. Do you know why they will not work for my family? Is it just the skeletons we spoke of? Mrs Holt said there was also an accident with a footman, years back?'

'Well . . .' He paused, fingers twitching at his lip. 'It seems to be a mixture of folk tales and superstition. I quite forgot to fetch you those records I mentioned, Mrs Bainbridge, but I remember there was some balderdash about a suspected witch.'

Sarah sat forward with interest. 'That could be the diary I am reading! Anne Bainbridge, my ancestor. She had a talent with herbs and made brews for good luck. She seemed to think she had a power. Did the villagers really believe she was a witch?'

Mr Underwood sighed. 'It is very likely, Miss Bainbridge. People were not rational back then. And your family have been unlucky with their servants. Several have died in accidents, and of course the village wants someone to blame ...' He held up his hands. 'This is how rumours are born. But I have hopes that, with education, we might eradicate superstition in the next generation. I must admit, Mrs Bainbridge, to being a trifle radical in my notions. I believe every child should have an education, regardless of their circumstances. They should be given the tools they need in this world.'

'I could not agree more.' She recalled little Jolyon with his abacus, tongue stuck out in concentration. It created a painful knot in her chest. 'Perhaps you should set up a school here?'

The smile lighting his face was so wide and genuine that for a moment she saw why Sarah admired him. 'Would you help me?'

'When I can. Miss Bainbridge would be more fitted to the task. She will be out of mourning in less than a month. She can do many things that would not be seemly for a widow.'

'Oh yes, do let me help, Mr Underwood!' Sarah clapped her hands together. Her bandage muffled the sound. 'I think it's a wonderful idea. Mrs Crabbly left me a little legacy, and I will make a donation. We must help the children.'

Suddenly the gravestones were before her eyes again. Buried under a borrowed name. Those poor little girls . . . She would not keep all of Rupert's money for her own baby. There were other children: unprotected, vulnerable.

The thought made her queasy. A sour taste was filling her mouth. She rose abruptly to her feet. Things shimmered, became uncertain and shifting. 'Will you . . . Please excuse me? I must . . . go and see after that tea.'

Out of the corner of her eye, she caught a glimpse of the first companion. It had never looked so much like her. Her own face, watching her.

She had to hurry from the room before she was sick.

Wooden railing bordered the gallery, cordoning off the drop into the Great Hall. Elsie had to walk all the way around the edge of the square to reach the water closet. Ordinarily, that was not a hardship, but nausea made the distance feel tremendous. She reached out and used the rail to support herself. It creaked. She thought of the footman Mrs Holt mentioned, toppling to his death, and withdrew her hand.

A floorboard moaned across the gallery. Helen was hurrying towards her from the opposite direction, her cheeks as red as apples. The strings of her cap were untied and flapped around her shoulders.

Elsie sucked in a breath. 'Helen? Where is the tea tray?'

'Mrs Holt's making it, ma'am.' Helen jogged the last few steps, her chin wobbling over the collar of her dress. 'I hope you'll pardon me but I wanted to speak with you . . . alone.'

Just then, Sarah tittered from inside the parlour. The companion's face floated back into her mind.

'Helen, fetch me a chamber pot. Quickly.'

Once Elsie had expelled her burden and drunk a glass of water, she became aware of her surroundings. Helen had sat her on the worn baize of the billiard table with her feet dangling over the edge. Next door, in the parlour, she could hear spoons clinking against china. Mrs Holt must have finally served tea.

'I told Mrs Holt I needed to stay with you, for a bit, in case . . . in case you go again.' Helen spoke in a whisper, her eyes continually darting to the wall. 'I don't have long, ma'am. May I speak to you now?'

Elsie was hardly in the mood to deal with staff, but Helen had saved her from vomiting and fainting in the corridor. She owed her an open ear, at least.

'Yes, I can spare a moment. Please go on.'

'I . . .' Helen stopped, at a loss. She looked down and began playing with her apron. 'I don't really know how to start, ma'am. Only . . . Mrs Holt told me you've been in the nursery.'

Heat, creeping across her scalp. 'Yes.'

'Did you . . .' Another twist of the apron. 'Did you see anything, ma'am?'

Elsie grabbed the edge of the billiard table. A joke, surely? Mrs Holt had let slip her reaction to the nursery and the maid was teasing her.

The housekeeper in Rupert's London home had tried to trick Elsie into serving dinner as early as two o'clock, to make her look common in front of the guests. Servants could tell she only had trade money – or *shop money*, as they called it. Without breeding, they thought her fair game.

'What, exactly, is it you expected me to see there?'

She waited for the description she had given Mrs Holt of the crib and the toys. But instead, Helen said, 'Writing.'

'*Writing?*'

Helen dropped her apron. 'I shouldn't have said anything. Please, ma'am, forget I spoke.'

'Have *you* seen writing in the nursery, Helen?'

She made a frantic hushing motion. 'Don't let Mrs Holt hear you. She hates anything like that. Even bought herself a black cat to prove superstitions are nonsense. But ever since the master came down, something's been . . . strange, here.'

If she was acting, she was good. She had the jittery hands of a woman unnerved.

Elsie chose her next words with care. 'I think you found Mr Bainbridge, Helen? After he died? It is only natural that you would feel on edge after a death in the house. Perhaps . . .'

Helen shook her head. 'I thought of that, ma'am, when Mabel never noticed it. And I thought how there's enough camphor to kill a cat in that nursery, so the fumes might be sending me giddy. But the master . . . he saw it too.'

Elsie wobbled on the edge of the table. 'Writing?'

'No . . . not exactly. It's only me that sees the writing, in the dust. Like a finger did it. But Master's was different. He saw the wooden alphabets, laid out in a word.'

'What word, Helen? Could you read it?'

'Oh yes. Mrs Holt taught me my letters.' Even now, a touch of pride. 'Mabel still don't know hers.'

'Never mind that, what was the word? What did it say?'

Helen grimaced. '*Mother*. It said *Mother*.'

THE BRIDGE, 1635

I am not nearly as organised for the royal visit as I wish to be, what with the snow – *snow!* – at Whitsun, which prevented any travel. That terrible frost destroyed most of my plants. All will need reseeding, or replacing with full-grown blooms. Thank heaven the London hothouses managed to send us roses and lilies! Pray God we can keep them alive in the next three months. Another small mercy was the survival of Hetta's herb patch. Those little green sprigs have proved hardier than most and the blue-grey stalks of the thistle thrive.

My anxiety increases with Josiah's burgeoning hopes. He is already drawing up plans for a new wing to the house. This morning he came into my rooms as I dressed, carrying a parcel wrapped in silk.

'What is that?' I asked his reflection in the mirror. I had the sense of something cold behind me, something ice-bright.

'It is a gift, my lady.' He placed a hand on my shoulder. 'Can you guess it?'

'It is a jewel to wear when the King and Queen visit. A . . . necklace?'

He chuckled. 'My little prophetess.'

He began to unwrap the package. I squinted, not seeing but feeling his hands at my throat. The necklace jangled and touched my collarbone. Sharp, cold. It was like a band of snow.

'Open your eyes,' Josiah laughed. 'Lizzy, pull the curtain, your mistress is half blinded.'

I heard the curtain swish behind me and slowly rolled my eyelids open.

I had predicted the object, but not the quality. Diamonds ringed my neck and dropped down into my bosom. The shape was a bow with three pear drops. Every stone clear-cut, pure as water. The necklace might have belonged to the Queen herself.

'Josiah . . .'

I caught a glimpse of his face in the mirror. He glowed with pride. 'This will go down to our descendents, Annie. To James's wife and his son's wife after that. Every great family needs an heirloom. These will be the Bainbridge diamonds.'

My lips parted. It was on the tip of my tongue to say I already had jewels from his mother but there was a heaviness, a prickle in the atmosphere that warned me against it. 'They are very beautiful. Can we . . .' I shot a look at Lizzy and lowered my voice. 'Can we afford it, dearest?'

He frowned. 'Why would you worry about a thing like that? The Midsummer rents will be in soon.'

Rents we had put up since last quarter, I recalled.

'Of course.' The diamonds lay heavy on my chest. When I moved them against my skin they were painfully cold. 'Forgive me, it is only . . . I have never owned anything so fine! In truth, I am a little afraid of it.'

I could not help but recall how Mary spoke of diamonds, many years ago.

'They ward off the evil eye,' she told me. 'Protect you from the darkest magic.'

Was that why Josiah placed them about my neck? Did he suspect my stillroom housed more than simple herbs?

Feeling queasy, I touched my throat and looked at his reflection in the mirror.

His cheeks lifted as he smiled. 'You must become accustomed to the best jewels, my lady, as will befit your station as my wife. I wish to see these diamonds upon your person every day.'

A hint of the diamonds' ice in his voice. Not merely a wish: a command.

Behind him, Lizzy stood at the window. One wrinkled hand lay on her collarbone, as if she too felt the chill creeping across her skin.

I swallowed. The diamonds moved.

'As you desire it, my lord.'

Today I took a trip into Torbury St Jude. The weather is not warm, but at least it is drier. The flood waters have receded and the roads are passable. We travelled between shops in the carriage, for remnants of puddles oiled the streets and the wind whipped up and down the alleys most violently.

'I have the new napery,' I told Jane, checking off the list on my fingers. 'The silver is being polished. The dresses should arrive from London next month.'

'Mrs Dawson looked scandalised you didn't order from her shop, mistress,' Jane said.

She did, poor dear. But what did she expect? This is no country ball. The *King* and *Queen*, upon my soul! They will expect fashionable slashed velvet, the most exquisite lace.

'I cannot concern myself with Mrs Dawson at present,' I said. 'There will be time enough for her later. For the moment, I am only concerned with pleasing Queen Henrietta Maria.'

'Mistress, the Queen can't help but be pleased with all that fancy decoration in her bedroom and the improvements you've made. It's enough to put her head in a spin.'

I smiled, proud. 'It looks fine to *us*, Jane. But she is the Queen. She grew up in the Château de Saint-Germain-en-Laye. It will take a mighty effort to impress her. She likes curiosities, strange things no one else has seen.' I looked out of the window. The oppressive milky sky made our little town appear bleak indeed. Our horse lifted its tail and dumped a load on the cobbles. I sighed. 'Where will I find exotic things like *that* in Torbury St Jude?'

'Mayhap just up the way here, mistress. There's an establishment I heard talk of at the market.'

I turned to see the shop Jane indicated on the left. It was a small place, pushed back from the straggling, uneven row of buildings that lined the street. The lower storey was made of brick; the upper consisted of old beams and plaster.

'Hold!' I called. The horses pulled up. As the click of their hooves ceased I heard the shop's sign groaning in the wind. I could not make the picture out, but I thought I saw the words *Fancy Goods* painted above the mullioned window. 'Jane, I do not know this place. How long has it been there?'

She grinned. 'I thought you knew everything, mistress.'

I let her sauciness pass. In truth I sensed a strangeness about the shop which I could not put into words. I knew I should not be able to drive on without going inside. There was something important, something there . . .

I have felt that way but once before: it was on that freezing January day, some nine years ago, when I opened Mary's old leather book and recited its words over the mashed herbs in my stillroom. It was the exact sensation: the apprehension, the certainty.

'Let us go in.' I rapped on the roof. The footman sprang down and tried to open the door. It did not want to yield. I put my fingers on the handle and attempted to help him, but it was as if the wind was an iron hand, pushing against me. Barring my passage.

Straining with all my might, I pushed back. The door gave way, blowing open with such force that it slammed back into the body of the coach. I tumbled into the footman's arms.

'Are you well, mistress?'

I was embarrassed, but unharmed. My skirts were in much disorder; the wind snatched at them and tore a ribbon loose from my hair. I watched it sail off into the grey oblivion of the sky. 'I am perfectly well. Jane, you will need to take my arm to the door.'

I was thankful for Jane's stoutness and her thick, country waist. An odd pair we must have looked, heads down, battling against the wind; Jane in her dirty green kirtle and I billowing in satin and lace.

The wind made instruments of all it touched. From behind came the clink of the horses' harness, beckoning us back; ahead, the sign creaked as it swung. Its moan grew louder with each step, until at last I could hear the horses no more.

Jane thumped the shop door open with one of her broad shoulders, setting a bell jangling. 'You first, mistress.' She all but pushed me in – I paid it no heed, for I was glad of the shelter.

A short, balding man leapt up as we entered. A much-worn maroon jerkin stretched over his stomach. He had small, hot eyes – pig's eyes, I thought – which fluttered at the sight of us. 'Good morrow, ladies. You gave me quite a start.'

'I do apologise. We were somewhat blown in.'

'Is it breezy out?'

Jane banged the door shut behind us. The bell jangled again. 'Breezy? It's fit to blow a gale!'

'Indeed?' He smiled, seemed to recover his composure. 'In that case, I expect you are in need of some refreshment. Let me fetch the wine and sugared plums. Every customer is treated like a duchess in this shop.'

Above his left shoulder hung an ornate gold mirror, carved with cherubs and flowers. My reflection stared back, thoroughly dishevelled. I did not feel much like a duchess.

As he fetched our wine, we had leisure to look around us. The shop was much larger than it had appeared outside, but curiosities packed every inch of it. Dusty cases hung from the walls with displays of crystal and stone lurking beneath the murky glass. Strange, stuffed birds from foreign climes glowered at us, their feathers brightly dyed. Suspended from the ceiling was a skeleton I have never seen before – some monstrous creature with a large horn, like a unicorn, only it protruded from the nose. Even the air tasted unusual, warm with spices.

'Thank you,' I said, taking my glass of wine from the shopkeeper. I noticed that it trembled in his hand. 'I am surprised we have not come across your shop before. Are you new to Torbury St Jude?'

'Just arrived.' He proffered the tray of sugared plums. Jane was quick off the mark to seize one and stuff it whole in her mouth. 'My name is Samuels. I have spent my days travelling the world, madam, and now here I am, with all its rarities laid out before you.'

It was good wine. Another import, I suspected.

I ran my fingers across a cabinet and tugged on a velvet tab attached to the drawer. It slid open. Rows and rows of birds' eggs lay before my eyes: blue, speckled, some minuscule, one the size of an apple. Nature's jewels. Not even the diamonds at court could rival treasures rare and delicate as these. 'In faith, it must be hard to part with your collection. Is not every item a memento of your journey?'

'There are some memories one does not wish to keep.' His face hardened for a moment. 'Besides, I like to share what I have found. People always want a curiosity to show their friends.'

Carefully, I picked up a sugared plum. Its granules stuck to my fingers. 'I confess, I am here on such an errand. Come August, we will entertain some illustrious guests.'

'Ah! This way then, madam. I will show you the ivory. Exquisite pieces beyond all compare. Any guest will swoon.'

I popped the plum in my mouth and followed him.

It was a giddy half hour, picking and choosing from the world's treasure chest. I found dried tulips mounted in frames and a mechanical cannon that fired shot. I was carried away, I confess. I felt quite ashamed when I turned and, in the low candlelight, saw another customer waiting.

'Oh!' I cried. 'Pray, forgive me.' I turned to Mr Samuels. 'That must do for now, I am keeping you from business.'

His small eyes followed mine. For a moment, I thought he was afraid. Then he laughed.

I saw my mistake: it was no customer standing in the corner but a board, painted to resemble a person. So splendidly was it worked that you would not notice it was a piece of art, at first glance. The subject was a woman resting with her hand on her hip. Shadows were painted on her face at the exact angles light would hit from the window of the shop.

'You have run ahead of me,' Mr Samuels said. 'I was coming to these.' He walked over to the object. I could see, by the light of the window, beads of sweat stood upon his brow. 'These counterfeits can trick the best of us. Do you know the meaning of *trompe l'oeil*?'

'A trick of the eye?'

'Precisely. A playful deception. Come hither.' He pointed to the shoulder of the cut-out. His finger hovered an inch away from the wood. 'See the bevelled edges? They stop it from looking flat.' I peeped around the back, still surprised to find it was not solid. She was not real and yet I felt I could not touch her, could not meet her eye. 'I have more of these I can show you. Children carrying fruit. Maids and sweepers. A lady with her lute.'

'Wherever are they from?'

'These were given to me in Amsterdam. They call them "silent companions".' He cleared his throat. 'Those Dutchmen, madam, they love their little deceits. It's not just the tulips they are mad for. They have perspective boxes and pretend food – even doll's houses fitted out finer than a duke's palace.'

I turned to Jane. 'They are good sport, are they not? I can imagine guests coming across these boards with a little cry. A moment of shock, then laughter and conversation.'

'I do not know if Her Majesty would wish to be shocked,' said Jane.

Mr Samuels looked at me with a new respect. 'Her Majesty, say you? The Queen?'

I coloured again, this time with pleasure. 'Yes. We are greatly honoured. So you see why it is important that I choose—'

He held out a hand. The fingers were fat, like sausages, and marked by the weather. 'Yes, yes,' he interrupted, 'you must have the best of everything. May I humbly recommend these items?' Once more he gestured to the figure, but he did not let his hand make contact with it. I deduced the item was expensive, even too precious to touch.

'They are unlike anything I have seen before. I shall certainly consider them.'

'What is there to consider, dear madam? They are just the thing to please Her Majesty.' There was a plea in his voice, in his eyes. Perchance business was not going as well as he had hoped.

'I have taken a quantity of goods already,' I said, trying to tally my spending. Something this rare would surely stretch beyond my purse? 'It would be fitting to consult my husband before—'

'But your lord will only counsel you as I do. I doubt any man in England has seen the like of these.'

I thought of Josiah, of the way he pined for recognition from the King. 'We may desire one or two . . .'

'But the effect will be diminished. Come, I will let you take the whole collection.'

Usually, I would be wary of a person desperate to peddle his goods, but I wanted Mr Samuels's strange toys. They were calling to me, watching me, baiting me to take them with their painted eyes.

'I am unsure whether . . .'

'For a special price.' He smiled. 'I promise you, there is no better method to surprise the Queen. She will never forget the companions.'

I bought them all.

THE BRIDGE, 1865

'Its eyes moved.'

'What?' Elsie's pen jerked and spluttered over the page. Ruined: her letter to the builder was ruined. 'What do you want, Mabel?'

After two weeks of resting in bed, Mabel had resumed dusting and other light tasks. Elsie was inclined to think she could manage a lot more. She played up to her misfortune, dragging herself about like a child with a club foot.

Today she stood in the open doorway of the library, her posture crooked, favouring the uninjured leg. Her right hand clasped a dirty cloth and there was a smear of soot on her nose.

'The thing. Its eyes moved and looked right at me.'

Elsie laid down her pen. 'What thing?' she asked. But she already knew. It was as though she had spent the last fortnight just waiting for this to happen.

'The wooden thing.'

'The companion?'

'That's it.' Sweat spangled the thin line of hair showing beneath Mabel's cap. Her throat worked. 'I won't clean it no more. Its eyes moved.'

Words formed in her mind; a thousand cutting remarks. She could not utter a single one of them. 'The gypsy boy?'

Mabel shook her head. 'T'other one.'

'Show me.'

They walked downstairs in silence, stiffly, like marionettes. Wind gusted through the cracks in the floorboards and skittered leaves against the windows. From behind the house, Beatrice gave a mournful low.

Helen stood waiting in the Great Hall, her knuckles clenched around a duster.

'You have moved them again,' Elsie said, looking at the scratches on the floor. 'Why do you keep moving them?'

'*We* didn't move them,' cried Mabel.

Both companions stood beside the fireplace. There *was* something different about the boy, but she could not place her finger on it. He regarded her haughtily, staring to his left. He was taunting her, daring her to notice a change.

Something . . . The angle of his face . . . She shook the thought off. There was no change. Paintings did *not* change, it was a ridiculous fancy.

The little girl looked exactly as Elsie recalled her: the white rose pressed to her breast; her mischievous smile and the olive silk. Her green-brown eyes still carried the same warmth of expression – they had not moved.

She let out her breath. 'You do not appreciate good art, Mabel. The skill of a painter is to make the eyes look as if they are upon you, no matter where you stand. Go walk past the portraits upstairs. The same thing will happen.'

'I weren't walking. Didn't move a muscle. I stood still, right there, and they *slid*.'

It was too horrible to imagine. She would *not* imagine it, or believe any more of these servants' ridiculous stories. 'Did Helen see it?'

'No, ma'am,' Helen croaked. She wrung the duster. 'But . . .'

'Let me guess: you found writing?'

'No. I felt . . . strange. Like someone were watching me.'

'We have all felt like that, Helen. It was probably Jasper.' She turned away from the companions. 'I think Mabel had better go to bed. She is clearly still unwell. And since we are here, Helen, I would rather you put the boy back wherever you found him. Miss Sarah only asked for the girl to go on display.'

'I'll put it in the cellar if you wish, ma'am. Still can't get into the garret.'

'Yes, I was in the middle of writing to Torbury St Jude for someone to open the garret when Mabel started this folly. You put the gypsy boy in the cellar and I will return to my letter.' She was heading for the stairs when Mabel's voice stopped her.

'What about t'other one?'

'Miss Sarah wants the girl companion, Mabel. Have Helen clean it if it scares you so.'

'No.' Mabel pointed a soot-caked finger. 'That one.'

On the oriental rug, where Rupert's coffin had lain, stood a third companion.

An old woman seated on a chair. It was worse than the gypsy boy; not just sneering but decidedly malevolent. She wore a white coif and a black partlet. Propped in her arms was a doll-like child, unnaturally stiff and blank-faced.

'Where did that come from? Why . . . why would anyone paint such a thing? That face!' Her words rang out through the hall and bounced back at her.

Helen trembled.

'Put it *away*, Helen. Where on earth did you find it?'

Helen's lips quivered. 'Here, ma'am. Right here, this morning.'

THE BRIDGE, 1635

I knew from the moment I awoke that this day would be one of conflict: it was written in the muggy air. Battlements of cloud crowded out the light and a silent tension hung over the gardens. It was oppressively hot. I longed all day for the clouds to break and relieve my headache but still they glower down at me, primed. Nothing outside stirs; there is no breeze.

If it is like this when the King and Queen arrive, we will all be sweltering and cross. How can we look becoming in our beautiful outfits, with the sweat pouring off our faces? No one will hunger for a roast swan. Oh, if only this weather would give way!

Josiah has made me feel melancholy about the visit. He came to me soon after dinner and sent the maids away.

'I need to speak with you,' he said. The set of his jaw, the lines in his forehead, spoke for him.

'You have decided about Hetta,' I said.

'Yes.' He ran a hand down the length of his beard. 'Annie, you will not like what I have to say.'

'Then do not say it. Change your mind.'

He sighed. 'I cannot. It is for the best. Henrietta Maria may attend the feast. She has worked hard enough for it. But as for the rest of the entertainments . . . The answer is no.'

My hands curled into fists. I knew I should select my next words with care, but I was not mistress of my emotions. That hot, tingling sensation welled up inside me and pushed tears into my eyes.

'She is young,' he went on. 'I am not sure it would be suitable, even if—'

'You are ashamed of her,' I said.

He hesitated for an instant. It was enough. 'I pity her . . .'

'She is a miracle! The midwives said I would never bear another child, not after Charles. And yet here she is. Your only daughter, Josiah. A miracle.'

'I am mindful of that. No one thought you capable of carrying another. Perhaps that is why she has her . . . her difficulties.'

Behind his words I heard the accusation that is always simmering beneath the surface: it is my fault that Hetta's tongue did not grow. My womb failed to nurture a complete child. There was something lacking; either in me, or the mixture.

'She is touched by God!' I cried. He looked at me. Just one look, and it set my anger ablaze. 'You think not? You think the other way?'

He held up his hands in surrender. He was tiring of me. 'Calm yourself. Of course I do not think Henrietta Maria has a demon. You are speaking hysterically.'

'I am not. You are hiding my daughter away!'

'Everyone will see her at the feast, Anne. I will not *hide* her, but I must protect her.' He began to pace the room, the leather of his boots creaking as he walked. 'We will introduce her to society slowly. She is not ready yet. She is too wild, too girlish. We have indulged her and let her run around the house in her own way. But that must stop now. She will be instructed.'

'Instructed?'

'In court manners. There is no time to train her up before the visit. We cannot afford a mistake. Not one! I dare not imagine the consequences. Would you see me banished from court, for Henrietta Maria's blunders? Everything must go perfectly.'

My temper frayed beneath the creak, creak of his boots. For I did not hear squeaking leather: I heard trees in the night, waving their arms above a cloaked figure picking herbs; a pestle and mortar grinding together; mystery and temptation in the words of an old spell. 'You seem to imply that our daughter is not perfect.'

'You know that she is not.'

It winded me. How could Josiah say such a thing, of his own child? I do not think I have ever hated him as I did at that moment. 'This news will break her heart,' I told him.

'Then I will tell her, if you do not like to. Where is she now?'

'In the garden.'

I walked over to the window, wanting to see her at peace before he shattered her hopes. Everything outside looked strange. The plants glowed unnaturally bright under stormy skies. My new fleur-de-lis hedges were transformed into vivid green spears; the roses, clots of blood. Behind them, my Hetta knelt on the ground, tending her herbs. Her ankles showed, smeared with green. I did not mind that. Her face was full of light, despite the clouds. She looked happy; she smiled as she nodded and tilted her head up to . . .

'Who is that?' Josiah's voice blared over my shoulder.

I cursed under my breath. 'It's that gypsy boy again. It is time he had a good hiding. I have warned him to stay away.'

'See? Do you see, now?' He gestured out of the window. 'Playing with gypsies! This is exactly what I am talking about.'

I whirled round, too angry to contradict him. 'I will deal with it,' I said, and stalked from the room.

My feet pounded on the stairs. Blast that gypsy and his impudence, blast him for making poor Hetta's father think ill of her!

I burst out into the gardens. The air was like stale breath. I could not wonder that the plants did not thrive; even the soil was pale, dry and cracked.

Lizzy was nowhere in sight. What was she about, leaving Hetta unattended in such a manner?

'Hetta! Is that boy bothering you?'

She sprang to her feet and came to take my hand. Her palm was dirty, but without sweat. The humidity that frazzled me and the gardens did not touch her.

'What is going on?'

She smiled, slowly. Her eyelids fluttered and I real-ised she was staring up at my diamonds. One small hand extended, reaching towards my neck.

'Not now, Hetta. Your hands are filthy. You can look at my necklace later.' I swatted her away and glared at the boy. He held his ground, unwholesome urchin that he was. 'As for you . . . You should not be here. You know it well. This is your last warning.'

Belatedly, he snatched his cap from his head. 'Please, mistress. I'm only come looking for work.'

'Gypsies do not work—' I began, but Hetta tugged at my arm. She gave me one of the signs we have made between us. *Horse*. 'He has stolen my horse?'

She shook her head vehemently. Her lips puckered with frustration, as they always do when she cannot make herself understood. *Horse. Boy. Horse.*

The boy squirmed. He spoke to her in his canting gypsy language. It sounded infernal; all tongues, like something demonic. But she seemed to understand him, for she nodded and grunted.

'Miss Henrietta Maria . . .' He looked at me, eyes black as pitch. 'Miss thinks you'd let me work here. With the horses.'

I wondered how he knew that; how he dared to presume he understood Hetta when I did not. 'I would not let you within a hundred yards of my horses,' I scoffed. 'You would steal them.'

Hetta dropped my hand.

'Please, mistress. Please. My people are good with horses. Now your steward has cleared us off the common, what will we do? How will I eat?'

I paused. He really did look pitiful, cringing there all ragged. Hetta signed to me again. *Nothing*.

'I know they have nothing, Hetta. It is not my fault.'

No, that wasn't it. *Boy. Nothing*.

'We have stolen nothing,' he said softly. Her eyes lit up and for an instant I begrudged him that. What communion was it he shared with my daughter – *my* creation? I did not want him near her. 'In all the years we have lived on this common for the summer, we have stolen nothing from you.'

'That may be. But I will have the King's horses in my stable. Do you understand? How can I risk that? What would he say, if a gypsy took his horse? He would hold my husband responsible. It would ruin us.'

Hetta held out her hands.

'You will need extra hands,' he said. 'For the King's visit. Plenty of stable hands. You will be rushed off your feet.'

'Then we will employ men. Not a gypsy boy.'

Hetta stamped her foot. To my astonishment, she put her hands to my leg and shoved me.

My temper flared. I was no longer in the gardens of The Bridge but at home, years ago. Mary was dashing for the tray of sweetmeats, pushing me aside. Laughing as I fell. Fury burnt into my hand.

The noise of our skin connecting was louder than any cry. I gasped. My handprint was red on Hetta's cheek. I have never struck her before.

I shall never forget the hurt – the passion nearly akin to hate – burning in her eyes. 'Oh Hetta! Pray forgive me. I did not mean to – you should not hit me! You are being so wilful today.'

Furtively, my eyes sought the window. Thank heavens, Josiah was not there. He did not see my daughter act like the hoyden he accused her of being.

'I didn't mean to cause trouble, mistress.' The boy put his cap back on. 'All I wanted was to work. I'll be going now. Goodbye, Miss Henrietta Maria.'

A sound tore from Hetta's lips: an awful noise, like an animal in pain. She ran after him and grabbed his coat. I cannot say what passed between them. He spoke resignedly in that heathen language and she responded with hand signals I have never seen before. At last, she let him go.

Hetta turned to her herb patch and began to clip the thistles. She did not look at me, but I saw her profile. The resentment had drained from her face. Everything vital had gone, leaving naught but sorrow.

My heart squeezed in my chest. She did not even know she was banned from the masque. I watched her bend low over the ground and water the rosemary with her tears. Dark spots appeared on the parched soil, slowly seeping into the roots.

No mother's heart could withstand that sight. It would be bad enough with an ordinary child, wailing and sobbing. But watching my poor mute girl, so quiet in her misery, snapped my resolve like a tender branch beneath the weight of a wood pigeon.

'Wait,' I called out. The gypsy boy stopped still. I risked another look at the window – clear. 'Wait.'

THE BRIDGE, 1865

'Mabel? Mabel, may I come in?' Elsie pushed the door open.

With the garret sealed up and an empty house, the maids had taken to sleeping in the guest bedrooms of the west wing, on the third storey. They were modest chambers, but pleasant. Blue carpet covered the floor. Small prints hung on the walls, giving it a homely feel. A washstand and a hip bath huddled next to the fire. It was a fine, comfortable place for a girl accustomed to the austerity of a workhouse, better than any maid's quarters, but Mabel sat rigid in bed with the covers pulled to her chin. Her face was drawn, haunted.

'Mabel?'

'Oh it's you, ma'am!' she exclaimed. Her pupils shrank back to their usual size. 'Sorry. I got muddled and I thought you was . . . I'd dozed off.'

'Pardon me. I did not mean to startle you.' Elsie perched on a corner of the bed. 'How are you feeling?'

Mabel grimaced. She ran a hand over her dark, tousled hair. 'Shook up, ma'am. I don't mind telling you, it gave me the collywobbles.'

'I must admit, I felt a little strange myself.' She looked down. *Strange* was an understatement. Unravelled, opened up, exposed: they were more accurate words. Fear pushed so much out of a person – she had forgotten that. 'I think that I will call the physician in. Your cut ankle may have become infected.'

'Tain't an infection making me go queer. I *saw* it.'

'I do not doubt that you did.' She paused. A memory flowed back in liquid fire. She saw it again: the red eyes and the parched, gaping lips. 'My mother, Mabel, had the typhus. Have you heard of it?'

Mabel inclined her head.

'Poor woman. How she roasted. Once, I felt her head and I thought—' Her voice caught. 'I thought she was burning alive. From the inside.' Mabel's legs twitched beneath the bedclothes. 'It was bad enough being so ill in the body. But she was tormented more in the mind, by the things that she saw. I won't go into detail. The illness painted demons around the room. She saw them clear as day, but they were not there. I sat beside her the whole time. None of it was there. Yet to her it was very, very real.'

'I ain't going mad, ma'am. I ain't got no fever.'

'No.' She folded her hands and tried to compose herself. The image of her mother remained burnt on the back of her eyes. 'But I would like to make quite sure, just in case. Until we are certain, Helen will do your chores and Sarah can assist where necessary.'

'I can't sit here doing nothing, ma'am. All alone, thinking of them *things*.'

Elsie thought for a moment. Mrs Holt's generosity must be catching, for the first idea she had was so wildly kind that it took her aback.

Should she give Mabel a chance to become something better than a workhouse girl?

She was still wary of putting Mabel around a young child. But perhaps, if Elsie invested time now, she could improve the maid before the baby arrived. Education – that was what Mr Underwood said, wasn't it?

She drew in a breath and took the plunge. 'Well, while you recover, might you like to train in some gentler work? Something less strenuous?'

'Like what, ma'am?'

It was like moving rusty filings in her mouth, but she managed it: she managed to put on her sweetest smile and say, 'I am in need of a lady's maid.'

'A what, ma'am?'

'A lady's maid. Someone to do my hair. Bring my breakfast, draw my bath. Washing and mending will be required too. Tell me, did *you* get that mud out of my bombazine dress the day I arrived?'

'Yes, ma'am. Mucky as a pigsty, it were.'

She let that pass. 'Good. It shows you have aptitude. Would you like to train up, Mabel? It will set you in good stead for the future. A girl with skills will not always need to stay at The Bridge.'

Mabel's eyelashes flicked up and down. 'Look after all your clothes and fancy things? Your diamond necklace?'

'Yes.'

'A lady's maid,' Mabel repeated with wonder. 'That's one of *them*, ain't it? The fancy sort Helen talks about?'

'The role is that of an upper servant, yes. Much higher than your current position.'

Mabel grinned, all traces of fright evaporated. 'All right, then, ma'am. I'll do it.'

These drugs were stronger than the last. She felt them suck at her bloodstream as she lumbered down the corridor beside Dr Shepherd.

Shapes and faces melted beneath her eyes. Everywhere she turned were the slack jaws and wet mouths of idiots. They shrieked like witches, looming large in her vision then swirling away again. Hideous phantoms haunting the place as surely as the stench of piss.

'It is most beneficial, don't you think?' he asked. 'Walking gets the blood flowing. I see no reason why you might not enjoy the same benefits as the other patients, under my supervision. Nothing has been proven against you, after all.'

Another of his 'helpful' prescriptions. It was more of a penance than a treat. Imprisonment was never the real punishment: it was the people you were stuck with. Lunatics were the worst; jabbering, yammering, moaning. Some couldn't even control their bladders. That's why she'd thrown her dinner over the old woman and given the nurse a black eye along with the plate. It was nothing personal. The only way to get privacy, and a quiet sleep, was to be branded 'dangerous'. It meant the dark, padded cell for a few days, but also stronger medication. A fair trade, she thought.

'But I must take care I do not tire you too much. I hoped we might have a little conversation once we are back in your room with the slate, Mrs Bainbridge? If it is agreeable?'

Agreeable? She had a notion these manners were a device of his, constructed to reawaken the social, genteel side of her character. If there still was one.

Aromas served as landmarks. Burnt porridge told her they were near the eating hall; soap, cold water and fear signalled the bathrooms. When she smelt musty bedclothes and felt her feet squeak against floorboards, she knew she was back in her own cell. It was almost like coming home.

The world was hazy as she slumped onto her bed. White walls rippled. Dr Shepherd offered her the slate and chalk. When she tried to take them, her hands seemed to waver before her eyes, slowed by the drugs.

'Do remain lying down if you need to, Mrs Bainbridge. So long as you can write, you may pick any position you choose.'

There was no choice about it – she didn't have the energy to rise.

'Several interesting developments have occurred in your story. I would like to concentrate upon one for the present. You have written that your mother died of the typhus. Your father, I think, predeceased her?' She nodded. 'And how did he die?'

Pa's face tried to manifest itself before her but she wouldn't let it. She clamped her eyes shut.

'Mrs Bainbridge? Do you remember how he died?'

The chalk grated as she wrote, *No.*

He cleared his throat. 'I expected that might be the case. You see, Mrs Bainbridge, I am of the opinion that your current silence was not simply triggered by the fire at The Bridge. I believe this has been building for a good while. In fact, I believe the malady may have started with your father.'

Her eyes sprang open. She turned her head on the pillow, stared at his wavering shape.

'Yes. I am sorry to tell you that the manner in which your father died was highly distressing. It occurred less than two months after your brother's birth.' She heard him rustle paper, although she could not focus clearly. 'The police were involved. You yourself made a statement.' A pause. 'Shall – shall I read it to you?'

It was as though he had frozen every drop of blood in her veins. She could not move, she only blinked, but he seemed to take that for assent.

'"Elisabeth Livingstone of Livingstone's Match Factory, Bow, London. Twelve years of age. I am the daughter of the deceased. I have been assisting the workers in the factory since I was a girl. On the afternoon of August 2nd, about three of the clock, I was tying bundles of splints when I perceived a fire on the factory floor. It was a small fire, located beside the circular saw. I did not see how the fire began. Knowing the danger of fire in a factory, I ran to extinguish it, but I did not have a blanket or sand to assist me. I tried to beat the flames with my hands and was injured. I do not believe I called out, 'Fire.' Another worker may have done so. Shortly after, I saw the deceased running towards me with a bucket of water. The water sloshed from the bucket and he must have slipped. I was tending to my injury. I heard a sound like a shoe squeaking, then a clang. I looked up and realised that the deceased had fallen into the circular saw.'"

He let a respectful moment pass. How she wished he would not – in the silence she heard it again, that dreadful sound.

'Quite a horror for any person to witness, I should think,' he said at last. 'Let alone a girl of twelve years.'

He had no idea.

Dr Shepherd began to pace. She was relieved: the pad of his steps replaced the roaring inside her ears.

'From your story, I gather this event somewhat unbalanced your mother – as well it might. Do you remember?'

She nodded.

'Was she perhaps – almost – mad, with grief?'

Ah, Ma, loyal to the end. How she loved him. She saw him at his worst, yet still she loved him – loved him far more than she loved Elsie.

Another nod.

'And do you not think, Mrs Bainbridge, that the same unfortunate circumstance may have affected you in a similar manner? That there may have been a tendency, within your family? Don't forget, you suffered a terrible loss too. And more followed.'

The irony was that she had *not* lost her mind completely. Every feeling, all that was good and pure in her world had been mangled, and she was still stronger than those wretches pissing themselves out in the corridor. She knew it.

'Madness, as we call it, manifests itself in many ways. People do not always wail and shriek as you say your mother did. But it does seem to run in families, I have observed, particularly through the female line. Hysteria – womb to womb. Diseased blood will out. There is no hiding from it, I am afraid.'

Slowly, she let the slate and chalk drop from her hands.

She could feel the past stealing up on her, the way a river inches up its banks in the rain; gradually lapping at her chin, filling her mouth.

There is no hiding from it, I am afraid.

He was right about that. Now she had begun to tell her story, there was no hiding at all.

THE BRIDGE, 1865

Advent brought with it a decided decline in the weather. Mist prowled over the hills and steamed up the windows. Every time the front door opened, wind gusted in with the silver-grey scent of rain. But Elsie had promised Mr Underwood she would start attending services again, and you couldn't break a promise to a vicar, especially near Christmas.

In October, at Rupert's funeral, she had barely noticed the state of All Souls Church. Concentrating on the awful presence of the coffin and the body trapped within, Elsie had let her surroundings blur to nothing. But now she saw the structure take a solid form around her. It was wretched. Cold, damp and in dire need of repair.

The family pew was at the front. Elsie and Sarah were a little late and had to shuffle past rows of threadbare villagers to take their place. All the wretches looked, but none met Elsie's eye; they gave furtive, sideways glances beneath their eyelashes. Perhaps they still considered a widow bad luck.

Thankfully, the Bainbridge pew was built up and screened at the back with wood. Holes pocked the structure – she had to dust down the seat before she dared to sit on it.

'Worm,' Sarah whispered, wrinkling up her nose.

The pew door thunked shut beside them. Elsie shuddered. Locked in a wooden enclosure with the worms – it was not much different to being buried alive.

Worms were not the only discomfort. Cobwebs laced the arches and there was a relentless drip from the leaking roof. Although holly from The Bridge gardens decorated the windowsills, the place looked dreary, far from festive. It carried a mineral smell, slick and wet.

Sarah looked queasy as she surveyed her surroundings. She still wore a bandage on her hand. The apothecary at Torbury St Jude said the cut was not infected, but Elsie had her doubts. It was nearly two months now. Surely the wound should scab, at the very least?

'Are you a little off-colour, Sarah?'

'Yes . . . It is this church. When I think of my poor cousin Rupert, resting forever in such a place!'

Elsie could not answer for tears.

When she was young, she'd liked going to church. It was a place where she could walk in a higher atmosphere and breathe a higher air. But at some point – it must have been around the time Pa died – her feelings had changed. Church became a giant magnifying glass focused on her face with a crowd of people peering through. Today was not much different. The Fayford poor might not meet her eye but they were alert to her presence, like hounds scenting blood.

They went through the usual routine: hymns; a gospel reading; Mr Underwood's thoughts; the lighting of the Advent candle. By the end Sarah was trembling from cold. Elsie heard her voice shudder over the words for 'Rock of Ages'. She stretched out her arm, meaning to put it around

Sarah's shoulders, when a twang in the pit of her stomach pulled her up short.

Sarah looked at her, pop-eyed. 'Mrs Bainbridge?'

She placed a hand to her bodice and felt it again beneath the buttons: something within, kicking back.

'Is it the baby?'

'Yes. It quickens.'

Sarah beamed. Without asking for permission, she placed her palm on Elsie's belly.

A curious sensation: Sarah's heat on the surface of her skin; the child pushing back on the wet, slippery side within. Horrible, in fact. One Bainbridge on the outside, one locked away behind flesh, and she was no more than a thin barrier, a wall through which they could communicate.

She looked down at the black crêpe of her dress and at Sarah's gloved hand, grey against it. She had the strangest feeling that it was not her stomach at all – not any more. It was only a shell. *She* was a shell, and another body, a foreign body, was growing inside.

Elsie decided to walk back to The Bridge. Movement, she thought, would get her blood flowing and dispel the peculiar sense of invasion. Helen agreed to accompany her. Sarah was half-dead with cold and Mabel's leg could not carry her such a distance, so they took the carriage with Mrs Holt.

Rain had fallen during the service, leaving the footpaths slick, plastered pewter with dead leaves. Snails crept out from the undergrowth to stretch their necks. Once or twice

Elsie had to step sharply aside onto the wet grass to avoid crushing them.

'Dear me, ma'am, Mabel will have to change your clothes as soon as you get back,' Helen said. 'Won't do for you to catch cold, not in your condition.'

'Thank you, Helen, I will make sure she does.' Her ankles felt cool and numb. Another ruined pair of stockings. She only prayed her crêpe did not shrivel in the damp air.

Her boots tapped in a discordant rhythm as they crossed the bridge with the stone lions. Fine, white vapour rose up from the river. It put her in mind of the match factory. If she closed her eyes, she could imagine the smell of phosphorus, haunting her. She loathed that odour, but somehow she needed it; it was bound up in home, in Jolyon.

What would Jolyon be doing now? Making the arrangements for new girls in the dipping rooms, perhaps, and getting ready to leave the place for Christmas. Once he returned to The Bridge, she was bound to feel like herself again. This interlude without him had unsettled her. It was not natural to be separated from him.

Helen cleared her throat. 'Ma'am?'

'Yes, Helen?'

'May I ask something?'

Elsie ducked her head to avoid the dripping fingers of a branch. 'Very well.'

'What happened to your hands, ma'am?'

'Whatever do you mean?'

'Your hands. I've never seen you take your gloves off. I thought perhaps . . . maybe you hurt them?'

They prickled and throbbed beneath her black lace gloves: echoes of Helen's own hands; calloused, with swelling joints and stains ground into the skin. 'You are right, Helen. There was an accident. They were burnt.'

Helen whistled between her teeth. 'That's bad luck. You can't be too careful with fire, ma'am. Knew a woman in Torbury St Jude, once. Her little daughter's dress caught light on a candle and up she goes in flames.'

Elsie felt the cold creeping into her bones. 'Is it much farther now?'

'Not overmuch. Two more bends and you'll see the gardens.' Helen wiped the moisture from her face with the back of her hand. The chill, damp air only made her red skin look rosier. 'But while we're out here, ma'am, I did wonder . . . have you been back in the nursery?'

'Certainly not. I have had no occasion to go there.'

'Oh.' A short pause. 'Ma'am, can I ask another thing?'

'Good lord, I thought this was a walk, not an inquisition.'

'Sorry, ma'am. Only I wondered if we'd be getting some more help when the baby comes? What with Mabel being promoted and all the extra clouts and such, I won't have time to catch my breath.'

Or ask so many questions.

'Naturally, I will hire nurses for the baby at Lady Day. I have other expenses for the present.'

They must be drawing close now; she could hear the sound of shears clipping in the gardens.

Hopefully they would make it inside before another onslaught of rain. The clouds were building in formation, ready to attack. With the sun shining behind them they glowed, gunmetal grey.

'We had better send the gardeners home for the day,' she said. 'They will get too wet working in this weather.'

Helen raised her eyebrows. 'I didn't think the gardeners were come today.'

'Of course they have come, can't you hear them? Listen.'

Helen shook her head.

'They're deadheading flowers or trimming the hedges. You really cannot hear it?' The sound was growing louder, like a blade against a whetstone. *Snip, snip*. Elsie stopped walking and put her hand on Helen's arm, forcing her to pause. 'There.'

Helen blinked. She looked thoroughly witless. Elsie had never seen a more witless look – she wondered if Helen practised it.

'Never mind.'

Just as Helen promised, another two turns brought the gardens into sight. Evergreen foliage showed vivid against the backdrop of the sky. Elsie spotted a crow hopping between the dying hedges, but no gardeners. They must be working around the other side.

'I hope you won't be too downcast this Christmas, ma'am,' Helen said. 'What with the poor master and all . . . The first Christmas is always difficult.'

'Yes.'

'Master were only a few years older than me. Seems so cruel . . .'

Of all the servants, it was Helen who mentioned Rupert the most. Perhaps it was, as she said, the similarity in their ages, or the fact that she had found his body.

'You sound as if you were fond of your master, Helen. I am glad to hear it.'

She gave a half-hearted smile. 'He always spoke kindly to me. I thought it was nice of him, to notice his staff.'

Heaven knew the London ones didn't deserve his notice. Spiteful ingrates, they were, for all their efficiency.

'And then,' Helen went on, 'he'd tell me little things about his day. Like reading that book, and finding the letters in the nursery.'

The nursery again. Elsie shuddered as a raindrop fell from a branch and trickled down her back. 'You must give up this fancy, Helen. You have already told me that Mr Bainbridge presumed the letters were left that way by the previous occupant. *He* did not think it was a ghost.'

'No,' she admitted. 'But he didn't know I'd tidied them up the week before and put them all in a box. And he never saw the writing in the dust. *Mother*, it said, that day. Usually it's a whole sentence.' Elsie did not want to hear that sentence, but Helen was clearly going to tell her. '*Mother hurt me*, it says.'

She couldn't answer.

They were nearing the house. Elsie clopped around the dew-sprinkled hedges. They gave off a green, mossy smell. She could still hear those relentless shears, and the sound began to grate on her nerves.

As they drew level with the stone fountain, Helen chirped up again. 'What do you think it is then, ma'am? Writing to me?'

'It is Mabel,' she snapped, irritated. 'Playing a joke on you. She writes it and then pretends she cannot see it. Nothing could be simpler.'

'Mabel? But she can't even read her own name, ma'am, let alone—' The end of Helen's sentence disappeared in a gasp.

Elsie snapped around to face her. 'What? What is it?' The roses had fled from Helen's cheeks. Even her lips were pale. 'Are you unwell?'

Helen extended a finger, pointing.

Elsie didn't want to see. She didn't want her eyes to follow the direction of that finger, but they *would* drift, slowly, without her volition, trained by some fatal instinct.

The wooden girl stood looking out of the card-room window. Shadows like twigs obscured her face. Antlers – they were antlers. She was placed directly underneath the stag's head. But that was not what caught Elsie's eye: it was the window to the left.

The rectangle with a muddy hand printed on the glass.

'Perhaps the gardeners . . .'

'No.' Helen swallowed. 'Look, the mark's on the inside.'

It was difficult to breathe. The baby was moving, turning somersaults in her stomach. Still the air rang with the sound of those damned shears: *snip, snip.*

Elsie shook herself. *A mountain out of a molehill* – that's what Ma would say. Mabel, or even Helen herself, could have made the mark by accident.

'Nonsense. You cannot see if the print is inside or out from all the way over here.'

Elsie strode forward with more determination than she felt. Helen's voice pleaded with her to stop, but she could not change course now. Her feet moved without her – she was left behind.

Another step and the muddy print bobbed closer, coming into focus. Too small. It could not be a gardener. This was a child's hand.

She drew to a halt just before the window, so near that her breath misted the glass. As it cleared, she saw her own face reflected back, overlaying the wooden features of the companion. Only it was not her face – not really. It was pale and warped, ugly with fear.

Trembling, Elsie reached out her glove and placed her palm against the mud hand. Helen was right. The print came from the other side.

'Ma'am? Can you see it? Is there writing?'

She opened her mouth to reply when a flicker, a small movement behind the glass, drew her attention. She recoiled.

'Ma'am? Are you all right?'

She managed a nod; she could not speak.

The companion no longer looked out across the grounds. She stared, dead and unblinking, right into Elsie's soul.

Mabel had not been lying. Its eyes *moved*.

———

Draughts flowed down the maroon corridor. Shadows rocked across the flock wallpaper as the gas lamps fired up with a roar. Elsie huddled in her shawl, cowering against Sarah's shoulder. She had never felt so overpowered, so *swallowed* as she did in this house.

'This one,' said Sarah. She extended a finger and let the tip hover an inch away from the painting. 'Do you see? Behind the woman's skirts?'

It was a baroque piece, close to the style of Vermeer. A plump blonde woman with tired eyes sat before a birdcage. She held out her hand to a sparrow perched inside. Light hit them from the left, falling full upon her face. She was pretty, if a little jowly. Coral ribbons threaded through her hair, echoing the shade of the fur-trimmed mantle about her shoulders. Butter-cream skirts tumbled out from her waist, and clutching at them was a girl. A fey girl with that odd, puppet-like appearance prevalent among children in early portraiture. She did not look at the sparrow but gazed, intently, up at the lady's face.

Giddiness washed over her. 'It's *her*. Sarah, it's her. It's the same girl as the companion.'

Hiss.

Elsie's fingers clutched Sarah's sleeve, wrinkling the lavender fabric. 'Do you hear . . .?'

'The builders,' Sarah said softly.

Elsie gulped a breath. Air rushed into her lungs, soured by the taste of paint. Of course, it was not the sound that came at night, so reminiscent of a saw – it was a *real* saw. Real decorators, ready to make her house presentable. 'Of course. I forgot.'

Sarah returned to the picture. 'I thought she looked like the companion too. Perhaps a bit younger. But here is the really interesting thing. Look at the writing on the frame.'

'Sixteen-thirty,' Elsie read.

'Yes. And the name. *Anne Bainbridge with her daughter Henrietta Maria.*'

'Henrietta Maria.'

'But they called her Hetta.'

'How do you know?'

'She is one of my ancestors! Hetta, the gypsy boy, the companions – they are all in the diary we found in the garret. Poor Hetta was mute. Her mother wasn't meant to have any more children, but she took some herbs and Hetta was born without a proper tongue. Poor girl! You know how it was in those days, they thought afflicted children were cursed. She was left out of everything. Just a sweet, lonely girl . . . I *cannot* believe – I mean, even supposing that her eyes did move . . .'

'They moved.'

'Well.' Sarah's brows drew together. She had never laughed – Elsie was eternally grateful for that. Sarah tackled the problem as if it were a complicated sum that needed to be solved. 'What if the wooden figure is channelling the spirit of this Henrietta Maria Bainbridge? Does it follow that she means us harm? I cannot believe it.' She shook her head. 'Hetta just wants someone to look after her. A friend. She was so alone. I know how that feels.'

Elsie shuddered. 'Is this what we have come to now? Talk of ghosts and spirit possession?'

'Do you not believe in the spirits?' Sarah looked astounded. Elsie might as well have said she didn't believe in colour. 'I can assure you they are real, Mrs Bainbridge. I've seen them. A mesmerist visited Mrs Crabbly, and a medium, to contact her dead husband. All the rich old ladies do it in London. It's quite safe. It's a science. There's nothing to be afraid of.'

Then why did her pulse beat so thick? 'I *am* afraid. I'm afraid of the gypsy companion and the woman with the child on her lap. There's something the matter with them. They feel . . . wrong.'

'Perhaps what you saw on the glass was Hetta's hand, reaching out to us? We should try to make contact with her. I've read a book about séances. I attempted to summon my parents once—'

Elsie groaned. 'In God's name, no! You must stop talking as if this is a real child. I had Mrs Holt lock her in the cellar with all the others, for goodness' sake!'

'It's not as foolish as it sounds. There *was* a real child. This picture and the diary prove it. I am trying to recall what happened in the last diary entry I read . . . Anne's husband gave her your diamond necklace, I remember that. Did you know it was commissioned especially for the visit of Charles I?'

'That is hardly relevant right now.'

'No, I suppose not . . . Oh yes, poor Hetta was forbidden to attend the court masque! Her father was afraid she would shame him.'

Elsie took a steadying breath and tried to conceal her irritation. 'I doubt a spirit would take the trouble to haunt us over a court masque she missed two hundred years ago.'

'No,' Sarah said thoughtfully. 'There must be something else. I will have to finish reading the diary. If only I had grabbed the second volume before the garret door jammed!'

'The man is working on the door now. When he is done we will fetch the book and see if we can find a clue.'

There was a way forwards, she just had to keep her terror under control for a while longer. In two weeks it would be Christmas. Her new dresses would arrive and Jolyon would come down. He would bring plum pudding, oranges studded with cloves, parcels wrapped in coloured ribbon; all the warmth and vibrancy she had lacked. Everything would be all right once Jolyon arrived, she told herself.

Then she heard the scream.

'Mabel! It sounds like Mabel.'

They tumbled down the corridor to the Lantern Gallery. Mrs Holt and Helen galloped up the staircase from below to meet them. Helen still had a wet apron and a wooden clothes-beater in her hand. She wielded it like a weapon.

'Mrs Bainbridge! Miss Bainbridge. What is the matter?' Mrs Holt looked stricken.

'We don't know,' Sarah said. 'We think it's Mabel, upstairs.'

Their feet thumped on the risers. Elsie was out of breath and her bodice cut under her arms, but she managed to gain the landing first. She took three steps before colliding with a shape hurtling in the opposite direction.

'Mabel! Mabel!' The girl looked almost feral. Tears streamed down her face. Elsie seized her shoulders and held her steady. 'What has happened?'

'How could you? How could you?' Her fists pounded against Elsie's breast. 'How can you be so wicked? Oh, oh!'

'What? What are you talking about?'

'You know! You know!' Mabel's knees gave way; she crumpled to the floor. 'It weren't funny. I was that scared ...' She began to sob.

Elsie released her and looked helplessly from Sarah to Mrs Holt and then to Helen. 'Helen, can you try to get some sense from her?'

Helen laid her beater on the floor. Tentatively, she placed a hand on Mabel's shoulder. 'Hush, now. What happened? It wasn't ...' She dropped her voice to a whisper. 'Did you see another one?'

'She – she—' Mabel could barely speak. '*She* must have put it in my room. Knows I hates them! All part of some – some joke!'

Prickles darted up and down Elsie's skin. 'What is in your room, Mabel?'

'As if you don't know! One of them *things*!'

She looked at Sarah. 'No. That cannot be. Mrs Holt locked all the companions in the cellar. I saw her do it.'

'Not this one. I never seen it before.'

Blood thumped in her ears. 'No. No, I will not believe this.'

Rigid with determination, Elsie stalked down the corridor. She would see it with her own eyes. She would prove them wrong.

The door swung open with ease, revealing Mabel's narrow bed, the washstand and the prints on the wall.

It was standing in the hip bath.

A stout woman, brushing her hair. Her kirtle was the colour of pickled gherkins. She wore dirty linen oversleeves and an apron that fell to her ankles. Her expression teased as she swept the brush through the ends of her wavy brown hair, the other hand smoothing behind. It was a flirtatious look, yet somehow hostile.

'Go on then,' Elsie croaked. She was light-headed with a sense of her own bravado. 'Move if you're going to do it. Move, damn you, move!'

The eyes remained still. But she heard, just at the edge of her consciousness, the sound of bristles tearing through dry hair. The scent of roses flared up, thick and choking. Suddenly it was very warm.

Her mind would not stand it. Whirling round, she slammed the door shut and ran back down the corridor. Her legs refused to move with their usual speed. She was slow now, weighted by the baby. Vulnerable.

The others were waiting on the landing. They had coaxed Mabel onto a chair and she was dry-faced, very pale.

'It was locked,' Mrs Holt said. 'I swear it was locked. Mrs Bainbridge doesn't have the key, Mabel. I just don't understand how this has happened.'

'Mabel.' Elsie tried to keep her voice steady but it was a strange, swooping thing, beyond her control. 'All of you. I want you to think, very carefully. Who has been in the house? We have had tradesmen and workmen. Gardeners. I want you to make a list. Someone, somewhere, for whatever reason, is playing a trick upon us. Putting handprints on the windows and . . .' She frowned, distracted by a glint of light. 'Mabel, are you wearing my diamonds?'

Colour flared into the maid's cheeks. 'I were warming them, ma'am. That's what Helen says they do, in the fancy houses. Ain't it, Helen? Warm the mistress's pearls.'

'Warming them?' Sarah cried. 'A likely story! Mrs Bainbridge cannot even wear them during her mourning.'

Elsie had ridden a crest of anxiety all day. It had to break. Anger flickered through her fear and she seized it with both hands. 'Take them off!' she shouted. 'Take them off at once!' Fresh tears spurting, Mabel grappled at the base of her neck, but her hair was tangled in the chain. 'If you don't take them off this minute, I will send you out of this house!'

Helen stepped in with her steady, chafed hands. She unfastened the clasp and pulled the necklace away. Threads of Mabel's dark hair still clung to the chain.

'Didn't mean no harm,' Mabel muttered, rocking. 'Didn't mean no harm, didn't deserve no bloody thing in my room.'

There was a bang, then a shout rang out in the east wing.

Elsie's eyes met Sarah's. 'It sounds like they have prised the garret door open,' she whispered. 'Go and get the second part of that diary.'

Sarah went at once.

Mrs Holt paced up and down, pressing her hands together. 'Dear me, dear me. What a to-do! And the laundry not even finished . . .'

Elsie looked at Mabel, shivering in Helen's arms. She felt calmer now; slightly ashamed of her harsh words. 'Look, Mabel, whatever you think, I did not place that companion in your room. I am starting to hate them just as much as you do.'

Mabel looked up at her, but she could not read the expression.

Sarah returned at a run, breathless and empty-handed. She looked queer. Pale, shivering like a whippet.

'Sarah, what is it? Has the book gone?'

'No, it's there but she didn't . . .' She gulped down a breath. 'She didn't want me to take it. I could feel that the poor soul didn't want me to read it.'

'What are you talking about?'

'She was in there.' Sarah's chin trembled. 'Hetta was in the garret.'

———

It was cold enough for snow, but Peters and Stilford sweated as they stood in the yard, swinging down the axe-heads again and again, *thunk*, *thunk*. Piece by piece, chunk by chunk, the wood splintered away, first brown then maggot-white, stringy and harder to cut. Peters rested for a moment, one hand on his hip. A miscellany of body parts lay heaped before him: wooden heads, severed wooden hands.

Elsie huddled by the kitchen door with Sarah and the female servants, wearing her heaviest cloak. She wished she were a man. If she had strength to pick up an axe she would do it; hack that gypsy boy's face to bits. She thought of the circular saw in the match factory, newly cut splints rattling from its teeth into the trough. A shiver ran through her.

'It seems such a shame,' whined Sarah. 'They are antiques! My ancestor Anne Bainbridge bought them in sixteen thirty-five. Could we not at least have tried to sell them?'

'Who would pay good money to have a bunch of dolls give them the willies?' Mabel cried. 'They'd have to be touched in the head, ma'am.'

Sarah bit her lips. She was unhappy and it made Elsie feel uncomfortable. By rights, the companions belonged to a descendant of Bainbridge blood – not an interloper, a mere Bainbridge by marriage. She was destroying Sarah's heritage. But what else was she supposed to do? Have them cropping up all over the house like jack-in-the-boxes, scaring the life out of them all?

'The extra firewood will come in handy for the winter,' Mrs Holt put in.

Elsie's skin itched. 'No. I do not want to burn them inside the house. I do not think that would be . . . wise.'

'Could I give it to the villagers then, madam? In Fayford?'

The axe whistled through the air again, followed by the clop of falling wood.

'Perhaps it is best if we just burn them here, in the yard.'

Mrs Holt did not reply, but Elsie heard her little cluck of disapproval.

Was she being foolish? It did seem silly, now the companions lay dismembered on the cobbles – a nervous reaction from an overwrought female. And yet the horses were uneasy, their ears flat, the whites of their eyes rolling. Beatrice the cow was keeping well back in her stable, lipping another clump of hay from her net. The animals knew. Animals always sensed these things.

'Right then,' Peters panted. Perspiration ran into his eyes. 'Last one.'

They all turned to look at the one Sarah called Hetta. Poised, silent and alone, she gazed over the massacred remains of her fellows; her smile serene, the white rose against her breast.

Elsie did not think she could watch Peters chop this last one up. What would it be like to see the lineaments of that face, so like her own in childhood, fractured? The past amputated, then going up in flames.

Peters took a step forwards.

'No!' It was Sarah. 'No, please. We cannot! Not Hetta. She has suffered enough already.'

Elsie averted her head so that the side of her bonnet hid Sarah and the companion from view. 'We have to, Sarah. There is something about these things, something . . . wrong.'

'How do you know it is wrong? You only know that it scares you.'

A child's hand on the window, the slide of those eyes . . .

'Yes, it scares me. That is reason enough. What do you think it is doing to my baby, having all these jumps and frights?'

'But Hetta is my ancestor. I've read about her, I feel that I know her.' Sarah's voice slid from pleading to desperation.

'What if she is trying to contact us? If she is asking me to right an injustice? I cannot fail her!'

They said that, didn't they? That the murdered could not rest but wandered, seeking justice. Elsie knew for a fact it was nonsense. It must be that old woman Mrs Crabbly, putting notions into Sarah's head. Mesmerism, indeed!

'Miss Sarah,' said Mrs Holt, 'if I may be so bold as to say so . . . I've lived in this house since I was a young woman. We never had any ghosts!'

Helen sniffed.

'But you are not related to Hetta!' There was a fanatic energy about Sarah. 'She would not try to reach *you*. We are alike, she and I. Please let me keep her. At least until I have finished the diary.'

A sound came from the pile of companions – a dry creaking, like beams settling. She had to decide. Soon it would grow dark.

'Do it,' Mabel whispered. 'Hack her up and burn the buggers to hell.'

Mrs Holt whirled round. 'Mabel!'

Elsie sighed. The world was full of them, past and present: sad, lonely little girls. *She has suffered enough already.* Was Sarah talking about Hetta, or herself?

Elsie had already taken Sarah's house and her diamond necklace. There was no doubt what Rupert would want her to do now.

'Sarah may keep Hetta, if it is so important to her. But mark me, I want it kept locked up in the garret, not in my house, not anywhere near my baby.'

'Oh thank you, thank you, Mrs Bainbridge!' Sarah squealed. 'I know you are doing the right thing.' A red circle glowed on either cheek. Her eyes were glittering, like frost.

'In the garret, do you understand?'

'Yes, yes. I will keep her in the garret, that is no trouble at all.'

Sarah seized Hetta as if she were snatching her from the jaws of death. She held the painted side against her body, but she could not manoeuvre it with her bad hand.

'Who will help me move her upstairs?'

Both Mabel and Helen stepped back.

'For heaven's sake!' cried Mrs Holt. She jangled her keys and unlocked the kitchen door. 'Come along then, Miss Sarah. My girls have become afraid of their own shadows.'

As soon as they were inside, Elsie withdrew a box of matches from her pocket. Peters held out his hand, but she shook her head. She wanted to set the fire herself.

'About time, too,' whispered Mabel.

Elsie approached the woodpile. The wind picked up and her veil billowed out behind her like dark smoke. She had a vision of herself, standing there, black and solemn.

The companions were a jigsaw of parts: the gypsy's hair, scalped; that horrendous stiff baby, severed in half. They could not scare her now. Withdrawing a matchstick, she scratched it along the sandpaper.

A spark, a flare of blue, then the orange flame. Warmth prickled through her gloves. She watched the light bob in the breeze, feeling the power there in her fingers, ready to release with a single flick. She could smell the smoke already.

'Do it, ma'am,' Helen urged.

She let the match fall.

Wood cracked and the pile burst into a blaze. An eye watched her from beneath a flicker of flame. It melted, bleeding down the cheek, the colours running.

THE BRIDGE, 1635

I thought I had done the right thing. I thought all was well.

The gypsy boy, who calls himself Merripen, is established in the stables. He has taken a solemn vow not to leave doors unlocked or abet his thieving kin. I know what these people are like.

Ever since I relented towards her friend, Hetta has been all sweetness and light, running up and down the stairs with her spaniels bumping after her, cutting swathes of herbs for the kitchen and marvelling over my diamonds. I was surprised by her glee, but I was also proud of her. I thought she had conquered her disappointment like a lady. I assumed it was enough for her to have her friend in employment. *How well Josiah has managed her*, I said to myself. How was I to know? How could I dream that he had not even told her?

It all started when the boys arrived. The weather was sultry, uncomfortably close. All morning the magpies chittered, cackling their secrets. But my sons were in high spirits, tumbling from their carriage on their gangly legs, slapping one another on the shoulders.

James led the way into the Great Hall. Henry towered over him. He has shot up this year, tall and thin like a reed, like one of Hetta's saplings. And Charles—! I never can believe that Charles came from my body. He is wide, sturdy and built with the strength of a mastiff. No wonder he wreaked so much damage; no wonder the midwife said . . . But that does not matter now.

We were full of embraces, full of news. Dinner passed in a happy, raucous blur and Hetta was smiling, smiling all the while. Once we had eaten, she showed her brothers the preparations for the masque: trap-doors and levers; platforms made to look like clouds. She tried a pirouette and James swept her into his arms, flying her around the painted backdrop of a blue sky.

It was then that another man arrived from Mr Samuels's shop with boxes.

'More!' Josiah pretended to be scandalised, but I saw he was pleased with every single choice I had made.

'We will astound the Queen with our curiosities,' I said. 'The Bridge will be the greatest showpiece she has ever seen.'

This time it was the counterfeit people – the wooden figures Mr Samuels called his companions. What wonders they are! The lady from the shop was there, and many more besides: a sleeping child; a lady with her lute; a gentleman with a doxy on his lap.

'God's blood! Did you ever see the like?' Charles went over and touched one with his fat hand. 'A person stepped right out of a portrait!'

Hetta gave a high, loud squeal of delight, like a dog when it sees its master. She bounded over to Charles's side and gazed up at the figures, wonder written all over her face. As the boys chattered, she weaved in and around the boards, fingering their edges.

'Hello,' said Henry. 'Henrietta Maria's playing hide and go seek.'

So that's what we did all day while the servants worked to make the house perfect: ran about like children, placing the companions in the strangest places, trying to make each other jump.

'They need to look real,' I said. 'I want people to come upon them and start. I want the King to bump into a companion and beg his pardon!'

We found a thousand nooks and crannies in the house, a thousand corners to position them just right. As the light fell, the wooden figures watched me from their hiding places and they seemed to smirk, complicit. They promised to give the Queen the surprise of her life.

'It will be a triumph,' Josiah laughed. 'The whole thing a triumph.'

It had grown rather late, but none of us could settle for a quiet hour of reading before supper; we were feverish, highly strung. In less than forty-eight hours, royalty would be in our house. Already the place was coming alive in a way it has never done before. We had prepared as far as we could. Now there was nothing to do but wait.

'When do we rehearse the masque?' James said, pale and anxious in the candlelight. 'I practised the steps you sent me but I would rather do it here.'

'Tomorrow,' I told him. 'The players are coming tomorrow.'

'*The Triumph of Platonic Love*. It sounds very well, doesn't it?' Henry stroked the lace at his cuffs. 'Not that we will rival Mr Jones's pieces in any way, but I'm sure the Queen will be pleased. Do you dance, Charles?'

The three boys erupted into laughter. I have seen Charles dance but twice since he was a small boy: it is not a performance designed to inspire maternal pride. He has no sense of time or grace, and his stout figure makes him most comical.

Charles took the jibe on the nose, though he pretended to glower and shook his fist at his brother. 'Oh, wouldn't you like to see it? But I have no wish to put the Queen in a fright. I swagger on and do my speech, that's all. And what a speech!'

I was so busy laughing with the boys that I did not notice Hetta stealing up to where Josiah sat on the chair before the fire. It was only when I heard him speak that I turned to see her beside the armrest, tugging on his sleeve.

'Yes, Henrietta Maria? What is it?' She blinked her big eyes, green splintered with gold and brown in the firelight. 'Well? What is it that you want?'

I should have known then. I should have paid attention to the shadows scurrying over her face and the queer, frightening hush. But I just sat there, dumb, and watched them; watched Hetta point to her chest, her eyes alive with expectation.

'How now?' Charles called. 'Speak up, little Hetta!'

The boys hooted again.

'Leave her alone, Charles!' I snapped, but it only made them laugh harder. They were so excited, I believe they would have laughed at death itself.

'It is only in jest, Mother.'

'I really cannot understand what Henrietta Maria is trying to communicate,' Josiah said. 'Anne, have you any idea?'

Slowly, carefully, Hetta rose onto the tips of her toes and turned a perfect pirouette, her arms arched above her tortoiseshell head. She looked like a dream, like a French courtier dancing ballet. I had not known she could dance like that. But the sight did not fill me with pleasure or a mother's pride. I saw the light in her face, and the guilty scowl upon Josiah's, and all the pieces slotted into place.

'She wants to know her part!' Henry bleated. 'What part will Henrietta Maria have in the masque, Father?'

No, I thought. *Not like this. Not in front of her brothers*. But Josiah did it anyway. He swirled the drink in his glass and said, very quietly, 'Henrietta Maria will not be in the masque.'

She dropped back to the flats of her feet. I could not look at her face. I stared into the chasms between the logs on the fire, wishing they would swallow me.

'Not even a little part?' Charles's voice – too loud, too jovial. 'I'm sure we could slot her in somewhere. Not a speaking part, mind!'

James and Henry guffawed.

'She is too young,' said Josiah. 'She is still too young for these things. She will feast with us and then she will go to bed.'

The boys had been away for too long: they did not recognise the warning in their father's voice. Drunk on their own humour, they called out ideas.

'Make her a cupid.'

'Love is blind, so why not silent?'

'Have her act in the antimasque.'

'What, as a devil? Do they have tiny devils?'

'Oh yes, they're the fiercest. Mr Jones always makes them erupt from a cloud of smoke.'

'Doesn't he do that with the Queen's dwarves?'

'Aye, but there's always a shortage of good dwarves. Dress up a girl and paint on a beard, that's what I say.'

'Heigh-ho! We'll stick her in the menagerie! Her Majesty likes to collect queer and curious people.'

'I warrant you, there's none more curious than my sister.'

'Enough!' The drink slopped out of Josiah's glass as he sat forwards in the chair. 'Enough, all of you.' His growl cut through the chatter, through my skin. 'What is this knavish talk? I thought you had grown into men.'

The boys hung their heads, chastened.

'We were only—'

'It does not matter, Henry. The King and Queen will be here soon, do you understand? I won't have my sons behaving like fools.'

'No, Father.'

'I have said that Henrietta Maria will not stay for the entertainment, and that is an end of it.'

I might have borne it if she had stamped her foot, if she had cried, or shoved me as she tried to do that time in the garden. But she did nothing. She dropped onto her knees by the side of the fire and folded her hands into her lap. She did not sob. She did not move. She stared into the fire, as I had done, fixated on something within its depths.

They all went to bed, but neither Lizzy nor I could move Hetta. We could not make her look at us. She might have transformed into one of the wooden boards, for all the expression on her blank face.

'Your diamonds?' Lizzy suggested.

I placed them about Hetta's slender throat, to no avail. They simply flickered against her skin, red and orange in turn.

We had to leave her there, watching the logs dwindle into ashy piles. My daughter, alone in the dark with the dying flames.

———

I cannot sleep. My ears are alive with tunes that will not fade, playing over and over, on and on. When I close my eyes I see champagne satin, scarlet taffeta and gold-tipped lacing. My body feels as though it is dancing still. I know that my heart is. Josiah was right: it was a triumph.

They arrived a little after noon, with their heralds and gentlemen-at-arms forging the way. A magnificent sight: a glimmering ribbon of horses, armour and riches, winding beside the river and over the hills. No Fayford Puritans interfered with the cavalcade, but neither did they come out to cheer. I had planned for that. I hired common folk from Torbury St Jude to wave banners and give the loyal address. They did it creditably.

Barges on the river blasted a fanfare as the royal couple crossed the bridge. Jackdaws scattered before the pound of hooves. The fountain flowed with wine, ruby red, spilling out of the stone dog's mouth to patter in the basin.

I found the King shorter than I expected and slender too; almost dainty. Dressed all in black, he had a sharp beard and sleepy eyes. He looked older than his years. Around his neck gleamed the only relief of colour in his sober apparel: a silver lace collar, delicate and fine as a spider's web.

And she! I thought I should faint to see the Queen's elfin figure skip down from her horse. She was dazzling and bright and utterly infectious; laughing, singing, talking all day long. Her hair gleamed like jet, her dark eyes danced. Lizzy calls her a papist conjurer and perhaps she is, for a moment in her company bewitches the senses.

We feasted at trestle tables in the Great Hall. Quail eggs, salmon, cock's-combs, sweet potatoes, dates, artichokes laid out on gold plates; everything perfectly seasoned with Hetta's herbs. I did not realise until then how hard she had worked.

She has been very solemn, very correct in her behaviour since the night Josiah forbade her from the masque. All through the feast she sat watching with a curious expression as the courtiers ate and gossiped. I expected her to giggle, to try and touch the ladies' bouncing curls, but she did not. She simply cocked her head like her pet sparrow and observed. I wish I could decipher the tangle of her thoughts. I wish that I, like our Creator, could read the mind of the girl I have made. How is it I can hear Josiah, but not her?

She did not appear to enjoy the feast – with her small and misshapen tongue, food is seldom a great source of enjoyment to her. Yet when Lizzy came to take her off to bed, a most rare expression took possession of her features. She left with a smile screwed to her face – but such a smile! It was a blast of cold air, not her usual ray of sunshine.

It did not trouble me much then, to think of her upstairs. Like a heartless woman, I was enjoying myself too much to notice. But now the image makes me tearful: the silent girl sitting with her pet sparrow while shrieks of laughter and notes of music drift up to her from below. Poor child. It should not have been her, marooned like a leper: it should have been me.

All I wanted was a daughter to keep, a female companion to fill the void left by my sister Mary. I wanted her so hungrily that I did not care how I begot her. It was *I* who scorched my fingertips with witch-craft; I who mixed the draught and took God's power into my own hands. Why should Hetta be punished for my greed?

She missed the acrobats in the Lantern Gallery, the tumblers dancing on wires above the Great Hall in their shimmering costumes. She did not see the fire-works leap into the sky and explode over the gardens. She could not join in the squeals and surprise as our silent companions made the guests jump, again and again. But perhaps it is as well that she missed the masque.

I did not realise until the performance began how the house had transformed itself into a pagan glen full of nymphs and satyrs. My chariot of shells glided onto the stage in the Great Hall and I performed my dance with the diamonds blazing from my neck. Mermaids pranced in diaphanous dresses, singing their siren song. Petals fell from the gallery. The air was thick with burning orange water. What would Lizzy have thought, had she seen it, never mind the Puritans of Fayford!

Perhaps it *is* wicked, perhaps it is wrong, this court of endless luxury. But oh, it is intoxicating! And now I have witnessed it, I do not know how I will ever do without it.

My eyes are heavy after all this writing. Each time I begin to drift, I see the antimasque: the evil magicians and their minions cavorting from a fiery cave. Awful creatures: strange, stunted men with overgrown heads. Cackles drifting through the orange smoke. If I fall asleep with these images, I will have hideous dreams.

I was shocked by the Queen's freaks; I own it. I had not seen things like that before, things unnatural and somehow obscene. I would say they should not exist, they should not *be*, but then I remember Hetta and I am ashamed. For people say the same devil that disfigures them stunted my daughter's tongue.

Who can compare Hetta with one of those cursed creatures? They are not beautiful; they are strange and unbalanced. Especially the one who never unmasked but haunted the dances with his leering red face, capering, like a many-legged insect, and frightening my guests. I scc him when I close my eyes; moving quickly, winding around dancers, his short body swallowed by wafts of smoke.

Outside banks of cloud are building up, grey spectres against the black. I think we will have rain at last. Thunder prowls around the trees and in the distance, off towards Fayford, I see a fork of lightning sizzle through the sky. If it rains too hard, perhaps the court will not be able to leave. Perhaps we will be allowed to keep them.

The thunder cracks outside. My fevered imagination hears a cry, rising up from the night. Yet there is nothing, not even a fox outside my window.

Lightning floods the room with white light. I see my face in the glass, fleeting, afraid. 'Hetta is nothing like the freaks,' I whisper to it, before I blow out my candle. 'She is *nothing* like them.'

THE BRIDGE, 1865

Sarah sat at the piano, clunking out festive tunes awkwardly with one hand. The window behind her stood open, letting in frigid air. Her fingers trembled on the keys.

'Close the window, Sarah. You look chilled.'

Her gaze rose above the top of the piano. 'I like the air. I like to feel as if I am . . . outside.' A few discordant notes clanged. She looked back down to the keys.

So Sarah felt it also: this strange pressure; the stuffy, cloying warmth that infused the house. The smell, too. Ever since the bonfire, Elsie could not shift the smell of burning from her nostrils. It reminded her of the wooden baby, sliced in two, no anger or hurt in its eyes – just that awful, chilling blankness.

She sighed and returned to wrapping Jolyon's present. At least her dear boy would arrive soon with news of London, the rational world. What would he make of her improvements to The Bridge? New paper was up in the nursery: a corn-coloured background with birds and branches in the oriental fashion. The drawing room had new panelling, set with gilt roundels. Best of all she'd arranged for the gardeners to set up great fir trees in pots around the grounds and string them with lanterns. As a boy, Jolyon had stared round-eyed at the shop windows at Christmas, mesmerised by candles and mechanical toys. Now she finally had the money to spare for frivolities. She was going to give him the Christmas he deserved.

She was adjusting a ribbon when a high note chimed from the piano, echoing up to the moulded ceiling. It lingered on its own, pathetic and fragile, before dying out.

'Mrs Bainbridge,' Sarah whispered. 'Mrs Bainbridge, look.'

She froze. Her sweating hands made her gloves clammy on the wrapping paper. Inch by inch, she raised her eyes, steeling herself for something awful.

It was a sparrow. Only a little sparrow, perched on the lid of the piano. He tilted his head from side to side, regarding them. Tiny black eyes darted above his beak.

'He's beautiful.' She kept her voice low, trying not to startle the bird. 'Better not let Jasper see him.'

Sarah smiled. 'Have you any crumbs left? We could lay them along the piano for him to gather up.'

Elsie looked to the side table. The plate there was speckled with grains of cake, perhaps a dozen or so. 'I do. But I don't want to get up and frighten him.'

The sparrow hopped forwards. Pulling back his wings, he puffed out his chest and parted his delicate beak, ready to sing.

At that instant, three blows fell on the front door. Quick as a dart, the sparrow flew through the open window. A single brown feather drifted down on the piano.

'Who could that be?' Elsie went to the window and tried to peer around the brick mass of the east wing. She could only glimpse the drive – no carriages.

'I think . . .' Sarah began tentatively, 'I think it might be Mr Underwood.'

'Mr Underwood? I do not recall inviting him.'

'No.' Sarah closed the lid of the piano over the keys. 'No, you didn't. I'm terribly sorry, Mrs Bainbridge. It was me. I invited him.'

'Oh. I see.'

'It's just that . . .'

'You might have mentioned it.' She felt wrong-footed. In some way – she was not sure how – she had been insulted. 'I am not prepared to receive guests.'

'But I did not invite him as a guest.' Sarah stood and nervously began to smooth her hair. 'More as an . . . advisor.'

Another trio of knocks, quicker this time.

'Whatever do you mean?'

'I want to ask him about Hetta.'

Dread bobbed in her stomach. 'Sarah—'

'I thought perhaps he would know what to do. The Church performed exorcisms, in the past.'

Exorcism. The word was guttural, too far back in the throat. Saying it aloud was like gagging, like beginning to speak in demonic tongues yourself. What was Sarah *thinking*?

'You are not seriously going to ask him to perform some kind of ritual?'

'No! Oh no, I don't think Hetta needs *banishing* or anything like that. I simply want his advice.'

The house-bell jangled.

'Clearly, no one is going to answer the door,' Elsie said. 'I had better do it myself.'

She was relieved to have an excuse to leave the room and escape Sarah's intense expression. At least Mr Underwood would set her straight. He was a man of faith but not, she thought, of superstition.

The Great Hall was dingy and chill. The fire, though lit, did not draw well. No light glinted on the ceremonial swords or the suit of armour; they were dull, pewter grey. Air whipped in through the open front door. Underwood stood on the threshold, holding a long box.

'Good day, Mrs Bainbridge. Forgive the intrusion. I rang the bell but the door was ajar and I found this, lying on the step.'

'It will be my new gown! I've been expecting it from Torbury St Jude all week.'

'Just in time for Christmas. How fortunate.' He came in and placed the box onto the oriental rug for her. She knelt down – no easy task these days, with her budding stomach – and ran a hand over the package. There was no tag, no label, only a ribbon of olive and gold.

Mr Underwood removed his hat. It had squashed his blond hair flat against the scalp. 'I wonder, is Miss Bainbridge at home? I received a note from her, asking to speak with me. I must say, I was alarmed. Her message sounded . . . confused.'

'She is in the music room.' Elsie stared down at the package. She had an urge to confess everything: tell him about the splinters on Rupert's neck; the nursery; the garret; the handprint; the eyes. But to speak of such things made them a farce. You could not explain fear; you could only feel it, roaring through the silence and striking your heart still. 'I feel I should warn you, Mr Underwood, that Miss Bainbridge wishes to discuss her beliefs. They are . . . unconventional. She used to work for a very old, very fanciful lady. I gather she was part of some spiritualist circle.'

'Ah.'

'I hope you will support me when I say I am – cautious – about such things.'

'Absolutely. While the Church does not deny the existence of spirits, it is strongly against meddling in that field. Consider the Witch of Endor and the curse on King Saul for consulting a medium.'

It came to her in snatches of Sunday-school memory: King Saul, desperate for the advice of his prophet Samuel, begging the woman to resurrect him. *Why hast thou disquieted me, to bring me up?*

The disturbing recollection was, she had done it. The thing had been possible.

Elsie cleared her throat. 'You must understand Sarah is particularly susceptible to these sham mesmerists and mediums. Her parents died when she was young. Without family she is vulnerable . . . May I trust you to try and dissuade her from these rash methods? With gentleness?'

'You have my word upon it.' She looked up from where she knelt on the floor. He regarded her softly – almost, she feared, tenderly. 'It is as I once said to you: I want to school Fayford and eradicate superstitions like this.'

'I have been thinking, Mr Underwood, about Fayford. My brother will come up from London for the holiday. If you could recommend some likely girls from the village, I might persuade him to take them back as apprentices. The wage is not high, but all our children get schooling – at least two hours a day. They will have employment, food and a roof over their heads. A dry one, without leaks. Proper clothing. And at the end of their term, they will have learnt a trade. What do you say?'

'I say it is the best gift I could possibly receive.' A beatific smile illuminated his face. 'In fact, I can think of some suitable children already. Their parents cannot object to your factory. It is this house that they fear. Which reminds me.' He drew a brown paper parcel, tied with string, from his inside pocket. 'Records from town. A rather dry read, I fear, but some of it may interest you.'

She looked at the string, twined tight. Her chest felt the same. *It is this house that they fear.* She was beginning to think they had reason. The bundle of paper might provide answers but, then again, it might tell her things she did not wish to know.

'How kind of you to remember. Perhaps you could leave it in the music room when you speak to Sarah? I will sit there later and peruse it.'

He extended a hand. 'Come with me. Let us go and persuade Miss Bainbridge out of these fancies together. Between us, I am sure we can make her see sense.'

She hesitated. 'Thank you. But . . . I have already tried with Sarah. I think it would be best if she spoke to you alone, without my interference. These spiritual matters require a degree of confidentiality, after all.'

He let his hand fall and put it behind his back. 'Yes. Of course. Very wise of you to observe, Mrs Bainbridge.' He looked over his shoulder. 'This is the music room?'

'That is the drawing room. Walk through and take a right. You cannot miss it. I doubt you ever saw a chamber so pink.'

He sketched a bow. 'Thank you. I shall leave you to open your package.'

She watched him walk away, the tails of his threadbare coat swinging in time with his step.

Shifting her legs, she got into a more comfortable position and prepared to open the box. A new gown might prove just the distraction she needed. This would be her finest dress – her Christmas Day outfit.

It was difficult to untie the bow with her gloved hands but she managed. Her fingers found the edges of the lid, sweaty with anticipation. Crêpe and bombazine, braided with silk. Three-pieces, tasselled and fringed. She could not wait to see. She pulled the lid free of the box.

Screamed.

Ribbons of black material lay heaped together with dead leaves. Thistles prickled up, sticky and congealed with blood. In the midst of it all rested something black, white and furry, dotted with flies. She made out lumps of mangled flesh, bone. Veins like skeins of red silk. Then the drooping ears, the closed eyes. Blood smeared down the fur at the forehead. A cow's head.

Beatrice's head.

The stench caught in her throat and made her gag. She fell onto her back and scrabbled away, hands squeaking against the floor. She was going to be sick. She was going to be sick and yet she could not take her eyes from the box. *Beatrice. Poor Beatrice.*

Her head collided with a hard object. In utter panic, she whipped round. Hetta stood behind her, smiling still, the rose pressed to her bosom.

'No, no.'

Pitching forwards, she sent Hetta clattering to the floor. She found her feet – her legs were jelly but somehow she forced them on, up the stairs, two at a time. Her skirts caught around her ankles. She stumbled, tripped and picked herself up again. She had no idea where she was going, only that she must climb, climb – to the roof if she had to. Put as much distance as possible between her and that awful sight . . .

Dimly, she heard Mr Underwood enter the Great Hall and call her name. Then the throttled sound of Sarah's shock. But she could not stop. That scent of roses: it was following her, getting thicker and thicker with each step –

She jerked to a halt one stair short of the landing. Barring the way was another flat wooden face. A new companion, but one she recognised.

A moustache like a wire brush hung above its lip. Macassar oil smoothed the hair, a single curl falling over the left eye. Broken veins rippled on the cheek. And the eyes . . . The expression of torment in the eyes chilled her blood.

'Rupert.'

It could not be. She shut her eyes – if she looked any longer, she would go mad. But still she saw it; felt it, close to her face. Getting closer.

'No, no.'

She took two steps back. The train of her dress coiled around her ankles like a rope. Panicked, she thrashed her feet and stepped into thin air.

Three jolting knocks. Then there was only black.

THE BRIDGE, 1635

This morning I heard a man scream for the first time in my life. It is not a sound I wish to hear again: guttural, shameful, travelling across the stable yard and up through the lantern tower.

I awoke in a sweat of ice. Josiah lay in bed beside me, staring at the ceiling with the same horror I felt all over my skin. Memory fell with a sickening blow: the King and Queen. It could not be – please Almighty God – it could not be that some harm had befallen them?

The dreadful noise came from outside. It set the dogs barking. I flung myself out of bed and ran to the window. Raindrops spotted the glass, I could not see out clearly. A gauzy haze hung in the air after last night's storm. Puddles steamed in the morning heat.

'What is it?' Josiah demanded.

The reply did not come from me – it arose from that place where the dreams brood, where knowledge arrives fully formed. 'Someone is dead. Life has left this house.'

He was up in an instant, the coverlet thrown back and his bare feet thudding on the boards. I saw him snatch up his sword before he ran into the corridor.

We were not the only ones awake. Guests milled about in their nightclothes, bleary-eyed, their hair tangled from the night before. As soon as Josiah saw them, he assumed an air of calm.

'Do not be alarmed. Pray, return to your beds. I will go and find the cause of this disturbance.'

They mumbled, rubbing their eyes. Tired as they looked, they did not seem inclined to obey him.

I followed Josiah down one flight of steps, desperate to see the children safe. I found them gathered outside the nursery with Lizzy, all deathly pale. Hetta's sparrow screeched from within. Hairs raised on the back of my neck. Mary once told me that sparrows carry the souls of the dead.

'We do not know what the commotion is,' I told them. 'Your father has gone to deal with it.'

'Mistress?' Lizzy tried to catch my eye but I would not look at her. One glance, and I knew I should lose hold of my composure.

'Not now, Lizzy.'

I must appear every inch the mistress, in command. I turned my back on her to face the children. Despite her early night, Hetta looked more exhausted than the boys. I felt her forehead. She was burning up.

'Go back to bed,' I ordered. 'All of you, back to bed.'

The boys groaned. I did not heed them; could not stop to argue with them. A strange energy stirred me, a kind of nauseous excitement, and I returned the way I had come, intending to reassure the guests.

Crackling beneath all the fears in my mind was the one I could name: the plague. There had been sweltering temperatures and reports of sickness in London. Now my child was aflame with fever. I prayed to God it was not the plague.

We lost Mary to a sweating sickness. People told me it was a kind, swift death, but they did not see it. If my sister died in kindness, I dare not imagine cruelty.

She was well in the morning. Yet as we dressed, I felt it for the very first time: the sense of foreboding I have come to trust above my other senses. Our eyes met and I knew Mary felt it too. By noon she was abed.

It began with shivers. Then came the heat, scorching through her skin, running off her in rivulets of sweat. Before the night had passed, her jaw was bound. Gone. Dead at only twenty years old.

My bare feet crunched against the rushes on the floor. Beset by memories of Mary, I did not notice Jane running up the stairs. I collided with her and we both fell back, blinking, bewildered.

'Oh, mistress, forgive me.' She did not look like herself. She had been up earlier than us, I realised. She had been awake and about her duties before the scream sounded.

'Jane! Jane, tell me what has happened.'

She burst into tears.

I wrung it from her piece by piece. I did not need to go down to the stables, to smell the blood and see the

flies for myself; it was all there gleaming in the pupils
of her eyes.

There was a dead horse in the stalls. Not just dead
– mutilated. Its tail was cropped and nailed outside
the door, its mane attacked with a frenzy of scissors.
The ostler found a score of lacerations scratched in the
skin, like a tally you might carve upon a tree.

'Which horse, Jane?'

'Oh . . . m-mistress!' she sobbed.

'Not my grey mare?'

Jane shook her head. I saw a glimpse of the truth
shining back from her wet cheeks. 'W-worse.'

'No. You are not saying . . .'

'The Queen's horse!' she cried.

My legs gave way; I slumped against the wall and
then slid down it, straight to the floor. 'But who
would . . . Puritans?'

'I don't know, mistress, I don't know. Mark says
someone's missing from the stables.'

'Who?'

'A boy. A gypsy boy. Bless me if I knew we had
one! What was he thinking, taking on a nasty, dirty
beast like that?'

My blood froze. Merripen. Merripen had done it.

I do not know how. I do not know where a boy of
nine or ten years old would find the strength for this
infernal act. Where, in his young mind, would such a
hideous urge come from?

The Queen's horse! The *Queen's*!

My head splits with agony. It is my fault, mine. We
are ruined. The court will never return here. Josiah . . .

Dear God. Josiah will find out. He will know what I did, that I have destroyed his life's ambition with my foolish whim. Can a marriage withstand that? Can my heart?

God forgive me in my wickedness. I wish it *had* been the plague.

THE BRIDGE, 1866

Elsie awoke to three explosions of pain. The first in the small of her back, raking down into her thighs. The other beat her skull, at the top towards the crown, where it then radiated into her face. She felt her lip, swollen where her tooth had punctured the skin.

But these injuries were nothing compared to the third: the ripping claws in her belly.

They started softly, plucking at her internal chords, steadily building the rhythm until she screamed. Whoever nursed her pressed a bitter, sour-smelling liquid to her lips. She felt a scalding torrent of blood between her legs then fell back, exhausted.

She slept without dreams. Something hovered at the edge of her consciousness – as a scavenger hovers over a dying animal, waiting to swoop – but it did not strike.

She was caught in an ever-shifting kaleidoscope: she smelt the stale tang of unwashed skin and syrupy blood; tasted aloes and castor oil; heard Jolyon's voice and another she did not recognise. She only gleaned a few sentences, but they were sufficient.

'Wood? *Inside* her?'

'In there with the baby. Poor thing was splintered. I never saw anything like it.'

The baby.

It was missing. Amputated. She could not feel its motions or the bubbles inside.

I am no longer two. I am alone.

Christmastide must have come and gone, for when she crawled out from the fog one dreary morning Sarah was sitting in the room, soberly dressed, eating a collection of cold meats that looked like leftovers. Mabel fussed about the wardrobe, wearing the new uniform Elsie remembered buying for her Christmas box.

Her mouth tasted horrific. She groaned. 'My tonic. Give me . . .' *Drugs.* She cared not what; opium, morphine, chloral.

Sarah started at the sound of her voice. Dabbing her mouth with a napkin, she hurried over to the bed and took Elsie's hand. She had lost weight, making her face look longer and more horse-like than ever. There were shadows around her eye sockets, the irises glittering with unshed tears.

'Tonic,' Elsie said again. Her breath grated in her chest. In another moment the pain would rise up to meet her; she felt it building, gathering its strength.

Sarah shook her head. 'The doctor says not to give you too much.'

'The doctor! He has not felt anything like this.'

'He says you must eat. I can give you bread and water, or beef tea . . .'

'I'm not hungry.' Her tongue yearned for the astringent taste of opium; her head begged for sleep. It was aching now, turning over jagged objects and trying to pound them into memories. She wanted to cry – but no, that would hurt more. 'For the love of God, give me the tonic.'

'The doctor—'

'The doctor is a man. He can have no comprehension of this pain.'

Tears spilled onto Sarah's sallow cheeks. She squeezed Elsie's hand so hard that it hurt. 'Oh, Mrs Bainbridge. I'm so sorry. It would have been a little bit of Rupert, wouldn't it?'

Pain flooded back, but not into her stomach. 'Where is it? Where is my baby?'

'With his father. Mr Underwood was very kind. He christened the little stranger and laid him to rest in the family vault. He was not supposed to. It will be our secret.'

A little stranger. Grown in secret, buried in secret, always in the dark. Elsie felt her mouth open like a wound – wet, raw. 'But then – I will never see him!'

'We wanted to wait for you, but you were so ill. We could not delay any longer.' Sarah shifted. Her corset creaked. 'I can tell you what he looked like. He was very small. Dainty. We could only just tell that he was a boy.'

'And . . . splintered?'

'Who told you that?'

'So it *is* true! I thought, I hoped, that I'd dreamed Jolyon saying it. Sarah, how could he possibly . . .'

Sarah shook her head. 'I cannot tell you how. Even the doctor cannot say. I only know what I saw.'

'What . . . did you see?'

She looked away. 'Please, Mrs Bainbridge, I do not wish to speak of it. Do not make me.'

'It is my *child*.'

'His skin had splinters,' Sarah whispered, closing her eyes. 'All over.'

Pictures tried to form but Elsie would not let them, could not endure them. 'His name. What did they christen him?'

'Edgar Rupert.'

'*Edgar!*'

Sarah blinked at her. 'Was – was that wrong? Mr Livingstone said it was your father's name.'

'Yes.' She sank back against the pillow, nauseous. 'It was.'

Mabel closed the wardrobe. Pressing herself against the walls, she glided round the room and through the door.

'Was Jolyon very angry?'

'Angry? God bless you, Mrs Bainbridge, why would he be angry? He has shown nothing but concern.'

No doubt that was true, but he would rue this lost opportunity as bitterly as Elsie did. She had lost the heir, the future of their business, lost him in a moment of – what? *No, Ma, not carelessness*. Something worse, something lurking at the back of her mind . . .

'Beatrice,' she gasped. 'Beatrice.' Sarah's hand grew rigid beneath hers. 'Oh Sarah, tell me I imagined it.'

'I cannot. The poor creature. The dress . . . Mrs Bainbridge, what happened? You were not out of my sight for ten minutes.'

'It was delivered. Mr Underwood . . . He said he found it on the front step.'

'Yes, he told me. But how then were you at the top of the stairs?'

A cold finger lay across her heart. 'Oh God. Did you see it? Is it still there? What did you do with it?'

'Hush, hush.' Sarah tried to hold her hands steady, but she was trembling too. 'Do you mean Hetta?'

'No. Rupert.'

Sarah dropped her hands with a cry. '*Rupert?*'

'There was one of him.' She closed her eyes, trying to push away the memory, but it was no use. 'A companion of Rupert, Sarah. He looked . . . Oh God, he looked wretched.'

'No! No, you must be mistaken, Mrs Bainbridge. That is not in the house. No one has seen it.'

'It was right on the top step.'

'Good God.' Sarah's lips trembled, wilting rose petals ready to drop. 'I never meant – I'm so sorry, Mrs Bainbridge. You know, don't you, that I would never put Hetta in the Great Hall? She was in the garret, I promise. She was locked up in the garret, I do not understand how . . .' She fell silent. Muscles twitched in her face, as if she were fighting with an emotion. 'The truth is, it happened in the diary. Anne's diary. A horse was mutilated, right after she bought the companions. And I'm starting to think that maybe . . . maybe Anne was a witch, after all. She writes about these potions she used to conceive Hetta . . . Perhaps that's what Hetta is trying to do: warn us of her mother's power.'

Elsie closed her eyes. Every inch of her throbbed. She was beginning to wish she had never woken up. Sleep was simple, safe. 'Sarah, have you mentioned any of this to Jolyon? Or to Mr Underwood?'

'Yes.' Suddenly her tone hardened. 'I told your brother, and I begged Mr Underwood to perform an exorcism. They would not believe me. They had a talk, and then they made me see the physician.'

'What did he say?'

'Oh, he gave me some beastly medicine. He was more concerned with this.' Sarah held up her hand, still bandaged. 'The skin has gone white and soft around the cut. He thinks it is infected.'

An infection making Sarah see things. The medical men always had some explanation, but this one was insufficient. Elsie did not have an infection – nor did the maids. How could he rationalise what *they* saw?

'The worst of it is,' Sarah cried, 'they want to separate us! Mr Livingstone is taking you back to London at the end of the month.'

'London?' Elsie's eyes snapped open. Right now, London sounded as far away as Heaven.

'To convalesce. He says a change of scene will be beneficial.'

'But what about you?'

Sarah was struggling to hold in tears. 'The gentlemen say I am nervous. They think the trip would be too much of a stimulant for me and I had better rest here. Without you.'

Elsie scoffed. 'Rest? In this house?'

'I used to love this house, I thought it was where I belonged. Until . . .' Sarah met her eyes, beseeching. 'I don't know what to do, Mrs Bainbridge. You will be in London while I am here, alone, with . . . Whatever it is. Whatever *they* are. Tell me what to do.'

'Burn it. Burn Hetta.'

Sarah hesitated. 'As you burnt the others?'

'Yes.'

'You *did* burn them, after I took Hetta inside?'

'Of course.'

Sarah's hands were in her hair, distractedly tugging it out of its pins. 'You are *sure* that you burnt them?'

'Of course I am sure! Peters and the maids watched me.'

'Good God.'

'What? Sarah? What is it?'

'They are back, Mrs Bainbridge.' Her voice broke. 'The companions are all back in the house.'

THE BRIDGE, 1635

I do not suppose there ever was a shame like ours. I can barely breathe for the despondency that lays upon my spirit, the guilt I cannot scrub off.

Again and again, that morning circles in my mind. I remember the shocked silence all around; how the courtiers were no longer gay but grave, stern as judges. I hear the humiliation ringing shrill inside my head as the Queen sobbed. She loved that horse. Of course we gave her my mare, but how insufficient it was compared to the fine-blooded creature she had lost. It looked like a poor woman's horse. They rode away with a double guard, leaving us alone at The Bridge. Alone, with the echoing taunt of our failure.

My disgrace is twofold. I have failed not only my King but my lord and husband, my heart's dearest hope. He was not aware of my treachery – at least, not the nature of it. He came to me soon after they left and gripped my hands. When he stared into my face I saw that his own was drawn and quivering, as if the muscles themselves shook for fear.

'Anne, you must tell me the truth.' I could not speak. 'I know we never mention it, but we must now. The time has come.'

My guilty mind flew straight to Merripen. 'Josiah . . .'

'I know you have always seen things. Sensed things, before they are there. Those tisanes you gave me . . . I thought it a gift from God. But . . . Tell me truly.'

'Tell you what?'

He had difficulty pushing the words up his throat. 'You had a daughter. They said it was impossible to birth another child, but you had a daughter. I rose faster in court than any other man of my station. Was it herbs? Or . . .?'

I know I coloured, conscious of my transgression, of drawing my skirts a little too close to the flame of sin. 'How can you ask me such a thing?'

'I know you would not do that awful, that wicked act in the stables,' he ran on hurriedly. 'But do you think that you might have accidentally . . .' He glanced at my diamonds. They flashed as I swallowed. 'I do not know. Is it possible that some dark force has its eye fixed upon you?'

'Josiah!' I cried.

'Answer me, Anne. For I looked at that animal and I cannot believe this is the work of human hands.'

So I told him. I told him the excruciating, miserable truth: that it was his wife's stupidity, not her cunning, that brought a demon upon him.

He has not spoken to me since.

I cannot summon the strength to cry. I do not resent his hatred. Nothing can burn hotter than the contempt

I feel for myself. I ripped off my sparkling diamonds, ashamed to think how much my poor Josiah spent, how much he invested in me.

He is confined to the country now; he cannot show his face at court. His acquaintances no longer answer his letters. He has nothing to do but stomp about like a caged bear, shoot our grouse and pick quarrels with the villagers as we prepare for the harvest. They do not want to work our land after what has happened. They are afraid that the gypsies have cursed us.

Heaven grant that the servants do not follow suit. For now they seem minded to stay and revel in the gossip, yet when all is said and done only Lizzy can be trusted to remain with us. Not that Lizzy is *quite* content – her every glance reproaches me for keeping Merripen a secret from her. Dear Lizzy, she never can accept that I am a lady grown. She does not realise how many secrets my traitorous heart can keep.

The house falls silent as a tomb. No guests, no decorators, not even my sons to cheer the gloom. Years ago, we placed the boys in noble households so they could learn how to run vast estates. They are back with them now, but I do not suppose Josiah's relatives will be prepared to keep them for much longer. It is a risk to be allied with us.

Even Hetta is not the comfort she once was. As I sat in the Great Hall today it was heartbreaking to see her skipping around those wooden cut-outs, as if the prospects of our house and our family had not gone up in smoke around her.

I have spent nearly nine years of my life yearning only for her smile, but today I could not stand it.

I watched her, playing as she does for hours with the painted boards, and unleashed the wicked torrent of my thoughts. I thought that I should be happy today, were it not for her and her gypsy friend. I should be on my way into the service of the Queen herself but Hetta was the reason – the only reason – that no one else in The Bridge smiled today.

'How can you?' I burst out. 'How dare you smile and prance like that? You know what has happened.'

She cocked her head at one of the companions, as if it had spoken. Then she went on playing.

My rage mounted. God forgive me, I know it was wrong, I know she is only a child. But I could not help myself. 'Listen to me! Do you not understand what this means for us?'

She should do. But it seems she does not fully comprehend. Perhaps she *cannot*.

'Merripen!' I cried, pushed to the end of my endurance. 'Your friend Merripen has done this to us!'

The smile dropped from her face, quick as a curtain falling.

'He has killed the Queen's horse,' I said, 'because we moved his people off the common. He has made your father most unhappy.'

She glanced at the nearest companion and then at me.

'You made me employ that heathen and now he has ruined us, ruined us for good!'

I could not read her expression. She opened her mouth and, for one wild moment, I thought she was actually going to speak. Then she ran from me.

I heard her feet pattering on the stairs as fast as rain, as fast as my tears fell. I slid down into my chair, feeling like a knave.

Hetta was the only one left who did not hate me. And now I have pushed her away.

Somewhere in the distance, thunder booms. I do not know how long I have sat here rueing my fate, begging for the strength to go on. But the storm must have nudged closer, for the light has clouded and the hall has fallen into a bruised, grey-yellow murk. Drops of rain hit the window. A companion, the sweeper, watches me.

Her gaze has become shameful, degrading; as if she knows every secret of my soul.

I have ordered them returned to Mr Samuels first thing in the morning. All of the fine objects, returned. I cannot stand to have his treasure in my house any longer. I hate every piece of it.

———

A very curious thing happened today. My cart rumbled back from Torbury St Jude with my servants, but the goods were still tied down.

'What is this?' I barked. 'I told you to leave these with Mr Samuels.'

'I know,' said our man Mark, 'and I'm sorry, mistress, but it weren't there.'

I looked at Jane. 'What does he mean? Did Mr Samuels refuse to take delivery?'

'No,' she said shakily. 'No, not that.' Lines of confusion furrowed her brow. 'The shop – it wasn't there.'

How could that be? A shop so full and well stocked only last June!

'What? Is the shop vacant?'

'No, mistress.' Her voice was high now, close to tears. '*It was not there*. The shop. We must have driven up and down a dozen times but I swear . . . It's as if it never existed.'

I could only gape at her. The beef-witted girl! I never heard anything like it. She went into the shop with me herself. Shops do not simply disappear!

Perhaps she is ill; there is certainly something amiss about her, for she has been all aquiver since they returned.

I must go into town to settle the business myself, and soon. Until then I am stuck with our misbegotten companions. I cover their faces with sheets but I know they are there, watching. As if they know what has happened. As if it amuses them.

THE BRIDGE, 1866

'My diamonds. Where are my diamonds?' Elsie raked through her jewellery box, scattering chains and pearls across the dressing table.

'Elsie.' Jolyon sounded tired. He slouched against the bedpost. 'Leave that. You must rest.'

'But I cannot find my diamonds.'

'They will turn up.'

'Rupert wanted me to have them.' She dug faster. She had lost Rupert. She had lost the baby. She would not lose the diamonds too.

'Elsie.'

'I am not being hysterical, Jo. Rupert heard it too. He wrote me a letter but I can't—' She shuffled through the belongings strewn over her dressing table. No one had cleaned it during her illness. The surface was coated in that coarse, beige dust. 'I cannot find it right now.'

'You need to calm down. This is not you speaking. You have been very ill.'

Ill. A laughably inadequate word. 'This is not a nervous disorder. The wood inside me! And Sarah saw the companions,' she whispered. 'She saw them too.'

'This is not like you, Elsie. You are no neurotic girl.'

'Then why don't you pay me the courtesy of believing me?' Without warning, she burst into tears.

Jolyon came to her side at the dressing table and placed a hand on her shoulder, bringing with him his familiar scent of bay leaves and lime. His fingers trembled on her collarbone. Of course, he was not used to seeing her cry. All these years she had hidden her sorrow from him, held herself tight, strong. But now a chamber inside her had unlocked and she could not seal it up again.

'What you are asking me to accept, dearest . . . It is impossible. You see that, do you not?'

It was all very well for him. His pressed suit, his necktie and shining shoes proclaimed his place in a world of order and sense, figures and business. He did not know what it was to ferment out here with a malicious, nameless fear.

'I am not blaming you,' Jolyon went on. 'I do not think you made it up. Poor, dear heart, you have been cruelly deceived.'

She stared at him. 'How do you mean, deceived?'

'Consider it. Could a person butcher a cow and deliver it to your door without any witnesses? *Someone* must have seen something. Did Peters not notice Beatrice was missing? What about the gardeners? And where were the maids, all that time? Why did they not answer the door?'

'You do not think . . .'

A thought was forming, drawing memories together as a poultice draws filth. *The maids.*

He removed his hand from her shoulder and ran it through his hair. 'To be honest with you, I think the maids were playing a joke. Perhaps they did not mean for it to go this far.'

'No . . . they would not.'

'You got rid of all the servants at the factory after Ma died,' he said gently. 'You are not used to managing such people. It would be quite simple for the maids to move things, keep spare dummy boards hidden. Write in the dust. Consider. They could have orchestrated every move.'

It was too horrible to believe. 'But . . . why?'

He shrugged. 'They resent you. Your very presence in the house. Once their work was easy and slapdash. Now, with a mistress, and the prospect of a baby . . . No doubt they thought it amusing at first, but they have overstepped the mark.'

Could two women enact such spite? Slaughter a cow and shred a dress just to get back at her? Elsie struggled to imagine it. And yet . . .

Mabel took the carriage home from church that Sunday before Christmas, didn't she? She had plenty of time to set up Hetta and place the handprint on the glass. It was Mabel who came running to say Hetta's eyes had moved, Mabel who screamed about the companion in her bathtub. She could have put it in the bath herself.

'No, that doesn't explain it. I saw things, Jolyon. I saw a pair of eyes move and I heard that one in the bath, brushing her hair!'

'Did you?' he asked softly. 'Or did someone plant that idea in your mind? You have been ill and grieving, very open to suggestion. Maybe the maids just prompted you. They knew your frightened imagination would provide the rest.'

She experienced a shrivelling sensation in her chest as she remembered Mabel, standing by the wardrobe, looking guilty as Elsie and Sarah cried over the baby.

She looked at Jolyon, his dear face, hazy through her swimming eyes. 'But . . . I raised Mabel up.'

'And she has betrayed you, my poor love. I would wager she took your diamonds, too. She has the key to the box, does she not?'

Her clever boy. Nothing got past him. He had grown stronger than her, sharper than her. And here she was, an utter blockhead, thinking she had helped those in need. She had only helped them to rob her.

She covered her eyes with her hands. 'Oh, Jo, I've been such a fool. Will you ever forgive me?'

He put his arms around her and drew her to him. Her head rested on his chest. How tall he was now. 'Forgive you? Goose! What have I to forgive *you* for?'

She buried her face in his waistcoat and did not answer.

Her boxes were all packed and tied, ready to be loaded into the carriage. The tight-faced servants stood clustered around them in the Great Hall. Elsie walked past and thanked God she was leaving: leaving this horrendous place and all the ghastly things that had happened here. Leaving the companions.

They faced the wall, like children put in the corner for failing to learn their lessons. Had Mabel positioned them like that? Elsie could not bring herself to look at Mabel, think of Mabel. She felt sick just sharing the same space as her.

Shakily, she went to the mirror and arranged her bonnet and veil over her widow's cap. The face reflected below the brim was misshapen, strained with dread. She felt awful. Her body was in a state of flux. Tender breasts pushed hard against her corset, confused as to whether to ripen or deflate. And all the while her baby lay cocooned in a derelict church, bearing a name that was not his own.

It was Mabel's fault. Helen's fault. Mrs Holt must share the blame for failing to supervise them. Or perhaps she was laughing up her sleeve at Elsie, too.

The splinters. That hellish thought went round and round in her head like a child's spinning top. It did not tie up with the rest. Scaring her and making her jump – that was one thing. But meddling with an unborn baby . . . She knew the maids would not do that.

What in the name of God had happened to her?

Jolyon's steps sounded on the flags. She did not turn, but heard him pull on his gloves. 'Did you find my sister's diamonds, Mrs Holt?'

'No, sir, I'm afraid not. I am sure they will turn up.'

'They will not.' He took a breath. 'Mabel has taken them.'

Mabel gasped. 'I never did!'

Elsie whirled round, her fury leaping like a flame. 'Oh, you did. I saw you with them once before, remember?'

'I were warming them.'

'Without permission.'

'Tell me, Mabel,' said Jolyon. He was calm, in control. 'Who else has access to my sister's jewellery box? Besides you?'

Mabel's eyes slipped to the door. 'Miss Sarah?'

Sarah's mouth flew open, but Elsie did not let her speak. 'I trust Miss Sarah.'

'I am sure it is all a mistake,' Mrs Holt soothed. 'I am sure—'

Jolyon put up a hand, stopping her. '*I* am sure that your maids have been playing tricks upon their mistress. All this nonsense about *companions*! Mabel has access to the kitchen, does she not? Access to the largest knives?'

Mrs Holt blinked. 'Sir, you are not suggesting the cow—'

'You've gone barty.' Mabel threw up her chin, but she was all puff. Elsie could see her lips quivering and the alarm stretching her eyes. 'If you think I swiped them diamonds and killed the cow then you've lost your mind. Sir.'

Jolyon gave her a long, hard look. 'Have I? We shall see.' He placed his hat on his head. It made him look taller, more imposing. 'Mrs Bainbridge and I will return at Easter. If the diamonds have not been located by then, I will report my suspicions to the police.'

'But I don't know where they are!'

'Please, sir.' Mrs Holt wrung her hands. 'Mabel has worked here for over two years. I cannot believe she is a thief.'

Jolyon softened his tone. 'Dear Mrs Holt, you are too trusting. You did not see what was going on under your nose. I think you and I need to sit down and discuss hiring some more . . . suitable servants.'

'But—'

'Do not be alarmed. Your employment is safe.'

'Dear me. Dear, dear, me.' Mrs Holt's throat worked convulsively.

Bumbling, foolish old woman, Elsie thought. If she had supervised her maids properly, if she had *considered* what sort of girl she was taking on in the first place, all this unpleasantness might have been avoided. Elsie's baby might still be alive.

Jolyon picked up a suitcase, his expression level, collected. 'Take comfort, Mrs Holt. We will talk again when I return from London. In the meantime, Miss Bainbridge will be in charge of you.' He passed his case to Peters and went outside with the man to supervise the loading of the carriage.

Sarah came forward. She could barely look at Elsie. 'Mrs Bainbridge . . . This is all such a mess. I—'

'Hush. You weren't to know. We both got carried away with fear and our grief. Neither of us suspected the maids.'

She bit her lip. 'Do you . . . Do you really believe they did it all? Every last bit?'

Elsie swallowed. 'Jolyon believes it, and I trust him.'

'But in the diary—'

'Enough. I cannot bear to speak of it any longer. Return to your diaries, and your study of the family home. You will scarcely notice I am gone.'

Sarah trembled for a moment. Then she pitched forward and kissed her on the cheek. 'God speed your journey. I am so sorry, Mrs Bainbridge.'

'Well. I suppose you might call me Elsie now.'

It was not until Elsie was settled in her seat, waving good-bye to Sarah, that she saw it: another face, intent on their departure. On the second floor, staring out of the window that belonged to her own bedroom, was a companion.

This one she knew. Anne Bainbridge. Unmistakable: the same coral ribbons from the portrait in her hair; the same plump cheeks. Her yellow gown flowed and rippled where her arms lay, crossed over her chest. And there, painted on her throat, was a necklace. One glittering bow supporting three pear-drop diamonds.

Elsie's diamonds.

THE BRIDGE, 1635

Hetta's birthday. In accordance with my custom, I went to All Souls Church to give thanks for the daughter they told me would never come.

I say I am giving thanks. But deep down, I wonder. Am I praising God or serving a penance? For each time I step into the church there is a nagging guilt at the core of me. When I pray, there are two voices inside my head, gabbling over one another. One cries *thank you*; the other *forgive me*.

Today I felt, more powerful than ever, the weight of God's disapproval pressing down on me as I slipped into the deserted church and took a pew. A force loving but sad, intolerably heavy.

Saints gazed upon me from the old stained-glass windows left from Queen Mary's reign. They seemed to shake their heads. I clasped my hands tighter. And as I closed my eyes, the words came to me in a torrent: *How dare you?*

My eyelids snapped open. I felt suddenly very small. But even as I dropped to my knees, the voice came again. *How dare you?* My gaze flew to the front of the church, to the cross, soaring up before the altar. *Who are you to create a life where I have refused it?*

I knew then that it was an answer to my prayers, to the nights I have spent on my knees asking why our family has suffered such humiliation: it was my fault.

And I see it now. God has a plan for each and every one of us He creates. His plan for Josiah was a brilliant one, set at the centre of court. But that plan did not account for one factor: Hetta.

Hetta befriended the gypsy and I, weak again, gave in to her demands. My sin looms so large that it has changed the path of my life.

This idea haunted me all the way home. As I walked through the swirling leaves, as I tasted the musk of late October on the air, I kept asking myself why I had done it. I had three boys. Three! My mother would have given her right arm for only one. But I had wanted a girl. Another Mary to sit with me and walk with me, a mirror of my own childhood springing up at my feet. And wrong as it may be, I want her still.

When I returned to The Bridge, I went straight to the nursery. Lizzy sat in her rocking chair beneath the trailing vines, darning one of Hetta's torn stockings.

My child wore the gown of olive silk I commissioned for the royal visit. It becomes her well, bringing out the coppery tint to her hair. She let me kiss her, but I could not keep her for more than a moment. As soon as my lips met her cheek she was off again, running between her companions.

It hurt me. I put my soul in peril, I paid the price of my future – and I receive one meagre kiss.

I sat down heavily beside Lizzy. 'I hope it will not be seen as odd for Hetta to spend so much time with these boards. She never was an ordinary creature and now ...'

'No, no.' Lizzy snipped off a thread. 'Don't go fretting about that. It's only natural she should take to the things, not having any friends of her own age. She doesn't have to speak to the boards.'

Hetta is not like me. That is not her fault, of course, but every difference I find is a little chip in the dream I had of my daughter. The close confidante, who was to be the repository of all my secrets, can confide none of her own. She isn't at ease with me. I am not to her what I am to the boys.

Perhaps it is part of my punishment. A check to my hubris. With herbs and ancient words I can create a daughter, but I cannot make her love me.

'Remember,' Lizzy went on, turning the stocking over, 'when you were Hetta's age, you could run about with poor Mary. God rest her soul.'

'And after that, I always had you to talk to, dearest Lizzy.'

She smiled up at me, her old gums dotted with black. 'Though there were some who thought that unfit, weren't there, because of my station? So you see, there's nothing strange about Hetta playing hide and go seek with wooden people.' She began a new stitch. 'What I *do* find strange is Mr Samuels, disappearing so suddenly like that. Have you found no trace of him in town?'

I shook my head. Mark and Jane were right: the shop simply is not there. I cannot see how it has happened, but it has. Even that man and his premises have fled from us. I am stuck with my cursed treasure.

Lizzy sighed. 'A mystery. I thought maybe there was news of Samuels, when the master rode off so fast.'

I jerked round to face her. 'Josiah is gone?'

'Aye. Didn't you know?'

'I was at church.'

'Oh.' Without looking at me, she threaded her needle. 'Rode out about an hour ago, he did.'

Foreboding hit me, as keen and sharp as the wind hurtling over the hills. 'Fast?'

'Aye.' She pursed her lips. 'As fast as if the hounds of hell were on his tail.'

———

I waited in the Great Hall. The day wasted fast. Indigo clouds blushed pink underneath as the sun slipped away. Blackbirds chimed until the light extinguished, then the owls began to mourn.

At long last the gravel crunched. I heard voices in the stable yard and the tramp of feet. Moments later Josiah strode through the door, splashed with mud.

I flew to him. 'Josiah, what is it? What has happened?'

His look was guarded. He removed my hands from his cloak and held them at a distance. 'The boy has been found.'

'Merripen?'

'Yes. It was our own man, our own Mark, who found him.'

'Thanks be to God.'

'Finally, I have some news to send to the King.'

What a blessed relief to picture that evil spirit captured and shackled! I had never supposed that the devil would sup with a child so young. I remembered Merripen's eyes, dark and blazing like a brazier of flaming pitch, and it struck me cold.

Foolishly, I thought that would be an end to it; that Josiah and I could go on as before. But he released my hands and swung off his cloak, turning from me as he said, 'The boy will be confined in Torbury St Jude tonight, and tried tomorrow. I shall attend.'

'Tomorrow is All Saints' Day.'

'The day after then,' he said irritably.

I knew I should leave it there; congratulate him and flee from his sight. But a raw uneasiness in my soul compelled me to blurt out, 'What will happen to him?'

He stared at me. His pointed beard made his mouth appear mocking, somehow cruel. 'That will depend on the verdict.'

Guilty. It must be guilty. Josiah will not let them find anything else. His reputation stands on the line. If he cannot catch and punish the miscreant who offended the Queen in his own house, his shame will know no end.

My throat grew tight, tight enough to choke me. I remembered the man who had his ears cut off. 'A traitor's death, then? Will they truly bestow that upon a boy?'

His crack of laughter made me jump. There was no mirth in it. 'A boy! Can a human boy do *that* to an animal? Oh no, my lady. Mark my words, he is possessed of a demon.'

'Indeed he must be. At that young age!' He is only a little older than my Hetta. I pictured him, so short beneath the scaffold. How thickly the rope would pile around his small neck, how smooth and flat his little stomach would lie beneath the blade. A child hung, drawn and quartered. 'Do you expect the King to show mercy?'

'Mercy?' He spat the word out like a thing vomited. 'Would *you* extend mercy to the fiend?'

I stuttered. 'No . . . I do not know. Deeds so wicked cannot go unchecked, and yet . . . Does not something within you baulk at this? Do you not feel the execution of a child will hang heavy upon your soul?'

'In nowise.' His eyes glittered. I did not like the thread of steel in his voice. '*I* am not responsible for this. The only person responsible is *you.*'

It hit me like a blow to the face.

'*You* let him into the stables, *you* put the horse in his way. This would not have happened were it not for you.' His glare pinned me to the spot. 'If anyone has that boy's blood on their hands it is you, Anne, and you alone.'

LONDON, 1866

The change in the texture of air was remarkable. As the carriage trundled through familiar streets, smog descended in a tobacco-coloured mist. Black smuts flecked the windows. Elsie tasted the biting scent of sulphur upon her tongue long before it invaded her nostrils.

Soon the factory materialised: one tall chimney flowing with smoke and behind it rows of slanting gables, like the dorsal fins of sharks. Iron railings enclosed the courtyard. Through the rails Elsie glimpsed a wagon delivering deal wood for the splints. A boy, one of their sellers, emerged from the building and walked past the horses with a tray bobbing at his waist. The merchandise seemed so much bigger than the boy himself.

A man opened the gates and they drew into the factory complex. Elsie heard metal clang behind her, locking her in. After The Bridge, this felt like another world. Alien. She looked with the eyes of a stranger at the place that had once been her home. Through the steamed factory windows she could see the cutting machine glinting like a hay knife as it whisked back and forth; sparks from the petulant matches that would not co-operate. The splinters of light hurt her eyes. She had to look away.

'Right,' said Jolyon as they stopped in the yard. 'Let us get you up to the living quarters and rested. You must be exhausted after that journey.'

'But what about the girls from Fayford? When their wagon arrives they will need to be settled in and shown what to do.'

'Miss Baxter will take care of all that. Who do you think has been running around after the apprentices since you married?'

It nettled her, to be supplanted. This was hers. She might marry and move away, but she would never let go of the factory – she would always be mistress here. God knew she had earnt that title. 'Well, Miss Baxter might look after them today, for I really am fatigued. But once I have rested I will start helping again.'

Jolyon chewed his lip.

'It will benefit me,' she explained. 'I need to be where there is noise and bustle and life. At The Bridge I feel like a piece of taxidermy underneath a bell jar.'

'We shall see. But first a cup of tea and a lie-down.'

She could not argue with that.

Firmly secured on Jolyon's arm, she alighted from the carriage and turned left, past the dipping rooms and drying sheds, towards a small, grey-brick house commanding the west side of the courtyard. Dusty, frowzy women with tassels missing from the fringes of their shawls nodded their heads in acknowledgement as she came by. A fine white vapour, garlicky and pestilential, arose from their shoulders.

'The windows could do with a scrub,' she told Jolyon, as she regarded the house. 'Look what happens when I leave you alone. I dread to think what kind of bachelor's den I am walking into.'

He smiled. 'You will find it just the same. The same as it always was.'

The front door squealed as Jolyon's housekeeper opened it up to them. Mrs Figgis had a plump figure and a pudding face – no trace of cheekbones under the large pores on her skin. Her unwieldy bosom went before her. Elsie wondered how her apron stretched over it. She tried not to stare as she entered her old home.

Mrs Figgis was a new fixture, hired after Elsie's marriage to do those womanly tasks she had always taken care of. Elsie was pleased to see how kind and motherly the woman acted, ushering them into the parlour, where the fire was already simmering, beneath the coals before she hurried out to fetch the tea tray.

It was a strange reversal of Elsie's arrival at The Bridge. She found the mantelpiece clean. The windowsills, too. That was no small feat for a servant working in the yellow cloud of a factory. Thin powder – not precisely dust nor sand – got into everything, even under your nails and inside your nose.

'I stand corrected,' she said as she drew her bonnet off and sat before the fire. 'You are being cared for extremely well.'

'Indeed I am. Mrs Figgis is a treasure. Not, of course,' he added swiftly, placing his hat on a stand and taking Elsie's from her, 'that she makes up for having you around.'

'Flatterer. I don't believe a word.'

Leaning back, she glanced around at the parlour. Jolyon was right – it was all the same. Faded wallpaper with a

repeating pattern of rose bouquets, a few well-chosen orna-
ments on the shelves and crocheted antimacassars draped
over the backs of the chairs. The usual chemical smell of the
factory, heightened by her absence from it. The room was
the same. Only Elsie had changed.

She could not help but notice how small everything
was, after The Bridge: the chairs too close together, the fire
feeble and insufficient. As if she had grown too large to be
contained in such a place.

Mrs Figgis brought in the tea with some bread and butter,
before tactfully leaving them alone. Elsie raised the cup to
her lips. There was a chip missing from the rim.

'I want you to take a drop of laudanum and sleep for the
rest of today,' Jolyon told her. He picked up a slice of bread.
'Tomorrow, I shall make enquiries about your treatment.'

She nearly dropped her cup. 'I saw a physician at The
Bridge. He said I was well enough to travel.'

'That is not a full recovery, though, is it?'

'I will admit that I am still weak, Jo, but I don't require
more than rest and a glass of wine a day.'

'You have had a nervous shock. It does not do to let such
episodes pass unheeded. The physicians have all manner of
therapies these days that can soothe you – steam inhalations,
cold sitz-baths.'

She sipped the tea, but it was sour in her mouth and hurt
when she swallowed it down. 'I thought we agreed. I was
not . . . It was all a ghastly joke.'

'Yes.' Jolyon chewed his bread and butter, purposefully
avoiding her eyes. 'I am not implying otherwise. But it is
still a nasty blow to the nerves. And together with all the
rest – Rupert passing, so suddenly, like that.'

'Jolyon—'

'And now look what has happened! The loss of your child. It would be unnatural if it did *not* shake you up. There is no shame, you know, in receiving help. Just a little something to steady your nerves, reanimate your spirit.'

'I know that.' She set her cup down on its saucer. 'But it's quite unnecessary. Please do not waste your money. I've dealt with things like this all my life.' He opened his mouth to speak, but she got there first. 'This is what happens to me, Jo. I trust people and they abuse that trust. It is time I pulled myself together and learnt from it.' She realised she was shaking. Hurriedly, she folded her hands in her lap.

'At least,' he said gently, sitting forward in his chair, 'accept some help in "pulling yourself together". It is my duty, Elsie, as your brother, to look after you. You are so brave that I often forget you are a member of the fairer sex. You were not built to withstand these things.'

She sat on her retort, because she knew it would hurt him. At twenty-three he wanted to feel grown, the man in charge.

'You have already discharged that duty.'

'No, I have not.' His brow contracted – he was serious, now. 'I am worried for you, Elsie. We need to be careful. After . . .' He struggled for a moment, his throat working. 'After what happened with Ma.'

Her eyes locked on his: his hazel irises, flicking minutely from side to side, and the shrinking pupils. But she could not pierce deep enough. He gave nothing away.

She realised she had forgotten to breathe. 'Ma?' she whispered.

'Because of how she went at the end.'

'You were too young to remember that.'

'I assure you, I recall it vividly.'

How could she hide it – this unaccountable trembling in her fingers, the twitching deep in her bones? 'I didn't know. I am sorry for it, Jo. It was a terrible time. I would have spared you the memory.'

There was a long pause.

'I remember,' Jolyon said, carefully, 'how bad she got. Seeing goblins and devils. And then, at the end, such terrible stuff. She used to whisper me over to her bed and accuse you of all sorts.'

'Me?'

'Oh, she was quite mad. I understood *that*, young as I was. But she was our mother, Elsie, and these things can be hereditary.'

Her face quivered back into life. 'She had the typhus! A fever like that would send anyone off into Queer Street.'

'Her confusion got worse with the typhus, but it didn't start with it. You told me yourself. You said she'd been that way since Pa died.'

'Yes. I did say that. Of course, the grief changed her. But she was not mad, exactly. At least, I don't think so.'

Did people know when they were going insane? she wondered. Did they feel the weave of their mind ripping apart? Or was it like passing into a gentle dream-world? She would never know, for she and Ma had never discussed the subject. And if she were honest, back then, she did not care if Ma suffered – in fact, she rather desired it.

'Is it worth taking the risk? Is it not better to see a doctor?'

A strange lethargy washed over her. What did Jolyon know about risks?

'You cannot make the comparison, my dear Jo, but if you had known our parents better, you would realise that I do not share any characteristics with them.' The old ache lodged in her throat. 'Nothing, do you understand?'

'You do, Elsie. You cannot help it. They are always with us, in our blood, in our very being. Whether we like it or not.'

She shuddered. 'Yes. Yes, I suppose they are.'

Her heart was beating too fast. It made her eyes cloudy, her lips dry. A faint singing started up. She could not tell if it was her ears, or the women working outside.

Daylight sifted in through the smog, prying at the curtains and splashing the tea tray yellow. The moment it touched her knee she stood, abruptly. Her cup and saucer rattled.

Jolyon stared up at her.

'I'm sorry,' she said. She pressed a hand to her forehead. It was slick with sweat. 'Forgive me, Jo. I've come over terribly unwell. I think I had better go and lie down.'

January passed into a raw, wet February with wind shrieking over the factory buildings, blowing smoke from the chimney in a diagonal stream. Elsie scarcely noticed the days go by. Whether it was the sleeping draughts prescribed by Jolyon's doctor or the red lavender tincture she took in her wine every evening, she felt a sense of cushioned well-being, detached from day-to-day cares.

She made rounds of the factory, but she had no real responsibilities. She could idle past the dipping room and watch the boys paddling a phosphorescent mixture on the stove.

Frigid gusts of wind carried the fumes up over the gates and out into the thicker smog of London. Occasionally her nostrils found snatches of the sulphurous odour, but it did not trouble her as it used to do. The scent was a pinprick, a little jolt, rather than a knife blade.

When it grew too cold to peer through steamed-up windows, she would enter the factory proper, where the splints were made. Here she moved and breathed freely, a fish put back in water. The steam, the whirr of the machinery, the woodchips and factory chatter were all as familiar to her as Jolyon's voice. She looked down on her employees, dashing to and fro, and the seething glitter of the saw, and felt she had been resuscitated. Brought back to life.

By March she was restored and had begun to mentor the three young girls she had rescued from Fayford.

'Here,' Elsie said to the smallest, a little girl with freckles who was struggling to tie up her bundle. 'Take this measure and put it under the spout. Each one is designed to hold eighteen hundred splints. That will be just the right amount for your bundle.'

The girl's friend looked alarmed at the prospect of having to count to so great a number, but Elsie helped her while the freckled girl darted off, teaching her the best knot to secure the bundle with.

'I used to do this myself,' she smiled, 'when I was your age.' Of course she was not as dexterous, these days, with her scarred hands.

The girl did not reply, though it was evident from her face that she did not believe a word of it. Perhaps it *was* odd, for the owner's daughter to labour amongst the employees, but Pa said you didn't know a factory until you had worked it.

As far as Elsie could recall, that was the only truly useful thing Pa had ever said.

When Elsie walked away from the girls, she noticed her shoes left prints on the floor, like a person walking in sand. Machinery whirred and splints sprayed into the trough, casting forth a nimbus of dust. The freckled girl from Fayford coughed. Gradually, the dust cleared. And just like that, Elsie's footsteps were gone.

Curious to think of all the hidden steps, all the moments the factory floor had known, buried then swept aside with a broom.

She mounted the stairs leading up to the office and stopped halfway, leaning against the iron banister, where she could look out across the entire factory. Women filling frames and supervising the machines, all their vitality burning off with the steam. Sparks from rogue matches that snapped and died out. How quickly it happened, the fizz and transformation from one state to the other. One moment the match was a stick with a proud white head; the next a charred, wasted thing with a forlorn appearance. Shrivelled.

Handcarts ferried the bundles to and from the dipping room. Beyond that were the drying sheds, not quite visible through the windows.

There. That patch there, near the circular saw, just concealed from view. If you scrubbed down to the surface you would find it black and scorched. That was where the fire began. Where Pa ran to douse it, frantic. And then . . . where the blood had flowed. Copious amounts of blood. Red blooming on the sawdust. Red trickling between the table legs. A strange deep red, like claret. Thick.

Vinegar and mops had taken up the worst of it, but Elsie imagined a remnant lingering there beneath the sawdust. Brown, not red now. Brown like molasses.

Jolyon was only six weeks old when it happened. Pa hadn't even changed his will to include a son yet. If Elsie had been determined, she might have found a way to retain the entire ownership of this factory until her marriage took place. But it was not natural to keep anything from Jolyon. She needed him to help her shoulder the burden of such an inheritance: a legacy born of blood.

Slowly, she deflated and sat down on the steps, her cheek pressed against the cold banister. Yes, there were terrible moments in the history of this place, but somehow the movement of the factory eroded them, wearing them away like the sea smoothing a stone. In their stead came another memory, far sweeter.

She had been walking down these very steps – not dressed in black, then, but vivid in fashionable magenta – when Jolyon ushered three gentlemen through the main doors. One wore a bowler hat, the other two toppers. They were roughly the same age – in their middle years, or a little older – but it was Rupert who caught the eye with his bright, active face. He looked more like a young man, damaged by a rough decade. His companions were what Ma would call *badly preserved*, their skin wrinkled, pickled.

'Ah,' Jolyon had said when he saw her. He was nervous but trying not to show it. A dark patch appeared beneath his armpit as he gestured. 'Here is my sister come to assist us with the tour. Mr Bainbridge, Mr Davies, Mr Greenleaf, may I present Miss Livingstone?'

They bowed. Only Mr Bainbridge smiled. Well, she assumed that was the case – Mr Davies and Mr Greenleaf sported such monstrosities of facial hair that she could not be sure they even possessed mouths.

Mr Bainbridge was her instant favourite. He had a tidy, salt-and-pepper moustache, and was nattier than the others – even his trousers were checked, blue and green. He had a habit of toying with his watch chain as he walked.

She had taken Jolyon's arm and shown the trio around the factory, giving prompts where required and explaining the women's work. Jolyon talked about machines and production rates. Between them, they had it rehearsed as thoroughly as any play. The acts ran according to the script; their potential investors nodded at the right moments, asked the questions they were supposed to. It was only when they went to the office, and Elsie sat opposite Jolyon at the head of the long, mahogany table, that the first problem arose.

'Forgive me, gentlemen, I thought we proposed to talk business?' Mr Greenleaf had put his bowler hat on the table, glancing from Elsie to a decanter full of brandy and back again.

'And so we do,' said Jolyon. 'Please, proceed.'

'Hardly gallant, with ladies present.'

Elsie screwed up a smile. 'I assure you, Mr Greenleaf, the factory is a topic of which I never tire. You need not be afraid of boring me.'

He inclined his head. Of course, boring Elsie was not what he feared – she knew it, he knew it.

'Dear madam, let me be plain. The language in these meetings can grow a trifle coarse. It would be far better if your brother simply recounted the parts suitable for your ears at a later time.'

Rupert's laugh was a single breath. 'Upon my word, Greenleaf, I don't know what sort of meeting you're intending to have. Here I was, prepared to be mannered and civil.'

Jolyon coloured. His hands began to hover about his pockets. 'You must understand this factory is Miss Livingstone's inheritance, as well as mine. She has a right, I feel, to be present at any—'

'Pshaw, no one's disputing her right, man. But is there a *need*? Spare the poor lady the formal horrors.'

She could feel her heart pounding in her neck, furious at this fat old man, stuffed with prejudice and money. *Horror.* What did he know of horror? Only the thought of Jolyon held her tongue.

'Bad language and formal horror,' commented Rupert, swinging his watch. 'I start to doubt whether I wish to stay here myself.'

'Bainbridge, you know well enough what I mean. Figures of speech and business formalities we take for granted could prove shocking, not to mention tiring, for a lady.'

The worst of it was that Greenleaf would never admit the truth. He would not insult her intellect. He would not argue her place. Instead he took up this degrading charade, mimicking chivalry, pretending to object for her own dear sake.

Greenleaf went on. 'I really see no reason, Livingstone, why your poor sister should be forced to suffer this. No reason at all.'

'Unless,' Davies put in slyly, 'it is for yourself. Young man that you are, you might require an elder sibling's presence?'

Jolyon turned scarlet. That was the trigger. She stood up and seized the decanter of brandy.

'Well, gentlemen, you've had your say and I'm sure you've enjoyed it. As for Mr Livingstone and me, we have business to attend. Anyone who invests in this factory will have a master *and* a mistress to deal with, and that is not up for debate.' She poured herself a finger of brandy and tossed it back. 'If you're too squeamish to talk business with a lady, you had better leave now.'

The speech seemed to have said itself. Elsie felt a flame in the back of her throat and gazed down at the brandy glass, unable to understand how it had got into her hand.

Mr Greenleaf and Mr Davies left. Rupert stayed.

And after all that commotion it was Jolyon who spoke for most of the meeting, detailing their plans to change from lucifer matches to matches with safety heads, and their proposed improvements for the welfare of staff. It was Jolyon who explained ventilation fans, Jolyon who made the case for a separate drying house. But it was Elsie whom Rupert remembered.

'A remarkable woman,' he said to Jolyon, when he thought she was out of earshot. 'Your sister has an acumen for this business, Livingstone, I hear it in every word she says. You are quite right to involve her.'

'Elsie.'

But that was not what Jolyon had said in response. It was not a voice from the past, but from the here and now.

'Elsie.'

She blinked, making an effort to draw herself back to the present. The image of Rupert and Jolyon shaking hands melted away. In its void rose another Jolyon. He bore no resemblance to the young man she had just seen; his face was distorted, shocked; his voice hollow and unreal.

'Elsie, what are you doing here? I've been looking all over.'

She stood, walking down the last few steps to take his hands. They were slick and hot. 'Whatever is the matter? You look terrible, Jo.'

'A damned awful business. Pack up your things. You need to go back to The Bridge. Today.'

The contents of her stomach shifted. 'Why? What on earth has happened?'

'It's Mabel.' He gripped her gloves, tight. 'Mabel is dead.'

THE BRIDGE, 1635

He will die tomorrow.

It is my fault. All of it. Every morning I wake sick to the dregs of my stomach with guilt. But I have not suffered enough, I will never suffer sufficiently to please Josiah. He must push my face to it, like a dog that has messed in its master's house. So we are hosting a celebration.

Since Mark caught up with the runaway, my husband has decreed that the servants be rewarded with a feast. All day the spits have been turning, flooding the ground floor with smoke. My eyes sting from it.

Josiah has granted them use of the Great Hall. They sit there now, clinking glasses, ripping meat from bones with their teeth as if they are ripping apart Merripen himself.

I have resigned myself to the kitchen with Lizzy. It is my penance to sit here in the choking smoke, sweat dripping from my forehead, watching the animal skins blister and bubble as they turn above the fire.

We try to make conversation but it seems too glib a thing, too ordinary an occupation. Can such trifles continue after all that has passed?

'It don't seem right,' Lizzy sighed. She mopped her face. 'Carrying on like that because a lad will be stretched in the morning. Even an evil lad.'

I listened to the fat dripping and sizzling. Would Merripen roast like that in the fires of hell?

'I was so foolish to trust him. Yet he did not seem like a wicked boy.'

'Aye. But the devil takes on many guises. The way he attacked that poor horse . . .' She came and patted my hand with her own sweating, calloused palm. 'Perchance it's better this way. Put an end to him before he can turn his spite on a human soul.'

But what an end.

We watched the fire together. To my eyes the logs resembled charred limbs; a poor soul burnt at the stake. God grant they never discover the way I begot Hetta. If they hang, draw and quarter Merripen, what would they do to me?

'How is Hetta?' I asked at last. 'Does she know what will happen to her friend?'

Lizzy heaved herself onto a bench. 'I didn't tell her, but she's sharp. Knew there was to be a big feast. To and from the garden all morning she was, gathering herbs for Cook. I suppose it helps her to keep busy.'

'And now?'

She glanced at the clock. 'Now I had better be fetching her in. Didn't have the heart before, so I let her sit where she was at peace. But there's a vicious nip in that air. Can't have her catching cold.'

I put up my hand as she made to rise. 'Let me go, Lizzy.'

She nodded her consent.

The frozen air was pitiless when I left the heat of the kitchen. I did not realise how cold it had grown. It was cold enough for snow. Frost glittered on the twigs that snapped beneath my slippers as I made my way to the herb patch.

My once fine garden had turned into a collection of bony branches scoured by the wind. The sky stretched above, colourless as salt. No lilies grew, no roses survived. Only the topiary remained, a green ghost of my summer hopes. And Hetta's herbs.

I thought I was chilled before I saw her. But the moment my eyes fell upon my child, my heart froze within me.

She sat on the frosted dirt with her skirts pooled around her. Perfectly still. Although her gloved hands were empty, she held them in her lap with the palms facing up towards the sky.

Her basket remained on the path. She did not look up as my feet crunched beside it. Her eyes stared blankly ahead.

'Hetta? Hetta, what are you doing? You'll catch your death.'

I tugged at her shoulder. She was like a doll in my hand, floppy and senseless. Crystals of moisture sparkled on her hair. How long had Lizzy let her sit here in the damp?

'Hetta. Give me your hand and stand up.'

The last flicker of twilight danced upon the icy herbs and dazzled my eyes. I reached down and felt that Hetta's gloves were sticky, stained with the juice of plants. They released the fragrance of thyme and something deeper, something bitter, as I seized them and pulled her to her feet.

'Have you been gathering herbs with your hands?' I looked to the basket. It was filled with creepers and thistles. 'Where are your little scissors?'

She reached into her apron. Cold light flashed off the blades as she moved them, *snip, snip*. They looked rusty, a brown substance caking the handles.

'You shall have to get the knife-boy to clean them.'

I jostled her towards the house. She looked more dead than alive; her skin waxen and her eyes a dull, singed green. My breath plumed out and shivered on the air before disintegrating but her breath was shallow, barely there at all. Only once did a wisp curl from her nose, thin as the smoke from a snuffed candle.

I changed her clothes and loaded her bed with furs. I banked up her fire with my own hands. Then I covered her sparrow's cage and positioned one of the wooden companions by her side, just as she likes it.

While the wind groaned down the chimney we sat looking at one another, us two, complicit in our guilt. Together we had ruined the family. And still the wind howled, warning of further torment to come.

Hetta raised a hand. She was reaching, reaching for me, wanting my comfort . . .

No. She did not even see me. All she wanted was my diamond necklace.

I pulled away from her.

When at last Hetta slept, I crept back down to the kitchen. Lizzy was asleep at the table, her head on her outstretched arms. I sit now beside her dear, warm body and listen to the breath whistling from her nose. It strikes me that this old woman with the lines gouged in her face is the only true connection between Hetta and myself. After all my efforts to make a precious daughter and friend, this is all that we share: the love of a servant and the death of Merripen.

I had almost dozed off when shouts came from the hall. Footsteps followed, heavy and uneven. I touched Lizzy's shoulder. 'Lizzy, wake up. They are coming back to the kitchen.'

The fire had burnt low. A chill crept in through the stone walls. The wind was wild now, shaking the door, banging at the window. I looked up and tried to see outside, but ice marbled the glass.

'Lizzy.'

She grunted and stirred. 'What time is it, mistress?'

'I do not know. Time for us to be a-bed. Come, I cannot stand to bide here. They might burst in singing.'

We were nearly at the servants' stairs when a blow fell upon the door to the stable yard. I froze. Who could be out in that storm?

Glass rattled in the window frames. The chimney gusted.

The knock came again.

Lizzy moved towards the door, her servant's habits ingrained. I grabbed her sleeve.

'Lizzy . . .' I could not say what I feared. Panic rose from my chest to my throat.

The noise of the servants grew louder.

'I must answer it, mistress. A body could freeze to death in that blizzard!' Her woollen sleeve rubbed across my fingers and was gone.

She reached the door to the yard just as the servants burst in from the other direction. Mark staggered into the roasting jack, his face blotched red. Next came Jane, giggling, then Cook and a string of footmen who looked quite foreign to me, out of their livery. At their heels, haunting every step, wafted a sour cloud of alcohol.

'Lackaday! What's this? Mistress in the kitchen?'

Lizzy darted a glance at them before she turned and pulled the door open. It blew inwards, thudding against the wall. Snow flurried onto the tiles, melting in an instant as the fire gibbered, casting shadows on the ceiling.

Roars of disapproval came from the drunken servants.

'Why did you open that door, damn you?' hollered Mark. 'It's cold as a witch's tit out there.'

I could not see who had knocked for admittance; the snow was too dense. I squinted, shivering. Something moved in the flurry. Something the height of Lizzy's waist.

'Oh! God save us, what is it?' Lizzy reared back, stumbling into Jane. Now I saw it: the queerest creature; black as the devil, but dotted all over with white. It lurched forwards, mumbling in tongues. Jane shrieked.

'Mercy.' A single, comprehensible word. Everything fell still. The creature held out its dark hands; the atmosphere prickled around it. 'M-m-mercy.'

And I saw it was no demon, but a meagre child, her hair loose and torn by the wind, dripping from the tips.

'No beggars here!' barked Lizzy. I had never seen her so afraid. 'We don't want your sort.'

I opened my mouth to say that she could sleep in the stables. Then I remembered what had happened the last time I let a stranger into those stalls.

The girl shook her head. Something in her black eyes was familiar. 'Josiah Bainbridge,' she stumbled over the name – it was clear that she did not use her native tongue. 'I see Josiah Bainbridge. Mercy.'

Mark bumbled forward, pushing Lizzy behind him. 'You'll get nowhere near my master. Now hop it.'

I could not stop myself. The question flew from me. 'Mercy . . . Mercy for whom?'

Those dark eyes turned in my direction. Diamonds of snow stuck to the long lashes. 'Brother.'

The floor spun away from me. Gooseflesh crept over my skin and I knew in that moment what it really was to have the second sight. Not my strange forebodings and dreams, but the power in this girl's ink-black eyes. I did not need to hear the name, yet she gave it.

'Brother. Merripen.'

Jane shrieked again.

'God's blood! It's that gypsy,' Mark roared. 'It's the kin of that foul boy!'

'Take her through to the master,' cried Cook. She steadied herself against the wall and belched. 'String her up alongside him, he will.'

As one, the servants surged. There were fewer than a dozen of them, but they had become legion: a mass of grasping fingers and furious red faces.

Lizzy was jostled sideways. Her black partlet ripped. She clung onto the brick chimney, a plea passing from her eyes to mine. *Stop them.* I started forwards, but they grabbed at the child, clumsy and rough in their liquor.

'Stop!' Lizzy launched herself from the chimney and tried to wrench their hands away. 'Run, child!' she cried. 'Run!'

I added my voice. They did not heed it. Who was I to halt them, now? The disgraced mistress, the wife Josiah treated like refuse in a street kennel.

Lizzy managed to free one of the child's wrists. Scratching and hissing, the girl pulled the other one to liberty. Just then, a stray fist caught the side of Lizzy's head. She went down – there was nothing between the girl and the mob.

I have never moved so fast in all of my life. Heedless of the benches, of my skirts, I darted into the space Lizzy had left and made my decision. They would not dare to strike me, but I could not hold them at bay for long. I had to get the girl away.

Planting both hands on her bony shoulders, I shoved her back through the door, into the waiting claws of the storm. Her hands flailed and caught at my throat – I felt my diamond necklace lift from my skin. Our eyes met again for the shock of an instant. Then she was gone, obscured by a drift of snow.

I whipped around and slammed the door shut behind me. My spine was firm against the wood, my arms out to bar the way.

'Back!' I shouted. 'Get back!'

Mark met my gaze. His face twisted. 'I will tell Master of this.'

One by one they fell away; either to their rooms or to the floor. Jane lies now, stretched snoring before the burnt-out fire. It is deathly cold. Yet Lizzy and I sit here together by a single candle, unable to stir ourselves.

All we can do is listen to the wind as it chitters and thumps through the woods. Nothing shows through the window: it is coated with snow, and we are buried.

'It is very cold,' Lizzy says, every so often. 'It is very, very cold.'

———

End of the first volume

THE BRIDGE, 1866

Elsie sat rock solid on the squabs, staring straight ahead as the carriage rumbled towards Fayford. Outside, the weather was mild. Pale, soft light showed buds in the hedgerows and blossom on every tree. But this year spring was a spiteful mockery.

Her cheeks felt hard, like set wax. A thrush trilled in the woods and it seemed the most painful, jarring noise she had ever heard.

How could this have happened?

An accident, Mrs Holt said. Mabel was washing greens for the servants' dinner and didn't take the time to dry her hands before preparing the meat. The cleaver must have slipped.

Slipped. A convenient word: out of control; hard to hold, even in the mouth. Too fast. You could not prove a slip. Elsie knew that well.

But if Mabel's hand had slipped, why didn't she run for help? Why did nobody hear her scream? How could it be that no one knew about the accident until Helen found her in a pool of blood on the kitchen floor, a vertical slash running from her wrist to her elbow?

Only one answer offered: she did not want help. She had intended it.

'This is my fault.' Jolyon had sucked on a cigar and exhaled forcefully through his nose as he paced up and down the office. 'I was angry. I accused her of those dreadful things. Easter is approaching, she must have been so afraid of returning to the workhouse that she . . .'

'I do not know that you were wrong, to accuse her as you did.'

'How can you talk so?'

'Think, Jolyon. This suicide – if suicide it was – confirms, rather than disproves, your suspicions. So often, this type of thing is an act of remorse. If she played a trick on me and it killed my baby . . . Well, who *could* live with that?'

He took another sharp puff. 'Either way,' he said into the smoke, 'my words have pushed a girl towards self-murder. There is blood on my hands.' And he had stared at his fingers, shaking on the shaft of his cigar. 'You must go down at once, Elsie. I have business to finish here, but I will follow you as soon as I can.'

Whatever the truth, they would maintain Mrs Holt's conclusion: an accident. The least they could do was ensure Mabel was buried in hallowed ground.

To think of all that life and bold-faced cheek, gone. Death lent the girl a dignity she had never possessed in life. They would stand around her coffin silent, respectful, expecting her to wake up any moment and ask them what they were moping about.

A cold hand twisted her gut as they approached the village. The spring sunlight did nothing to improve the cottages. Weeds sprouted from the mouldering thatch on the roofs. She shifted on the seat, feeling something unwind deep within her. She was wiggling back into all her old fears, donning the superstitions like an old cloak.

She put up her veil and looked out at the chestnut trees brooding over the church. White blossom wilted between the new leaves on the branches. Was that Sarah, by the south entrance? She peered through the window but the figures behind the stone wall were so small and blurred that she could not make them out. Of course it was possible that Sarah would be at church, making arrangements. What would she say about the death? What would Mr Underwood say? It was such a terrible mess.

Her carriage trundled over the bridge. Water gurgled beneath, seeming to laugh at her misfortune. There was something wrong about The Bridge. In London, she had learnt to scoff at her fear as nonsense, but now she was back she could feel it, creeping, slithering. Something dark and insidious, all the way down to the roots of the plants that grew in the garden. It was not just the past, those strange events Sarah spoke of from Anne Bainbridge's diary. The very fabric of the building was bad. Elsie could face the match factory where she had suffered as a child, but this . . . this place made her nervous.

When Mabel was buried, she would take Sarah back to London with her and shut up the house for good.

As the carriage turned and wound down the drive, the sun flared over the hills, burnishing the grass. From this distance everything was made up of shadow and light; the shrubbery glowed, the bricks fell dark, the windows blazed.

It was not until Peters drew the carriage round before the fountain that the flames died in the windows and Elsie saw the sight that struck her heart cold.

It could not be.

She threw the carriage door open and stumbled, blinking, onto the gravel.

'Ma'am?' Peters sounded anxious. 'Wait there, I'll come and help you.'

'No,' Elsie moaned. 'No, you're dead.'

Watching, as she always did, just watching.

'Ma'am?' A crunch as Peters jumped down from the box.

Ma couldn't have, she didn't *enjoy* watching?

'Are you unwell?'

Elsie paid him no heed. She had never noticed before, but she saw it now – that flicker of morbid excitement in the pupils. It was the look of someone before the scaffold, come to watch a hanging. Bloodthirsty.

'Oh, no, Ma.' The thought was worse than anything else, worse than the act itself.

Peters was shaking her arm now, his voice tight. 'Mrs Bainbridge? Mrs Bainbridge? What's wrong, what are you staring at?'

'The companion. Look!'

'Companion? No, ma'am. I chopped them up, remember?'

'Not that one.' She extended her hand. There was a kind of satisfaction in pointing her out, like a victim accusing her attacker in court. 'It's my mother.'

'What?'

'In the window! Look, man!'

But Peters stepped back, shaking his head. 'There's . . . there's nothing in the window, ma'am.'

It couldn't be true. She clutched her forehead with both hands. 'Look again.'

'I'm looking. The window's empty.' Peters was moving slowly, holding out his hands, the way he might try to placate a dangerous dog. 'Let me fetch Mrs Holt, ma'am. Sit you down, get you a nice cup of tea.'

'No. No! She's in there, I'll show you.'

'Please, ma'am!'

She was beyond reason, beyond even fear. She ran up the steps to the front door and streaked into the empty Great Hall. Sawdust scented the air. A fire popped and crackled in the grate.

'Ma! Ma!' She marched on through the drawing room, calling out for her mother. A thousand echoes rang in that cry: childhood pleas from years ago. Now, as then, only silence responded.

The music room. 'Ma!' Her voice bounced back from the high, moulded ceiling. She shouldn't be surprised. Ma never came to help, not even when Elsie was bleeding and desperate and screaming her name. 'Please, Ma, just this once!'

Tears burnt in her eyes as she stumbled into the card room. She never should have done it. She never would have *had* to do it, if Ma had only —

A voice erupted from deep within her, rumbling up, pouring out of her mouth in a raw scream. She fell to her knees.

'Mrs Bainbridge!' Peters's boots on the carpet beside her. 'Mrs Bainbridge, what's – oh, good God!'

He staggered against the wall, holding it for support, as he saw what she saw.

The stag's head no longer hung against the wall. It had fallen, antlers first. But it did not fall unimpeded.

Helen lay there beneath it. Impaled, skewered, penetrated.

Blood welled from a dip where her eye had been. The muscles around it still twitched, as if they could blink out the horn lance sticking through the eyeball, pinning Helen to the carpet.

Fluid ran from her lips. They were moving – trying to move – but she was drowning. A hideous gurgle left her at the same time Peters threw up.

Elsie swayed. Images were blurring, vanishing. Or rather, *she* was vanishing – withdrawing from the carnage before her to hide somewhere, deep inside.

ST JOSEPH'S HOSPITAL

The pencil was sharp. Dr Shepherd had trimmed it with his penknife. She didn't like the way it wrote now: scratching along the page; snagging; threatening to snap when she pressed too hard. She had to hold it delicately, as if it were made of glass.

But it was not made of glass, it was made of wood. It smelt of wood, after the trim – she recognised the unsettling scent of trees cracked open.

Over and over again, the same words. Perhaps they would blunt the lead. Make it soft and shining so she could pick up her story again. She refused to continue while the letters looked like this: crisp and startling in their clarity.

Could she blunt her senses also? Once upon a time, the drugs had done that. She remembered shambling down the corridors with Dr Shepherd, barely able to stay awake. But now her traitorous body was growing accustomed, as it had grown accustomed to so many ordeals.

She began to sense the sadness ingrained in the hospital's bleak white walls and cold tiles. Her whole existence dwindling to a lone, barred cell. Why did chemists manufacture medicines that awoke people, when reality was dismal and hopeless? Better the laudanum dreams, the tranquillisers. For now she felt like a woman in bed on a baking summer's night – desperate to sleep but turning over and over, unable to rest. Writing the same two words, over and over.

Jolyon. Protect Jolyon.

Her incantation since the day he was born, her twelfth birthday. *Protect Jolyon.* Yet he was not here and he had not come to visit. That could only mean one thing: she had failed.

The observation hatch slid open. 'Mrs Bainbridge? Do I disturb you? May I come in?'

She saw Dr Shepherd's spectacles, glinting behind the gap in the door. The pencil dropped from her fingers.

He shot the bolt from its cradle and entered the cell, closing the door behind him. The stack of papers he carried was thicker than ever.

'Why don't you sit upon the bed, Mrs Bainbridge? I am quite willing to stand.'

She did as he asked. The covers were still warm from her body, laced with her own scent. Strange, how a bed had come to mean safety and escape for her. It was not always so.

'I thought it best that you sit down, Mrs Bainbridge, because I fear our talk today may prove upsetting. Your story has progressed to the point where I begin to understand the pattern of your mind. We have come to the crux of it now.'

His words sank to the bottom of her stomach. She had an urge to pitch herself off the bed and run. Her eyes darted about the room, from the barred window to the heavy lock on the door. No escape.

'You have written of these "companions", as you call them. You say you were afraid of them. But do you know what really scares us? It is not things that go bump – or even hiss – in the night. Our fears are much closer than that. We are afraid of the things inside us – be they memories, sickness or sinful urges.' He tilted his head. His spectacles slid to the left. 'You, I deduce, are afraid of becoming like either of your parents.'

They were bound to come, of course: the pinpricks of light in her vision and the rush like water in her ears. Childish memories, childish thoughts, that if she squeezed her eyes shut, somehow Dr Shepherd would not be able to see her.

'I understand what you are feeling. I cannot pretend to be ignorant of the hints you drop, however much natural delicacy would prefer to draw a veil over the subject. And I think that's what you have done, Mrs Bainbridge: drawn a veil. First through coercion and then through a sort of mental necessity, you have hidden the fact that your parents mistreated you.'

If she still had a voice she would scream, *No, no, speak of anything but that.* Or would she? A part of her, a small treacherous part, must want it to be known or she would not have written it, she would not have told him.

He cleared his throat. 'Believe me, Mrs Bainbridge, I feel deeply for you. A betrayal of trust at such a young age, from those instinct prompts us to hold most dear . . . And a mother, who should nurture and protect, but instead . . .'

She'd hoped to outlive tears, move beyond them to an arid landscape where they never flowed. Yet here they came; hot, sliding down to her chin, restricting her breath. Had they been lurking there all along, just waiting to thaw?

'I wanted, more than anything, to tell you that this is a *positive* development. Naturally, it does not feel so – it is forcing you to face a world of distress. Yet you *are* facing it, Mrs Bainbridge. You have had strength enough to recall these unnatural abuses of your trust. I know you will also find the strength to remember what happened at The Bridge the night of the fire. Then we can make our report. We can clear your name.'

Surprised, she met his gaze: eyes the soft green of buds in spring; pliable, forgiving. And she realised, with a relief so sharp it was almost pain, that he was on her side.

THE BRIDGE, 1866

The room was tender with Elsie at first. Objects retreated to a considerate distance, hazy around the edges, withholding their full weight. Panic hovered in a place she could sense but not quite feel.

Light played upon the ceiling in ripples. She fluttered her eyelashes.

'Elsie.' Pressure upon her hand. 'Mrs Holt, make a hot posset! Quickly! She's awake!'

Clanging downstairs. It was all too sharp, penetrating the soft fuzz.

'Elsie, dear Elsie. Thank goodness.' Gradually, Sarah's strong features became defined.

'I am not . . .' Her mouth tasted metallic. She tried again. 'Why am I . . .' No memory would stay still long enough for her to catch hold of it. She saw a deer, then a match . . . They darted away again.

'Do not try to speak. The doctor says we must keep you quiet. I have telegrammed for Mr Livingstone, he will come at once.'

She looked around. It was all there: the heavy bedposts carved with grapes and flowers; the washstand; the triple

mirror on the dressing table. Features of The Bridge returning like a long-forgotten dream. She could not process them.

Jolyon was coming. Jolyon, her constant, her ballast. She
must hold on to that. But why was he not here with her
now? He was upset, wasn't he? Mourning over something.
Ma. No, Mabel. Mabel. *Helen*. She jolted upright, drenched
in cold sweat. 'Helen! She was – she—'

Sarah's hand pressed on her shoulder, laying her back
against the pillows. 'Hush, hush. I know.' She swallowed. 'We were at the church, Mrs Holt and I, talking
to Mr Underwood about Mabel's funeral. But now it
seems . . . Now we will have to hold two.'

Elsie shut her eyes. It was with her still: Helen's strawberry face staring up from the carpet in all its mangled
horror. 'How? How could this happen?'

Sarah took a trembling breath. 'We had the constable
come down from Torbury St Jude. Then some inspectors.
Peters gave a statement. From all they can conjecture, it was
some kind of terrible accident. Helen must have been cleaning the stag, they said, when . . .'

Lights flashed behind her eyelids. 'But you don't believe
that, Sarah. I can hear it in your voice. You don't believe a
word of it.'

She felt Sarah edge closer. 'No, I don't.'

'Tell me.'

Sarah burst into tears.

Elsie's eyes snapped open. Sarah's face was scrunched
into a wet, red mess. She struggled to breathe through her
heaving sobs. 'Sarah? What is it?'

'This is my fault. It is all my f-fault.'

'How can you possibly think that?'

Sarah's jaw quivered. 'I – Oh, how can I tell you? It was me, Mrs Bainbridge. I t-took your d-diamonds!'

Vomit rose to the back of her throat. Mabel did not steal the diamonds: she was innocent. Innocent and pushed to a desperate act through Elsie's mistake.

'I just wanted something f-from my f-family. Then Mabel got into trouble and I – I didn't know what to do. I never thought . . .'

Blood, running hot over her hands.

'I was going to tell you at Easter,' Sarah gabbled on. 'I was going to tell everyone the truth, I swear it. But then Helen decided that the companions must have stolen the necklace! She . . .' Sarah screwed up her mouth, pained. 'She wanted to burn them again. She took Hetta from me and threw her onto the kitchen fire!'

Weak and sick, Elsie pressed her hands to her temples. 'I don't understand. Why did she suspect the companions?'

'That's what Mrs Holt didn't tell you. There was a companion, Elsie, in the kitchen with Mabel. One I have never seen before, some kind of cook.'

Pinpricks ran up Elsie's arms. 'I saw a companion of my own mother, Sarah, standing in the window. Right where the handprint was.'

'You see? They are multiplying. I think fire only makes them more powerful. And there never would have *been* a fire, were it not for my stupid, stupid—'

'You could have asked me for the diamonds,' Elsie cut in. 'I would not have refused you.'

Sarah hung her head. 'I am so ashamed. It is almost as if . . . I could not help myself. But it is not only me. Hetta was obsessed with them too, obsessed with the companions and the diamond necklace. I've been looking at the records Mr Underwood brought, finding out all I can about Anne. Usually there is scant material to go on for a woman in the sixteen-hundreds, but I found records on Anne because . . . because of the way she died.'

Elsie could not bring herself to ask.

'She was burnt,' Sarah whispered. 'Burnt at the stake for a witch.'

'A witch? *She* is the witch the villagers still fear?'

'Yes. And with good reason. The records say she killed people, Elsie. But in the diary, she is not wicked. She thought she was using white magic, the old herbal remedies of the wise-women. But she must have made a mistake. Her poor daughter was born without a proper tongue and something else, something *evil* . . .'

Elsie didn't want to believe it. At the factory, she had talked herself out of believing it. But here, back in this house where Rupert had died, where his siblings had died, she could *feel* it. The old, old fear. No amount of reason or logic could erase that feeling. She had known evil from a child – recognised its velvet voice.

A knock fell on the door. They both jumped.

'Hot posset.' Mrs Holt.

'Come in,' Elsie croaked.

The steam entered first, laced with warm nutmeg and treacle. Mrs Holt appeared carrying a tray and a cup spilling over with clouds of heat. New lines dragged around her mouth and made it look hinged. The whites of her eyes, always jaundiced, were now shot with ribbons of red.

Elsie took the cup. Milky, sweet scents teased at her nostrils. Her stomach begged for sustenance, but she couldn't bring herself to drink. She didn't want to swallow anything from this house. She didn't want it inside her.

'Miss Sarah, I think you had better leave the mistress be for now. Remember, she needs her rest. The doctor said so.'

'But—' Sarah started.

'I really must insist. Pardon me, miss, but Mr Livingstone will never forgive me if he arrives and finds I haven't followed the doctor's orders.'

Sarah stroked Elsie's hair. Leaning in close to her ear, she whispered, 'I will be back later. We should sleep in the same room from now on. I don't feel safe alone.'

Elsie nodded. She did not ask what Sarah meant by *alone*. No one was truly alone. Not ever, not in this house.

Sarah swept up her skirts and left the room. Elsie heard her footsteps, treading the familiar boards to the library. Mrs Holt remained.

The housekeeper's gaze possessed a hardness Elsie had not detected before. 'Will there be anything else, madam?' The *madam* was a forced, horrible sound.

'Oh, Mrs Holt. I am so sorry. I cannot imagine what you are feeling. First Mabel and then Helen.'

'I loved those girls like my own daughters. There was no harm in them. And now they are stiff and stretched in the cold larder, and I will have to bury them. Both of them!' Mrs Holt broke down. Elsie averted her eyes and let her cry it out. The noise alone was terrible.

'I was wrong to blame them,' Elsie ventured at last. 'They did not trick me or kill my cow. I know that now. There is something else at work, something in this house.'

A spasm crossed Mrs Holt's face. 'I have kept this house for nigh on forty years. We never had any hauntings or deaths before you came along.'

'Before Rupert came along,' Elsie corrected her softly.

'They'd still be alive if it wasn't for you. If you hadn't come storming in, clomping about, throwing open doors that were meant to stay shut.'

'What do you mean?'

'It doesn't matter.' Mrs Holt snatched her eyes away.

'"Doors that were meant to stay shut?" I don't understand you. Are you talking about the garret?'

The elder woman's ribcage rose and fell, jangling her cameo brooch. 'I was meant to keep it secret. The old Mr Bainbridge ordered me, right from the day I arrived here, to keep the garret locked and never discuss it.'

'But why?'

'I don't know. He said there were things in there, things that troubled his wife. Books.'

'A diary?'

As she said that, she remembered that there were two diaries. Two volumes. Sarah did not mention if she had ever retrieved the second one. Perhaps it was still there.

'Maybe. I don't recall what books they were. I never had reason to recall until you turned up.'

Elsie's grip tightened on the cup. 'What – what happened to Rupert's mother? How did she die?'

'Blessed if I know.'

'You must have an idea. What were her symptoms?'

'I tell you, I don't know! For all anyone told me, she could be drawing breath yet.'

Elsie lay stunned. 'You were there,' she said, incredulous. 'You said. You talked of *when you lost the mistress.*'

Mrs Holt closed her eyes, seemed to wrestle with her memories. 'No. No, she didn't die. She was . . .'

'What?'

'We lost Mrs Bainbridge, but it wasn't to death. It was her mind. Her own mind got her in the end.'

Elsie's hands started to shake. The cup clattered against the saucer. 'Are you saying that her husband put her in an asylum?'

Mrs Holt gave her a long look. 'We never told Master Rupert. Just said that she'd died, and it was true, in a sense. That lunatic wasn't Mrs Bainbridge, not any more. I've seen hysteria, madam. I've seen a woman driven mad with her novel reading and her brain fevers. I've seen that look in your eye before.'

'But *I* am not mad!' Mrs Holt did not reply. 'You know I am not. You were there, Mrs Holt. You saw the companions. You saw them burnt to ash and reappear from nowhere.'

Mrs Holt shook her head. 'Maybe it's losing a child that does it to your poor mind . . . God help me. I didn't listen to the ravings of the last Mrs Bainbridge and I'll be damned if I'll listen to yours.'

Turning on her heel, she strode from the room and closed the door. Elsie heard her sharp steps echo through the corridor and down, down, descending the spiral staircase behind the wall.

———

The night hung heavy and interminable. Sarah lay beside her in the bed, her mousy hair spread out on the pillow. Her chest rose and fell beneath her ruffled nightgown. How could she sleep?

One window stood ajar, letting a gasp of air into the stuffy room, but it was not refreshing; it smelt warm and herbal. Outside, a barn owl screeched to its mate.

Rupert's mother waltzed in circles around Elsie's head. She had slept in this house, walked in the gardens. A lunatic? Or a fellow victim? She remembered that tattered, plundered crib in the nursery and shuddered.

Sarah shifted in the bed. Her body made the sheets too hot, but Elsie did not move. She kept her eyes open, waiting. Knowing it would come.

Yes.

Hissss. It was so soft, it might have been a breeze passing through the room. But there was no breeze tonight.

Hiss. She couldn't stand it any longer. She had to find out. She had to get the second volume of that godforsaken diary and discover what Rupert's mother had known.

Carefully, she slid her feet out from under the covers and placed them on the carpet. The bed rustled, but Sarah did not stir. Elsie reached beneath the pillow for the matches she kept there every night, like a talisman.

There was a snuffed-out candle in the holder on the dressing table. She picked it up as she passed. It made more sense to light the wick when she was outside in the corridor – then she could leave Sarah asleep, safe from the danger she was walking into.

Hiss, hiss.

She moved one leg after the other, forcing herself on, her hand out before her, feeling the way. Expecting, at any second, the sickening touch of wood.

Her palm collided with something. She flinched – it was the bedroom door handle, just the door handle. She leant against it and listened, stretching her senses to locate the next hiss, but nothing came.

She struggled to open the door, her nails clicking against the handle as she gripped it. She pushed down and eased the door open a fraction.

A wall of heat met her. It was like opening the door of a kitchen range. The scents of rose and thyme entwined about her, insinuating themselves into the fabric of her nightgown. *Light the candle, light the candle.* Neither light nor fire would protect her but she needed them, needed them like air.

The match flared in her trembling hand, sending shadows snaking out into the corridor. She would not look up, not until the candle was lit. It took every ounce of concentration to connect the flame with the wick. At last it caught; she shook out the match and let it drop steaming to the floor.

Quickly, quickly. She had to move but her hand refused to raise the candle, refused to do anything but grip the metal holder until her knuckle turned white. Close to tears, she finally managed to thrust the candle out ahead of her. The breath sealed in her chest.

The maroon corridor stretched before her, cross-hatched with shadows. Silver pools of moonlight dotted the path to the stairs. Three companions stood waiting, their eyes gleaming with a revolting hunger.

She would not scream, she would not scream. They were only pieces of wood.

Pieces of wood that can move.

She would have to move quicker – that was all. She could make it, she could do it. It was like jumping, like lighting a match. *One. Two. Three.*

Her tread was steady, far steadier than her careering heartbeat. Each time her foot hit the floor, the candle jogged and bumped in its holder. Light surged and retracted but the flame didn't go out.

Sawdust bloomed from the carpet as she approached the first companion. Through the candlelit haze she made out the figure of a woman. A woman without arms.

Her throat squeezed as she drew level. The woman had long, matted hair and eyes alight with a ghastly vivacity. Familiar, somehow. She had seen those eyes before, knew them well . . .

Rupert.

Rupert's mother, the other Mrs Bainbridge. A strait waistcoat concealed her arms. She was helpless, begging Elsie with an expression so lifelike that it cut her to the heart. Beneath the clumsy rhythm of Elsie's pulse came a wail, thin and pathetic. She could hear her. Elsie could hear Rupert's mother, crying.

Her skin pricked, tensed for the shock of contact – it did not come. Somehow, her feet kept walking; she passed by, unscathed, and moved towards the next companion.

This must be the cook that Sarah spoke of: she gripped a meat cleaver in her doughy hands. Blood streaked her apron and the coif that covered her hair. *Red paint, just paint.* Yet it carried the rancid smell of the real thing. Combined with the scent of roses and thyme it was a nauseous mixture, unbearable.

Again Elsie overtook the companion, this stab of fear deeper than the last. Terror knocked her vision aslant. She barely saw the last companion, the old woman with the child on her lap. Guided by memory, she turned past the

Lantern Gallery and made her way to the stairs leading to the garret.

The staircase was empty. Relieved, drunk with a sense of her own bravery, she broke into a run and took the steps two at a time. Shadows wheeled around her, scuttling back to the corners. She had beaten them. She would get that diary.

As she rounded the newel post and gained the landing, a sound stopped her in her tracks. Her eyes shot back down the staircase. They were all there – every companion she had walked past – staggered like children in a game of grandmother's footsteps; one on the treads, the other two at intervals down the corridor.

They had followed her.

Hiss.

Her gaze flew up: more companions had appeared, drawn to her like flies to a corpse. They were guarding the whitewashed passage that led to the garret. *Hiss.* Back again – the companion on the stairs had moved, ever so slightly.

Inch by inch, step by step, they were coming for her.

'God help me, please help me.'

She could not watch them all at once.

With a cry of agony, she wrenched herself away from the banisters and charged down the corridor. The candle blew out but she did not stop, could not stop; she kept going, pushing her way on. They didn't want her near the diary, and that was exactly why she must read it. She would read it if it was the last thing she ever did.

She shoved past the companions, hitting them with her shoulders, sending them rattling against the Dutch tiles. *Nearly there, nearly there.* She stubbed her toe and almost cried out for joy. It was a step – the first of the steps up to the garret.

She scrabbled for another match. The pack fell skittering to the floor but she managed to grab one stick, tight in her fist. She struck it on the wall and relit the candle.

The door to the garret was open.

Hiss. The sound made her nauseous. She could not stop – they were coming up close behind her. She stormed up the steps, whipped round and slammed the garret door shut. Just in time. Through the closing gap, she caught sight of a sinister painted smile and wide, vulpine eyes.

Her lungs seared in her chest. It was a labour to breathe with the dust and that dank, below-ground smell tainting the atmosphere. She felt close to fainting, and there was still the long run back to the bedroom. If she could get there. What if they barred her way out? What if they came through the door?

She spun around frantically, looking for the diary. Dust flew up like feathers in a hen-coop. As it cleared, she saw two glowing emerald eyes.

'Jasper!'

She had never been so pleased to see a creature in all her life. She ran to the table where he lay and put her candle down. Greedily, her fingers burrowed into his fur. The warmth of his skin, the beat of blood behind his ear, was comforting beyond measure. Something else alive – naturally alive. He could not help her, but she would rather face the companions with him than brave them alone.

Mewing, Jasper stood and bowed in a long, luxurious stretch. His claws extended and retracted again. As they went in, they took a nick out of the surface below him.

Leather. Worn and faded, but the scent was unmistakable. Jasper leapt elegantly to the floor and revealed what he had been sleeping on: 'The Diary of Anne Bainbridge'. Elsie seized it and pressed it to her chest. It was still warm.

She should read it here – here, now, while she had the chance. Her fingers flicked through the pages but it was no good. She could not focus, could not read. It was all a jumble to her.

Just then, she felt it on her shoulder: sharp as the lick of a knife. Screaming, she whirled round. In the instant before the candle went out, she saw a wooden mouth grinning at her.

'No! Jasper!'

His mew sounded at the other side of the room; his claws tapped as he swatted the door open and slunk away. He could see in the dark. She just had to follow him.

Lurching forwards, she gripped the diary in her hand and fumbled back the way she had come, towards the door and the staircase beyond. Or at least, she thought it was the way she had come. She could not see an inch before her nose. Companions must be massing round the door – she sensed them in the air: the force pressing down; malevolent, full of hate.

Her hand knocked against a table – papers slid to the floor. She couldn't see, she couldn't breathe . . .

All at once, the floor tilted beneath her. She grabbed at the air and felt a scream boiling out from her lips. Then she fell.

A corner of the diary jolted into her ribcage as she came to an abrupt stop. Her legs burnt, her chest squeezed. What had happened? Groaning, she kicked her feet out. She could move them. They were free, but she was stuck fast.

Understanding slammed into her: the floorboards had opened again. She was caught in the hole Mabel had fallen down.

Hiss, hiss.

Trapped, cornered. And all the while, the companions were coming closer.

She kicked wildly. She had to pull herself up, but one hand was clamped hard to her chest, nursing the diary, while the other waved uselessly in the dark, unable to catch hold of anything solid.

Hiss, hiss. She heard rather than saw them move: the slow, painful scrape of the wooden base against the floor. Pinpricks ran down her neck. Something hard pressed against the back of her head.

'No, no, no!'

With a final desperate convulsion, she flailed her legs.

There was a long, low creak. Then suddenly she was falling, falling, until her spine smacked into the floor.

She lay paralysed by shock and pain.

At last, with great difficulty, she turned her head and saw the rocking horse sway at her side. The floor had given way. She was in the nursery.

ST JOSEPH'S HOSPITAL

It started with the blast of a whistle: shrill, nasal, ripping her from sleep. The world was hazy as she struggled to her feet.

Sounds echoed: boots slapping against the floor, shouts. Only the shriek of that whistle was distinct until the door banged open. Attendants piled into the room; she did not know which ones. They were difficult to distinguish, all hard-faced and lined with endurance. Their muscular arms seized hers and pulled them behind her back.

'Mrs Bainbridge.' Dr Shepherd's voice. Relief alighted on her for an instant, but he shook his sandy head. 'Mrs Bainbridge, I did not expect this. What has happened?'

What *had* happened?

He gestured to her left. 'What has happened to the desk?'

She writhed in the attendants' grip, twisting to see. Her desk had imploded. Drawers lay scattered on the floor; some upside down, some with the bottoms punched out. There were scores on the wood. Tooth marks? Yes, tooth marks. But whose?

Dr Shepherd approached it and squatted down, as if he were inspecting a scientific specimen. 'Remarkable. Quite remarkable. How did it get like this?'

That was the question. Had another patient slipped into her room, while she slept? Surely she would have heard them? It would have to be someone with a key, the ability to lock and unlock doors, to move soundlessly when—

Dear God, no.

Wood; they always came from wood.

A gaunt nurse with cheekbones like blades stepped forward. 'It's what she does, doctor. She smashes everything to pieces.'

'I am not certain that she did,' muttered Dr Shepherd.

'What?'

Confusion flickered over his features. She recalled it well: the exact moment she had started to doubt her own senses. 'For a start, I do not believe Mrs Bainbridge is strong enough to do such damage. And then, look at her arms. There are no tears in her gown, no sign of blood or splinters on her hands.' He withdrew a pencil and prodded a drawer. 'I do not comprehend how a person could do this without injuring themselves.'

'So you're telling me the desk went and did this all by itself?'

'No.' He unbent his legs and bit on the end of his pencil. 'No, that is, of course, impossible. But did you hear the crash? What was it that prompted the whistle to summon us here?'

'I blew the whistle,' the nurse said, raising her chin. 'I heard an odd noise in here, and she's usually quiet as death.'

'A banging noise? She must have been going at it a good while, to get the desk in this state.'

'No, not a banging. I only heard it for a few minutes. It sounded like – I don't know. A scrape, like she had some kind of saw.'

He looked straight at Elsie. 'Would you say,' he asked, still addressing the nurse, 'perhaps, that it sounded like a hiss?'

Her knees buckled.

'Yes, that's it, doctor. A kind of rasping hiss.'

God, what had she done? She should never have written her story, never have tried to remember.

Dr Shepherd pursed his lips. 'Never mind. Just have someone come and clean up this mess. Until the room is suitable again, we will have to find Mrs Bainbridge some alternative accommodation.'

An attendant's breath burnt in her ear, alight with the scent of ale. 'Want us to put her out, doctor?'

'No, no,' he said. 'Leave Mrs Bainbridge be. I shall take her to my office.'

'To your office,' the attendant repeated in disbelief.

'Yes. Unhand her, if you please. She will take my arm.'

He offered his elbow, pristine and white. She grasped at it like a drowning woman.

The nurse and attendants muttered as he drew her from the room.

It had been a long time since she'd walked like a lady, escorted by a gentleman. She could not appreciate it now. Terror frayed her senses. It was fortunate Dr Shepherd was strong and young, for he practically had to carry her down the endless corridors to a passage where the echoes were dull and the paint peeled from the walls.

'Just in here,' he said.

In her story she had been defiant, fighting against the companions. Now Dr Shepherd had to heave her through the door and push her into a chair as though she were paralysed. She could not talk and now she could barely move. Was there anything left inside of her but fear?

Dr Shepherd's office was smaller than she had imagined it. The walls were the same green and white that pervaded the rest of the hospital. It housed a good, sturdy desk and a brass lamp, but little else. She noticed a bell beneath the coving, the type used to summon servants. There must be a clock somewhere too for she could hear it ticking, measured, so much slower than her hammering pulse.

'I am sorry that this has happened, Mrs Bainbridge. Please do not fret over it. In hindsight, I should have realised something of this nature could occur.' He sat down on the other side of his desk and exhaled. He was a little paler, these days. His eyes sunk further back into his head. The hospital was taking its toll. 'The hints are there in your file. When you can no longer flee from unpleasant memories, your natural instinct is to fight them. Quite understandable. A release of anger, if properly directed, can be cleansing.' He drummed his fingers on the surface of his desk. 'But it is preferable for you and me to work through your feelings together, rather than release them. I must include all my observations in my report and . . . well, violent acts do not present themselves in a favourable light.'

She shook her head, incredulous. The hiss! How did he explain the hiss? And he had said himself that she should have scratches or cuts if she had wrecked the desk. She reached out her hands to tell him, but they were empty – the chalk and slate remained in her room.

'Yes,' he said, noticing her action. 'I thought we might leave them behind. From what Nurse Douglas says, you have begun to articulate. Even if it is only noises from your own story . . . I am beginning to believe that this "hiss" has more significance than I first anticipated. Are you able to repeat it?'

Did he truly believe she would try? She would do anything never to hear it again, but even if she deafened herself it would still be there, waiting in her dreams.

'Mrs Bainbridge?'

To appease him, she opened her mouth, exhaled and shut it.

Dr Shepherd sighed. 'Well, perhaps not yet.' He opened a drawer. It made an awful wooden *clunk* that set her teeth on edge. 'While we are here, I have something I want to show you, Mrs Bainbridge. It is an old file of ours that I came across while locating your own. At the time I did not consider it of any importance that we treated another Bainbridge here. But when your account touched upon Rupert's mother, I had another look.' He pulled out a file and placed it on the desk. Its cover was stained and partly ripped. 'This, indeed, was her. Julia Bainbridge.'

A small explosion in her chest. The crying woman with Rupert's eyes.

She extended a shaking hand but Dr Shepherd put his palm firmly on top of the file.

'There are no photographs, I am afraid. Not common in those days. But I have read through it and am prepared to give you a summary.'

He didn't want her to see inside. Why?

Distractedly, Dr Shepherd began to smooth the edges of the file. 'In your story, you seem concerned that the other Mrs Bainbridge suffered from a similar malady. That the same circumstances troubled her and, ultimately, confirmed your ghostly fears. But I thought it would help you to know that Julia was, in fact, a very different case. She was plagued by melancholia her entire life. It grew particularly bad whenever she was confined in childbed.'

The tenor of those sobs, so different from Sarah's or even Mrs Holt's. She closed her eyes, trying to forget them.

'The fatal break occurred one summer at The Bridge. Her child, a boy of five years, attempted to jump a hedge on his pony. It was far too high. The animal was injured past help and had to be destroyed. The boy lingered a while longer but there was too much swelling in the brain . . . Eventually he passed away.'

The patchwork quilt. He must have lain beneath it while Julia hovered, tortured, by his side.

'It was unfortunate timing. Julia had given birth to a daughter just three months before. Her state remained . . . unstable. She developed a peculiar mania in regards to the rocking horse. She had found it scratched, she said, days before the accident, in the same places the pony received its injuries.'

This was bad enough, but there was something worse. She could feel it hanging between Dr Shepherd's lips. Slowly, she opened her eyes.

He was staring down at the file. He seemed to be looking through it, gazing into Julia Bainbridge's troubled past.

'After this, the details are conflicting. I have the official report, the somewhat stilted correspondence from the lady's husband . . . and the record of a conversation between one of our admitting physicians and Edna Holt.'

She held her breath.

'I was encouraged to find Mrs Holt confirmed many particulars of your story. For instance, she was not present at the death of either child, but she nursed Julia through her illness. That is, perhaps, the only solace to be found in the sorry tale.' Dr Shepherd met her gaze. His lips compressed, unsure. Finally he said, 'Officially it was suffocation. Babies do suffocate in their sleep, from time to time. But from hints thrown out by Mrs Holt and Mr Bainbridge, I gather that Julia drowned her baby daughter in the fountain.'

Empty lungs, pressure on her chest: she felt it too. *Mother hurt me.*

'Tragic,' he said. 'I deduce the matter was successfully hushed up until, of course, your own husband was born. Both the father and the servant became concerned for the child's welfare. Julia spoke of "protecting" him. These were the same words she had used about little Alice. You cannot blame them for taking drastic measures.'

She thought of her baby, and the antler sticking through Helen's eye. Perhaps drowning was kinder.

Dr Shepherd drew the file towards him and folded his arms upon it. There was no real need for him to bring it out, he seemed to know the contents by heart. 'Despite the hospital's best efforts, there was no recovery. She remained here for a score of years. Julia died, it seems, like your husband, at around forty years of age, from a heart condition.'

Poor woman. It was a wonder she had any heart left to break.

Dr Shepherd sat up straighter in his chair. His gloomy demeanour fell away. 'Strange as it sounds, Mrs Bainbridge, I actually told you that little history to raise your spirits. I feel it is proof we are drawing some authentic memories from you, whatever other . . .' he waved his hand, 'embellishments come with them. Progress is being made.'

She thought of the desk, the hiss. Right inside her room. Something was making progress, certainly.

She only hoped that it was her.

THE BRIDGE, 1866

It hurt to breathe. Try as she might, Elsie could not shift into a comfortable position. Every time she moved, a dagger slipped between her ribs.

Her nose felt bent. One of her eyes had swollen until she could only see a thin strip of light through it. There was no doubt in her mind now: she was not mad. Something was coming for her, as surely as the tide inching up the shore. But it would not come quickly. No. They enjoyed making her run.

She turned her head. A pillow puffed beneath it; she was not in the nursery. Someone must have heard the crash and found her in the rubble. She could not remember. Everything blurred beneath snatches of pain.

Footsteps sounded in the corridor, accompanied by a voice. A male voice — one she recognised.

'Jolyon!' His name a croak, barely audible. She made an agonising attempt to move. Pillows supported her on either side, she was propped sitting up at an angle.

The feet came to a halt outside her door. Elsie waited. Nothing happened. No one came in.

Straining her ears, she heard Jolyon and Sarah in conversation.

'She is still asleep?'

'I think so.' Sarah sounded spent. 'Heaven knows she was drugged enough, Mr Livingstone.'

'This is my fault. I should never have let her come back here, alone.'

'You must not blame yourself.'

Jolyon said something she could not make out. Then Sarah spoke again. 'The doctor said she cracked two ribs and sprained her left knee badly. It's a miracle nothing was broken. There is some damage to the face, but only cosmetic. Lots of scratches and contusions—'

'No,' said Jolyon – or perhaps it was someone else, for surely the tone was too harsh? 'That is not what I mean. You cannot pretend this is acceptable behaviour, even after all she has been through. What was she thinking, capering around attics at midnight?'

Sarah mumbled incoherently. It must have been something in Elsie's defence, for Jolyon shot back, 'You must not encourage her, Miss Bainbridge.'

The door creaked on its hinges. Elsie shut her eyes, knowing she would not be able to hide the hurt burning inside them.

Steps padded across the carpet.

'Elsie? Are you awake?'

She murmured and moved her head in the direction of the door, but she did not open her eyes.

'It's Mr Livingstone, Mrs Bainbridge, come to see you.'

Blindly, she stretched out her hand. It was not until Jolyon took it that she realised her gloves had been replaced with bandages.

'Elsie. How do you feel?'

She wet her lips. They were swollen and parched. 'Like I've been in the ring with Tom Sayers. I came off the better, though. You should see the state of the nursery.' She tried for a jovial tone, but it fell to the ground like a dead bird.

'I *have* seen it,' he said. 'Terrible damage.'

Carefully, she cracked open her one good eye. Jolyon floated into her vision. He looked ghastly. Uncombed hair straggled behind his ears and stubble covered his chin. Purple marks sat beneath each dull eye.

'Oh, Jo.' A tear slid down her face. She wanted to reach out and stroke his cheek, but there was something else beneath his concerned expression, something too hot to touch. 'I am sorry you've had to come down here and deal with this. We've had nothing but bad luck since the day Rupert died.'

'So it would seem.' His lips pressed together. 'What were you doing in the garret, Elsie?'

'Looking for something. There was a . . .' She trailed off as she glimpsed Sarah behind him, shaking her head and signalling madly with her bandaged hand.

'A what?'

Sarah was right – she could not tell him about the diary. He would take it away, say it excited her too much, and she would be back to the red lavender, back in the cold sitz-baths.

'An ornament,' she improvised. 'Helen saw it up there and took a fancy to it. I thought it would be a nice gesture if . . . if we buried it with her, in the coffin.'

'Oh.' A cold sound, impersonal. 'I see. And that could not wait until the morning?'

She had lied to him all his life. Why was it so difficult now? Perhaps the drugs Sarah had mentioned were slowing her down, numbing her faculties. 'I . . . couldn't sleep.'

'No?'

'We can none of us sleep,' Sarah cut in, shrill. 'Not with the goings-on in this house.'

'No. I expect not.' He released Elsie's hand and hooked two fingers in his waistcoat pocket. He looked, but he did not see her. His gaze was slack, insensate. What was going on in that mind of his?

Once she had known him, through and through. Her darling boy. Only he wasn't a boy any longer, was he? He was a young man, six years older than she had been when Ma died. Capable of all the things she had been capable of, back then.

Keeping secrets from Jolyon was second nature. But what if *he* hid things from *her*?

'Look at the clock – it will soon be time for dinner,' Sarah said. 'Shall I have Mrs Holt bring up a tray for you, Mr Livingstone?'

'No, I will come down and dine with you. Just one moment more.' His eyes lifted, suddenly, pinning Elsie to the bed. For one ghoulish moment, he looked just like Pa. 'Elsie, I need you to tell me what happened with Helen.'

'She . . . I do not know what happened. I came into the card room and she was there . . . like that.'

'Peters said you were acting strangely. Agitated.'

'Was I? I don't recall.'

'It must have been memorable,' he said, still in that cold, dead voice. 'It made quite an impression upon Peters. He has given me his notice.'

Well, Peters was never stupid. With the way things were falling out for servants around The Bridge, he would be a fool not to abandon ship.

'Is that so? I will be sorry to lose him. He has been an excellent driver.'

Jolyon nodded. 'Yes. Mr Stilford and the gardeners have left too. With all these deaths, one can understand it. Our household is sadly reduced since the winter.'

'Mr Livingstone.' Sarah moved towards the door, twirling a strand of hair anxiously around her finger. 'I have just heard Mrs Holt ring the gong.'

'One more word, and I have done. We bury Mabel and Helen on Friday, Elsie. We cannot in conscience leave it any longer. I wish for you to remain here, resting.'

'But—'

'There is no *but*. I will not have you put through unnecessary strain.' He moved his mouth, trying out a sentence, tasting it before he spoke. 'You are my sister. I will be . . . obeyed.'

Obeyed. The word roped around her throat.

'Get some sleep, now.' He bent to kiss her cheek. His lips were cold, dry. 'Mrs Holt will carry something up for you to eat later.' He walked to the door and offered Sarah his arm. 'Shall we, Miss Bainbridge?'

'Yes, certainly. Let me just say goodnight to Mrs Bainbridge first.' Sarah came forwards and repeated his kiss. Her breath was warm against Elsie's ear. 'The diary is under the mattress. I didn't have a chance to read it, I just hid it from Mrs Holt when I found you. Please, look while we are at dinner. Find out how we can stop this before it is too late.'

THE BRIDGE, 1635

I toiled up the stairs towards bed about five o'clock. Even then the snow fell ruthlessly. It would not stop until it had obliterated every object in a shroud of white.

I had grown so cold that I no longer felt it. Numb, inside and out, I climbed as if in a dream. I thought it was part of that dream when Josiah materialised on the landing in his nightshirt and bare feet, staring out of the window at the drifting snow. But he was real; the breath of life plumed from his nostrils and misted the frozen glass. He wheeled round at the sound of my step.

'God's blood! Anne, what are you doing up at this hour?'

'I could not sleep,' I said. His head flicked back and forth, from me to the window and back again. With a pang, I knew his mind: he was looking at the storm and wondering if I had whistled it up. 'Did the wind awaken you?'

He did not meet my eye. 'No. I am awake by design. I will leave within the hour. I intended to set out a little later, but this weather will slow us down.'

'Leave?' I had not slept – I was not thinking clearly. My temples throbbed with exhaustion. 'Wherever will you go?'

'You know where.'

It came back to me: Merripen. Josiah was going to watch while the boy danced on the end of a rope, while they cut his belly open to steam in the winter air. I had a vision of his innards, rotted to coal black.

'Josiah, you cannot go! You cannot travel in this weather! It is madness.'

'I must try. I have sent men out to dig a trench to the bridge already.' These are the men that ride with him – not the household servants invited to last night's feast. A fortunate circumstance, for I am sure if he sent Mark out with a shovel this morning, the man would topple sideways into a snowdrift. 'I wish to be the first to tell the King that justice has been served.'

My hand rested on his shoulder for an instant before he flinched away. 'Truly, husband, it is not worth the risk to your health. I doubt they will proceed with the execution on a day like today.'

'You would like that, would you not?' The ice crackling in his voice felt infinitely colder than the weather. 'Have done, Anne. I am going and I will make sure that it is accomplished.'

Fear wrapped its fingers around my heart. Something terrible would happen. I sensed it, as surely as I sensed him by my side. 'Josiah!' I begged. 'Do not act so rashly! You could die!'

It was then that I saw it: the old gesture I have seen a thousand times. But never from him. I never dreamt to see my own husband cross his fingers against me, as if I were a witch. 'Do not ill-wish me. You have done enough, my lady.'

He turned and strode back to his room.

My own chamber was remarkably cold. No fire had touched the grate, with the servants revelling downstairs. Even the ink I use to write my journal had frozen in its bottle, so I cradled it between my palms as I climbed, fully clothed, into bed. The sheets were so chill that they felt damp.

I must have slept, for I awoke with a sensation like falling that jerked my body up. Cold white light shimmered through the windows – I had forgotten to close the shutters. The sun was rising but no servant fetched my morning drink.

Wearily, I climbed out of bed, knowing I would not fall back into sleep. Something was wrong. I felt it, worrying at me, like a strip of torn skin. Perhaps I would go to the kitchen. If there was a fire anywhere in the house, it would be there.

I stumbled bleary-eyed down the steps. I was in luck. Orange flames danced in the kitchen's hearth and a pot hung suspended over them. Jane was no longer stretched out on the floor, but sitting at the table with one of Josiah's men. Both of them looked as pale as whey.

'What is the matter?' I demanded. They leapt to their feet at the sound of my voice. 'You,' I said to the man, 'why are you not out riding with your master?'

He inhaled. 'I was,' he said. 'The master sent me back here with a message. There is something that must be . . . attended to.'

Jane stared at the knife-scarred table.

'What?'

'An unpleasant circumstance. Do not trouble your-self, mistress, we will arrange . . .'

My stomach wallowed. 'What?'

A look passed between him and Jane. It was etched in their brows: their suspicion of me. They did not know how much they could conceal.

'There is something by . . . something *in* the river,' he said.

Understanding dropped into me, as heavy as lead.

'No,' I cried. 'No, no!'

I blundered over to the door. It was hopeless, I knew, yet I had to see for myself.

I inched the door open against the snow and waded into the yard. Nothing moved. There was no sound. A white spell had fallen over all.

Bracing myself against the bitter air, I followed the path cut by Josiah's men and their horses, a patina of fresh snow already covering it, step after laborious step. In a few minutes my shoes were wet through. Although I held my skirts bunched in my hand, high above my ankles, they soaked up the snow and weighed me down.

My teeth chattered. Snowflakes so cold that they stung like cinders battered against my face. A spite-ful wind snatched at my hair. I knew that if I stayed outside much longer, I would catch my death.

At last, the stone lions of the bridge reared up. Icicles hung from their roaring mouths. I staggered next to one, my nerves taut and braced for horror.

There was nothing. Only an empty bridge twinkling with frost, and the river, frozen solid.

Exhausted, I leant on the stone lion. It was so cold that my glove stuck to it.

I paused, panting, summoning up the strength to trudge back home. My lungs were raw. I was too tired to feel anything like relief.

It was then that it caught the tail of my eye. I blinked and looked again at the river. Peered closely through the murky, silver-grey ice.

A face stared back from beneath the solid water.

Two dark eyes turned up to the sky. Black hair spread like tendrils around her shoulders. She must have tripped on the brambles sprawling beside the river and fallen in, for they were all around her, holding her. Her lips and hands pressed against the ice in a hideous imitation of a child peering through a window. The open mouth gasped for air that would never come. I heard it speak, as I slumped to my knees in a bank of snow.

'Mercy.'

———

I was a coward. Unable to bear the sight of the poor gypsy girl, I crawled back to heat, life and comfort. I did not give any of my own directions for retrieving the body. With craven silence, I let events wash over me. Josiah's men did what needed to be done.

'I will return to bed,' I told Jane. Not to sleep – if I closed my eyes, that wasted face would surface before me. But at least in bed I could hide, submerge myself beneath the warmth of blankets and lock the door.

Jane rose clumsily to her feet. I noticed she held the table for support. 'Will you be needing me to unlace you, mistress?'

'No, I will cope. In truth, I do not think you would be able to manage a bodice.' I touched her hands, which quaked with tiny tremors. She did not seem able to control them. 'Are you so cold, Jane?'

'I think I am, mistress. My legs are numb.'

I frowned. The fire was stoked high. Heat returned to my own frozen skin with painful jabs. 'Sit yourself by the fire and heat some spiced wine. I cannot have you catching a chill.'

She thanked me, called me a kind mistress. I wish I could say my kindness came from some inner store of goodwill, but it was rank fear that made me generous. Fear that I had already let one girl freeze to death and I could not stand another on my conscience.

My skirts left a slick trail over the flagstones as I dragged them through the Great Hall and up the stairs. Exhaustion began to overpower me. Feverish and shivering, I clambered through the empty house. No servants stirred. All that remained of last night's festivities were the hacking coughs that sounded from the garret and the occasional retching sound. Jane had informed me that one or two of the men had cast forth vomit overnight. I detected the scent – sharp, sour and noxiously creamy. A broom and bucket lay abandoned on the landing of the first floor, but I could not see their owner.

Perhaps, another time, I would have been vexed. After all, Josiah had only given them a holiday for the day of the feast – he had not excused them from their duties the day after. But who am I to talk of duty now? Our family lies in ruins and two gypsy children are dead – all because of me. I cannot scold my servants.

I regretted my compassion to Jane the moment I gained my room. It was an abominable business, manoeuvring my numb body out of sodden clothes. I let them fall to the floor in a heap and stared at my skin – still wet, with a light sheen. I dried my arms with a clean shift, banked up and lit the fire, then retreated to bed with my journal. I have remained here ever since.

The book does not comfort me as it usually does. I thought I would be able to write at length about the remorse that consumes me, inch by inch; explain how the needling details of last night go round and round in my head. *If only I had done this.* But now I find that some regrets are too deep for words. Language is insufficient. I can do no more than remember that face. It is the *image* I need to confess my crime. All my fathomless, sprawling guilt is expressed in those two glazed eyes.

She must have tripped. She must have tripped on the thistles and fallen into the river. I see her when I close my eyes: stumbling in the snow; trailing plants wrapped tight about her ankles. Did she take my diamonds with her to her watery grave? Those stones which Josiah chose with such hope and pride? It is apt if she did. The man who bought those diamonds and the woman who wore them have gone. I do not know them any more.

Unnerving silence fills the house. Every time a sound is heard, it echoes as if it has some deep significance. Drips fall from the window as icicles melt away. Above me, sporadic thumps from the garret. There is a clatter from downstairs – Jane dropping a pan with her shaking fingers, I expect.

I wonder what Hetta is doing in the nursery with her wooden companions. I should go to Lizzy, I know, and tell her what has happened to the gypsy girl. She deserves to hear it from me. But dear God, I cannot bear to witness her dismay.

Did I really leave it there? Safe and tired in my bed? That is where I should have stayed. Looking back, I was happy then.

I would give kingdoms not to gaze over my shoulder and see the events of the last few hours. But I do not have kingdoms; only burdens I must shed. The truth must be laid down here.

Images swirl and I cannot sort them into order. I must think. Where was I? In bed? Yes: asleep in bed, for the strain of my late night and the trudge across snow finally caught hold of me. I awoke to the sound of sobs; heartbreaking in their very softness.

I clambered out of bed. The frigid air awoke me at once. Taking a dry mantle from the press, I flung it around my shoulders and opened the door. No one stirred. The cries rose and fell in a gentle tide.

With a shrinking emptiness inside, I concluded that it was Hetta. Crying for Merripen, or just for her own lonely existence.

A tiny piece of my heart cracked with each gasp I heard. But even then I was too selfish, too afraid. I did not go to comfort my daughter – I could not face her. Heading back into my room, I dressed in a day-gown and made my way downstairs.

Still no servants moved. It troubled me. Judging by the sun, it was well after midday. No one had fed me or checked if I needed attendance. It was not like my household.

Before I reached the kitchen, I heard a thud and a clatter like the sound of pans. That would be Cook, I thought. My stomach groaned – it had been many hours since last I ate. But to my surprise, when I unlatched the door and stepped into the warm glow from the fire, I found the room empty.

I sniffed – a strange, musty scent hovered.

The kitchen showed signs of recent occupation: a block with Hetta's herbs lay on the side, the stems half-minced and the knife still wet, green-tinged and gleaming. Perhaps Cook had gone down to the larder?

I passed through the inner door into a damp passageway. I felt like I was in a cave. I had forgotten to bring a lantern and it was difficult to see. I picked my way in a strange, halting manner, unable to move with any haste.

The door to the cold-larder stood open. No sounds of movement came from within. I gave a short knock. Nothing.

I poked my head inside. It was a cavernous room with a row of meat hooks at the far end. Dead animals stared back at me with their dull pebble eyes and there was a scent so strong, so primal, that it sent gooseflesh up my arms.

I could not see Cook.

I edged inside. 'Hello?'

The splayed ribcage of a doe took up most of the space on the table. I noticed the cleaver, still sandwiched in a hunk of meat.

Another step. My head knocked against a dead bird suspended from the ceiling. I flinched and pushed it off, spitting out feathers. The creature was half soft, half bobbled, as if someone had begun to pluck it but given up. And now that I reflected, there were many chores like that around the house today: the abandoned bucket; the partially chopped herbs.

A carcass creaked as it swayed on its hook.

'Hello? Cook?'

No answer. Almost frightened now, I walked in the direction of the hooks. I don't know what I expected – for someone to leap out at me from behind a carcass, perhaps, or for one of the animals to suddenly twitch alive. Focused on these fears, I did not think to look down. My foot slipped on something soft and, in a trice, my body smacked against the stone floor.

It took the wind from me. I lay for a moment, bewildered.

A long, lumpy shape stretched at my side. Revolted by the notion that it might be a dead cow, fallen from its hook, I kicked out a foot to push it away. But the black mass simply rolled over, an arm unfolding.

It was human.

My scream echoed. I levered myself into a sitting position, scrabbling backwards with my arms. I saw the face now: it was Cook.

Pushing down my gorge, I extended a shaking hand and tapped my fingers against her cheek. The skin was as cold as marble. There would be no saving her.

I had to get out of the room. Grabbing the bloody table, I hauled myself to my feet. They shook but they did not give way. *Fetch help*, my mind screamed. *Jane, Mark, anyone*.

I hurtled back down the stone passages into the warmth of the kitchen.

Still that musty smell tainted the air.

'Help!' I screamed. 'Somebody help! I am in the kitchen.'

Silence reigned.

Was it then that the sly, terrible thought crawled through my mind? Some part of me must have known, for my feet took me out through the servery passage and into the scullery.

The smell hit me first: vomit and the acrid reek of a midden. In a pool of viscous fluid lay shattered pieces of crockery, stained knives and, beside them, my two young scullery maids.

Bloodshot eyes stared blindly at the ceiling. Dark marks stained their lips and a yellow and red pattern mottled their skin.

'No,' I gasped, 'no.'

Hardly knowing what I did, I ran back to the kitchen. Stopped. The room undulated like water around me. As my eyes cleared, the chopping block loomed into terrible focus. On the half-cut herbs, I saw what I had failed to notice before.

'No.' My fingers turned over the wet stems. They were pocked with purple spots.

I grabbed the knife and groped for the door. It could not be true. If I had to run ten miles in the snow with the bitter wind tearing at my gown, I would prove it were not true.

Hetta's garden lay beneath a dusting of snow and frost. I plunged my bare hands into the herbs. The thistle entangled all. From the corner of my mind, Harris's words echoed back at me: *it creeps*. I wielded my knife and hacked my way through.

Scratched and bleeding, I clawed until all the snow fell away. And there, hidden beneath the blue-grey thistle, grew the plants I had failed to see – I, who prided myself on second sight. Poisonous henbane, monkshood and water pennywort. Vervain for sorcery. Last of all, growing at the back, the dark berries of belladonna.

My fingers fell slack; the knife dropped without a sound into the snow.

It *was* true. And it was worse than I ever imagined.

Memory flooded me with a force that would not be denied. I saw flashing images: the potion; rusted scissors; Hetta's cold, impassive face; an antimasque of smoke and red lights, and capering through it all, the masked devil of a child's height.

'Dear God,' I whispered. 'Dear God.'

I do not recall how long I knelt there with the bitter greens my daughter had sown. I barely felt the cold pinching my face, or the ice pooling to water beneath my skirts.

Josiah was right all along. Through my potions and spells, I called forth something wicked. I *created* her. I am worse than a witch.

My baby. Rotten to the core. Every memory of her childhood takes on a sordid, shameful appearance. Was she a demon from the very womb? But of course she was. What else could she be, at once unnatural and misbegotten?

Now she is nine, her power is full. The ninth hour, the time Christ died. Yet even before that she was plotting. What I mistook for friendship with the gypsy must have been a lure. She set him up to take the blame while she killed the horse. And now she has killed my servants.

I do not know if a child created by human hands possesses a soul. Yet this I do know – the penalty for Hetta's sins will be required of *me* on Judgement Day. *I* murdered those servants when I mixed my brew: it was only a different combination of herbs.

I must have made a mistake. A proportion of a mixture, a word in the spell. I did not create a child. I made a monster.

I wish I could say that I built up the nerve to come inside and face Hetta, but it was the chill that conquered me in the end. The sun set early, powdering the clouds pink and grey like mother-of-pearl. My shaking fingers sought the knife by my side.

My skirts had frozen stiff. It was as though I dragged a chain around my waist as I stumbled back towards the house, and my thoughts crawled too, unable to plot the course I must take. Whatever would I say to my family? Lizzy doted on the girl, she would never believe me.

Then the thought bowled me sideways.

Lizzy.

I ran. Stumbling, tripping, unable to control my limbs, I barrelled through the yard door. The house reeked of death. Coughing against my sleeve, I dragged myself on into the Great Hall.

My skirts threw out shards of ice as I thudded up the stairs. Fear clenched in my chest as I drew nearer to the nursery.

I reached the door. Hetta's sparrow chirruped from within. Once it was sweet to hear the bird sing, but now it was calling, calling to the dead, calling to their souls that it might carry them away.

I hesitated. Then I pushed the door open.

My eyes did not want to process what they saw. They took in the leaves on the floor, the silent companions ranged about the room like an audience at the play, and Lizzy, laying on her back. *Sleeping*, my eyes said. *Sleeping*. But with something draped about her neck. Vines. A rope made of vines and creepers.

I remembered the catches of breath I had heard earlier. It was not Hetta crying, gasping for breath – it was Lizzy.

Hetta turned to me. When her eyes met mine, everything came into focus. I saw my oldest friend, the woman I had loved like a mother, with the life throttled from her body, and standing over her, the goblin I had once called *daughter*.

There was no apology in her face – only a loathsome, gloating triumph.

I still held the knife in my hand.

God forgive me.

Now all is quiet. The sparrow sits motionless in his cage. Around the house, bodies stiffen and corrupt while Hetta's blood creeps across the floorboards to the feet of the companions, her only true friends. I watch the red pool curdle with the vines and turn to a rusty brown – the same brown as the potion I drank, so long ago.

I know what will happen to me: Josiah and his men will find me alone in a house of death. They will send for the witch-finder. The whispers have followed me for long enough. I shall burn.

It is the most horrific of all deaths. I could avoid it – the knife is still sharp. I should draw the tacky blade across my wrists now and save myself. But that would be too good for me.

I summoned the demon. I need the cleansing fire of God's wrath.

I need to feel the flames.

THE BRIDGE, 1866

Morning came and the clock in the Great Hall chimed ten before Sarah returned. Sunlight streamed through the open curtains and stretched her shadow, bending it up the wall. In her lavender gown, her frame appeared shrunken. She did not smile as she came into the room, trailing bandages as if she were a mummy burst from the tomb, and holding a bowl of water.

'Sarah, thank goodness. I thought I should never see you.'

'I've come to change your bandages,' Sarah answered, loudly. 'It must be done to avoid infection.' She kicked the door shut and dropped her voice to a whisper. 'There, that will buy us a bit of time.'

Elsie watched her lay the linen strips and the bowl on the dressing table. 'What is it, Sarah?'

Sarah glanced at the door. 'In a moment. Come, give me your hand.' She sat beside the bed and took Elsie's hand into her lap.

Elsie winced as Sarah peeled a piece of fabric, dried on with blood, away from her palm. 'I read the diary,' she whispered.

'And? Tell me!'

She paused, knowing she would never be able to convey the despair and chilling guilt in those last pages. The voice she needed belonged to Anne, belonged to another time. 'You were right. About Anne. She never intended to cause harm. It was all one terrible string of events she could not control.' Her breath snagged, but she did not need to conceal it – at the same moment the bandage fell away, exposing her wounds to the air. Most had scabbed over, but one or two still wept.

Strange, that Elsie's hands were healing faster than Sarah's single cut. Even an infection should have settled down by now.

'But what happened to poor Hetta?'

'Anne . . . Anne killed Hetta.'

'She killed her own child!'

'She had to!' A defensive flare that had nothing to do with Anne. 'The evil you spoke of. Something about a potion and a spell? It was in Hetta. Bound up in her. Anne had to kill her and save what remained of her family. She had to save her boys.'

Sarah frowned, thoughtful. She wet a cloth in the bowl of water and passed it gently over Elsie's palm. The wounds sighed with relief. 'Then it is not Hetta's ghost, haunting us?'

'Not that exactly. It is more than that. I think . . . The companions were there when Hetta died. Anne wrote that her blood flowed to the feet of them. They absorbed it, do you see? The evil moved into them.'

'But what does it want?'

'I have no idea.' Did evil have wants and needs? Surely not, surely that would make it too human. No longer a tug from the depths of the abyss, but something sentient that could surface in anyone. In her.

'Perhaps the evil is seeking something.' Sarah's breath came hot against her skin. 'Seeking . . . a more permanent host.'

A queasy silence fell as they considered the implications of that. Splinters. On Rupert, on the baby. Something trying to get in.

Sarah unrolled a fresh bandage and pressed it to the centre of Elsie's palm. 'While it stays in the companions, it is trapped inside the house.'

'Then we have to stop it, before it can escape.'

Sarah bound up Elsie's wounds and tied a knot in the bandage. Then, at last, she exhaled. 'We cannot stop it. We do not have time. All we can do is flee.'

'Flee?' Elsie cried. 'We can't just run! What if it hurts other people?'

'Perhaps it *will* hurt other people, Elsie! But I am not concerned for other people. I am only concerned for you.' Elsie wanted to withdraw her hand. There was something in Sarah's eyes that demanded too much. 'Listen to me, please. I have been alone all my life. You could not call Mrs Crabbly family, not with her scolding and her horrid cross ways. And Rupert . . . Well, there was a time when I thought Rupert might marry me. I thought he might sweep in and save me from the life of a lady's companion. But you know what happened there.'

Elsie did not know what to say.

'Then I met you. And you were kind to me. I started to think perhaps . . . you might let me be your friend, after all. That I could be of use to you.'

'You have been, Sarah. You are the only person in the world who believes me, who understands. You have been the best of friends.'

'I have never had a friend before.' Her grip on Elsie's injured hand was painfully tight. 'And I'll be damned if I let them take you away from me.'

'The companions?'

'Not the companions! The doctors!'

Her body stiffened beneath the sheets. 'Why would . . . why would doctors take me away?'

'I'm sorry, Elsie. I didn't want to tell you, but Mr Livingstone has made up his mind. He said it himself, at dinner last night. He's written to an asylum.'

Panic stretched its arms deep into her chest. It must be a mistake. Of course, it must be – Jolyon would never have her committed! But Sarah's depthless brown eyes told another story.

'What, exactly, did he tell you?'

'That you were very ill.' Gently, she folded Elsie's hand back onto the bed. 'He said he had suspected it for some time. Then he asked me to pack up all of your things because some men were coming, some medical men, to examine you. That they would take you with them and you would probably be gone for a good while.'

Falling – that was what it felt like. Plummeting off the side of a cliff with nothing but rocks below. *Jolyon*, betray her? The boy she had bled for, surrendered her youth to raise. No, he would never . . . Unless. Unless he had not been asleep after all.

'You are sure of this, Sarah? You are *absolutely* sure?'

Sarah nodded. Strands of hair drooped, listless, fallen free of their pins. 'I went to the library. I saw the letters he has written.'

'But *you* know I am not mad!'

'Of course I do. And that's why I've decided.' She threw her chin up, defiant. 'I am going to get you out of here. Tonight.'

Elsie had a terrible urge to laugh. That shocked, hysterical laughter that only came when all hope was gone. 'How do you propose to do that? Think of my leg.'

'I've found a walking stick. You can use it to lean upon.'

'It will make a noise. They'll hear it on the stairs.'

Roses bloomed in Sarah's cheeks. 'There is something . . . something I can do at supper. I used to do it for Mrs Crabbly, when she was griping.' Elsie stared at her. 'A little drop into the drinks, to make them sleep heavily.'

Elsie had the feeling she had misjudged Sarah all along. 'Did you really? Did you really drug Mrs Crabbly just to get some peace?'

A roguish grin spread over Sarah's face. 'We have all done things we are a little ashamed of, Mrs Bainbridge.'

———

Night fell swiftly. All afternoon rain pattered against the windows. Each time Elsie awoke from a doze, the clouds had grown a little darker. She closed her eyes to a gunpowder sky, and opened them to find it had deepened to tar black. It was time.

Elsie staggered out of bed before she had the chance to fall back asleep. With great difficulty, she tied on the cloak Sarah had left out for her and put a fresh box of matches in the pocket. A laudanum haze filled her vision. Every muscle protested at her folly. How would she even make it down the stairs?

The stick was too fragile, trembling under her weight as she limped to the door. If the companions came, she would not be able to run.

But what choice did she have?

Two soft thuds on the door. Elsie's head jerked up.

'Come in,' she whispered.

The door opened silently and Sarah slid in, bringing with her an aura of golden light. She carried an oil lantern in each hand.

'Here.' Shadows cavorted across her face as she handed a lantern to Elsie. Her pupils reflected the light.

'Are they both asleep?'

'There was a small problem,' Sarah said. 'Mr Livingstone went to the library. I'm afraid he's drifted off in there. He will have a stiff neck when he wakes.'

Worry bunched in her chest. Now it came down to it, she was weak. She did not want to leave him behind. 'Sarah . . . Perhaps we should wait. We need to plan it out. Where will we go, what will we do?'

Sarah stared at her. 'There is no time. We have enough money between us to get on a train.'

'But . . . I can't just abandon Jolyon. What if the companions go after him? What if they use him as their host?'

'Will you be able to stop them, if you are here?'

'No . . . But—'

'Will you be able to protect him from inside an asylum?'

Elsie closed her eyes. There was no way to win. Whatever choice she made, she lost Jolyon. And what was her life, then?

'I can't . . .'

'You are not betraying him, Elsie. It is *he* who has given up on *you*.'

Reluctantly, she nodded. Better to take her chances with Sarah than spend a lifetime trapped behind high walls. She would not let someone force her, not ever again.

Sarah led the way. Elsie limped after her. Everything was in gloom. Not even the gas lights burnt.

All she could hear were Sarah's footsteps and the steady *tap, tap* of her stick. The lantern in her hand bounced to her uneven gait, illuminating flashes of maroon carpet.

Suddenly, Sarah froze. Elsie could not stop in time. There was a thud and the sound of glass breaking, oil spilling. Shadows flooded in as the corridor grew a shade darker. Sarah had dropped her lantern.

'Quick.' She jerked round and snatched the remaining light from Elsie. The moment she held it aloft, they gasped.

Seven companions skulked beside the stairs.

It was too dark to make out their faces. Only silhouettes loomed, large against the wall as the lantern trembled in Sarah's hand. Elsie cast a glance over her shoulder, remembering how they had come before, from both sides, like a pack of wolves. She could see nothing solid, only a trickle of yellow running down from the ceiling at the end of the corridor.

'Sarah, what—' Before she finished, she heard Jolyon's snore. Confused images slotted together and then she realised: the yellow stripe was a lamp burning in the library. The library door was open. She clutched at Sarah's gown. 'He's in there all alone. I can't leave him, not with them out here.'

Sarah's eyes were fixed on the companions. 'What do you mean?'

'Jolyon!'

'But you being in the house won't stop them!'

Her bad leg started to shake. 'He's left the door open.'

'What difference does it make?'

She was right. There was logic, but then there was also the heart: the heart of a woman who had raised a boy alone from when he was five years of age. Elsie couldn't leave him. At the very least, she had to shut the door.

'Keep watching them,' she cried, and pivoted on her stick. Thinking only of Jolyon, she plunged back into the corridor.

Her stick tapped in time to her frantic pulse. She heard Sarah's shout of alarm, but already it sounded far away. She was drowning in darkness. Her eyes flew about, seeking relief from unrelenting black. *Jolyon. Just concentrate on Jolyon.* Despite the pain scalding her ribs, despite the numb weakness of her left leg, she pressed on towards the crack of light.

She thought she would drop. Pain, fear and laudanum engulfed her. Only the unnatural chill rolling out of the library and the dank, mouldy smell cut through the haze. She stumbled gasping across the threshold. Jolyon sat slumped at the desk in the alcove, his head resting on the polished surface.

Hobbling closer, she saw the movement of his eyes beneath their lids and the slow thump of a pulse in his neck. Alive. He was just sleeping. His breath fluttered the paper beneath his cheek.

It was only by chance that she noticed the letterhead. She was on the point of turning away, but her eye caught at the script, printed like a scream.

St Joseph's Hospital for the Insane

For a moment everything fell still. Then her heart kicked back in, drumming blood into her head with painful beats. She stumbled from the room.

That one word ricocheted around her skull: *insane*.

She could not doubt Sarah any longer. Jolyon really did think she was mad. He had given her up. The pain of that was worse than the cracked ribs. Slamming the door shut, she turned and fought her way through the darkness, back along the corridor.

'Please, Elsie!' Sarah's strangled voice led her forward. 'Are you there? I can't stare at these things any longer.'

'Have they moved?'

'Only their eyes. They were watching you.'

Elsie shivered.

If only she could see clearly. She could not relight the broken lantern, for the oil had soaked into the carpet. Dare she fire up a wall lamp? Surely the light of just one would not wake Jolyon?

With her free hand, she pulled on the lever.

'Here, Sarah, take my matches. I'll hold the lantern while you light the gas.'

Sarah obeyed and the flame leapt into life. Light splashed on the red flock wallpaper, the marble busts. 'Oh my. They look a little closer.'

'We cannot stop watching them,' Elsie told her. 'I'll go down the stairs first with the lantern, to watch out for any in the Great Hall. You walk backwards and keep an eye on these ones.'

Sarah's fingers tightened around the matchbox. 'Backwards? Why me?'

Elsie thumped her stick impatiently on the floor. 'It will be hard enough for me going forwards.'

They stood, back to back. Thank heaven they were dressed simply, with no puffing crinolines. Elsie felt Sarah's shoulders against hers, the damp sweat through her gown. 'Ready?'

Sarah's gasp of air. 'Ready.'

She scooped her skirts into the hand that held the stick, the material giving grip to her slippery palm. 'Come on, then.'

Her legs were shaking – not just the bad one. One step. Two. Slowly, slowly, Sarah's heels bumping at hers. The lantern's cloud of light careered around the stairwell, showing flashes of carpet and wallpaper. No companions.

'Last one,' Elsie whispered, and they stumbled onto a small landing. One flight down, another to go.

Hiss, hiss.

Sarah's shoulders turned rigid. 'I can't see them any more. The gas lamp . . . it's too far away.'

'Light a match. It's just a little farther.'

From above them came a slow scratch. Elsie pictured them, dragging their monstrous bases across the floorboards.

Exhaustion threatened to swamp her, but she couldn't surrender to it. *Thump, thump* went her stick on the stairs, her leg nearly buckling. With each step Sarah bumped into her, sending pain spiralling through her chest. And all the while, shadows rolled up behind them.

Hiss, hiss.

Finally the lantern glinted on metal and flashed over the blue and gold Bainbridge coat of arms. The Great Hall was in sight. They were nearly there.

'Elsie! Elsie, I *feel* something!'

They were on the last step. Elsie hurried to reach the safety of the floor, but she stumbled.

No, no. Her stick skidded, the lantern wavered. Fire shot up her bad leg. Sarah screamed. There it was: the floor, hard and level beneath her shoes. Elsie tottered and somehow managed to regain her balance.

They had made it into the Great Hall.

'Dear me! Miss Sarah!'

Light, sneaking in from the far side of the Great Hall. Elsie's heart leapt to her throat.

'How could you?'

Gasping, squinting, she turned to face the voice. The green baize door to the servants' side stood open. Mrs Holt outlined in fire, lit from behind. She fumbled, there was a pop, and then a lamp sprang to life.

'Well, well.' Mrs Holt's footsteps sounded on the flags, clipped, judgemental. 'Who would have thought? I might have expected it from *you*,' she gave a sharp nod in Elsie's direction. 'But Miss Sarah! You ought to know better.'

Disorientated, Elsie let the lantern fall from her hand. Mrs Holt lit another lamp.

'You!' Sarah, shrill, behind her. 'You're meant to be . . . Why aren't you asleep?'

'God forgive you, girl, don't you think I know poppy tea when I smell it? I knew you were up to something, but I never imagined you would try and take *her* out! Whatever possessed you?'

Where were the companions? The Great Hall materialised around her. Suits of armour, swords, the oriental rug.

There were no companions. There was only Mrs Holt and the pant of the gas lamps.

'You are trying to take her away from me!' Sarah screeched. Her hand latched on Elsie's arm. 'I won't let you. She is no lunatic! They were right here, did you not see them? Didn't you *hear* them, you foolish old woman?'

The fight was still in Sarah. Not Elsie. Feeling had ebbed away, leaving her an empty shell. There went disappointment. Fear laid pooled at her feet. The last dregs remaining were something like relief. At least now, she would not leave Jolyon.

'I heard nothing. There *was* nothing.' Revulsion twisted Mrs Holt's features. 'Heaven above! You're just as crazy as she is!'

Sarah's jaw jutted. For a moment, it really looked as if she would strike Mrs Holt, but then furniture crashed upstairs and footsteps clopped, unsteady, until Jolyon appeared in the gallery. He looked like a man in his cups: flushed, his hair out at angles. 'What is this?' He blinked at them, wrestling words from his drugged sleep. 'I heard a scream and – Elsie? Is that you?'

'It is both the ladies, Mr Livingstone,' Mrs Holt called up. 'I caught them trying to escape.'

'Escape!'

'I'm afraid they drugged you, Mr Livingstone. They are cunning. Far more dangerous than we feared.'

Elsie would never forget the expression on his face: the blend of fear and wrath. For it was no longer Jolyon staring at her behind those red-rimmed, hazel eyes. Her dear boy spluttered out of existence with Mrs Holt's words. In his place stood someone else, someone she'd prayed never to see again so long as she lived.

It was Pa.

———

'Let me out!' Elsie's palm slammed into the wood again and again, rattling the door on its hinges. Each blow vibrated through her ribs with white-hot pain, yet she did not stop. She *could* not stop. 'Jolyon, unlock the door this instant!'

'I cannot do that.'

'Please! Let me out! I have been in here all night!' Her voice soared off pitch. Hysterical, crazed. Even to her own ears, it sounded like confirmation of his diagnosis. 'Jolyon!'

'You are not well. I should have known.' She heard his shoulder shift against the door. 'I should have suspected long ago.'

Her hand hovered an inch away from the wood. She was filling up with smoke; behind her eyes, her stomach, underneath her tongue. Bitter, choking smoke that was the past and the present, engulfing her with acrid fumes.

'What are you talking about?' How false it sounded. A line given to an actress in a play.

'After Ma—'

'No!'

'I saw you, Elsie. I saw you put the pillow over her face—'

'It wasn't like that!' she shrieked, jangling the handle again. 'Listen to me, I can explain—'

'I cannot believe a word you say!'

'She was in too much pain. She was already on death's door, it wasn't a sin.'

'Not a sin!' he exploded. 'Good God. Maybe poor Ma was right all along. Maybe she was not mad. The things she accused you of . . .'

'All I ever did, I did for you.'

She heard a sob break from him. 'You did not do that in my name. You did not kill my mother for my sake.'

'Jolyon, look. There are things I never told you, things—'

'Stop!' His hand knocked back from the other side. 'Please, do not make me listen to it. Your words will send me mad too. Help is coming. I just need to keep you safe until the men arrive.'

'Men from St Joseph's?'

'Mrs Holt has gone with the telegram now. It is the best place for you. They might be able to . . .' He trailed off.

Tears streaked down her face. How could this be happening?

Each day the impossible became a reality, but it was easier to believe in wooden assassins than it was to accept that Jolyon, her Jolyon, was against her.

She pressed her forehead to the door. Under the white paint, she could make out the pattern and knots in the wood, as if it were not just a barrier between them but a living thing, complete with veins and sinews.

'Jolyon, consider again.' She struggled to keep her breath steady, to sound like a sane person. 'You know this is not in keeping with my character. With your own lips, you told Mr Underwood you would stake your life on my nerves.'

'They are broken, and my heart with them.'

She laid her palm flat, imagining his head pressed to the wood. If only he would look at her. If he looked into her eyes, he would know she was telling the truth. 'You are too hasty. Ask Sarah—'

'I have sent Sarah to her own suite! I cannot have her coming to your room, encouraging you in your delusions.'

She slid to the carpet, landing painfully on her bad knee. 'You cannot confine Sarah,' she tried again. 'You have no authority over her. You cannot treat us like prisoners.'

'It is for your own safety. I know what is best for you.'

But he didn't even know who she was.

She remained on the floor, empty and spent. Presently, Jolyon's footsteps sounded in the corridor. The library door opened and then closed.

Shadows of trees lay on the carpet by the window. Inch by inch, they lengthened across the floor. A detached part of her wondered which would get her first – the companions or the asylum. Perhaps Mrs Holt had sealed her fate by now; spelt out her doom in wires and crackles and clicks. Already, she felt the cold of a hospital dormitory closing in around her.

Did she deserve it? Perhaps she did. Not for the companions, but for the other things. Pa, Ma. She could blot them out but they never left her; they ran, dark, in her bloodstream. In Jolyon.

It was perhaps an hour later when she heard the noise: soft, at first, a crackle like logs yielding to a flame. She darted a look at the fire but the wood had burnt out. Again it came: a scratching, whispering sound. Right outside her door.

Elsie cocked her head, listening. This time she heard little clicks. Then a door, creaking open.

Jolyon's wordless exclamation made her jump. Perhaps it was Mrs Holt returned? But there were no footsteps, no voices. Just that distant rustle, like twigs snapping. Or tiny bones.

She lay down awkwardly on the floor. The sliver of light under the door only revealed a stretch of maroon carpet.

Jolyon screamed.

She bolted upright, wincing as pain seared along her ribs. 'Jo?' She tried the door handle. Still locked. He cried out again, a strangled word that sounded like her name. 'Jolyon!'

Now the sounds were amplified. Twisting, slithering. She thought of animals thrashing in the undergrowth, ensnared by branches. Dear God, what was happening?

'Elsie!' An anguished scream, bubbling with liquid.

Furiously, she pumped at the handle, hammered on the door. She couldn't get to him. She couldn't get out.

No torture could be more maddening: to hear and not to see; to be powerless while he howled. The air became stifling, impossible to breathe, pressing in close, close.

Elsie cast about the room for an object to batter the door with. Her roving eyes fell upon the dressing table and she shot up a prayer of gratitude. Why hadn't she thought of them before?

She dashed over, ignoring the pain in her knee, and seized a handful of hairpins. With sweating palms, she bent the first pin and tried to get it in the keyhole. It missed. Again she lined it up, and again it skidded out of control. 'God damn!' Her hands shook as if she had the ague.

Glass smashed.

'Come on, come on.' At last, she threaded the pin into the hole but it rattled and she couldn't feel the tumblers. 'Please!'

Hiss. The pin fell from her hand. *Hiss.*

There was another shout, and Jolyon's voice died out. The silence was deafening.

Seizing another pin, she bent it with her teeth and thrust it in the lock. Relief surged when the tumblers clicked and moved, and the door yielded to her hand.

In the corridor everything was still. She hobbled out, gritting her teeth. Footsteps pounded to her left. When she turned, she saw Sarah hurtling in her direction, wild-eyed, Jasper at her heels.

'Elsie! What happened? I heard screaming.'

'Jolyon,' she gasped. 'Jolyon.'

Sarah's eyes widened. 'Not *them*?'

A noise burst from her lips: keening, animal. She had never known a pain like it. 'No! Please God, no.'

Without another word, Sarah nudged her shoulder under Elsie's armpit and helped her to the library.

It was a wreck. Books lay spreadeagled on the floor with their pages hanging loose. The carpet was a graveyard of paper, glass and shrivelled leaves. As they stumbled farther into the room, Elsie saw rips in the curtains which fluttered and danced in the breeze.

'Jolyon?' It did not sound like her voice – did not sound like his name.

Ink splattered across the desk, splintered with shards of green glass from the lamp, but the chair behind stood empty.

'Elsie! Over there!'

She whirled round. The gypsy boy with his crook loomed before the fire. Something inhuman flickered in the flat face. Her eyes followed the direction of his crook.

The middle window was smashed to a spider web. Cracks radiated from a central, ragged hole. Something snagged on one of the points. Material. Hair?

The tattered curtains waved, frantic, motioning her away. But her feet moved without her permission, hopelessly drawn across the carpet, crunching on glass, to stand where the wind could slap her face.

Dozens of Elsies stared back at her from the shattered window, each one a different shape. Elongated, squashed, missing mouths; her face melting. And she saw that the cracks were edged with blood.

Taking a deep breath, she peered down from the sill.

Her Jolyon, her boy, lay face down on the gravel, his neck at an impossible angle. Dead.

The curtains gusted around, embracing her as she screamed.

––––––––––

Once, when she was very young, Pa had burst her eardrum. It created a noise, a noise so intense that it was somehow more than sound, drowning everything but its insistent ring.

After the noise had come severe pain. Burrowing into her head and making her dizzy, slackening her face. She felt everything and nothing.

It must have happened again, for she could not see or hear. Time slipped past her as if she were no longer there.

Suddenly she slammed back into herself, finding herself propped up behind the desk in the remains of the leather chair. Horsehair prickled through slashes in the fabric, rough against her tender skin.

Sarah was on her left, waving a bottle of smelling salts under her nose. To the right stood Mrs Holt.

'Another terrible accident?' she was saying. 'My eye! It's her, you daft girl. She's not right in the head. I'm going for the police.'

'It was the companions, Mrs Holt! Elsie had only just come out of her room, I saw the door open. There is no conceivable way she could have got in here and . . .' Sarah saw Elsie stirring back to life, and put the smelling salts down.

'I reckon Mr Livingstone missed a trick when he wrote that telegram,' Mrs Holt muttered. 'He ought to have had you both committed.'

Even his name was a blow to the gut. There was no Mr Livingstone now, no good to come of all her sorrow: there was just the wreck of a handsome young man lying splayed on the gravel like a fallen bird. 'My baby,' her numb lips said. 'My boy.'

'See?' Mrs Holt jerked her head. 'Crackers.' She leant in close so Elsie could see the nets of wrinkles around her eyes and smell her old, peppery breath. 'You might have lost a baby, madam, but that is nothing to losing a daughter full grown, the hope of your life. Seeing her skewered like a piece of meat on a roasting jack!' Her face looked frightful, distorted with tears. 'God knows I should pity you for your malady, but I can't. I can't do it. I only pray I'll see you swing for what you did to her.'

At any other time, her mind might have put the pieces together. But Elsie found herself staring at Mrs Holt with the same confusion that was lining Sarah's brow. 'What are you talking about? What daughter?'

Mrs Holt ran a hand over her ravaged face. 'I suppose there is no need to keep the secret, now. There was a reason

Mr Bainbridge called me his angel. There was also a reason that I came out here to the middle of nowhere.'

'Oh!' Sarah breathed. 'You were carrying his child.'

She closed her eyes and nodded. 'I was. You see, my mistress was so unwell and he needed . . . He was not a bad man. He wanted to do the right thing by both of us.'

'So he advanced you. Gave you a house where you would be free from gossip.'

'I hid the babe away at first. Then later, I trained her up to work alongside me in the house. I wasn't daft, I never expected Helen to be raised with Master Rupert.'

'*Helen.* Helen was your daughter? And so . . .' Sarah placed a hand on her chest. 'My cousin?'

'She was. That wretched woman sitting before us has taken family from you too, Miss Sarah. You must let me go for the police.'

Elsie did not fear Mrs Holt's hatred. She yearned to cling to her as someone who had felt this same pain and survived. Or had she? The woman remonstrating with Sarah was not the same Mrs Holt she had met that first night. She was a hardened version, an iron version, bitter at heart.

'Go,' Elsie said. 'Please. Go for the police.'

Mrs Holt blinked her watery eyes.

'No,' Sarah cried. 'No, Elsie, you are not thinking straight. You have to get out of here before the people from the asylum come and—'

'Let them come. What does it matter, now?'

'It matters to me! I need you!'

Elsie laid her head back against the chair. 'I won't leave Jolyon. I won't have strange hands washing him and laying him out. I'll be there when he's buried as I was there when he was born.'

Sarah exhaled, her shoulders sagging. 'Then I suppose . . . Mrs Holt is right. We must go for the police, or the asylum people will send for them the moment they arrive. It will look worse for us all if that happens.'

'Three bodies in the house,' said Mrs Holt. 'Three.'

'One of them outside. Come, let us bring him in before I go to fetch the constable.'

'You?' spat Mrs Holt. 'Why would I trust *you* to go for the police? Only last night, you were trying to break her loose!'

Sarah laid a hand on Mrs Holt's shoulder and turned her away from Elsie, towards the fireplace. 'It is a long trek to Torbury St Jude. You have been there and back today already.'

'But will you honestly—' Her sentence ended abruptly. Something was changing, shifting beneath her expression. 'Did you do that?' she hissed.

'Do what?'

'That!' Mrs Holt's arm flailed out at the hearth. 'Was that you or was it her?'

'I do not understand you.'

But Elsie did. She saw the change that had taken place while their backs were turned to the fireplace. Her skin crawled.

'It wasn't like that when I came into the room. Look at it!'

Frantic white lines marked the wood. Deep, angry gashes. The eyes of the gypsy boy had been scratched out.

———

Needles of rain hurtled past the open door. The afternoon air smelt strange: peaty and rich. Elsie tried to focus on the scent, to lose herself in it; anything to distance herself from the terrible scene playing out before her eyes.

Neither Mrs Holt nor Sarah was strong. They half pushed, half dragged Jolyon's body across the threshold. His head lolled, grotesque. Flecks of gravel stuck to his cheeks and the lashes framing his open hazel eyes.

She had always tried to save him. God, how she had tried.

They laid him out like a broken puppet on the same oriental rug where Rupert's coffin had sat. Mrs Holt folded Jolyon's sprawled arms so that the hands rested, overlapped, on his stomach. She frowned. 'There are splinters on his fingers.'

Elsie flinched.

'There were splinters on Rupert,' Sarah said. 'And the baby.'

The housekeeper's lips twitched. Elsie could see her struggling with the unpalatable truth: believing; not wanting to believe; trying to prove herself wrong.

'Did Mabel or Helen have splinters?' Sarah asked.

'I didn't see. I didn't check.' Mrs Holt took a step. Stopped. 'I might . . . go and look.' She darted another glance at Elsie.

Elsie understood. The housekeeper wanted to hate her. She would rather find Elsie's bloody fingerprints around Helen's neck than a spray of splinters.

Poor Mrs Holt. Far better to believe your child was murdered quickly rather than stalked, living their last moments in a paroxysm of fear. She watched the old woman disappear behind the baize door and her heart went with her.

'I don't understand.' Sarah bit at a strand of her hair, agitated. 'What does this thing want? What did it fail to find in Rupert, or the baby? What does it need, exactly?'

She swayed on her feet. 'I do not know, Sarah, and I do not want to know. I am only thankful Jolyon is free of it now. I won't give it another chance. Fetch me some water, please. I am going to wash him.'

Sarah hesitated. 'I'm not sure that you can. If the police come to investigate, they will want to see him . . . as he was.'

'As he was!' A dry sob came out. 'Dear God, we all want that.'

Sarah hung her head. 'You do . . . You still want me to go for the police?'

'Yes! Someone has to help us. We cannot face this alone.'

'But they will not believe in the companions! What if they arrest us?'

Prison, the asylum. It was all the same, without Jolyon. 'Then let them arrest us. At least we will be out of this damned house.'

Sarah went to fetch her bonnet and tied the ribbons hurriedly beneath her chin. While she pulled on her mittens, Elsie gazed at the baize door. Mrs Holt had not made a sound since she had passed through it.

'Do not worry, Mrs Bainbridge. We will get through this, you and I. It seems impossible now, but . . . Somehow we will rebuild our lives. Together.' Sarah squeezed Elsie's shoulder. 'I think Rupert would have liked that.'

No doubt Sarah meant it kindly, but Elsie could not endure her saccharine words. She pulled away.

Sarah opened the door again, letting in a fine spray of rain. The gardens were soaked. The hedges dripped and water cascaded from the jowls of the stone dog like drool. Sarah put one foot out of the door.

'Wait!' Elsie reached into her pocket and gave Sarah her purse. 'Take this, in case you run into trouble. It will pay for lodging or a conveyance home.'

Bestowing one last look on her, Sarah ventured out into the rain. Elsie watched her go: a hunched, grey figure crunching over the gravel, growing darker and darker as the shadow of the house fell over her. She crossed the hills and disappeared from sight.

Less than ten minutes later, the mist descended.

She slumped down by the fireplace and sat with her legs stretched out, next to Jolyon. Or what passed for Jolyon: the cruel, blue-grey parody of him. She did not want to store this image of her boy: waxy and puffed; features imprinted with horror; vicious cuts to the dear skin. But she knew it would encroach, stealthily, and overwrite all the happier times. Death, once conceived, was rapacious. It took all with it.

Every tick of the grandfather clock echoed through the Great Hall. The rain drummed in counterpoint. Elsie sensed the clouds pressing down, blotting out the sun. Taking her head in her bandaged hands, she waited.

She did not dare to close her eyes. With her back to the wall, she kept a vigil. The companions might take Jolyon's life, but she'd be damned if they desecrated his body with more splinters. She knew how that felt – to be invaded, against your will. She would never, never let that happen to him.

Time crawled by. Nothing moved. All she saw was grey stillness; all she heard was the constant patter on the windows. It was a kind of torture.

Her mind wandered down the misty paths to Torbury St Jude; saw Sarah lost, falling into the river, dragged beneath the current by her sodden skirts like the gypsy girl in Anne's diary. She slapped her cheeks and tried to steer her thoughts in a better direction. They twirled for a moment and then, dizzy, stumbled towards Jolyon. *No.*

After two hours had passed, she thought she would lose her mind. Stiff in her joints, she clambered to her feet with a groan. Still the rain fell, light but insistent. Everything looked the same as it had in the morning. She felt she had lived ten lifetimes since then.

The air was turning. Odour rose slowly, like a blush from Jolyon's corpse, stealing the smell of bay leaves and lime that had always been a part of him. He looked so dirty and neglected: streaks of mud on his hands, fragments of glass sparkling in his tangled hair. Police be hanged – she was going to wash her boy.

She limped through the baize door into the servants' quarters. It creaked shut behind her, encasing her in cold stone.

Last time she entered this passage there had been a staff of five. Now the hallways carried an air of abandonment. Gone was the sound of the kitchen range and the smell of soap. No oil lamps shone.

As she edged towards the kitchen to fetch water, she passed the housekeeper's room. The door was shut. Had Mrs Holt sat there alone, all this time, in the dark?

Her hand hovered over the panels, unsure. If Mrs Holt wanted to be by herself, she had no right to disturb her. She had just made up her mind to walk away when she heard a sound from inside.

Not a sob, as she expected. Something lower, prolonged. A groan or a creak, like old bones.

She reached for the doorknob, but she did not turn it. The pulse drummed in her throat.

Creeeak. A draught crept under the door and touched her ankles. She had to get back to Jolyon, she had to—

Just as she turned away, Jasper cried out.

It immobilised her. That pathetic, reedy sound, so like a baby's wail. She tried to shove it aside and harden her heart but it came again, louder this time. Piercing. Then the same creak.

'Damn it, Jasper.' Berating herself, she turned the knob and pushed.

The room glided into view. Elsie tightened her injured fingers around the jamb, driving her nails into the wood.

Every drawer of Mrs Holt's desk stood open. Papers covered the little table with the floral cloth. Jasper sat on it, mewling, as the various receipts and recipes fluttered beneath him. Diamonds of rain spotted his black fur. The window gaped wide open.

'What . . .?' One of the chairs was missing. 'Jasper, where is Mrs—'

The creak sounded, right by her ear. She spun around. The air clogged in her throat.

It was the movement she saw first – gentle, like a tree swaying in the wind. Only then did she begin to make sense of it: the creak, not of wood, but of hemp; the swinging feet. Her gaze travelled up the black dress to slumped shoulders and a face that belonged to no one: blue-red; the eyes popping; the tongue lolling out. The housekeeper had looped a noose around a hook in the ceiling. All that had once been Mrs Holt hung there, suspended like a sack of grain.

Nausea pushed up from her stomach. As the skirts waved back and forth, she caught flashes of a wooden face behind them, a maid's face made terrible by fear. Helen.

She reached out and snatched Jasper from the table.

Fear dominated her pain as she skidded out of the door, through the passages, into the kitchen. *Hiss, hiss.* Oh yes, they were coming now. They had only waited for her to see Mrs Holt's nightmare before starting her own.

Her hand fumbled with the yard door. 'Come on, come on.'

Jasper scratched with her.

It creaked and groaned, but it would not move. The door was locked.

Hiss.

The housekeeper's room – Mrs Holt had the bunch of keys. She just needed to get in there and – no, damn it, she didn't need to rob a corpse of keys, she could climb out of the open window in the room. Why hadn't she thought of it before?

Hiss, hiss. Inside her brain, buzzing along her thoughts. *Hiss.*

'Shut up!' she screamed. 'Shut the hell up!'

She was forced to stoop down and place Jasper at her feet. Pain burnt: hot needles up and down her leg, flames raging in her chest. Then that feeling inside her head as the hiss came again, a firecracker going off.

Jasper mewed and trotted forwards, turning back to see if she would follow. With great difficulty, she limped after him.

Hiss, hiss. Different from the sound that haunted her dreams: now she heard the steam of the factory in it. A saw too, but not one cutting through wood. It ripped through some other substance, spraying liquid.

'No.'

The white-paint letters spelling *Housekeeper* swam into view. Those letters were on the front of the door – but hadn't she left it open?

Hiss.

Locked. Another door, locked. She threw her shoulder against the panels, crying out in pain and frustration. Her fists pummelled, useless, on the wood.

Hiss, hiss.

Jasper hissed back. He prowled off down the stone passage. Hunting.

'Wait.'

She stumbled after him. Pain flared and threw black shapes before her eyes. She had to ignore it, she could not give in now. This agony was nothing compared to—

Hiss.

Shock kicked her in the stomach, then in the chest. She *did* recognise the sound. It was in her, part of her, yet her brain was smothering it and refusing to let the memory rise.

Hiss.

Objects slapping into the trough. Not splints. Softer, wetter.

They reached the baize door.

Jasper gathered himself and pounced. The door burst open, magnifying the sound and the smell – not roses this time but phosphorus, burning wood and scorched metal. A sharp, sickly note rising high above it all. Blood.

She staggered into the Great Hall. The wind whooped, gleefully hurtling rain against the windows. Light was fading fast. The dying fire touched Jolyon's face with orange streaks, and beside him—

'No!' The word ripped from her, taking her insides with it.

Jasper screeched and arched his back.

Another companion: one she had carried for too long. His leering face, the hefty, brutal muscle of him.

Pa.

Hiss.

She could not feel the pain in her ribs any longer. Other sensations took control. It was so much worse than she remembered; not just the terror but the anger, impotence and disgust.

Hiss.

'You can't have him! Get away!'

She went to move but her bad leg crumpled beneath her and she was on her knees, retching.

'Get away from him!'

Hiss.

She stared at her hands, splayed out on the grey and black flags. Her bandages were peeling off. There, under the recent wounds, sat the scars of old – the sin seared into her skin.

Hiss.

The dam gave way. She remembered it all.

And she did not regret it.

She was there in the factory, twelve years old, crouching with her box of matches, her veins pumping with the beat of her heart. Lighting the fire, too hasty, all fingers and thumbs. Once again she felt its vengeful warmth answering the fury that raged inside her. And she did not mind that it had burnt her hands because then she became the blaze, became the flames, became the lure to her father who ran like a madman to try and put it out.

Did he see her? She hoped he saw her, as Ma did, that split second before he fell. The child he had abused barrelling into his leg, pushing him straight into the circular saw.

Hiss, hiss. The machinery struggling to cope, the clogged blades. Gore slopping into the trough. A kind of fizz as blood sprayed out across the floor, making the match girls shriek. But then the noise turned into a whirring, a clunking as bones jammed the teeth. Steam panted out from the machine. The saw gave a death rattle. All fell still, and Jolyon was safe.

Until now.

'You . . . can't . . . have . . . him!'

Jasper sprang before she did, claws flashing by the embers of the fire. The Pa companion toppled, leering still, into the grate.

A puff of smoke, a crack. Then he leapt up in flames.

Jasper skittered back from the fire. It was going too fast; snaking down the length of the companion, throwing out sparks like luminous fleas. No natural fire could burn like that.

Smoke stung her eyes. She grabbed Jasper and climbed, unsteady, to her feet.

A log popped and the oriental rug caught alight.

'Jolyon!'

But it had him in its grasp. Orange tongues jumped and writhed, reflected on the swords that hung on the wall. She watched it dance, fascinated, appalled, until she began to cough.

She wheeled around and saw the wavering outlines of companions everywhere: on the stairs, peering down from the gallery, standing in every door. Barring her way.

It was hot. So hot. Jasper's fur made her arms sweat.

Charred snowflakes of ash fluttered in the air. She could no longer make out which companion was which; she could not even see the front door.

There was nothing but the flames.

A window. Spluttering, she fought her way towards a rectangle shining through the smoke. The window overlooking the drive. This was where they had stood, Hetta and the gypsy boy, watching her. Knowing this would happen.

Cradling Jasper in one arm, she hammered on the window with her spare hand. Hot glass – unbearably hot.

'Come on!'

That old, familiar scorch on her palms. This was how she had won before – fighting through the pain. She could do it. She could make her body do anything. She had learnt the hard way.

She hit the glass again. Again. Her knuckles screamed and she brought them back, dripping blood. Again. The glass cracked.

The fire roared behind her. She felt its breath, wringing sweat out from the back of her neck. Of course, she had let the air get at it. She had made it worse.

'Quick, Jasper, quick!'

He was a muddle of flailing limbs and claws, trying to press his paws either side of the hole and stop her from posting him through it. But she was rough, impervious to him. The glass cracked again and she pushed him outside with it, yowling furiously.

Heat gusted up her back. She felt her skin lift and tighten. The pain. The *pain*, rummaging through her clothes with its burning hands.

She didn't think. There was no time to think – she took a few steps back and ran, as Jolyon must have done, straight at the glass. With her arms protecting her face, she hurtled into the window and shattered it to pieces.

A fork of fire lashed out behind her, but she was already on the ground, beating at her gown, rolling across the gravel and smothering the flames. Rain fell and extinguished the last of it. Too late. The damage was done – she could feel her skin blister and pop in the ruthless air.

Jasper had raced up the closest tree. His green eyes peered down at her as she crawled, steaming and half dead, into the damp gardens. She had to get away from the fire. From the house.

Her muscles were shrieking. Black smuts danced in her vision and threatened to take over. This was the limit: the fountain. Her body would go no further. She slumped over the rim, red-raw arms dangling into the basin.

A gust of wind blew across the hills. She smelt it on the breeze: roses and thyme, peppering the smoke. She coughed.

'Mrs Bainbridge!'

Sarah?

She peered through the shimmering, heat-hazed garden. But it was not Sarah she saw. There was a companion, by the topiary. The one who started it all: Hetta.

'Mrs Bainbridge! Good Lord!'

It *sounded* like Sarah's voice, coming from the other end of the gardens, although she couldn't be sure. She could hear two voices at once, one lapping over the other.

As she stared fixedly at Hetta a dark shape, a taller shape, ran through the gardens, over the gravel towards her. Human. Whether it was male or female, she could not tell. It seemed to her that two were moving there, not one. Both of them, holding out their hands for her.

'Mrs Bainbridge!'

When she came to there was another calling her name, a nurse with a face like a rat. Her surroundings were white and sterile. She smelt carbolic soap. Urine. Pain was stitched into her skin.

She cracked open her parched mouth to speak, but only a croak hobbled over her lips. Her voice was gone – gone with the memory and the smoke.

ST JOSEPH'S HOSPITAL

When he finished reading, he remained bent over the desk, staring at the last word. Then he pushed back and leant into his chair, making a hollow sound in his throat. That sound seemed to fall right through her, like a penny in a well, echoing as it hit the edges and landed with a dull thud in the pit of her stomach.

Failure. All that work, ploughing up memories and emotions until they were seeds on top of the soil for the crows to peck at, and still – failure.

Or was it? She watched him minutely, alert for the slightest change in his countenance. His green eyes had not moved, they were trained on the paper. A good three minutes passed. The space between them thickened, heavy with expectation.

She pictured his mind like a great machine, the pistons pumping, assembling her past into . . . what? Did she even want to know?

'Well,' he sighed. 'Well. It must have been Mr Underwood you heard, calling your name. He found you.'

Only a crumb of information but she leant forward, eager to take it.

'Although,' he went on, shifting in his chair, 'it was considerably later than you have written here. Full night. He saw the glow from your house on the horizon and raised the alarm.'

No one had told her that. No one had told her anything.

Flashes of aching memory came: not just sepia photographs of people but their voices, their scents, the feelings they inspired. Mr Underwood, Sarah, Jasper. What *had* happened to them?

She'd regarded the story as her secret. Now she saw it before her on the desk, pages and pages covered in her large, square writing, and realised it was incomplete. The end was not in her power. Dr Shepherd held the last act, locked inside him.

Hesitantly, she picked up his pencil and wrote a word at the bottom of the last page.

Sarah?

'That is the question. What befell Sarah Bainbridge?'

She tilted her head, trying to see the look in his eyes, but the light was wrong. The lenses of his spectacles were opaque, screening him from view.

'What you have written . . . I think, perhaps, that I can use it. But possibly not in the way you had hoped. It does not prove your innocence, or indeed anything except a great facility for invention. And if imagination were a malady, Mr Dickens would be a permanent resident here.'

Imagination! At least *madness* had power. It did not make her sound puerile, a girl dreaming of fairies and unicorns.

Sarah? She underlined the word, scratching through the paper.

'Yes. She is the only person able to collaborate your story. If what you write is true, she can confirm your whereabouts at the time of Jolyon Livingstone's death.'

344

A tear wet her cheek at the mention of Jolyon's name.

'Here we reach our difficulty, Mrs Bainbridge. Since you began to write, I have been scouring records in search of Sarah Bainbridge. Will you hazard a guess as to what I found?' He held out his hands, showing them empty. 'Nothing. I cannot trace a census entry, a death – not a thing. I even took out an advertisement appealing for information. Sarah Bainbridge has vanished.'

Another tear, falling to join and speed on the first. Poor Sarah never reached the police. They had not found her body. It could be lying in some ditch, corrupting, flies crawling in and out between her lips. Oh, Sarah. She deserved so much more than that.

Dr Shepherd coughed – not a real cough, but a modest clearing of the throat. A harbinger. It was coming now: his theory.

'One thing is clear to me from your writing, Mrs Bainbridge. You have a tendency to repress unpleasant emotions. It is your defence, your strategy to cope. The – incidents – with your father, for instance. Then episodes missing from the story. Elsie – that is to say, the Elsie on these pages – passes out on several occasions. I cannot help but feel each one represents a chunk of the past you refuse to remember.'

Down the corridor, a bell rang.

'Let us consider, for a moment, that you are actively submerging your harmful memories. Your anger at your parents, the guilt you feel for their deaths – whether qualified or not, I cannot say at this stage. All those dark emotions must go somewhere. I have read of them turning upon the patient's body and making them unwell. But there are also cases where they splinter off, so to speak, into what we can only call a double consciousness.

'Would you consider a possibility for me, Mrs Bainbridge? No doubt it will prove alarming, but I want you to open yourself up to the possibility that Sarah Bainbridge did not exist at all. That she was, in fact, an aspect of yourself.'

She grabbed the pencil, tried to keep her hand steady. *People saw her. They spoke to her.*

'So you believe.' His voice was soft, but not kind. Insinuating, tickling inside her ears. 'But we cannot verify it. The cast of your story are gone. The only people who could attest to the existence of Sarah Bainbridge now lie dead and buried.'

Mr Underwood.

'Ah.' He crossed his legs. 'I am sorry to say Mr Underwood also perished.'

Her fingers moved but all she felt were the vibrations of the pencil. *How?*

'By fire. It seems that when the rescue party arrived from Fayford, Mr Underwood sent some villagers to Torbury St Jude for help. But he did not wait for their return. Witnesses say he spoke of other people, trapped inside the building. That does tally with your story – he would not know about the deaths of Mr Livingstone or Mrs Holt, he would imagine them still inside. He ran into The Bridge to try and rescue them, but alas . . . Poor man.'

Jasper?

A relieved smile broke on his face. 'At least there, I have some good news. The little fellow did not leave you with your injuries. He fairly guarded you. By daybreak, our people had arrived in response to Mr Livingstone's telegram.

Given your condition, the police were willing to let us take you to our infirmary, and the little cat tried to follow you. One of the orderlies took pity on him, brought him back here. He has been living with our chief superintendent ever since. I've seen him. Very fat, he looks, and very happy too.'

Nine, she wrote.

'I'm sorry?'

Nine lives.

'Ah! Yes, quite.' Dr Shepherd uncrossed his legs and leant forward to rest his hands on the desk. He had short, even nails. Blond hairs grew on his knuckles. Beside him, her own burnt hand looked like a monster's paw. 'Fortunately, we do not have nine lives to account for. Only two. Mr Livingstone and Mrs Holt.'

At last, his eyes tangled with hers.

'Mrs Bainbridge, I do not believe that you killed them. I never did. And while I cannot believe all aspects of your story either, I *do* believe your love for Mr Livingstone. You would not hurt him. It seems to me the fire was an accident, as so many fires are. It consumed the lives of two, and it nearly consumed you, until Providence helped you escape. But you must comprehend, my belief is immaterial. A jury will look at this and see a woman whose father died in suspicious circumstances, whose husband died within a quarter of their marriage, to her considerable advantage. Two servants killed in mysterious accidents. Then, the very day a telegram is despatched to an asylum to say you are unmanageable and in need of restraint . . . You see how it looks.'

Murderess. The name did not match the Elsie in the story, but she had the face for it now: the pink, shining flesh;

cropped hair; eyes that looked like they had been screwed into the sockets. A monster, gifted to the crowds. How they would gobble her up, write about her, delight in little affected shrieks as she shambled to and from the dock.

'I have very few options, Mrs Bainbridge. I must make my report, and soon.' His fingers twitched. They would write the next words, the words that decided her fate. She regarded them, wary. Could such slim, tapered fingers hold her life safe?

'As far as I can see, there are only two ways for me to keep you from gaol. The first is that you submit to my theory. Accept you are a disturbed individual, damaged by a pair of cruel and unfeeling parents. You allow me to say that Sarah is a separate part of your subconscious, that you may have killed but you cannot accept what you have done, so you have invented these phantoms, these *companions*, to take the guilt for you. The verdict will undoubtedly be guilty, but at least we have a chance of pleading criminal insanity. That means Broadmoor rather than Newgate.'

Let everyone believe she murdered Jolyon? Have her name go down on the record as the destroyer of his life? She shook her head, vehement.

'You must dwell upon it, Mrs Bainbridge. Promise me you will. It may not be the whole truth but . . . It is our best hope.'

The pencil slipped in her sweating hand. *Other option?*

His mouth twisted. 'Well, there is one, but I fear it is not likely.'

Yes.

'My dear Mrs Bainbridge, your only other option is to pray that Sarah Bainbridge walks through that door, ready to swear to your innocence.'

She dreamt of Sarah that night. Lavender dress, grey cape, swishing in the rain. Branches writhed above her head, reaching out to her with a mute appeal. Her boots scuttled around the puddles that bubbled on the ground.

The landscape stretched ahead of her; ditches, black hillocks and the unruly mass of hedgerows. Behind lay the village of Fayford in shades of silver and grey, a daguerreotype of the place Elsie had known. There was no light.

Sarah stumbled. Mud clagged the hem of her skirt. Her ankles were soaked and her gown was wet, sticking to her legs. She looked utterly lost, utterly alone. Drowning.

A creak; long and low, like a moan of pain in the dark. Two heavy beats – *thump, thump*. Then the creak again.

Elsie's eyelids flickered. Was the sound from her dream? Or was it in the room? She could still see Sarah, cowed by the silver needles raining down upon her, but she could not smell damp turf, or the metallic tang of rain; a sweeter, heavier scent filled her nose. *Roses*.

She jerked awake. Instinctively, she twitched her arms. They were pinioned at her sides, weighed down by the tucked sheets. She tried to look around but saw only black.

The floorboards whined. Elsie heard it up and down her spine. Little pats, like the footfalls of an animal.

Jasper?

But no; Jasper was not here. She was not at The Bridge. She released her breath, relieved by that one fact: she was not there.

Bang, bang. She jumped. Someone at the door.

She would not answer it, she thought wildly, they could not make her. She tried to hide beneath the covers but they were tight, so tight. The knock came again.

Who could it be? Nurses, attendants, doctors – none of them *knocked* for admission.

The floorboards by her feet moaned. The sound was coming from within the room.

Fear squeezed her throat. She could not call out, she could not scream; she could only scuffle her legs at the end of the bed as the creak came closer and closer. Still the sheets refused to give way and it was hot; scorching like a breath from hell.

She felt sick. She wanted to cry. Made strong by desperation, she wrenched her arms loose from the sheets and groped under her pillow. *Please be there, please be there.* But no, that was the past. They did not let her keep matches in here.

Something touched her foot.

It burnt like a brand. Red-hot arrows pierced her skin, travelling up her veins. They sliced through Elsie's blocked throat and released her scream.

Footsteps pounded outside. Voices, real people, coming to help. She kept her eyes shut and screamed louder. They could not come fast enough.

She heard them jangling the chain, shooting bolts from their cradles. Why did it take so long?

Another brand on her leg. Up to the shin, now.

Bang. The door hit the wall. Gas lamps were on in the corridor; their light bounced into the room.

It was only a glimpse, caught in the snapping shadows, but Elsie saw it: Sarah. Wooden, painted.

She screamed again.

'Watch yourselves.' The low voice of an attendant.

Something hissed, then a gash of light tore across her vision. She shut her eyes, blinded. It was the lamp in her room – they had turned it on. Slowly, slowly she managed to open her scrunched eyes. Sarah was gone. In her place stood two burly attendants and a man wearing paper cuffs.

'Now!'

They pounced, seizing the tender flesh of her wrists. Two more attendants took her ankles. The bedsheets fell away easily now, no longer taut and suffocating.

She kicked and thrashed, but their hold did not give. They were insensible to her blows, deaf to her screams. She tried to bite. An acrid, dry taste filled her mouth as they stuffed it with a rag. Gagging, she tried to spit it out, but something covered her face, edging past her eyes; something coarse and stiff and reeking of terror.

Pressure squeezed around her ribs. Her clawing hands were plunged into sleeves without end. For a moment she was a ghoulish figure with long, dragging arms and no hands. Then the sleeves were crossed over her chest and secured tight behind her back. A corpse: she was tied in the position of a corpse.

The man with paper cuffs gave her a horrible grin. His teeth were rotten. 'Better fetch the doctor. Tell him it's a bleedin' miracle. The murderess can speak.'

She tried. The words were all there, queued up in her throat, clamouring for release: *run*; *Sarah*; *companions*; *coming*. But her dry, swollen tongue refused to move.

She made a wheezing sound and that was all. A pathetic echo of the companions' hiss.

'Don't look like she can speak to me,' an attendant said.

The man eyed her. His grin turned into a leer. 'Well, at any rate, she can scream.'

The padded room again. It must be. She could smell straw beneath the filthy canvas on the walls. Straw, body odour and fear: a pungent scent not easily forgotten.

Oilskin lined the floor and squeaked as her bare feet paced, back and forth, back and forth. She could hear it; could feel the buckles of the strait waistcoat grinding against her torso. Did they grind against Rupert's mother, too? *No, no, no.* All she wanted was to go back to the time when the world was still and safe. Why did she start to write in the first place?

Somewhere inside the hospital, a bell rang. Too loud, too real, even through the straw.

She needed to see Dr Shepherd. If he had woken her up, then perhaps he could send her back to sleep. Then she would not have these horrible nightmares about Sarah, or be forced to endure the next steps of the proceedings. An inquest? A trial? He was going to stand up on a platform and talk about her like she was a rare species of plant, exposing all she had hidden beneath the soil. Men like that potential factory investor Mr Greenleaf – fat, privileged and bristling with facial hair – would sit listening to him and decide her fate between them.

And what fate was that? Dr Shepherd said the best she could hope for was Broadmoor: fortress for the criminally insane. She had a notion it would make St Joseph's look like Claridge's hotel.

Maybe if the medicine was strong enough, like it was before, she could bear it. But to survive as she was now – alert, remembering? Impossible.

A lock clunked. Dr Shepherd flew into the room.

Something had happened to him. He wore no jacket or waistcoat, only shirtsleeves with a pair of beige braces on display. His hair was uncombed. She noticed a thumbprint on the lens of his spectacles and smears of ink on his fingertips.

'Mrs Bainbridge, forgive me. I should have come much earlier when I heard about your little outburst, but events have rather overtaken me.' He looked her up and down, truly seeing her for the first time. 'The strait waistcoat? I did not realise they had done that. My apologies, Mrs Bainbridge, I will get them to remove it and put you back in a proper room. Why would they think all this necessary? As I understood it, you only had a bad dream?'

He looked at her. She stared back.

'Oh, of course, you cannot write – your arms. I beg your pardon. I am not thinking coherently.'

Almost as an afterthought, he closed the door behind him. His eyes were bloodshot: it did not appear he had slept. But then, she could not be sure of the time in this windowless cell. It could still be the middle of the night.

'I was writing my report,' Dr Shepherd told her. Noticing his ink-stained fingers, he distractedly wiped them against the walls. 'You see the marks of that! I was putting forwards the theory we discussed about your parents and Miss Bainbridge when – Well, I will need to redo it. Or not write it at all, I can hardly say. This is most, most irregular.'

Never had she missed her voice so much. Last night she screamed, but it seemed that was all she could do. She remembered Anne's diary, the demon holding Hetta's tongue. That was how it felt: a strait waistcoat on her tongue with no one to loosen the ties.

Dr Shepherd plucked off his spectacles and polished them on his shirt. 'I must say, it is quite a blow to my pride. I thought I had it figured out, and the report read very well indeed. But in these cases one is glad to be proven wrong. You stare. But of course, I have not even begun to explain.' He jammed his glasses back on – they were still smeared. 'I would ask you to sit down, yet it seems my thoughtless colleagues have not provided a chair. No matter. I will just have to ask you, Mrs Bainbridge, to prepare yourself for something wonderfully strange.'

Was he in earnest? *Wonderfully strange?* Had he read her story?

'Late last night – or rather, early this morning – I received a telegram. It was in relation to the advert I placed enquiring for information about Sarah Bainbridge.'

The room seemed to dilate. She held her breath.

'You would not credit it, after all this time, but it was *from* Sarah. She exists, she is alive.'

Alive. So many possibilities in one word – it was a door opening from her cell, opening from the crypt.

She must have gone pale, for he grasped her shoulder tightly. 'Yes, I can see what you are feeling. It is miraculous. I am so, so pleased for you, Mrs Bainbridge. Congratulations.'

Sarah would swear that Jolyon's death was an accident. And although she was not there to see Mrs Holt hanged, she could testify to her state of mind at the time, the anger and dismay she had shown following the loss of her only child.

No one could call Elsie criminally insane after that. She was not a murderess. Or at least, not in that respect. Would Dr Shepherd reveal her strange narrative and the confession about the death of her parents? She did not think so. He was smiling from ear to ear, looking for all the world as if he had personally saved her from the noose.

'Communication by telegram is naturally rather stunted. I could not ask Sarah too many questions, but I can do that in person. She is coming, the day after tomorrow. The hospital have granted her an interview with us both. I understand that she intends to make herself known to the police, but she wanted to see you first.'

Sarah. No longer just a character in her story but a flesh and blood person who cared for her. The thought choked her with joy.

What had she said before she set out for Torbury St Jude? Something about rebuilding their lives together. Yes, they really could. With Sarah's evidence, Elsie might be set free. There would be someone to look after her, someone to live for. She would not treat Sarah as Mrs Crabbly had, a mere paid companion. They would start again as equals.

'Now,' said Dr Shepherd, 'I had better make myself presentable before I start my rounds. Sit tight, Mrs Bainbridge, and I will have someone come to untie you. The staff have no excuse now, no excuse at all, to treat you like a criminal.'

She did not mind when he closed the door, plunging her back into gloom. She did not even mind the strait waistcoat restricting the blood flow to her arms. She could endure anything now. This was only temporary.

They had bathed her. Dr Shepherd even persuaded the nurses to change her hospital dress for a newer one, not yet faded by the laundry. A blue kerchief was tied around her neck – respectable-looking, as lunatics went. But Elsie could not contain her cramping anxiety. How would Sarah react when she finally arrived?

With its tile floor and aqueous light, the long room reminded Elsie of a mortuary. A metal table had been set in the centre. She and Dr Shepherd sat on one side; a chair stood ready for Sarah on the other. Elsie had a view of the door in the left corner of the room and, opposite it, a round mirror hanging just below the ceiling. It was angled so that a doctor or attendant entering could see the far corners – could see, in short, if a lunatic were about to pounce on them.

The mirror didn't show a distinct view of Elsie's face. It only reflected the colour of the skin, like sausage meat. She looked diminished, a wreck of the woman Sarah had known. A white cap covered her head, hiding the frazzled tufts of her hair.

Had they prepared Sarah for the shock of seeing her?

Dr Shepherd laid a hand on hers. 'Courage, Mrs Bainbridge. She will be here in a moment.'

Her stomach churned with nerves. She half feared Sarah would take one look at her and scream. But this was Sarah, who cared for old women, who even pitied Hetta. She was kind. She would see past the disfigurement. Once the initial upset was over, they would go on as before – only this time, they would be free of fear.

What had Sarah said, once? *Fire makes them more powerful*. It hadn't. The Bridge was burnt and gone, and the evil along with it. No companions were found in the debris, Dr Shepherd confirmed that. Only bones and ashes.

The door joints whined. Dr Shepherd jolted to his feet. Elsie could not trust her legs to stand – she simply gripped the edge of the table.

'Miss Bainbridge for you, doctor,' said an attendant.

Elsie was so concerned about her own appearance, she had not stopped to think how Sarah would look. She expected the same poorly dressed, drab girl she had waved away. But the lady who walked into the room wore a silk gown of arsenic green buttoned up to her throat. Its fringed bustle rustled behind her. The mousy hair that had always fallen out of its pins was combed back clean from her face and arranged in a pile of cascading sausage curls. Perching on the side of her head was a black hat with a green feather and a net face veil.

An imposter.

But no – the face was the same. A little plumper, perhaps, and improved with cosmetics, yet the cheekbones were still too high and the mouth, which smiled to greet Dr Shepherd, was still too wide.

'Oh! Mrs Bainbridge!' She swept forwards to grip Elsie's hands in her own. They were soft, encased in tight-fitting kid gloves. 'Good heavens, I had no idea it was so bad. Your poor face! What you must have been through.'

There was a note to her voice Elsie had not caught before – more girlish now and fluting. But perhaps she did not remember it correctly.

She squeezed Sarah's hands, trying to convey all her emotion through the pressure. She could not look Sarah full in the face, not yet. She did not want to see the pity and revulsion there.

'I think perhaps I mentioned to you, Miss Bainbridge, that my patient has experienced difficulty with speech since the incident. I will act as her interpreter, if that is agreeable to you.'

'Yes, of course.' Sarah withdrew her hands and took the chair Dr Shepherd pulled out for her. The boning of her gown gave her an upright posture. 'It is hardly surprising after all that has happened.'

Dr Shepherd walked back round to his own seat. Elsie stole a glance at Sarah's face, but she was watching the doctor.

'Indeed, it is common when a patient has endured trauma,' said Dr Shepherd. 'But in this case it has proven rather inconvenient. Without being able to question Mrs Bainbridge, the police have been on the back foot somewhat in their investigation. Speculation about what occurred at The Bridge has run out of hand.'

'That is why I am here. To tell what I know.' Sarah offered him a smile. It was somehow eerie.

'And not a moment too soon! The inquest is almost upon us. May I ask, Miss Bainbridge – forgive the impertinence – what it was that kept you from coming forward for so long?'

'I would have thought that was obvious, doctor. I was afraid.'

'Afraid? Whatever of?'

'Oh, no doubt it will sound foolish to a clever man like you.' She flicked a curl over her shoulder. 'But there was so much death at The Bridge! Then Mr Livingstone decided to put his sister in the asylum, and it seemed to me I must get far away from the place.'

The air rearranged around them. What – what had she said?

Dr Shepherd paused, his mouth slightly ajar. 'You . . . ran away, then? You did not get lost or hurt going to fetch the police?'

'I know what you must think of me, doctor. I have been a terrible coward. But I am willing to be brave now. After all these years, I have finally found my voice.'

Elsie stared at her. Her outline swam, wavering beneath the tears that filmed Elsie's eyes.

Sarah had left her? On *purpose*? She had lied to her face, taken her purse, and run off to leave her for the companions? Of all people, *Sarah*?

The sense of betrayal brewed so dark and strong that she could taste it. Her own words came back to her. *This is what happens to me, Jo. I trust people and they abuse that trust.*

Dr Shepherd was rummaging through his notes, flustered. 'But, you – er – you did not think it your duty to make yourself known after the fire? When the police appealed for information?'

'It was unclear at that stage whether Mrs Bainbridge was going to pull through or not. I read of the poor thing's terrible injuries.'

Another blow. She had known. And even though the newspapers would have told her The Bridge was burnt to the ground, forever rid of companions, she had not bothered to visit. Elsie had been fighting for her life and Sarah had not lifted a finger.

This was the girl that just yesterday Elsie had hoped to live with, live for! How could she have got Sarah so wrong?

'Well yes, but surely that would not . . . I mean, regardless of Mrs Bainbridge's survival, you had information. Information about Mr Livingstone's death.'

'Yes, God help me.' Sarah drew out a handkerchief and dabbed at her eyes. Her dress was so bright that it reflected in her irises, lending a green tinge to the brown. 'I did not want to say it unless I had to. But now it is my duty, I see that. Other people may be in danger.'

'In danger from—?'

Sarah looked at Elsie. Her face crumpled. 'Oh, forgive me! You know that I must tell them!'

Tell them? About the companions, did she mean? She swapped a bewildered glance with Dr Shepherd, whose cheeks were growing redder by the instant.

'It appears we may be talking at cross-purposes, Miss Bainbridge. I did not set much store by it, but Mrs Bainbridge has told me of a furnishing you both seemed to fear, something she called a companion. Is this what you allude to?'

'You poor thing,' she whispered, 'you poor thing.'

'Miss Bainbridge?'

'That was why Mr Livingstone wrote to your hospital in the first place, doctor. She kept seeing these companions everywhere, when no one else could.'

Dr Shepherd cocked his head. 'I thought . . . she wrote that you could?'

'I may have gone along with it, doctor, to pacify her.' Sarah twisted her handkerchief. 'I didn't know what else to do. I was so afraid that if I crossed her, I would be next.'

'Next?'

'Those . . . accidents. It was so clear what was really going on, but no one wanted to admit it. The cow, baby Edgar, Helen. Mr Livingstone could not bring himself to face the truth until it was too late for him.'

'You – you –' Dr Shepherd began to stutter. Elsie saw her own confusion and dismay written all over him. 'Are you saying . . .'

'I saw her. I saw her push him from that window with her own two hands. And I have no doubt she killed poor Mrs Holt too, before starting the fire.'

No. How could they not hear it – how was her tongue not saying it? The word clanged so loud in her head it should be echoing off the walls, bouncing down the corridors. *No!*

It was not true, she would never hurt Jolyon! She was not a murderess!

But then why did Sarah glare at her like that?

She saw Dr Shepherd's certainty crumble, his courage slither away. 'Oh! Oh, I see . . .'

They were still sitting on the same side of the table, but they were not a team now. The space between their shoulders prickled like static. His mind must be racing with the same thoughts as Elsie's: why did I trust her; how could I be so foolish; why would she betray me like that?

'You understand, now, why I held back,' Sarah said. 'I loved Mrs Bainbridge, I truly did, and I was horrified when . . . I did not want to speak out against her if I could help it. But now that time has come.'

'Yes.' Dr Shepherd removed his glasses and rubbed his eyes. He would not look at Elsie. 'Yes, I believe the inquest is due next week. We must consult the police. Would you . . .'

'I am prepared to testify. I must put my personal feelings aside for justice.' She let out a little sigh. 'Even if it means watching my poor cousin's widow hang.'

'Hang!' Dr Shepherd repeated.

Elsie felt it around her neck: hemp squeezing tight. Wood, always wood, beneath her feet until they pulled a lever and the trapdoor clunked open.

'It is a possibility, is it not, doctor? Four people are dead.'

'Well . . . yes, in theory the death sentence could be bestowed. But you said she is not in her right mind. Surely a jury would find her not guilty by way of insanity.'

'That is my dearest wish.' Sarah glanced down her long nose at Elsie. The look turned her cold. 'But I suppose it depends upon what is said at the trial.'

None of it was real. These were actors standing and shaking hands, their conversation swirling around her edges. The squeal of the chair legs against the tiles; Sarah's breathy 'God save you, dear Mrs Bainbridge!' – these things could not be taking place. Not here. Not to her.

She gazed up at the mirror in the corner of the room. A mottled-skinned, scrawny woman sat hunched over the table, alone. Her hands resembled cloven hooves. She looked like a murderess.

Jolyon. In the maddest of fits, on the strongest of drugs, she knew she could never harm him. Mrs Holt, Mabel – well, perhaps. In extremis. But never, never Jolyon.

Dr Shepherd and Sarah had moved to the door. They stood there in conversation.

'I can accompany you to the station after my rounds here. I am sure you will not wish to go alone.'

'That is most kind of you. I do appreciate your time, Dr Shepherd.'

'Not at all. And you may wish for some support when they question you. Inspectors can be sticky chaps. They might get a little rough when they ask where you have been all this time.'

'It is a valid question. I have only myself to blame.' Sarah slipped a finger beneath her collar. Something glimmered there.

'Understandable, considering.'

'I do hope you will treat her kindly, doctor. For as long as you are able. I know she has done dreadful things but . . . I do not like to think of her suffering unnecessarily.'

Diamonds. There were diamonds at Sarah's throat.

'I will do my utmost. I cannot answer for Broadmoor, or Newgate, or wherever they may send her next.'

Sarah turned to call into the room. 'Goodbye, Mrs Bainbridge. God grant you some rest. I pray that in time you will understand what I have done. I cannot keep my silence forever. I must be free.' She sighed. 'Will you not at least wave me goodbye, my dear?'

But Elsie was not looking at Sarah. Her eyes were focused on the mirror and the two figures reflected in the doorway.

Everything was reversed. The arsenic-green dress, the bustle, the hat. Yet the face peering out beneath the brim was not a mirror image of Sarah's. The nose was shorter, the cheeks fuller.

Red-gold hair replaced the pile of Sarah's own mousy locks.

It did not look like Sarah at all. It looked like—

'Well, goodbye, Mrs Bainbridge. Thank you for all you have done for me.'

As she turned and closed the door, Elsie remembered where she had seen that face before.

Hetta.

Acknowledgements

There are many 'silent companions' hidden behind my name on the cover of this book. I would like to take this opportunity to extend my heartfelt thanks to them all.

Juliet Mushens, my wonderful agent, to whom the book is dedicated. You believed in my idea from the very start. I could never have come so far without your advice and encouragement. Thank you, thank you, thank you.

The team at Raven Books, particularly my editors Alison Hennessey and Imogen Denny. You are the most intelligent, lovely people I could possibly have hoped to work with. Your enthusiasm for the story has kept me afloat and made the publication experience a delight. To David Mann – that cover! I will always be grateful that you packaged my writing so beautifully.

My thanks to Hannah Renowden for alerting me to the existence of these creepy wooden figures and starting my mind rolling. Early readers Anna Drizen, Laura Terry, Sarah Hiorns and Jonathan Clark your feedback was invaluable.

I am indebted to Mimi Matthews and Past Mastery for comprehensive blogs that have assisted alongside my wider research. Also to the team at Harris & Hoole, Colchester, for keeping me caffeinated every day!

Lastly, and most importantly, my husband Kevin. You have helped with plot points, brainstormed ideas and supported me through numerous book-related meltdowns. I love you with all my heart.

A Note on the Type

The text of this book is set in Linotype Stempel Garamond, a version of Garamond adapted and first used by the Stempel foundry in 1924. It is one of several versions of Garamond based on the designs of Claude Garamond. It is thought that Garamond based his font on Bembo, cut in 1495 by Francesco Griffo in collaboration with the Italian printer Aldus Manutius. Garamond types were first used in books printed in Paris around 1532. Many of the present-day versions of this type are based on the *Typi Academiae* of Jean Jannon cut in Sedan in 1615.

Claude Garamond was born in Paris in 1480. He learned how to cut type from his father and by the age of fifteen he was able to fashion steel punches the size of a pica with great precision. At the age of sixty he was commissioned by King Francis I to design a Greek alphabet, and for this he was given the honourable title of royal type founder. He died in 1561.